MURDER AT DUNHAVEN CASTLE

ALSO BY NELLIE H. STEELE

Cate Kensie Mysteries:

The Secret of Dunhaven Castle

Murder at Dunhaven Castle

Holiday Heist at Dunhaven Castle

Danger at Dunhaven Castle

Jack's Journal Versions:

The Secret Keepers

Murder in the Tower

Lily & Cassie by the Sea Mysteries:

Ghosts, Lore & a House by the Shore

Duchess of Blackmoore Mysteries:

Letter to a Duchess

Shadow Slayers Stories:

Shadows of the Past

Stolen Portrait Stolen Soul

Gone

Trouble

Clif & Ri on the Sea Adventures:

Rise of a Pirate

Maggie Edwards Adventures:

Cleopatra's Tomb

Secret of the Ankhs

MURDER AT DUNHAVEN CASTLE

A CATE KENSIE MYSTERY

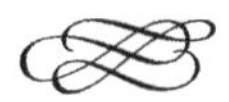

NELLIE H. STEELE

Cover design by Stephanie A. Sovak.

❀ Created with Vellum

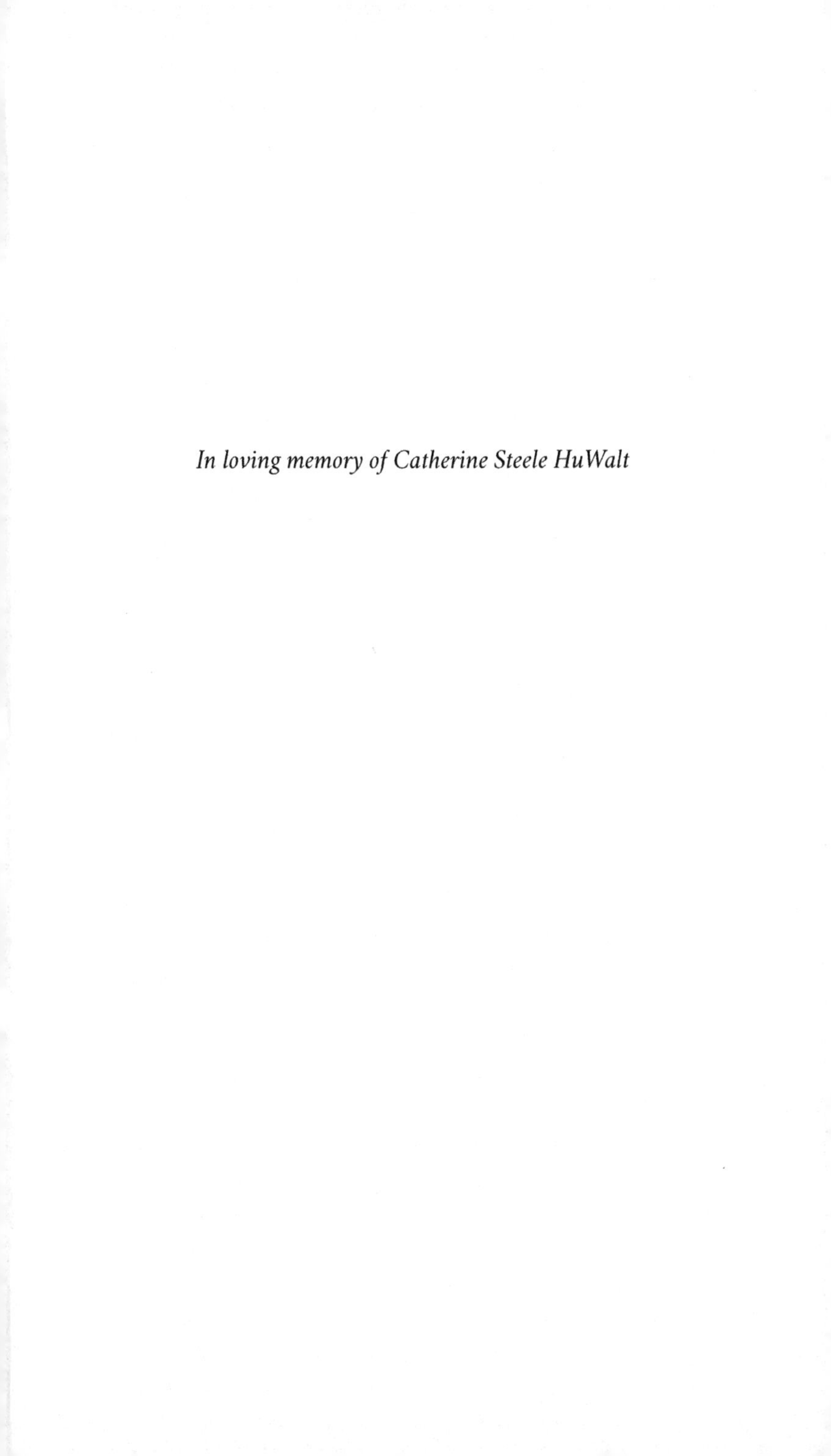

In loving memory of Catherine Steele HuWalt

ACKNOWLEDGMENTS

A very special thank you to everyone who made this book possible! Special shout outs to: Stephanie Sovak, Paul Sovak, Michelle Cheplic, Mark D'Angelo and Lori D'Angelo.

Finally, a HUGE thank you to you, the reader!

MacKenzie Family Tree

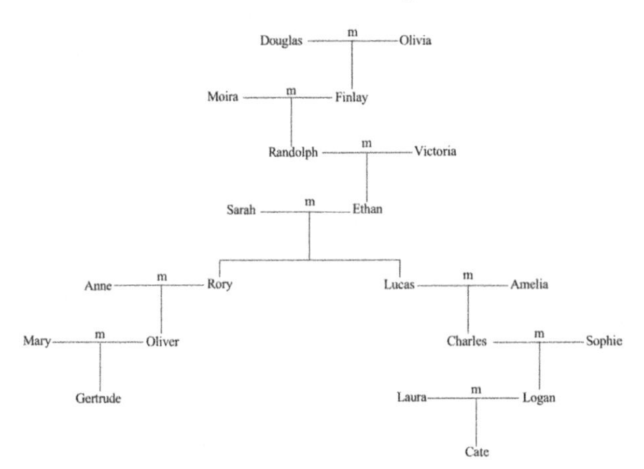

CHAPTER 1

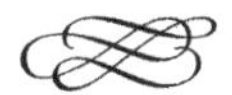

Lady Catherine Kensie sat on the banks of the loch with Riley, her beloved black and white dog. Dunhaven Castle towered in the distance, dominating the landscape. Cate stared at it, her mind still grasping to comprehend the whirlwind that had been the last few months of her life.

She was living a quiet life in a small college town in the United States, teaching history at a local college, struggling to make a go of her career when her life took an incredible turn. Out of the blue, Cate learned she had inherited a Scottish castle from a distant relative along with a fortune large enough to enable her to manage its upkeep and allow her to never want for anything. It was an incredible turn of events for her, despite the rumors that the castle was haunted. Cate chuckled, looking down at the timepiece that was part of her inheritance. Even she had given in to those haunting rumors when she first arrived. That was before she discovered the truth.

What people described as hauntings weren't hauntings at all; there were no remnants of lost souls roaming the halls of

Dunhaven Castle. Instead, what people experienced were what her ancestor discovered and termed "rips in time" that allowed people to slip from one time to another. The castle walls seemed to encase these anomalies, though Cate did not discern if Douglas discovered them before or after building the castle. The timepiece she held in her hand had been designed and maintained for generations to regulate and interact with these "rips," allowing the user to control when he or she would open the rift to another era and step back or forward.

At first, Cate wondered if she was losing her mind, but they confirmed the theory, not only with her own evidence, but by her estate manager's grandfather, Stanley Reid. The elder Mr. Reid worked on the estate and Cate's benefactor, the late Gertrude MacKenzie, swore him to secrecy until he was able to assess if the secret would be safe with her. Cate, a bit too clever for her own good, stumbled upon the secret, dragging estate manager Jack Reid into the situation with her. That was when his grandfather revealed the story, telling her about the "rips in time," the way the time piece controlled them, and how a Reid had been present on the estate to help protect the MacKenzie secret since the beginning.

It was an incredible story; Cate smiled thinking about how amazing it was. "Ahoy there, Lady Cate!" a voice with a Scottish accent called from behind her.

"Hello, Jack," Cate said, smiling as he approached. Jack was the youngest member of Cate's small staff, having taken on his father's caretaker position after his death.

"And hello to you too, good Sir Riley. Lost in thought over your research there, Cate?"

"I was just thinking about my journey."

"Your journey? You mean your time traveling journeys?"

"No. Reflecting on how different my life is now compared to the beginning of the year."

"Ah, yes, from mild-mannered professor to Scottish Countess. You've really come up in the world, Lady Cate," he joked. One thing Cate could always count on was Jack's sense of humor.

"Yes, and not just any Scottish Countess, but a time-traveling one," Cate teased back.

"You are way more fond of the time-traveling stuff than I am, Cate. If it were all the same to me, I'd stay right here in my present time."

"Yes, I realize that, but unfortunately, it's your solemn duty to make sure I'm safe and so is this secret. And that includes not only wherever I go, but WHENever."

"Don't remind me. You're too adventurous for your own good, m'lady."

"Speaking of adventurous, how are we looking for the costume ball?" Cate asked, turning her thoughts to her future rather than her past.

"Everything will be right as rain for the ball. Mr. Fraser and I will have the gardens closest to the house in tip-top shape for the guests to enjoy."

"Oh good! I can't believe it's only a month away!"

"I can't believe we have another month. Another month listening to Mrs. Fraser chew my ear off about her costume. I tell you I've never seen that woman so tickled about something as when she learned you wanted her to attend as your guest and not have to do all the cooking for it."

Cate laughed. "I'm glad she is enjoying her new role. Sorry that you aren't! Well, speaking of the ball," Cate said, standing and dusting herself off, "I better go attend to a few details for that. I have an appointment with Mrs. Campbell to go over some items."

"Okay, Cate. Enjoy the rest of your day."

"Thanks!" Cate said, scooping up Riley and carrying him back to the castle.

As she entered the castle, Mrs. Fraser, her housekeeper and cook, informed her Mrs. Campbell was already waiting for her in the sitting room. "Am I late?" Cate asked her, checking her watch.

"Nay, Lady Cate. She's early, 'bout a half hour early, too. If you ask me, that woman is insufferable, always showing up and poking around as if she's welcome anytime. Dinnae she realize people have other things to do? Bless your soul for helping her with this ball, Lady Cate. Although, if I may say so, I am excited for it."

"I'm glad you are, Mrs. Fraser," Cate said, smiling at her. Despite having a rough start when Cate first came, she and the woman grew close over the few months she had been here. She liked Mrs. Fraser and would be sorry to see her go when she retired. She was glad the couple's home was on the estate so she was sure they would continue to visit. Still, Cate dreaded the day when the woman told her she found her replacement. "Jack has been telling me about your discussions with him regarding your costume," Cate said.

"Giving away my secrets, is he?"

Cate laughed. "He hasn't given away any secrets, just that you're excited over your costume, which you won't have the opportunity to wear if I don't finish these details with Mrs. Campbell."

"Best be off with you then! Oh, why dinnae you leave the little pup here while you meet with her, I've got a nice bone for him."

"Oh, he'll love that," Cate said. "Okay, Riley, you stay here. Mrs. Fraser has a nice bone for you, buddy. Be a good boy for her, okay?" Cate gave the pup a scratch on his head and left the kitchen, making her way up to the main floor and to the sitting room.

The large sitting room off the main entrance was the picture of Scottish nobility, decorated with thick tartan draperies and heavy wooden pieces. In Cate's opinion, the room looked like something out of a movie, although to be fair, those sentiments extended to the entire castle.

"Mrs. Campbell," she said, entering the room. "What a pleasure to see you again."

"Lady Cate," the woman said, standing from the couch near the fireplace, "thank you for meeting with me. Pardon my early arrival, but I was concerned the details may take longer to work out than we expect."

She was a small woman, wearing a smart skirt suit. Isla Campbell doubled as the town's librarian and president of the historical society. The Halloween costume ball had been her idea. "What a lovely way for everyone to get acquainted with the new owner of Dunhaven Castle!" she said when proposing the idea. Cate learned in short order that her predecessor, Lady Gertrude MacKenzie, had been for the most part a recluse. While friendly enough, she rarely entertained visitors at the castle. Mrs. Campbell suggested Cate invite several friends and also to allow the historical society to sell tickets to the ball as a fundraiser. She was sure many of the townsfolk and others throughout the countryside would be interested in attending. She was confident they would sell out the event and have a successful fund drive even after covering their expenses.

While Cate was an introvert, she considered the idea a fun way to entertain friends who were interested in visiting the estate and involve the community, so she agreed to open the castle for them. At first, the idea did not thrill Mrs. Fraser at all, who assumed all food preparation for the soiree would fall on her. Although elated to find out not only was she not responsible for this, but that Cate hoped she would come as a guest and enjoy the party rather than work it, she still found Mrs. Campbell too pushy for her liking. The theme of the ball, crafted by Mrs. Campbell herself, was "Ghosts of the

Past." It tied in to both Halloween and the castle's history, she deemed.

"No problem, Mrs. Campbell, I was just settling Riley after a long walk."

"Oh, of course, your little pet, how is he? Adjusting to the move all right, I hope."

"He is doing well and yes, he loves it here."

"Not too many ghosts for him?" Mrs. Campbell loved to remind Cate about the haunting rumors that abounded in the town about the castle. Cate found it amusing considering she realized the truth.

"No, just the right amount for Riley," she joked. "Our last place was lacking in the ghost department. Anyway, should we get down to business?"

The women spent the next two hours going over many details for the party from entertainment to catering to décor and more. "Of course, we'll have to have another meeting in two weeks and then several more as the day approaches, just to be sure we have everything nailed down," Mrs. Campbell said, as they concluded their business and stood to walk toward the entrance.

"Yes, well, you have kept a very close eye on all the details, Mrs. Campbell. You've done an incredible job in putting this together," Cate said, complimenting her.

"Oh, oh, why thank you, Lady Cate. Well, this is quite an undertaking for our little historical society and I do want it to be a success. I'd love to make it an annual event, I trust you wouldn't object to that if all goes well?"

Cate recognized what she was doing. Mrs. Fraser's assessment was correct, she was quite pushy, but Cate lived in an incredible castle, she couldn't fault anyone else for wanting to have a glimpse at her home. Nor could she fault the historical society for wanting to capitalize on the biggest asset in their town. Cate nodded, smiling as the woman continued, "Or even a series of events. Oh!" She grabbed Cate's arm, staring into space as though an idea just struck her on the head. "Christmas with Lady Cate. Oh yes, what a magical idea. Perhaps that's a winner too!"

Cate patted her hand. "Let's see how successful this event is and take it from there," she said, not sure she was willing to begin auctioning her holidays to the historical society.

"Right, of course. Well, thank you for meeting with me. I'll be in touch!" Mrs. Campbell said, stepping out into the fresh air and making her way toward her car.

"Bye!" Cate called after her.

Cate closed the door and returned to the sitting room, sighing as she dropped onto the couch. The meeting left her drained. There were many details to attend to. What was she thinking when she agreed to this? Cate was grateful that Isla had a firm handle on most of it.

"Is the ninny gone?" Mrs. Fraser said, breaking her from her daze.

Cate let out a chuckle. "Yes, she's gone."

"Has she exhausted you or do you have a few minutes to go over a few details about your upcoming house party?"

"I always have time for you, Mrs. Fraser. Let's walk down to the kitchen, then I can retrieve Riley, too. I bet he enjoyed his bone."

"Oh, he did, Lady Cate, he did. Chewed on his bone almost the whole time he was down there. Now," Mrs. Fraser said as they walked, "I wanted to make sure I've got the timetable right so I can plan menus for everything and everyone. Ms. Williams is the first to arrive, and she's coming in on the Saturday before the party and staying on until the second Monday. She'll be here for dinner Saturday evening, staying the week and leaving after breakfast the following Monday, right?"

"Yes, that's right. Molly will be visiting for just over a

week," Cate answered. Molly Williams was the department secretary from Cate's old teaching department in the U.S. She had been Cate's only friend after moving to Aberdeen following her parents' tragic death in a car accident. Five years her senior, Molly was her champion, advocate and ally when she had none, much like an older sister. Molly was the first and only person she'd told about her move to Scotland and Cate promised her a visit. While Molly joked about how soon she could visit only weeks after Cate moved, she was astounded when Cate suggested October for a trip, explaining that she planned to host a costume ball at the castle.

Molly replied with a "heck yeah" adding "when am I ever going to get the chance to go to a costume ball in a castle." Now single following a surprise divorce, Molly said it was the perfect time for her to travel to "get her mind off of things."

"Then, Ms. Pearson is traveling in on Monday and will be here in time for dinner and staying on until the following Monday, same as Ms. Williams," Mrs. Fraser continued.

"Right, Gayle is coming two days after Molly and leaving at the same time as Molly," Cate confirmed. Gayle Pearson was the administrative assistant for her, and the estate's attorney, William Smythe.

"And last but certainly not least, Mr. Smythe will arrive on Wednesday, here for dinner in the evening and leaving with the ladies on Monday morning after breakfast."

"Right," Cate said as they proceeded down the stairs.

"Now, I'll put Mr. Smythe in the blue room as usual, Ms. Pearson in the same bedroom as the one she used when you first came and Ms. Williams in the rose bedroom near to Gayle's if you agree."

"Yes, that sounds perfect, Mrs. Fraser, thank you. Also, I hoped you and Mr. Fraser would stay Friday evening after the ball so you don't have to return home late. I realize your cottage is close but staying may be more convenient. And on Saturday morning, we can help ourselves to a cold breakfast so you won't need to prepare anything."

"Well, I'm happy to prepare food, but if you are certain that will suffice, I'll have some fruit and such prepared the day before and put into the fridge for everyone the next morning." They reached the kitchen. "Funny, I never imagined Mr. Smythe enjoying a party, he doesn't seem the type. I realize he was a friend of Lady Gertrude's but they never did more than have a nightcap." She was right. Mr. Smythe, while a good-hearted individual, was extremely straight-laced, rarely engaging in humor. Cate, too, was curious to see his demeanor at a party.

"That would be perfect, Mrs. Fraser, thank you, again. Well, Mr. Riley, how did you like your bone?" Cate said, glancing around the kitchen. "Riley?" she said, not spotting the little pup.

"Strange, he was here chewing on that bone when I came to fetch you."

"Riley! Come, Riley!" Cate called. "Oh, he's here somewhere, Mrs. Fraser. Probably hiding away with his bone so we don't take it from him."

They searched the kitchen but did not find him. "Perhaps he wandered into one of the other rooms," Cate said, calling to him down the hall.

They both moseyed down the hall, searching in each room. Both of them came up empty. "I don't expect he could have gotten upstairs, the door at the top is closed," Mrs. Fraser said.

"No, we must have missed him somewhere."

Upon returning to the kitchen, they looked around again before Cate heard a noise. "Did you hear that?" Mrs. Fraser asked. Mrs. Fraser and Cate strained their ears.

"Yes," Cate said, "Riley? Riley? Is that you? Where are you? I can hear him whining." Cate wandered around the room listening. "Sounds like it's coming from over here," she said, approaching the door leading outside. "Riley?" Another whine. "Is he outside?" Cate opened the door. The small dog was sitting outside of the door, his fur smudged with dirt. He jumped to his feet and trotted into the house. "Where have you been, mister?"

"Oh my word, Lady Cate, I'm so sorry, he must have gotten out of the door when I was shaking the crumbs off the towel." Mrs. Fraser was beside herself. "Where were you?" she said to Riley. "You had your Mum and me worried sick. And look at the mess you've gotten yourself into. Now come here and I'll clean you off." Mrs. Fraser wet a rag and bent down to clean his fur.

"Oh, here I can do it. I'm sure he was fine, most likely ran out with his bone to show Jack. The little imp gets away from me, also. As soon as he gets a whiff of Jack, he runs off to see him."

"Nay, Lady Cate, he got dirty on my watch and I'll clean him off," she said, wiping the smudges from his fur. "There we are, good as new. Now don't you go running off on me again!" She wagged her finger at him.

"You'd do well to listen to her, Riley," Cate said, picking him up. "And look, you've lost your bone somewhere. Oh, Riley, what are we going to do with you?" The little dog gave her a yip. "Yes, I know, feed you your dinner. I guess all your romping around made you hungry."

Cate fed him and took him for another walk before she ate her own meal. She loved to see the low sun paint the sky over the moors. Tomorrow's forecast promised rain, so Cate wanted to enjoy the outdoors as much as possible today. She planned to spend the next day continuing her research on the castle's history for the book she was writing. It would be a perfect day to spend fireside.

Dreary weather moved in the following morning as expected. Cate settled into her sitting room after breakfast with all the tools of her trade around her. Mrs. Fraser gave Riley another bone to keep him occupied during the rainy day, only allowing him to take it after warning him not to lose this one. Content, he settled with it in front of the fireplace. Cate pulled tables from all over the room to set up her laptop, folders, notes, pencils, pens, sources, and a few other odds and ends in an array around her. She dove into her research. She was making good progress, having learned a good deal about the castle and its inhabitants in her short time there.

Besides gleaning a factual history, the personal history of the castle also interested Cate. As well as having a private interest in her newfound family history, Cate speculated adding this information to her book may make the history more vivid and real to her readers.

In addition to discussing the ball yesterday, Mrs. Campbell dropped off several resources for Cate to peruse to assist in her research. Many of the items were old news articles about one of the castle's former proprietors, Randolph MacKenzie. He, as Mrs. Campbell explained, was quite a scoundrel and would make interesting material for her book.

From Cate's previous research she learned that Randolph MacKenzie was born in 1827, the son of Finlay and Moira. He took over the castle in 1854 upon his father's death. He married Victoria MacKenzie neé Winston in 1850 and the two produced a male heir, Ethan, born in February 1856. Victoria's beauty was renowned, considered by many to be one of the most beautiful women of her time. She captured the hearts of many but Randolph's continuous pursuance of her wooed her to Dunhaven. Cate found many love letters that Victoria kept in which Randolph not only made his intentions clear but wrote her poetry describing her beauty and its effect on his heart.

Mrs. Campbell alluded to Randolph's scandalous behavior when Cate interviewed her a few weeks after arriving in Dunhaven. According to her story, Randolph brought a girl back from his travels abroad to provide a release for his baser instincts. His reputation of being a rogue surprised Cate, then again, perhaps that had been what made his letters easy for him to write. Perhaps it was a case of "he says that to all the girls," Cate mused.

She settled in with her new sources, notepad and pen in hand. Cate opened the folder, finding in it several printouts of copies of the local newspaper from the 1850s. The first article, landing on the paper's front page, trumpeted the headline MURDER AT DUNHAVEN CASTLE. The subtitle read Footman to MacKenzie family found dead on the estate. Cate read the article. It provided few details beyond the headline. With the murder occurring only days before and the investigation in its infancy, details were few. It explained that a guest at the estate's Halloween Ball discovered the body of a young footman named Andrew Forsythe at the foot of the turret room, having fallen from a window there. However, the article informed the reader, the fall was not what killed him. His skull had been crushed with a blunt object several times. The man sustained several other injuries prior to his post-mortem fall including bruises and scratches. The murder occurred in 1856 on October 31, All Hallows' Eve.

Cate shuffled to the next article in the packet. This one followed the story of the murdered footman and the search to bring his killer to justice. The police arrived at the castle, intent on searching it from top to bottom, looking for both the murder weapon and any motive for the crime. In a stunning turn of events, Randolph MacKenzie confessed to the crime stating that he was in a fit of jealous, drunken rage because he perceived the footman shared too intimate a glance with his beloved Victoria at the dinner table.

The article continued on saying the confession took the investigators by surprise since Lord MacKenzie had provided police with an alibi at the time of the crime. Others on the estate corroborated the alibi. Despite thorough questioning about this, Randolph maintained his guilt in the crime, stating that he paid those to support his original story but that his conscience no longer allowed him to lie.

Further articles in the packet described the short trial that took place, the sentencing, and eventual fallout. Randolph was sentenced to prison to await the death penalty, almost unheard of at the time for a man of his position. This left his wife with their infant son to maintain the estate alone.

Cate had not read this anywhere in the materials she found on the estate. The family would have likely downplayed a scandalous event like this, choosing to leave it from the family history rather than face what many would have considered a stain on the family reputation.

Still, something didn't sit quite right with Cate. Even what Mrs. Campbell told Cate months ago didn't add up with the impression she formed when reading the intimate letters sent from Randolph to Victoria. This made even less sense to Cate. While Cate didn't have firsthand knowledge, her gut told her something was off.

Gathering up the folder, she wanted to stretch her legs. Riley was still enjoying his bone, so she left him to it while she went on her quick jaunt. "Be right back, buddy. I need a second opinion." She had a particular destination in mind. Since it was a rainy day, Jack and Mr. Fraser were working inside, repairing various things in the castle, focusing on those that needed fixed before the ball. She knew Jack was working near the grand ballroom downstairs so her stroll took her there.

"Lady Cate!" he said, as she rounded the corner and approached him. "And how are you today?"

"I'm good, how are you?"

"Well, I was fine, but you've got that mischievous look in your eye so I'm betting I won't be in a few minutes."

Cate frowned at him. "I have no such look."

"No? Then what's that in your hand? Just some random paperwork that you happen to be carrying about?"

"Just a few articles about a former castle owner. I just wanted to get your impression on it."

"My impression, huh?" he said, eyeing her as he accepted the folder from her. Opening it, he scanned the articles.

"Well?" she questioned as he closed the folder.

"My impression is this Randolph fellow got in a jealous rage and killed someone then he couldn't live with the guilt, confessed and they sentenced him to death."

Cate frowned again. "Really? It doesn't strike you as odd?"

"No? Perhaps he was a hothead or maybe his wife was having an affair. I don't find it that strange."

"It doesn't make sense." Cate mused aloud, pacing the floor. "It's all too convenient. He has an alibi then out of the blue he confesses? He leaves his beloved wife to raise his infant son alone while he rots in prison awaiting the death penalty. Why would he do that? He would have gotten away with murder by just letting his alibi stand."

"Possibly someone threatened to tell, or he didn't expect someone in his position would get that kind of sentence. Could be any number of things, who knows?"

"Well, Randolph knows and perhaps a few others."

"Cate..." Jack began.

"I'm just saying maybe something else was going on there and we should check into it."

"Caaaaaaaaate," Jack chided.

"And we have the capability to check into it. The year in the article was one of the access points that your grandfather told us about."

"CATE! Are you kidding me?"

"Come on, Jack! My ancestor was accused of murder and was put to death. What if he was innocent?"

"First, he confessed, he wasn't accused of it. And second, what if he wasn't? You're willing to risk our lives to find out if he's innocent?"

Cate made a face. "How are we risking our lives, Jack? All I'm suggesting is that we go back and take a peek around, perhaps prevent a murder, perhaps save an innocent man's life."

"Do you remember, Cate, the conversation we shared with my grandfather about not changing history when we first learned about this? Because I do. What if we change history so much that one or both of us disappear? We shouldn't be messing around with this stuff."

"I won't do anything that will jeopardize our lives."

"That's the point, Cate. You don't know what tiny thing you might do that would jeopardize our lives, there's a butterfly effect."

"Where is your sense of adventure?" Cate asked.

"My sense of adventure? My sense of adventure is ordering something other than the fish and chips at the pub. Not romping around in other time periods solving murders."

"So, you agree the murder needs solved."

"Bah, Cate. I won't win this argument, will I?"

"Probably not. Let's just look around at least. We have a month before the murder. We'll see who the players are and if anything seems amiss."

"Only that, huh?"

"Hey, I'd go myself but it's against the rules."

"Wonderful, now you're concerned with the rules. I guess that's something at least, you're obeying one rule. Okay, okay. So, when do you want to go?"

"Hmm." Cate considered it. "Well, it's September twenty-sixth, we have a little over one month before the murder. How about Sunday? Perhaps we can take a quick peek around while most everyone in the household is at church? Get the lay of the land before we move on to trying to figure out what happened?"

"Sunday it is, I guess."

"Excellent! Glad you agree!"

"Oh, I far from agree, I'm a conscientious objector, but I'll do it, if only to be sure I stop you from erasing some vital part of history by accident."

Cate rolled her eyes at him. She was a former history professor, holding a Ph.D. in History. It was doubtful she'd be so cavalier as to erase a vital part of history. "You're so dramatic." She laughed.

"Says the person who suspects a centuries-old murder, that has been solved, I might add, has some dark secret lurking in it that still needs to be solved."

"We shall see," Cate said. "I'll get everything ready for Sunday! I'll let you get back to your work."

This time Jack rolled his eyes at her. "Fantastic, on both counts" he said.

CHAPTER 2

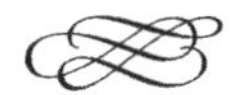

Cate spent the next few days making plans for their trip to 1856. She found period clothing for them to wear. If someone stumbled upon them, roaming around in twenty-first century clothing would put them in a stickier situation than they needed. She also researched as much of the family and the household as she could, making as many notes as possible about who lived there, how they fit into the family and other basic background information. She hoped to get through at least their initial visit without running into anyone, but just in case, it was better to be prepared.

Halfway through her research on Friday, she texted Jack suggesting that it might be a good idea for them to meet to go over some of her findings so he was as prepared as she was before they made the trip to the past. He responded with a straight face emoji but suggested they include his grandfather in case he could shed any light on the situation and suggested they meet over dinner the next evening.

Cate filled the rest of her Friday with checking items off her to-do list for the upcoming Halloween party. The number of details needing attended to amazed Cate again.

She didn't envy Mrs. Campbell's list of tasks to complete; the woman was a party-planning extraordinaire. Not only did she seem able to complete these tasks with ease, she seemed to enjoy it and was already looking forward to planning another epic party on the castle's grounds.

Using the ruse of discussing estate business, Cate, Jack and Stanley, Jack's grandfather, met Saturday evening over dinner provided by Mrs. Fraser. She even provided Riley with another bone to replace the one he had lost. Jack handed it to him, playfully tugging at it until Riley pulled it from his hands. "She's all yours, Riley. You're one tough little mutt!"

"Perhaps in his mind you owe him one since he lost his last one running around the yard searching for you."

"Oh?" Jack asked.

"Yes," Cate answered."Mrs. Fraser gave him one Thursday. When we returned to the kitchen to check on him, he was gone. We found him outside minus his bone. He must have run out of the door looking for you and lost his bone during his search. Did he ever find you?"

"Thursday? No, I was inside that day. I never saw him."

"Hmm, that's right. Funny he didn't realize you were in here. Oh well, at least he's got his replacement, he's happy," Cate said as they watched Riley settle on the floor, chewing his bone. "It's nice to see you again, Mr. Reid," Cate said, turning her attention to the older man.

"Aye, it's always a pleasure to see you too, lassie!"

"Has Jack brought you up to speed on my request?"

"Aye. I told him all about your insane plan," Jack answered before his grandfather.

"It's not insane!" Cate objected. Turning back to Mr. Reid, she said, "We were hoping you might have some information for us about that time period. Did you and either Mary or Gertrude travel back to that time?"

"Now, wait a minute, lassie, I want to discuss some estate business with you before you dive into this discussion and lose all sense of reality," Jack said.

Cate frowned, but gave in. Since their dinner was under the ruse of estate business, Jack reviewed some estate business first to ensure their ploy was grounded in truth.

"Okay, that's done," Cate said. "Now let's move on to the fun stuff."

"That was the fun stuff," Jack said, grinning.

"Only you consider bills and business 'fun stuff' and not time travel."

"Only you consider going back to a time when people died of typhoid in their mid-thirties and indoor plumbing was nonexistent 'fun stuff.'"

"Hey, consider this though, if you were estate manager back then you'd have one less thing to worry about!"

"You two make quite the pair, don't you?" Mr. Reid said, laughing at their bickering.

"Speaking of estate managers, I guess besides your ancestors, we may run into some of ours, huh?"

"Yes," Cate said, opening her research folder that contained the information she had amassed on this topic. "I charted your family tree. Your great-great-great-grandfather, Malcolm Reid, was the estate manager under Randolph MacKenzie. It would be him we'd have the chance to meet. Malcolm and Randolph grew up together before Malcom became Randolph's estate manager." She pulled out a small drawing of a family tree and placed it in front of him.

"Wow, look at you with our family tree!" Jack said, picking up the paper and perusing it. "Take a look, Pap!" he said, handing the older man the paper. "She's got us all mapped out."

"Aye, she has," he answered. "And it looks about right to me. Well done, Lady Cate, well done!"

Cate beamed. "It took a little work, but I was able to track everything down through household documents and some information that you gave me, Mr. Reid. You are a wealth of information!"

"Yeah, he is," Jack agreed. "If I'm lucky he'll even have enough to stave off your crazy plan."

"Crazy plan?" Jack's grandfather questioned.

"Yeah, Pap, Cate's got another one of her brilliant ideas to time travel."

"Ah, time traveling, what a rush that was," Mr. Reid said, reminiscing.

"Bah, don't feed into her Pap, you'll only make her worse," Jack chided.

Cate laughed. "So, tell me this crazy plan you've got, Lady Cate!" Mr. Reid said.

"Isla Campbell gave me a few articles from around the year 1856, one of the time periods that we can travel to, which makes them intriguing to begin with. But what makes them even more intriguing is the tale of murder that I read."

"Oh, aye, you mean the murder of that servant by Lord MacKenzie," he said, nodding his head as he remembered.

"Right. That's the story I mean, but I'm not convinced Lord MacKenzie murdered that man. Hence my desire to time travel. I want to investigate."

"Ah, you think he's innocent?" Mr. Reid asked.

"That she does, Pap, and she's dead set on proving it, too."

"What makes you think that, lassie?"

"A hunch. It doesn't add up. He first says he's innocent, he has a solid alibi, then out of the blue and in a complete reversal, he confesses to the murder and is sentenced to prison, leaving behind his infant son and beloved wife. It just doesn't make sense."

Jack's grandfather considered the information.

"Well?" Jack prodded.

"Well, she's got a point."

"Hey, whose side are you on?" Jack joked.

"I've been the voice of reason long enough, laddie, I'm retired! Now I can voice my opinion. And the lassie has a point."

"Isn't it more probable that old Randolph's guilt got to him and he confessed rather than live with it?" Jack questioned.

"What about his alibi?" Cate tossed back.

"Someone lied to protect him?" Jack answered in the form of a question.

"More than one someone, several people saw him."

"It's not inconceivable," Jack said.

Cate rolled her eyes at him. "We have a way to find out."

Jack looked to his grandfather for help. The older man shrugged his shoulders at him. "It's your show now, Jackie. Yours and Cate's."

Jack sighed, rolling his eyes. "Some help you are."

"Do you know anything else about this story, Mr. Reid?" Cate queried.

Stanley Reid glanced into the air above him, as if searching for an answer. "Not much more than you summarized earlier. Lady Mary and I traveled to that time. They had many a great party on the estate before Randolph's trouble. Lady Victoria was quite the entertainer! I don't know any facts about this though, we didn't speak with Randolph about it, nor did we do any investigating of our own."

Cate raised her eyebrows at Jack. "Well, it looks like it's up to us to do some investigating!"

Jack shrugged his shoulders at her. "Guess I'm not talking you out of it, huh?"

"Nope." Cate answered.

"And I guess you're not going to talk any sense into her?" he said, directing the question to his grandfather.

"To quote the lady, 'nope,'" he said, laughing.

"Ahhhh, well okay then, let's get on with the history lesson so I know the players," Jack acquiesced. "Malcolm was the estate manager for Randolph MacKenzie, you said?"

"Right, and Randolph was the son of Finlay and Moira MacKenzie, grandson of Douglas, who built the castle and discovered the time travel anomaly. The concept was probably still novel to them."

"Anything that we should know about Randolph except that he's a crazy murderer?"

"Hey!" Cate said, batting her hand at him, "that's my ancestor you're slandering there! And, yes, Randolph had quite the reputation before the murder."

"How so?" Jack asked, taking a sip of his ale.

"Womanizer," Mr. Reid chimed in.

"Yes, according to Mrs. Campbell, Randolph garnered quite the reputation. He spent a good bit of time overseas and the rumor was that he brought home a young woman with him. The rumor is he kept her in the tower room to satisfy his 'more base desires' in the words of Mrs. Campbell," Cate said.

"Any record of the girl existing?" Jack asked.

"None that I've found so far."

"So possibly just some tall tales from the village," Jack suggested.

"It could be, but there's usually some truth in a rumor, some reason that started it."

"Most likely an old big-mouthed biddy like Mrs. Campbell," Jack quipped.

Cate scowled at him. "She isn't that bad!"

"If you say so. Okay, so who else are we trying to avoid?"

"Funny," Cate said, groaning. "Also in the household was Victoria, Randolph's wife."

"Anything of note about Victoria?"

"Victoria MacKenzie, neé Winston, was from a well-known and powerful English family. She was also a countess, so she made a lateral move marrying Randolph, although some would have said she stepped down because she moved out of English aristocracy settling for a Scottish lord rather than an English one."

Jack stared straight ahead, then let his head drop to his chest, feigning snoring.

"Okay, okay, I get it, here's the juicy bit," Cate said, rolling her eyes. "Victoria had no shortage of suitors. Her family was not only wealthy and powerful, but she was renowned for her beauty throughout England."

"Aye, she was a real beauty, that one!" Mr. Reid added.

"So, what made the beautiful Victoria leave the English high society for Scotland?" Jack asked.

"She moved to Scotland and married Randolph because he spent countless months wooing her. He wrote her letters, poems, sonnets. He visited daily when he was within her vicinity. Even if she refused to see him, he'd leave her a love note and come right back the next day."

"Looks like his persistence paid off."

"It did, she eventually succumbed to his considerable charm and married him. They had a son, Ethan, in the same year that the murder occurred. He was only nine months old."

"So, when did he bring this supposed girl back?" Jack questioned.

"The rumor mill said he brought her back from his honeymoon," Mr. Reid answered.

"What? Oh, come on, he was so in love with the beautiful Victoria that he brought back another woman from his honeymoon?" Jack complained.

"Yes, it seems rather quick that he tired of her when he was so persistent, right?" Cate said.

"Which makes me think that rumor is just that, a rumor."

"I guess we could find out tomorrow, take a swing by the old tower room and check," Cate joked.

"Caaaaaaaate," Jack admonished.

Cate held her hands up in defeat. "Okay, okay, we won't go into the tower room tomorrow."

Jack grimaced at her, noticing that she only agreed not to go into the tower room tomorrow. "Anyone else?"

"Yes, Randolph had a ne'er-do-well brother that hung around the house many times. His name was Lorne. He wasn't a permanent resident at the castle. He would check in at times with a random woman."

"Perhaps he brought the tower girl?"

"No, that rumor was definitely about Randolph. Lorne seemed like the type that wouldn't bother hiding a girl in the tower room. He had numerous affairs none of which he kept secret. Other than those three, a random girl that Lorne brought home, and the staff, there shouldn't have been anyone else at the castle in those days. Randolph and Lorne had a sister, but she died of influenza when she was only fifteen."

"How did you find this information?"

"Various sources, some from Randolph's letters to Victoria that she kept, some from letters they wrote when he was in prison. Others from my book research, local legends, family histories, et cetera."

"Good work, Cate. Now, I think we need a few ground rules and a backstory, in case we run into someone."

"Rules?" Cate said, looking dismayed.

"Yes, rules. Rule one: we're only going to look around. YOUR words," Jack said as Cate opened her mouth to protest. "IF, and this is an enormous IF, we discover anything amiss, we return. Upon our return, we will discuss how to proceed, if at all. Agreed?"

"Okay, fine." Cate sighed. "I agreed to just get the lay of the land, so that's what we'll do tomorrow."

"And if someone catches us, what's the backstory?"

"Backstory?"

"Yes, Cate, the backstory, who are we? Why we're there? You can't very well say 'Hello, I'm Cate Kensie, I'm a time-traveling history professor and this is my friend, Jack. Mind if we have a look-see?'"

Mr. Reid chuckled at the conversation.

"Wandered in by accident?" Cate kidded, shrugging her shoulders.

Jack made a face. "I don't think that will work."

"We could say we're some distant cousin. Families traveled all the time to stay with each other, often they arrived without notice because correspondence was delayed or lost."

"Okay, so I'm some kind of distant cousin to the MacKenzies?" Jack asked.

"Well, both of us."

"Both of us? That makes no sense."

"Why not? We could be siblings."

"Oh, right, that'll work. Hello, I'm Jack MacKenzie," Jack practiced, pretending to shake someone's hand, "your distant Scottish cousin, and this is my American sister, Cate."

"I could try a Scottish accent, mate," Cate said in her best imitation of Jack's accent.

Jack glanced at his grandfather before both burst with laughter. "Do you want to get us caught?" Jack said when he recovered.

"I thought that was passable."

"Lassie, you couldn't pass for Scottish with that accent if you dressed head to toe in tartan, carried bagpipes and had your clan crest tattooed on your forehead," Jack said, still chuckling.

Still laughing, Jack's grandfather agreed. "Aye, lassie, that's terrible."

Cate rolled her eyes. "Okay, smarty pants, how do we explain me then."

"Ah, my wife?"

Cate frowned. "Hey," Jack said, sipping at his ale, "I saw that. I'm quite a catch, I'll have you know. Besides, it would make sense why you're American then and why we are together."

"Yes," Cate agreed. "It wouldn't be very proper if I was running around the Scottish countryside with a man."

"Nay, they'd think you're one of Lorne's girls," Jack said, letting out another big laugh.

"Okay, so there we are. We are the MacKenzies, distant cousins to Randolph in for a visit. Didn't you get our letter?" Cate practiced, looking shocked.

"And the Emmy goes to..." Jack teased. "Well, I guess we have everything then. Looks like we're ready to travel to 1856, or at least as ready as we'll ever be."

"I suppose I'll need to dig up a fake wedding ring, but other than that we're ready!" Cate said, raising her glass in a toast.

"Good luck to you two. Can I get a copy of this family tree? You've got it so neatly written," Mr. Reid asked, admiring the lineage.

"Sure! I'll make a copy for you now." Cate used her copier to make a copy, bringing it back to him.

"All right, I will see you tomorrow then, bright and early," Jack said when she finished.

"Great! Okay, let's say good night to Jack, Riley!" Cate said, turning to scoop up the little dog. "Riley?" she said, not finding him.

She turned, making a concerned face to Jack. "RILEY!"

she called again, as she climbed to her feet and began looking around the room. Both the little dog and his bone were gone.

"Perhaps he went to thank Mrs. Fraser."

"Well, one way to find out, we'll take our plates down and see if he's there or if we can find him anywhere along the way," Cate suggested.

"I'll wait here," Mr. Reid joked. "You won't get me to walk the length of this castle!"

The pair gathered up their dishes and made their way to the kitchen. They didn't find any trace of Riley along the way. When they got to the kitchen, they asked if Mrs. Fraser had seen him. She answered she hadn't seen the little pup at all, suggesting he may have wandered off with his bone.

"It's odd for him not to come when he's called though," Cate said, beginning to worry.

"We'll look around the house," Jack said. "He couldn't have gotten far and we know he wasn't along the way here. I'll grab some flashlights."

Jack was testing flashlights from the nearby cupboard when they heard a small whine. "Wait, listen!" Cate said, hushing the room to silence. "I hear him crying. It sounds like…"

"He's outside the door again," Mrs. Fraser chimed in, finishing her sentence.

She ran to the door, opening it. "Ah, here he is, Lady Cate. How did you get outside you little bugger?" she asked him as he made his way into the kitchen.

"RILEY!" Cate exclaimed. "Why do you keep running outside?"

"Perhaps he's burying his bone?" Mr. Fraser suggested.

"Maybe," Cate said. "He is a little dirty."

"Ah, that must be it, mystery solved!" Jack said. "I'm glad he's back."

"As am I," Mrs. Fraser said. "You need to stop worrying your mum! Well, is there anything else you need, Lady Cate?"

"No, nothing, sorry for the commotion. I'll see everyone on Monday!" Cate fibbed.

They all said their good nights and went their separate ways. Cate climbed the two levels to her bedroom, changing clothes, settling Riley into his bed and laying down in her own. She prepared for a sleepless night, sure she wouldn't be able to get any rest with the upcoming trip tomorrow.

CHAPTER 3

As expected, Cate was up before the sun the following morning, pacing her bedroom floor in anticipation as the sun rose over the moors. Jack planned to meet her early in the morning to travel to 1856 when she figured most of the household members should be at church services.

When the sun had risen, Cate ate a quick breakfast and took Riley for a short walk before beginning her preparations, trying her best to get her hair styled into what would pass for appropriate in the 1850s. Next, she went through the arduous process of putting her dress on. There were several trunks in one of the bedroom closets with period appropriate clothing for both of them. Previous MacKenzies placed clothing appropriate to the time period of where each time rip led.

The weight of the clothing always surprised Cate. It felt as though she were dragging around several extra pounds while wearing the dress. After she had all elements of her outfit on, she glanced in the mirror. When she was convinced her efforts would suffice at passing her off as a woman from 1856, she decided to check with the expert. She turned to Riley, asking, "Well, Riley, what do you think? Would I pass for a nineteenth century lady?" Riley cocked his head to the side as if considering the question.

Checking the time piece she wore around her neck, she noted that it was almost time for Jack to arrive. Cate locked the door to her room with Riley inside so she knew he would be safe while she was on her journey. She made her way down to the front door, carrying her skirts awkwardly. She hoped she didn't run into anyone in the past on this trip, they would never believe she had worn these dresses all her life the way she moved in them.

When she arrived downstairs, Jack was already making his way in through the front door. "Thought I'd let myself in the front door since I'm a MacKenzie now," he said, dressed in his nineteenth century garb.

"Funny. The clothes worked well," she said, eyeing him up and down.

"I'm not so sure about that, although, I think you look nice in your dress."

Cate curtsied dramatically. "Why thank you, kind sir!" she said, laughing.

"Boy, are these uncomfortable," Jack said, pulling and tugging at his clothes. "I'm glad I live in this century."

Cate smiled, holding in a laugh. "Mine aren't much better," she admitted. "Okay, ready to go?"

"No, but I don't think I've got a choice."

"You haven't, come on!" Cate said, leading the way upstairs, slower than usual thanks to her dress.

"Wow, so there IS something that can slow down the great Catherine Kensie," Jack joked.

"Yes, this dress is not comfortable, let me tell you. It weighs a ton! I'll have no trouble sleeping tonight after all the exercise from lugging this weight around."

They reached the bedroom they referred to as the "1850s bedroom" because of the rip in time leading to the 1856 time period. Cate held the timepiece in her hand as they entered the closet. She took a deep breath and said, "Okay, let's do this!"

Jack placed his hand over hers and together they rubbed the timepiece. Rubbing the timepiece in specific spots within the castle, as they had discovered, controlled the time rips and allowed them to travel back and forth between their present time and a past time period. The second hand began its characteristic slowing down, ticking slower and slower until its movement was imperceptible. They also learned, as they traveled to another time, time almost stood still in their present time period. The watch, engraved with the admonition *Always keep an eye on YOUR time*, continued to keep the present day's time.

As the watch slowed to a crawl, Cate and Jack glanced around. "Guess we're here," Cate said.

"Guess so," Jack said.

"Okay, well, let's go explore," Cate said, starting for the closet door which they found closed in this time period.

"Wait a minute, Cate," Jack said, grabbing her by the arm and pulling her back.

"What?" she said, holding her hands up and shrugging her shoulders.

"At least let me check everything out before we plow out into the house," he said, pushing her behind him and creeping to the door.

He cracked it open a slit, glancing into the outer room. Spying nothing, he opened the door and stepped out, continuing to scan the room. Cate followed him into the room. They crept to the door leading to the hallway. Jack inched it open, peering through the slit into the hallway. "Well?" Cate whispered from behind him.

"Coast's clear for the moment," he whispered.

"Okay, let's go!" Cate said, skirting past him and into the hallway.

Rolling his eyes, he followed her. "What are we looking around for, Cate?" he asked as he followed her down the hallway, recognizing Cate appeared to have a specific location that she was heading for.

"Anything that gives us some information about Randolph and company, like journals or handwritten notes. Anything that can shed some information on the stories that surrounded Randolph and the castle in Randolph's time."

"And where do you propose we search for this?"

"I thought we'd start in the office. All his correspondence is likely there. We can rifle through the desk."

They reached the office room and, after entering, Cate went straight for the desk. Papers covered the desk. She scanned the papers scattered on the desk. By the appearance of the desk, Randolph was not an organized person. She discovered nothing of interest so she tried the drawers.

"Jack," Cate whispered.

"Yeah?" he said, turning from the door where he was scanning the hallway.

"Check in those files over there for anything that might be of interest," she said, pointing toward a pile of files sitting on top of an old-fashioned filing cabinet. Jack strode over to peruse the files as Cate went through the drawers of the desk.

After searching each drawer, Cate joined Jack as he finished the last of the files in his pile. "Anything?" she questioned.

"Only employment records and investments and so on, nothing that would shed any light on your mystery. How about you?"

"Nothing," she said, holding her hands out.

"Okay, let's head back."

"Wait a minute," she said. "There are more places to check."

"Such as? I don't like gallivanting around here."

"We still should have time. The church service shouldn't be over. Let's check Victoria's bedroom."

Jack rolled his eyes again as he followed Cate upstairs to the bedrooms. They found the one Victoria inhabited and scanned her desk and wardrobe, again, coming up with little information. Victoria had kept a journal but, since the birth of her son, she had written little, so it didn't do much to shed any light on the current mystery.

"Okay, Cate, fun's over, let's go," Jack insisted. Cate plodded back toward the 1850s bedroom. As they passed the stairway to the tower room, Cate paused. "Cate, let's go," Jack said, pausing a few steps in front of her after detecting her hesitance.

Cate didn't answer, nor did she move to follow him. She stared up the curving stairway that stretched between the outer and inner stone walls. Despite being unable to spot the door at the top, she knew it waited around the bend. Jack could imagine the gears turning inside her head. "Cate, no, no way," he insisted.

"But this is why we came!" she contended.

"No, Cate. It's too dangerous."

"How is it dangerous?"

"What if someone is in there? What do you propose we do, Cate? Open the door, say hello and introduce ourselves?"

"No, but we could listen at the door and determine if it sounds like someone is in there, if there're any signs it's inhabited."

"Let's go home."

"Oh, come on, one little listen and we can go, I promise," Cate said, starting up the stairs.

"Cate? Wait! Damn it," he said, charging after her.

Cate reached the top of the stairs and pressed her ear against the door. Jack met her there moments later, huffing from running after her. "Well? Do you hear any signs of life?" he asked.

After a moment, Cate answered as she scowled. "No."

Jack raised his eyebrows. "Really? Aw shucks. Okay, let's go." Cate made a face at him. "Come on, you promised."

"Okay," she said, sighing.

The pair began down the steps. After a few steps, Jack stopped dead, putting his arm out to stop Cate. "What is it?" she whispered.

He held his finger to his lips, miming that he thought he heard footsteps. Within seconds, Cate heard footsteps, too. Her eyes wide, she stared at him, panicked. They were trapped with only a closet between them and the source of the footsteps. The room provided their only refuge to be undiscovered. They had to act fast to descend the stairs and reach the closet before the person approaching rounded the bend. She produced a key from her dress pocket. Jack recognized it as the skeleton key for the castle. Grabbing it, he raced down the few steps toward the door. He unlocked it and opened it, pushing Cate inside ahead of him before easing it shut moments before the footsteps came close to them.

Both listened, pressed against the door, holding their breath as the footsteps passed them. The sound continued up the staircase toward the tower room. Cate signaled Jack to open the door to identify who it was. Jack signaled "no" with a vigorous shake of his head. Cate pressed her lips together and nodded her head "yes" with equal vigor. He rolled his eyes again and eased the door open a crack.

The pair of them stared out of the small gap. From their angle, they could view the door to the tower room. The figure of a man stood outside the door, fiddling with a set of keys, a tray in his hand. On the tray sat a plate and a teacup. It appeared he was taking food to someone. After finding the appropriate key, he turned, glancing down the stairway before unlocking the door and entering the room.

Cate and Jack shrank back as he turned around. Cate gasped, covering her mouth to quiet any noise. "Who is that?" Jack whispered as the man's face came into view. He had dark, thick, wavy hair. Thick eyebrows shrouded deep-set, dark eyes housed in an angular and chiseled face.

"That," Cate whispered back, "is Randolph MacKenzie."

When they heard the door shut, Jack said, "We better make a run for it."

He barely had the words out of his mouth before Cate was already dashing as fast as her dress would allow down the stairs. Jack followed her and the two raced back to the bedroom. Hearts pounding and gasping for breath, Jack and Cate closed the door behind them, taking a moment to breathe. Not wanting to wait much longer, Jack grabbed Cate's hand and pulled her into the closet. "Let's go home," he said.

Without a word, Cate produced the time piece, and the two grabbed hold of it, rubbing it until it started its cycle of speeding up. Within moments, the timepiece was back to normal speed. Jack let out a long breath. "Oh, thank God," he said, running his hands through his hair then doubling over to rest them on his thighs.

"Close call," Cate agreed.

"Too close," Jack said.

"But well worth it."

"How do you figure that?"

"We have the answer to one of our questions." Jack screwed up his face. "Randolph MacKenzie is most definitely keeping someone in the tower room."

Jack groaned. "A fine time for him to be visiting that person too, when he's supposed to be at church service."

"He must have stayed home to visit her. What better time to do so? The entire household, including his wife, is away."

"Well, are you satisfied?" Jack said, loosening his collar.

"Not in the slightest, the mystery deepens! So we've established he's got someone in that tower. Why? And who?"

"Most likely a girl like the town gossips said." Cate didn't answer, instead, taking a few steps away, finger on her lips as she pondered the events. "Caaaaaaaate," Jack chided.

"I need to do more research before..." Cate began.

"Before you give up?" Jack asked, hope filling his voice.

"No, before we go back."

"I was afraid you'd say that."

"Look on the bright side, Jack."

"What's that?"

"You get to put off going back until I'm done researching all I can about this mysterious tower room tenant."

Jack rolled his eyes for the umpteenth time, hands on his hips. Cate flashed a smile at him. "Well, I am going to change, I've got my work cut out for me today!"

"I'd say good luck, but I'm almost hoping you find nothing."

"You should know me better than that, I'll keep digging until I do."

"Yeah." Jack smiled, then laughed. "Yeah, I know you will. So, I'll have to hope that you have to dig forever so I can stay in my favorite time period: my own. I'll see you tomorrow, Cate."

"See you tomorrow, Jack. Enjoy the rest of your day off." Jack started out of the closet. "Oh, and Jack?"

"Yeah?" he said, turning around to face her.

"Thanks, I appreciate your help."

"No problem, lassie, no problem."

CHAPTER 4

Cate returned to her room, unlocking the door to find an impatient Riley waiting for her. "Hey buddy, why the long face? I wasn't that long!"

Riley issued a small whine in response to her question. "Okay, okay, I get it. You didn't have a proper walk today. I'll tell you what, as soon as I get changed, I'll take you for a walk." Riley gave another whine then a yip. "I'm going as fast as I can," she said, unlacing her dress. "I'll NOT walk you around in this get-up!"

Cate changed as fast as the old-fashioned clothes would allow her and set the dress aside to put away later. She scooped Riley up into her arms and carried him down to the front door where she slipped on her boots and headed out with him. Setting him down on the front lawn, she asked, "Where do you want to explore today, Riley?"

In answer, Riley raced ahead of her to the side of the castle. "Whoa, buddy! Wait up!" Cate yelled dashing to keep up with him. As she rounded the corner of the castle, she saw the little pup dash into a clump of hedges in the side garden and disappear. Cate followed him, trying but failing to keep up with him. She emerged from the garden and glanced around over the rolling hills but saw no Riley. She called and called to him, but he did not dart out from any of the trees or hedges to run to her.

It was unlike Riley to disappear. He stayed close to her during their walks and enjoyed playing with his ball. Cate had brought the ball in her pocket. She planned to give Riley some exercise playing fetch, but he had not even bothered to demand one toss before he had run off. She hoped that he hadn't caught the scent of some small animal and run off chasing it.

"Riley! Riley!" she continued to call as she scanned the area. Still, she spotted no sign of Riley. After calling a few more times, she heard a small yip coming from her right. She made her way toward the sound, continuing to call out to him. As she crested one of the hills, she saw the little dog, milling around near a folly on the property. Cate sighed and jogged over to the area. "And what is so interesting about this folly today, Riley, that you didn't come when I called you?" she asked in a stern voice.

Riley looked up at her, his dark almond eyes considering her question. Within a moment, he returned to milling around the outside, sniffing the ground. He stopped a few times and glanced toward the interior of the folly, but never ventured in. "All right, Riley, let's move on," Cate said, "how about we play some fetch?"

At the last word, Riley's ears perked, and he stared up at her, catching sight of the little ball she held in her hands. "I figured that might get your attention," Cate laughed and tossed the ball away from the structure, watching as Riley chased after it. He scooped it up into his mouth and stood waiting for her to catch up to him for another round.

Cate and Riley continued their game until they reached the loch. Riley often enjoyed a restful nap on the banks after playing, so Cate settled in, sitting next to him as he curled into a ball, his head resting on her leg.

Cate lay back on her elbows. The trees danced in the autumn breeze and the wind rippled the waters in the loch. As she contented herself to enjoy the beauty of nature, her thoughts turned to what she had experienced earlier this morning. It appeared Randolph had someone in the tower room, but who and for what purpose? Were the stories about him true? Cate didn't imagine this was the case, though she couldn't say why. Jack would tell her she was being foolish, a romantic, that Randolph was the cad everyone assumed him to be. But Cate couldn't shake the notion there was more to this story than met the eye.

She considered her research and tried to plan where she would search for more information. The tower room was on the top of her list. She had been in the room before, it was where Mrs. Fraser stored the late Lady MacKenzie's personal items until Cate found time to sort through them and determine how to deal with everything. It was also another hot spot for the time piece. Cate wondered if this was related to Randolph's preoccupation with the tower room. She wasn't aware of which time rips Randolph was familiar with, but this was a possibility.

Perhaps if he was aware of this one, she mused, he was using the rip to travel through time while everyone else was out of the house. She questioned her theory though because of the tray of food he carried. Was he taking himself a snack for when he returned? Perhaps time travel made Randolph hungry. Cate laughed out loud at her latest supposition. Now that her theories were entering ridiculous territory, she supposed it was time to head back to the castle.

"What do you say, Riley?" she said, sitting up and stroking the dog's fluffy fur. "Shall we head back for some lunch?"

Riley closed his eyes again, giving a big sigh. Cate took

that as a "no." She gave him a few more minutes to continue his nap as she rubbed his head. After he caught a few more winks of sleep, Cate gathered him into her arms and stood up, brushing herself off. "Come on, little guy," she said, starting on the path leading back to the castle, "I'm getting hungry." Riley lay in her arms for a few moments then decided he wanted to use the walk back to explore. Cate set him down and allowed him to investigate the pathway back.

As they entered the castle through the kitchen entrance, Cate said, "That should tire you out for a while." She busied herself making her lunch and setting it on a tray to take to her sitting room. Cate set up camp on her chaise lounge with lunch and her laptop to stream a movie while Riley stretched out on the carpet for a nice long sleep.

When she finished, she checked her watch. It was almost one thirty in the afternoon. As much as she wanted answers, Cate decided that she wouldn't start any research this late in the day and opted to spend the day relaxing with movies and another long walk with Riley.

Cate found herself tired early that evening, figuring that it was a mix of her sleepless night and the adrenaline burst from this morning's adventure. She turned in early with the promise of using the next day for research.

Cate yawned, stretching as the sun rose over the moors outside of her bedroom window. Bright morning sun struck her in the face as she glanced out of the window. The warm glow painted the morning sky brilliant shades of orange, yellow and red, casting the scenery below in a rosy light. "What a beautiful morning for a long walk, Riley," Cate said, as she dressed for the day. The little pup crawled out of his bed, stretching his legs before sitting next to Cate, eyeing her expectantly.

"Okay, how about a quick pit stop outside before breakfast and then afterwards we can take a nice long stroll?" Cate asked. Riley bounded off the bed and headed for the sitting room. Laughing, Cate followed him. He had already settled into his new life at the castle. Cate remembered when she had wondered if Riley would feel at home here before they had moved. Now, she couldn't imagine the little pup anywhere but Dunhaven. Not only had he taken to the castle and its grounds, but he seemed happy here. Cate understood why, they lived in a museum with grounds that reminded her of a park and everyone in the household fussed over him. They had come so far from the little three-room apartment with its tiny patch of grass outside.

Cate let Riley out through the front door to take care of his business before heading to the kitchen to eat. She had gotten in the habit of having breakfast with Mr. and Mrs. Fraser and Jack on Monday mornings rather than eating alone in the large dining room. She found it enjoyable to have people around after having lived alone for so long and she enjoyed the conversation about weekend events. Cate stunned Mrs. Fraser when she had asked to dine with them after first arriving here, but now it had become part of the routine. Even Emily Fraser seemed to enjoy the mealtimes they shared.

"Good morning, Mrs. Fraser!" Cate said, entering the kitchen, with Riley trailing behind her.

"Well, good morning, Lady Cate. And good morning little Riley! And how was your weekend, little pup? Did you get lots of rest and relaxation?" Mrs. Fraser asked, bending down to the little dog and giving his head a gentle pat.

"He sure did," Cate answered for him. "Lots of playtime

and lots of naptime. Where are our intrepid groundskeepers this morning?"

"Ah, getting a few tools ready for the day while they wait on the breakfast. Wanted to get an early start on their work today. My Charlie is fussing to no end about having these old grounds just so for your big party."

"Oh, I appreciate that, but the grounds are always above par in my estimation," Cate said.

"Well, I appreciate hearing that, Lady Cate, and I know Charlie will too, but," she said, holding up her hands, "when he gets something in his mind there's no stopping him."

Cate laughed. "I know that feeling well."

"Darn right she does," Jack said, catching the tail end of the conversation as he came through the kitchen door with Charlie Fraser. "Good morning, Lady Cate. And where, oh where is my good friend, Sir Riley?" Riley dashed to him, standing on his hind legs and pawing at his leg. "Oh, there he is, and how are you today, little laddie?" Jack asked, picking up the small dog and tousling the dark fur on his head. "Oh, what's that?" he asked, leaning his head closer to the dog's mouth, "hungry, did you say?"

Cate laughed. "Good morning, Jack and Mr. Fraser. Yes, he's hungry, I'm still getting his breakfast ready," she said, shaking some kibble into his bowl. "Okay, little buddy, here is your breakfast." She set the bowl down out of the way as the rest of the group served themselves breakfast and sat down at the table. Cate had made great strides with the staff since she had come to the castle. Mrs. Fraser now let Cate serve herself oatmeal at shared breakfasts. Cate filled her bowl, sprinkled some raisins onto it and sat down in her usual spot at the table.

"So, Mr. Fraser, I hear you have quite the vision for the castle's exterior for the party," Cate said, winking at Mrs. Fraser.

"Aye, I do, Lady Cate. It's been a long while since we've had proper guests on the estate. She's got to be in tip-top shape," he answered her.

"Speaking of, that reminds me, Cate," Jack chimed in. "I'll have a few additional jobs for the lawn service the week of the party. I want the grounds to be perfect for the party."

Cate nodded, "Sounds good," she said, scooping up a spoonful of oatmeal, "Whatever you presume we need."

"Lady Cate?" Mr. Fraser asked.

"Yes?" Cate answered, thinking this might be the most she'd ever heard the quiet man speak.

"I had a… a…" He stammered. "A vision I guess you might call it for the outside, I was hoping to get your approval on it."

"I'm all ears," Cate said, excited to hear the idea.

"Well, if I'm not mistaken, there are some old family banners hidden away in the old servant's quarters. The kind that used to hang on the castle to announce the clan for miles around. I thought it would be just wonderful to hang them again."

"Oh, that sounds great. I bet that would look nice, especially given the party's theme."

"And," he continued, sitting straighter in his chair, encouraged by Cate's acceptance of his ideas, "the garden that's accessible from the ballroom, wouldn't it be lovely to have lights strung all the way around? We could open the doors to the garden if it's a nice enough evening to allow the guests to wander back and forth between the inside and outside. Adding a few tables could incorporate the garden into the event. My cousin owns a rental business with just such lights so we'd have no problem getting what we need, assuming you like the idea, Lady Cate."

"I think it sounds marvelous," Cate agreed. "Incorporating

the lighted garden into the party is enchanting. I think it'll seem magical."

Mr. Fraser dropped his eyes to the table, smiling, proud of his accomplishment. "Why, thank you, Lady Cate."

"I didn't realize you were such a party-planning pro, Mr. Fraser. I should have been inviting you to my meetings with Mrs. Campbell," Cate said.

"If it's all the same to you, Lady Cate, I'll let you do the talking to her."

Cate smirked, neither of the Frasers cared for Isla Campbell. Cate didn't blame them; the woman was an insatiable gossip. She was also one of the first stops on Cate's list for researching the tower mystery. If anyone wanted to spill any rumors, no matter how unsubstantiated, about what went on in the tower room in the 1850s, it would be the town crier herself, Mrs. Campbell.

"I will relay your plans at our next meeting on Wednesday. I'm sure she'll be thrilled to hear what you're planning," Cate said.

Mrs. Fraser gave a huff, insinuating nothing that simple could ever thrill that woman. Cate held in a giggle. They finished their meal making other light conversation about the party preparation. After breakfast, Cate stayed for a quick cup of tea, or cuppa, as they referred to it here, with Mrs. Fraser before taking Riley for his long walk around the grounds.

By lunchtime, Riley was tuckered out and ready for a nap allowing Cate to eat and begin her research unfettered. Leaving Riley napping, Cate climbed to the tower room. She would begin by searching for clues in the room itself. She didn't know what she expected to find there, but she thought it wouldn't hurt to take a quick peek around.

As she climbed the stairs, she thought of her last experience here in 1856. Her heart skipped a beat as she remembered how she and Jack had fled from the doorway of the tower room to the small closet steps away. She thought of how they had waited, holding their breath, hoping Randolph MacKenzie himself did not catch them. At least on this trip Cate would encounter no one, she mused.

She reached the top of the spiral staircase and opened the door to the room. Several stacks of boxes still littered the space, containing the late Lady Gertrude MacKenzie's belongings. Cate had made good progress sorting through Gertrude's effects, but she had not yet decided what to do with them. While some things she preferred to keep, many items she was still uncertain about. She did not want or need them, but she was reluctant to discard them as though they were meaningless. Her indecision resulted in a room filled with memories.

Cate sighed, at least she knew where she did not need to check. She surveyed the room. Beside the boxes, the room was rather bare. She would inspect the walls to detect if there were any markings or etchings made by someone held prisoner in the room. Barring that, the only other source of information would be the large wardrobe that stood against the far wall.

Cate had never looked inside of it before, assuming it was an unused piece of furniture, moved here to be kept out of the way. Now Cate beheld it with fresh eyes, wondering if it held a clue to her mystery. But first she'd have to move several boxes to get to it. There was no way to open it without moving them.

She would start with her examination of the walls first, Cate decided, putting off moving the boxes for as long as possible. She gave as thorough an exam as possible, pushing a few things aside, but everything looked normal on the stone walls. There were general scrapes and dings but nothing that indicated any significance. Cate wasn't sure what she had expected, other than perhaps the words "HELP ME" carved into the stone somewhere like in a gothic novel, but she found no traces of anything like that.

She stared over at the mountain of boxes in front of the wardrobe. She considered asking Jack to help her move them. "Boy, I'm getting soft," she said aloud to herself. Six months ago she would have struggled with a box of any size and never asked for help from anyone. "Time to toughen up, Cate," she said, resolving to move the stack of boxes herself.

After about thirty minutes, Cate patted herself on the back for a job well done. She now had access to open the wardrobe. The hinges creaked as she opened the wooden doors, and she held her breath as she waited to see what was inside. With the doors opened, Cate stared into an empty cabinet, disappointed. Toggling her cell phone's flashlight on, she checked the corners, but found nothing but cobwebs. Scowling, Cate sighed, tracing her finger along the dust that filled the bottom of the cabinet. While she had no expectations, finding nothing was disappointing.

As she traced her finger along the bottom, she felt a groove in the wood. She turned on her cell phone's flashlight again and looked at it. A layer of dust covered it but there was a faint line discernible only under the bright light. She blew the dust away and examined the crack further. She followed the edge around, it seemed to form a small rectangular box. Cate wondered if it was a compartment. She tried to slide the wood forward, backward, and side-to-side but it wouldn't budge. She peeked underneath the front of the cabinet, trying to see if it was accessible from the bottom. Blindly, she stuck her hand underneath and tried to feel the box from the underside or move it, but it would not budge.

Cate sat up, sighing, dust and cobwebs now adorning her hair after crawling around on the floor. Cate next tried to slide her fingernail under the edge and pry the board up. It wouldn't budge no matter what angle she tried. She stared at the little box, her lips pressed together as she thought. Perhaps it was a secret compartment, triggered by a mechanism somewhere.

She pressed on the box itself, hoping it was a spring-loaded mechanism. She pressed different areas, center, corners, sides, front, and back, to no avail. Next she tried areas around the box, nothing triggered it to open. She tried the decorative elements on the front of the wardrobe, pushing them, trying to twist them and turn them in various ways, none of it affected the box.

Cate was not ready to concede yet. If she couldn't solve the puzzle, she'd use brute force. She gathered herself up off of the floor and hurried to the library. Riley had awoken from his nap and entertained himself chewing on a stuffed moose he retrieved from his toy chest. She stroked the fur on his head and left him gnawing on his toy after retrieving a letter opener from the desk.

Making her way back up to the tower, she went straight to the wardrobe. Using extreme caution, she wedged the letter opener into the crack and pried. After some effort, the block of wood moved. She was encouraged, at least the block was removable, not just a crack in the wardrobe. However, it was still difficult and slow-going. The workmanship on the block was precise, it fit tight to the surrounding wood, making it hard for her to get any leverage. She was also careful not to damage the wood that surrounded it.

After almost forty-five minutes of delicate prying, pulling, teasing, tugging, and wrenching, she grabbed hold of the block and pulled it free. Careful not to drop it back into the hole, Cate extracted it, holding it in her hand as she took a moment to be proud of her hard work. Eager to see if there were any fruits for all of her labor, she switched on her cell phone's flashlight. She leaned forward to shine it into the cavity she had just opened.

She expected to see a hole, but, much to her surprise and delight, she saw a few pieces of paper at the bottom. A smile crossed her face, and she reached in and removed them with care. One of the small papers was blank. The second one was a charcoal drawing of a man's face. It was good; someone was a talented artist. Cate recognized Randolph MacKenzie's likeness in the unsigned sketch. The third piece of paper had writing on it. Cate skimmed it, setting the sketch aside. Her eyes grew wide as she read the short note.

R –

I am sorry, but I must go. Your family has already paid too heavy a cost. I will never forget what you have done.

– S

Cate drew in a sharp breath. This note must have been for Randolph. The drawing was the likeness of Randolph and the note was addressed to "R," it had to be him! To Cate, this offered irrefutable proof that someone had lived in this tower room, someone who had known Randolph. Part of the rumor must be true. What didn't seem to pass muster was that the person writing it was being held against his or her will. The writer was apologetic and indicated it was Randolph bearing some burden on their behalf, this had to have meant that they were not a prisoner, Cate surmised.

Excited by her find, Cate gathered the papers and her letter opener and returned to the library. She placed everything on the desk and checked her watch. "Should we go outside for a walk before dinner, Riley?" Cate said, her intentions two-fold. She wanted to give Riley some exercise, and she hoped to find Jack and reveal her find.

Riley discarded the toy in favor of "outside," trotting in front of Cate to the front door. Cate made her way around the path that circled the house and gardens. Riley seemed content to wander in and out of the various shrubs and bushes. About halfway through their walk, Cate spotted Jack watering a few flowering plants. "There's your buddy, Riley," she said to the little pup, "let's go say hello!" Riley, spotting Jack, raced over in front of Cate to greet him.

"Well, hello there, little Riley!" Jack said, petting his head. "My, my, Lady Cate, this is a new look for you."

Cate's brow furrowed as she approached Jack. She looked down at her clothes, they seemed standard, her usual leggings with a tunic sweater and an added cardigan for extra warmth. She finished the look with a pair of black riding boots. "Huh?" she said, confused.

Jack swept a few cobwebs from her hair. "Are you trying out your 'Ghosts of the Past' look?"

"Oh," Cate said, swatting at her hair and laughing, "I got a little dirty on my latest research mission."

"And where were we researching, Indiana Jones? The depths of a tomb?"

"No, the depths of the tower room."

"Find anything interesting? Maybe a signed confession from Randolph?"

"I did! But it wasn't a signed confession."

"Oh, no, let me guess. It's something that deepens the mystery and means you are hellbent on time traveling to find out more."

"It's like you're psychic, Jack. Has anyone tested you for ESP?"

"I think my sixth sense is about as strong as your comedy routine."

Cate grimaced. "Okay, all joking aside, I found a note hidden in a secret compartment in the wardrobe accompanied by a drawing. The sketch is of Randolph and the note is addressed to 'R'. The writer apologizes to 'R', saying the family had endured too high a cost already and would never forget what he had done."

"Who signed it?"

"I'm not sure, it just says 'S.'"

"S? Like the letter?"

"Yes, just the letter 'S.' I'll show you the note and sketch tomorrow after lunch if you have a quick second. It's quite something."

"I'll reserve my judgement for after I see it."

"Fair enough! Well, I think this is a great find, I'm encouraged. I'll let you get back to your watering though and we can discuss it more after you've scrutinized it."

"Okay, Cate. But don't get too optimistic, you know I'm a killjoy for time travel."

Cate laughed as she began walking away, calling Riley to come with her. "Oh, yes, I know," she said, turning around to wave before she left.

Cate opted for a movie with her dinner, still riding the high of her discovery. She looked at the note several times, reading everything possible into it, trying to shore up her case before she showed it to Jack. There was no doubt in Cate's mind he would try to argue it wasn't what she thought it was, but Cate knew she was on to something.

She wasn't sure the castle held any more information for her research. Her next step, after getting Jack's take on the note, was to see if she could wheedle any additional information out of Mrs. Campbell at their meeting on Wednesday.

CHAPTER 5

Cate spent the better part of Tuesday organizing information for her upcoming meeting with Mrs. Campbell regarding the Halloween ball. The details were overwhelming. But she felt remiss in her duties as hostess if she did not, at least, keep up with the details and make some meaningful contribution to the discussions. Mrs. Campbell had a heavy hand when it came to taking charge of the planning, but Cate still felt the party was her responsibility.

After a walk with Riley before lunch, Cate returned to the library to find an email waiting for her from Molly. The title alone made Cate laugh out loud. She clicked on the subject line that read "SO EXCITED!!!!!!!!!!"

Cate! We're less than three weeks away from my trip to SCOTLAND! I still can't believe I get to stay in a castle either. I can't tell you how excited I am! Oh, I'm also excited to see you and that cute little doggie of yours, too! ;) I started packing! And I have already gotten overwhelmed, so I was hoping to get your help with it before I end up dragging three suitcases across the pond. Are jeans and sweaters appropriate? Is it cold there? Do we dress up every night for dinner like Downton Abbey? *HELP! I'm not sure what to pack now that I'll be staying with and dining with an honest-to-goodness Countess!*

Also, thank you so much for renting a costume for me over there so I don't have to pack one. The way I am going, I won't have room for souvenirs on the way home!

Okay, I'll let you go before you disinvite me. Looking forward to hearing from you AND to my trip!!!

Molly

Molly's email had Cate in stitches as she read it. Same old Molly, she reflected. She was looking forward to seeing her too, she had missed her old friend. Cate was just about to hit the reply button when Mrs. Fraser arrived with her lunch. Thanking her, she ate lunch before answering Molly's email. After her lunch, she typed an email back to Molly.

Hi Molly – We are looking forward to seeing you, too! It will be nice to hear another American accent around the house. It's definitely cooler here than it is in Aberdeen! Sweaters and jeans would be perfect. Also, I'd suggest some comfortable shoes for walking and a light fall jacket or raincoat. Riley and I love to take long walks and we'd be happy to have you join us and see the entire estate. It's beautiful here.

As I mentioned before, I have two other guests coming later in the week. So, Wednesday, Thursday and Saturday, we'll have everyone for dinner and we wear smart casual for dinners. When we're here with just the girls, it will be casual dress. We might even dine in the library, no frills, if you'd like!

I'm just an email away if you have more questions!

Cate

Cate had just hit the send button when Jack appeared at the library door, knocking on it before entering. "M'lady," he said, bowing extravagantly.

Cate laughed, shaking her head. "Always so dramatic," she teased.

"Always," he said, grinning. "So where is this letter?"

Cate grabbed the papers from her folder, jumping up from the desk and making her way over to Jack. "It's more of a note than a letter," she said, handing it to him.

He glanced first at the drawing, then read the note. Cate waited with bated breath for his reaction. As usual, she found him impossible to read. "Well?" she asked.

"Well, nothing."

"Nothing?" she said, confused.

"Yeah, nothing. It looks like 'S' vanished and that was that. Seems like 'R' never found the note. He, assuming it's a he, probably wondered what happened to her, assuming it's a her."

"Assuming? 'R' has got to be Randolph. 'S' drew his picture and put it with the note, so I think it's a safe bet."

"Okay, so 'S' left Randolph a note he never found."

"And 'S' must have not been a prisoner, it looks like he or she left of their own free will after apologizing. So, the rumors about a person held captive in the tower room must be false."

"I think you're jumping to conclusions, Cate."

Cate scowled at him. "If I am it's not that far of a leap."

"We aren't sure 'S' isn't a prisoner. Look here, I'll never forget what you've done? That sounds ominous to me."

"No, it's like 'you're so great, I'll never forget what you did for me!'" Cate explained.

"Or, 'wow, you're a jerk, I'll never forget what you did TO me,'" Jack countered.

"What about the apology? And the stuff about the high cost for the family?" Cate argued back.

"Perhaps 'S' means the high cost because he's a jerk. I'm not sure, but I don't assume it means that Randolph isn't a murderer."

"Okay, point taken, perhaps he is a murderer, but who is 'S'? And what happened there? And why did 'S' leave? There are so many questions."

"And I don't have any answers." Jack shrugged, handing the papers back to Cate.

"No, I don't expect that you do but..." Cate said, a gleam in her eye as she glanced up at him.

Jack shook his head as though he didn't want to hear what she said next.

"We could find out the answers."

He sighed. "I'm not going to argue with you."

"Because you want answers, too!" Cate exclaimed.

"No, because I'll lose again. So, what is your plan?"

"I'm not sure. I have to consider it more. Give me a couple of days to come up with a plan for you to hate."

"Deal. You come up with the plan, I'll hate it."

Cate nodded her head, smiling. "For now, I'll hate the idea that you're coming up with the plan at all while I go find these banners with Mr. Fraser."

"Okay!" Cate agreed. "Oh, is there anything that I need to discuss with Mrs. Campbell tomorrow from your end?"

"No, nothing other than what I've mentioned already. If anything comes up, I'll let you know."

"Okay, sounds good! Thanks, Jack."

Cate looked over at the stack of notes, paperwork, samples, and other party paraphernalia on the desk. She groaned at how much more needed done. Wind rustled outside of the window, drawing her attention outdoors. Maybe a nice long walk with Riley before she finished her party-planning tasks. "What do you say to another walk, Riley?" Riley jumped to his feet, always ready to explore. Cate took full advantage of the pup's adventurous personality, spending over an hour and half allowing him to run around outside, play ball and enjoy the beautiful fall day.

After enjoying the hike around the property, Cate settled in to finish her necessary work before dinner. Then she spent a cozy night cuddled up with Riley under a blanket with a good book.

CHAPTER 6

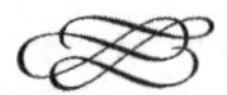

Cate spied the rising sun from bed the next morning, choosing to sleep in a bit to conserve her strength for her meeting later today. Isla Campbell was incredible in her efficiency for party-planning, but she was an exhausting woman to deal with. With some luck, Cate could use the meeting to her advantage to get some useful information from her.

Cate spent the first part of her morning walking the grounds with Riley. The morning was cool and damp, but they both enjoyed it. They entered the castle through the kitchen, greeting Mrs. Fraser for a second time this morning.

"Mrs. Fraser, do you mind if I leave Riley here with you while I meet with Mrs. Campbell?" Cate asked.

"Not at all, Lady Cate."

"Thanks. I don't think Isla cares for animals," Cate confessed.

"I dinnae think that woman cares for much outside of gossip," Mrs. Fraser answered. "The little pup will be just fine with me."

"Oh, Jack and Mr. Fraser are working right outside in the

back garden, so he might try to sneak out on you again. I'm sure he'll go straight to them, though, so no worries if he gets out of your sight!"

"Aye, he's very fond of young Jack. I dare say, young Jack is just as fond of him!"

"They do have fun together." Cate laughed, thinking of them playing fetch and tug-of-war. "Well, I had better get changed and get my notes together. If I know Mrs. Campbell, she'll be here early."

"You know it, Lady Cate."

Cate walked down the hallway to the stairs, listening to Mrs. Fraser chattering away to Riley. Cate smiled to herself, thinking she couldn't be any luckier. After changing and retrieving her notes, Cate met Mrs. Campbell at the front door just as she was about to ring the bell.

"Mrs. Campbell, I had a feeling you might be early!"

"Oh, Lady Cate! I hope it's not a problem?" she said, in a questioning manner.

"Not at all, I'm ready for you if you'd like to step into the sitting room," Cate said, motioning to the room on her right.

The two spent two hours pouring over the details, updating progress and discussing the rest of what needed completed. Mrs. Campbell suggested they meet four more times, two for planning and two for what she called "action items." Cate agreed, noting them in her daybook.

"Well, if there's nothing else, I suppose I should be on my way," Mrs. Campbell said, still sitting and making no move to stand.

"Actually," Cate said, "I was hoping you might have a few more minutes. I'd like to pick your brain about something I've come across in my research."

"Oh," Mrs. Campbell said, making a show of checking her watch, "well, I have a few more minutes, how can I help?"

"When I first interviewed you, you mentioned a rumor

about Randolph MacKenzie, he would have inherited the castle around the 1850s. Concerning a person in the tower room?" Cate prodded.

"You mean a *woman* in the tower room," Mrs. Campbell corrected, a smirk on her face.

"Yes, I recall you said the rumor mill claimed it was a woman. Do you have any more information? Perhaps how the rumor started, or what prompted it?"

Mrs. Campbell looked up to the ceiling as if trying to remember. "For as long as I've known, that's been the story, Randolph was a cad and kept a woman locked in the tower room. I'm not sure why or how that rumor began way back when but my best guess would have been a servant with loose lips. Most of the village rumors had similar starts, someone at the pub with a bit too much to drink or some pillow talk."

"I see, that sounds likely, yes," Cate agreed.

"Oh, there are many other lascivious rumors that have torn through the town from this castle. You read Randolph ended up in prison for the murder of a servant. Perhaps the one with the loose lips, you never know!" Mrs. Campbell said, rambling on about the dirty secrets of Cate's ancestors.

"Yes, I was just reading that in the materials you sent me from the historical society. Interesting story, isn't it? What's your take on it?" Cate nudged.

"My take? Oh, well, most likely that's the servant that let slip Randolph's secret and he killed him over it. He tried to cover it up, claiming he had an alibi but when a man has a secret like that hidden in the tower room, there's no doubt he'd be willing to kill over it. I am surprised the guilt ended up getting to him enough to confess, though."

Cate raised her eyebrows, how quick she was to judge Randolph, his motives, and his personality. "Well," Cate said standing, "we all have our own quirks, I suppose. Well, thank you so much for your time, Mrs. Campbell, I don't want to keep you any longer. I'm sure you are very busy."

"Oh, not at all, it's no imposition," the woman answered, also standing. "I'll see you next Friday?"

"Yes, next Friday, same time as today."

"Wonderful, oh, I can hardly believe the party will be only two weeks away the next time we meet!" she said, as they walked to the door.

"Yes, it's almost upon us!" Cate said, opening the front door for her.

"Well, enjoy the rest of your day, Lady Cate. We'll be in touch!"

"Thank you!" Cate watched her leave, waving as her car pulled down the drive.

She made her way to the kitchen. On Wednesdays, Cate lunched with her staff, another tradition that she had started after arriving. Cate smiled recalling the look on Mrs. Frasers' face when she suggested eating lunch in the kitchen with them.

"Well, I'm glad that's over with," Cate said, entering the room.

"As am I. I cannae say why, but I dinnae like when that woman is in this house," Mrs. Fraser said, shuddering.

Cate laughed, "And how was Riley? Any trouble?"

"None at all, the little fellow ventured out to visit Jack, but he came back, didn't even need to call him."

"Well, good job, Riley! I'd say that deserves a treat!" Cate said, clapping her hands at the little pup. At the mention of a treat, Riley leapt to his feet, dancing around with excitement.

Cate walked to the pantry room where she kept his snacks to retrieve a few treats for him. "I'll have to order more treats, it looks like. I could have sworn we had two bags, but I only found one."

"He's been begging too much, he'll eat you out of house

and home this one!" Mrs. Fraser joked, as Jack and Mr. Fraser came through the door for lunch.

"Hello, everyone, especially little Sir Riley!" Jack said. "What have we done to deserve the royal treatment today?"

"He ran off to find you and came back without having to be called!" Cate answered.

"Oh, is that what you told them? Sorry to say, he didn't come to find me."

"What?" Mrs. Fraser said, setting a tray of sandwiches on the table alongside a tray of cookies. "I had the door propped open for air and I heard a rustling. Like a streak of lightening, he bolted through the door, then returned. I assume he visited you and you sent him back."

"He didn't visit me! He must have found a new friend." Jack knelt down to scratch Riley's ears. "Have I been replaced, laddie?"

Cate wore a mask of confusion on her face. "That's odd, I was sure he went to you and back. Maybe he just made a potty trip," she said, brushing it off. "Anyway, shall we have lunch?"

"Yes, we shall, m'lady, I'm starving! And, I've been smelling these biscuits all day," Jack said, taking a bite of a cookie first.

Mrs. Fraser harrumphed. "You'll spoil your appetite! Now see that you get a sandwich next, not another biscuit," she said, placing one on his plate.

The four of them made light conversation over lunch, discussing the new details of the party and how quickly it was approaching. Mrs. Fraser mentioned she should get a start on preparing menus for the meals while guests were in the house, asking if Molly had any preferences or allergies that she had to be aware of. She was most grateful when Cate informed her that Molly was an adventurous eater, willing to try most anything once, so there was nothing specific that she needed to plan around. She suggested a few menu items which Cate approved. Mrs. Fraser was pleased, joking that she was glad Cate didn't expect her to serve hot dogs and hamburgers all week for the Americans.

After lunch, Cate decided she had been neglecting her primary research project: her book on Dunhaven Castle's history. With the upcoming weeks promising to be busy, she figured she would at least do a little work on it to ease her guilt. She dug out her laptop and notes and spent the afternoon working on her research. As always, she found it all-consuming, working almost until dinner. Only Riley's tiny paws on her leg, requesting a walk before dinner, snapped her back to reality. Guilty from neglecting the pup all afternoon, Cate took him for a long evening walk, watching the sun dip low in the sky over the loch before returning to curl up with a book.

Despite all of her work, Cate found herself unable to sleep that night. She pondered how to get more information about the secret tower resident. How could she discover the identity of "S?" Was "S" related to the murder? Did Randolph kill the servant because he had loose lips about "S?" The questions turned round and round in Cate's mind as she tossed and turned.

After a while, she decided she could no longer lay there. She got up to pace the floors of the castle while waiting to become tired enough to go to sleep. She wandered all over, no longer finding the moonlit castle as eerie as she had when she first came.

She meandered up and down the hall containing her bedroom, then downstairs to the main floor. She passed through the gallery containing portraits of many of the castle's former inhabitants. She paused in front of Randolph MacKenzie's portrait, willing it to tell her his secrets. Unfortunately, he was not talking.

Continuing on, she passed the library, where she had been reading earlier. She spotted a light streaming from under the doorway. Startled, she wondered if someone was in the house or if she had left the light on earlier. Since she presumed she had turned it off, her pulse quickened as she approached the door. She pressed her ear against it, listening for any noises. Hearing none, she steeled her nerves and opened the door. After breathing a sigh of relief from spotting no one on the other side, she made her way to the lamp and switched it off.

Leaving the library, she closed the doors again, satisfied that no light was coming from the room any longer. Then an idea struck her. They could travel back to 1856 and determine if someone was in the tower room. It had seemed like the room was occupied, based on Randolph's trip there with a tray of food. However, they had no confirmation. Perhaps Randolph worked in the tower room and took a snack for himself. But if they traveled back at night and checked for light under the door, they may confirm if someone occupied the room. It was a low-risk plan that Cate assumed Jack might agree to. It was a small step, but they had plenty of time before the fateful night to search for answers. With that settled, she made her way back to her bedroom and fell asleep.

CHAPTER 7

Cate awoke the following morning excited about her plan, not because she thought it would provide her with a lot of information but because she thought Jack wouldn't argue about it. After breakfast, Cate took her usual morning walk with Riley around the property. Cate loved spending most of her mornings outside with Riley, just as she often had before they moved to Scotland. Unlike her former place of residence, though, she wasn't just a visitor in a park. The grounds of her new home were park-like, making it seem to Cate that she owned the park. Riley could bound around as much as he wanted with Cate chasing after him, no other park visitors, no one else to worry about, not a care in the world. Cate enjoyed watching him, a goofy grin on his face as he chased after his ball, or found a new plant to smell, or when the two of them happened upon Jack.

This morning, Cate had planned to meet both Jack and Mr. Fraser to discuss some details from her latest meeting with Mrs. Campbell and gather the specifics for their plan for the exterior of the castle. Though Cate found party-planning with Mrs. Campbell quite the chore, she felt much more at ease with Jack and Mr. Fraser. So, she wasn't apprehensive about this meeting.

After promising Riley they would visit the loch after her meeting, she headed toward the back gardens that adjoined the ballroom where the party would take place. As they rounded the corner, Riley spotted Jack and raced toward him, springing onto his hind legs to greet him.

"Well, good morning, Sir Riley!" Jack exclaimed, ruffling the fur on his head.

Cate caught up with Riley within a minute, beaming at the scene unfolding in front of her. "Good morning, Lady Cate. He really loves that lad, doesn't he?" Mr. Fraser said to Cate as she approached, watching Jack and Riley.

"Good morning! Did you mean Riley loves Jack or Jack loves Riley?" Cate questioned.

Mr. Fraser glanced at the two of them again. "Well, you could go either way with that, I'd say, Lady Cate."

"Good morning, Lady Cate!" Jack said after picking up Riley to continue to rub his chin. Riley, enjoying the experience, appeared as though he had a smile on his face.

"Good morning! I'm glad the two of you could join us!" she said, eyeing the pup in Jack's arms.

"I was just checking with him to make sure he had his costume set for the party. Eh, what's that laddie?" he asked, holding the dog closer to his ear, "Oh, it's a secret, is it? Well, I won't tell a soul!"

Cate chuckled. "Oh, his costume is in order, it'll look like his bed and blanket. This little guy will most likely sleep through the party."

"Aw, am I going to lose my buddy for the night?" Riley looked up at him as though agreeing that he would never lose him as a friend.

"Well, unless we get some details nailed down, we won't have a party for Riley to sleep through!" Cate said.

Mr. Fraser took the opening Cate offered to begin. "Well, Lady Cate, running with your theme 'Ghosts of the Past' and the ideas we discussed over lunch, here is what I was thinking," he said, opening a group of folded papers that he withdrew from his pocket. Cate's eyes widened with amazement.

"Mr. Fraser! These are great!" It was clear from the drawings he had not only spent a good amount of time and care designing what he hoped to achieve but he was also an excellent designer. The plans showed the castle from all angles, with detailed drawings of the back gardens that connected to the ballroom.

From the front, banners waved at the castle's entrance. Lights were positioned to illuminate the castle at all angles. Cate imagined the castle would appear impressive lit up in the evening skies.

The sketches of the back garden made it seem magical. Lights were strung around the garden, lighting paths through the various foliage for guests to enjoy. A temporary water feature sat at the center of the garden. Gourds and pumpkins, some carved some not, decorated the pathways. Tall corn stalks also stood in various spots around the gardens and at the entrances to the ballroom. Hay bales, adorned with the fruits of autumn, were arranged around each of the doors that opened to the gardens. Banners put the finishing touch on the entryway.

The design delighted Cate, but also overwhelmed her. "I love this design," she began, "but I want to be sure you two are not taking on too much! Will you need some additional help to achieve all this?"

"Well, Lady Cate," Mr. Fraser answered her, "I think we'll be okay. The Bailey farm will supply most of what we'll need and help us set it up."

"That's wonderful! I can help, too!"

"A real hands-on lady, aren't you, Lady Cate," Jack teased.

"Yes, I am," Cate said, giving a slight curtsy. "And, I have an idea if you don't mind?" Cate probed.

"I'm happy to hear it, Lady Cate," Mr. Fraser answered.

"Well, I noted that your plans show some carved pumpkins. Perhaps we could all pitch in and carve them. We could put a small sign designating who carved each pumpkin to show the guests we're real people! I bet Molly and Gayle would love to help, maybe even Mr. Smythe. And with you, Mrs. Fraser and Jack, that would be seven of them."

"I think that's a fun idea, Lady Cate. We could even make it a contest. Let people vote for the best. I had better tell Emily now, she'll want to spend at least a week planning her pumpkin!"

"That sounds great!" Cate answered.

They spent another forty-five minutes discussing various aspects of the design and logistics. Cate grew more excited by the minute to see the plan materialize. After they had gone over all the details, Cate asked to make a copy of the plans to share with Mrs. Campbell at her next meeting.

"By all means, Lady Cate," Mr. Fraser said, handing her the plans. "Although I dare say she'll have something she wants changed once she sees it!" He chuckled.

"But I have the final decision!" Cate answered. "And I love every detail of this!"

"Want to leave Riley with us while you run in to make a copy?" Jack asked.

"Riley, do you want to stay with Jack for a minute?" Cate asked the dog. His eyes gleamed as he glanced at Jack, who brandished a stick, promising to play a game of tug of war with him. His tail wagged furiously. "I think that's a yes! Okay, I'll be right back."

Cate entered the castle and made two copies of the plans, one for herself and one for Mrs. Campbell, with the copier she purchased to keep in the library. She smiled as she placed them in her planning folder, taking one final glance at them before returning to the back garden.

"Here are your papers back, Mr. Fraser. Okay, Riley, time to finish that walk!" she said, approaching the two men. Notably missing was the small dog. "Riley?" she questioned, glancing at Jack.

"Ah, the little laddie is right over..." He paused. "Well that's odd. He was right here. He was right by this bush. It wasn't a moment ago."

"Disappeared, has he?" Mr. Fraser asked, concern crossing his face.

"Maybe he started the rest of the walk without me," Cate joked. "I'm sure he's fine, he rarely goes far."

"Well, I'll help you look for him," Jack offered.

Since she wanted to talk to him anyway, Cate took him up on the offer. "Thanks, Jack. I expect he's on the path to the loch, or over near that folly. I'm not sure why but he has a sudden interest in that spot."

"If you don't find him soon, let me know, I'm happy to help you hunt for him," Mr. Fraser said.

"Thanks, I will let you know if we don't find him and sorry for stealing Jack for the moment!"

"Not to worry, Lady Cate, we're just getting some measurements today to make the final calculations on how much of everything we'll need to make these gardens shine! Plenty of time to do that once we've located little Riley."

Cate smiled at him and she and Jack started down the path. "So, you figure the little laddie is on the path?" Jack said.

"Most likely, he rarely goes far, like I said," Cate answered him as she called to Riley. About a quarter of the way down the path, she spotted Riley bounding down a small hill. "There he is!"

Jack spotted him too. "You were right, coming from the direction of that folly."

"I told you. I'm not sure what it is about that spot he loves, but there's something. One day I'll have to investigate it and find out what is so enticing to him." Riley bounded toward them and Cate reached down to pick him up. "What were you thinking running off? Silly boy, come here." Cate cuddled him in her arms, giving his head a kiss and ruffling the fur on his back.

"Well, looks like you're all set then! Guess I'll get back to those measurements."

"Oh," Cate said, staring at the ground, "I was hoping to have a few more moments of your time to discuss something."

"Did you have a question about the party?"

"No," Cate said, tight-lipped.

"Did you want me to grab your hundredth order of the fish and chips from the pub for you?"

Cate snickered. "No."

"Oh, I've got it, you wanted to ask me what my costume was!"

"Well it does involve a costume of sorts, so you're getting warmer."

"Are you having a private costume party that you'd like to discuss?"

"That's one way of putting it, yes."

"And when is this party occurring?"

"In 1856?" Cate said, phrasing it as a question.

Jack scrunched up his face. "I was afraid that would be your answer."

"I have a low-risk plan to get us more information. Not tons of information, but some! Not even you can object to this one, Jack!"

"Try me, lassie."

Cate rolled her eyes at him. "It's simple. We travel back when the family is having dinner. We make sure ALL of them are accounted for then we check the tower room."

"Oh, that's it, huh? Just go back at night, mosey to the tower room and check if someone is in there, doing what, sleeping?"

"We can check for a light shining under the door!"

"Hmm, we can avoid everyone. This might be one of your better terrible plans, Cate."

"See! I told you! So, when should we go!"

Jack rubbed his chin. "Hmm." He paused. "Let's see. How about…" he paused again, "the fifteenth of never? Does that work for you?"

"You're hilarious, Jack. Now, seriously, we should go this coming week, before we get busy with the party. How about this Sunday again?"

"Oh, Cate." He sighed. "You are a handful."

"Is that a yes?"

"It's a reluctant yes."

Cate grinned at him. "Okay, it's a plan! And NOW you can collect those measurements."

"Yes, measurements, a nice, safe idea that won't ruin the course of history, my favorite! M'lady," he said giving her a bow before he returned to the garden as she continued on her way toward the loch.

Cate laughed, then turned her attention to Riley. "And where did you get yourself off to, Mr. Riley?" Cate asked, ruffling the fur on his head. Riley's eyes gleamed at her but didn't provide any information. "Not talking, huh? Well, then, I guess I'll have to investigate what's got you so interested in that folly." She set him down on the ground, watching him scramble down the path in front of her toward the loch.

As they reached it, Cate called to him. He stopped,

turning to glance at her, then came galloping back as he saw his blue ball in her hand. His eyes twinkled with anticipation as she tossed it. He sprang into a run, chasing it. He snatched it up, bouncing around in a circle, before returning it to her to throw again.

They made their way to the loch, with Riley enjoying playing fetch all the way. Cate settled on the bank, Riley curled next to her, spent from playing ball. Cate sighed, stroking his back. She gazed at the castle, her attention focusing on the tower. If she was correct, their Sunday evening visit would confirm if someone was living in the tower room. Her low-key plan depended on verifying the whereabouts of the rest of the family. That was a fact that she kept from Jack. She would never have convinced him if he knew they would be traipsing around the castle. She'd keep that one to herself for now.

She smiled down at Riley, who was rolling onto his back to allow her to scratch his belly. "Oh, Riley." She laughed, pulling him into her arms. He snuggled into her, not appreciating the cooler weather.

She spent another half hour enjoying the loch and surrounding scenery before the cooler temperatures chased her in. A mountain of work awaited her between her research project and party planning. She determined she could put off her party planning work since she didn't have another meeting scheduled with Mrs. Campbell for about a week.

Cate settled after lunch in the library with Riley. Mr. Fraser had built them a roaring fire and Riley curled up in front of it, intent on taking a long afternoon nap. Her laptop stared back at her after she opened it along with her notes to work on her research. After opening her working draft, she had stared at the screen for almost twenty minutes. She gave the laptop a scowl and placed her hands on the keyboard. She forced herself to type. Nothing would get done if she didn't try.

Another few minutes passed, and she found herself gawking at the screen again. The word "The" followed by a blinking cursor stared back at her. She sighed, it was useless. She couldn't focus. She poked around on the internet, searching for a new cardigan for the cooler weather. After finding one she was pleased with, she ordered it and checked her email for the confirmation.

She found the email confirmation waiting for her after she logged in. In addition, she found another email from Molly. Her subject line read TWO WEEKS! Cate opened the email, realizing the subject was a reference to the date that Molly would begin her trek from Aberdeen, USA to Dunhaven, Scotland.

Hi Cate! In TWO WEEKS, I will be on my way to SCOTLAND! Thank you so much for the packing tips! I think I have the packing under control now, although my shopping may not be. I'll confess, I felt I needed a few new sweaters for the trip. My Scotland sweaters should arrive any day now and I can't wait to put them in my suitcase! I'm giddy every time I cross a day off the calendar!

I keep reminding everyone in the department that I'll soon be seeing you and staying at your CASTLE. You know, in case they want to pass along their best wishes to you, but mostly because I'm just bragging that I'm staying at a castle.

I'm so excited, I can hardly sleep. Although, that might be because I've been watching a lot of haunted castle movies in anticipation of my trip. You promise that it's not haunted, right? Even if it is, I'm still coming!

Thank you so much again, Cate! I know I've said it 1000 times already, but I mean it. I really needed this. It's given me something to look forward to, so THANK YOU!

Molly

P.S. They haven't filled your position yet. Guess they couldn't find anyone willing to do all that work for none of the reward!

The email put a smile on Cate's face. She was so pleased that her old friend would soon join her and even more pleased at Molly's excitement for the trip. Molly had always been a good friend. She was pleased to return the favor and give Molly something to look forward to. Cate knew a small snippet about the recent misfortune that Molly had suffered through her divorce. Molly didn't deserve the treatment she had received. Cate hoped Molly's time away was just what the proverbial doctor ordered.

She pressed the reply button and began typing an email back to Molly.

Hi Molly! Riley and I are counting the days on this side of the pond too! We're excited to see you. I'm glad you have the packing under control, and I don't blame you for the shopping! You definitely need a few new "Scotland sweaters." You'll get plenty of use out of them here, we are cool and damp, sorry to say!

I PROMISE the castle is not haunted, you can put your mind at rest. Keep watching those spooky movies, that's the only Scottish ghosts you'll see!

I'm so glad that you're looking forward to the visit. Enjoy crossing those days off, it'll be here before you know!

See you soon,
Cate

Cate sent the email and a new idea entered her mind. She wanted to surprise Molly with a gift when she arrived. She decided to go shopping the following day. Riley would enjoy visiting the town again and Cate would enjoy the shopping trip. It would have a special significance for her since she was on a mission to find something special to cheer Molly.

An added bonus was being able to occupy her time before Sunday. Without something to divert her attention, Cate would go crazy with anticipation. Cate knew Jack's reluctance for these trips, but she couldn't help herself. She was so excited she could burst.

With her plans set, she returned to her laptop, hoping to get something done. As she typed her first few strokes, Mrs. Fraser knocked and peeked into the library.

"Oh, Mrs. Fraser! Is there something you needed?" Cate asked, surprised to see Mrs. Fraser. "It's not dinner time yet, is it?"

"Oh, no, Lady Cate, not yet! But I was hoping you had a moment?" she asked.

"Oh, of course, Mrs. Fraser, please come in!" Cate motioned for her to come in and have a seat near the fireplace. Cate pushed back from the desk and joined her. "Please, sit, Mrs. Fraser. Riley is really enjoying the fire. I'm thinking of curling up here with a good book, too. I'm not making much progress on my research."

"It is nice and cozy here. I'll tell Mr. Fraser the little pup is enjoying it. He'll be pleased."

"So, what did you want to discuss, Mrs. Fraser?" Cate asked.

"Right, well, Lady Cate, I was hoping to ask a favor of you."

"Sure!"

"I've been thinking, it may be easier for Mr. Fraser and myself to stay at the castle while your guests are with us. We will be available if any needs arise. Also, we will be on hand for the busy days prior to the party."

Cate smiled. Mrs. Fraser was well prepared with explanations for her request, although they were unnecessary. Cate was happy to have the Frasers at the castle anytime they wished to stay. "It's not necessary for you to ask or explain, Mrs. Fraser. You're welcome to stay here anytime!"

Mrs. Fraser returned her smile. "Thank you, Lady Cate. Well, I prefer to ask just the same. Well, with that settled…".

"Oh, just a moment, Mrs. Fraser," Cate interrupted. "I have one request."

Mrs. Fraser's brow furrowed in confusion. "Request?" she asked.

"Yes. I want to be sure this makes things easier for you and I do not want you working yourself to death trying to attend to all of us!"

Mrs. Fraser laughed, "Oh, Lady Cate, it will make it easier on me and you'll not worry yourself about overworking me. I'll be fine!" Mrs. Fraser stood. "Fine, that is settled," she said, with a nod of her head. "I'll leave you to your work, or your book!"

"Thanks!" Cate smiled at her. After sitting a few more moments by the warm fire, Cate had little desire to return to her work. Instead, she settled for reading a good book, nestled on the chair with Riley.

She spent the rest of her afternoon and evening enjoying quiet moments of relaxation, attempting to ease her mind from dwelling on her upcoming trip to the past.

Cate arose early the next morning, excited for her shopping trip. Cate departed following breakfast, although the stores would not yet be open. She spent the time before the shops opened letting Riley explore his favorite areas of the town. Riley also enjoyed the attention he received from the town's other visitors during his morning walk.

As mid-morning approached, Cate watched the sleepy town come to life as store by store opened its doors. Cate began her shopping trip by visiting one of her favorite shop owners, Harry Abernathy. He always enjoyed seeing Riley and Riley enjoyed receiving the treats Harry always kept behind the counter.

"Ah, good morning, Lady Cate! And good morning to you, Riley!" Harry said producing a treat for the little pup.

"Good morning, Harry! How have you been?"

"Cannae complain, Lady Cate! Are you enjoying the change in weather?"

"I can't say I'm enjoying the cooler temperatures, but I have always been fond of fall!" Harry's wife, Helen, appeared from the back storeroom. "Good morning, Helen," Cate said, as she saw her.

"Good morning! Doing some shopping today?"

"Yes, I have a friend from across the pond coming in soon and I wanted to get her something to welcome her."

"Ah, that's very thoughtful of you," Helen answered. "Is she coming in for the party?"

"Yes. She's coming early to visit and staying for the party."

"How are plans coming along for it?" Harry chimed in.

"Very well, thanks. Mrs. Campbell seems to be a professional at event planning, so I am following her skillful lead. She seems to have a fantastic handle on all the details. You both are planning to attend, aren't you?"

"Oh, yes, we wouldn't miss it! Isla is billing it as the event of the decade!" Helen exclaimed.

"I'm surprised she hasn't run you ragged yet, Lady Cate." Harry laughed.

"There are so many details, it is exhausting keeping track of them, but I think she'd be the one run ragged before me. She has thrown herself into this head first!"

"Aye, that'd be our Isla!" Harry agreed. "If we can help in any way, please ask!"

"Thank you both," Cate answered. "Have you decided on costumes yet?"

"We have," Helen said. "But we're keeping them a secret until the big day!"

"Fair enough! I look forward to seeing you both at the party."

"Have fun with your shopping, Lady Cate," Helen said. "I hope you find something your friend will enjoy."

"Thank you!" Cate said, turning from the counter to browse the store.

Cate spent the entire morning browsing stores in search of something she thought Molly might enjoy. By lunch she hadn't decided on anything. She took a break for lunch at the pub after settling Riley in the car for a nap.

She ordered fish and chips for the umpteenth time and used the time to mull over the gift options she'd narrowed down for Molly. After lunch she completed her purchases, choosing a tartan blanket that she paired with a copy of the book *The Mysteries of Scotland* which featured a blurb about Dunhaven Castle's supposed haunting. She also picked out a photo album featuring a picture of Dunhaven Castle on the front for Molly to fill with her memories.

Pleased with her purchases, she carried her packages to the car and headed back to the castle for dinner. It was Cate's habit to eat dinner with her staff on Fridays and she didn't want to miss it. She spent a pleasant evening discussing the upcoming party, her shopping trip and giving them a little more information about her friend, Molly.

As Cate climbed into bed, she was pleased to be one additional day closer to her Sunday trip. "One day down, one more to go!" Cate promised herself as she drifted off to sleep.

CHAPTER 8

Cate was on pins and needles Saturday, counting the hours until Sunday arrived. To distract herself, she spent much of her day working on her research project, gathering materials and writing sample outlines for several chapters. On several occasions, Cate found herself distracted, wondering who "S" was and what the note meant. She spent at least an hour looking through old employment records from that era for a clue. However, with only one initial, there was not enough information for Cate to solve anything. If only she could find something definitive.

As she searched through the old records, a question formed in her mind. The dates listed did not coincide with what she expected to be "work days" for staff. A quick search on her phone showed her that the dates in 1856 corresponded to different days of the week than they did in the present time. How could she have been so short-sighted, she mused? She and Jack had traveled back on a Sunday in their time, but it was a Monday in 1856. This may explain Randolph's presence in the house. She made a note to tell Jack about her discovery.

After what seemed like an eternity, evening arrived and Cate spent the time snuggled with Riley on her chaise, warmed by a fire and watching a movie. Cate dreaded night to come, sure she wouldn't be able to sleep. To worsen matters, Cate realized she had a long day of waiting ahead since she and Jack planned to go back in the evening, after dark.

Cate could have kicked herself for not insisting they go sooner. Either way, the decision was made. She would do her best to live with it and to get as much rest as possible. She retired for the night after a long walk with Riley in the cool evening air. The night air must have worked wonders for her because she fell asleep within minutes and Sunday morning arrived before she realized it.

She awoke refreshed and ready, excited for her evening trip. The crisp morning air made everything appear more vibrant to her as she took a long morning walk with Riley. They ended at the loch, playing several games of fetch with Riley's favorite ball before relaxing on its banks. Cate was able to fritter away most of the morning enjoying the outdoors with Riley.

After making a light lunch, Cate gathered Riley and made a trip to the tower room. She studied the area outside of the tower room, then scoured the room for any additional clues. She wanted to prepare herself for her trip later, figuring that having a good idea of the lay of the land would help her. She couldn't forget her skeleton key, in case they needed a quick hideaway again. She made a mental note to hang it around her neck as soon as she finished exploring.

She glanced out of the tower room windows, one by one. They may have a better view from the grounds below to determine if someone was in the tower room. Jack would not be pleased but Cate figured it might be their best option. She would convince him later when the time came.

Satisfied with her plan for the evening, she scooped Riley into her arms. "How about a nice long walk before Jack gets here?" The dog's ears perked up. Cate wasn't sure which interested him more: the walk or Jack. He loved both.

Cate wrapped up in her warm cardigan and bundled Riley in his tartan sweater before heading out. The two enjoyed the fall evening, watching the sun descend in the sky in a brilliant blaze of deep red. Cate peered at the tower room, half expecting to witness lights shining from within. Darkened, lifeless windows met her gaze.

As they approached the castle after their walk, Riley raced ahead, spotting Jack from a distance.

"Hello, Sir Riley!" Jack exclaimed as the dog rushed toward him. He caught Riley mid-leap, pulling him close to his chest as he rubbed his belly.

"Perfect timing!" Cate called, still a distance away.

"I'm not sure anything about this is perfect," Jack answered as Cate closed the gap.

"Stop being a stick in the mud! This'll be a quick one, just your style. Oh, by the way, I figured out why we may have run into Randolph."

"Oh?" Jack asked.

"Yes, we traveled back on a Sunday in our time, but in 1856 the twenty-ninth of September was a Monday," she explained.

"Ohhhh," Jack said, realization dawning on him, "the days of the week are different! Good catch, Lady Cate."

Cate beamed at him. "Thanks. Ready to go?"

"I'm with Gertrude on this one, I'm not a fan."

Cate rolled her eyes at him. "Well, we might as well head in and get ready, it'll be dark soon."

Jack handed her Riley so she could leave him in her bedroom suite while they conducted their business. "Clothes in the bedroom as usual?" he asked, referring to the bedroom they used to travel back to 1856.

"Yep! Meet you there after I've changed and settled Riley."

They separated for the moment, each heading to change into period appropriate clothing, just in case they ran into anyone. Cate swept her hair into an updo, the typical style for that time and donned her dress, making sure the skeleton key dangled with the time piece from her neck. After giving Riley a kiss on the head and ensuring that he was nestled in a blanket on her chaise, she exited her bedroom suite, closing and locking the door behind her.

She made her way to the 1856 bedroom. She was acutely aware of the difference in the clothing she was wearing. Unlike her sweaters, jeans, leggings, and cardigans, the weight of this dress made moving difficult. Moving was a challenge. Cate marveled at how women accomplished anything beyond the basics in this era.

She found Jack already waiting for her, fussing with his collar. "I wish we could travel to an era with more comfortable clothing," he said, continuing to fiddle with it.

"I'm sure I can make that happen," Cate assured him.

Jack rolled his eyes at her. "Very funny, Cate."

Cate grinned at him. "Ready?"

"As I'll ever be."

They entered the closet. Cate and Jack both placed their thumbs on the watch face, rubbing it. Within moments, the timepiece's ticking decreased. The second hand slowed to a crawl, indicating the slowed passage of time in their own century.

"Looks like we made it," Cate whispered. "Let's go!"

"Agreed, let's get this over with. Straight to the tower room and back, right?"

"More or less."

"Caaaaaaaate," Jack began.

Cate cut him off, "Come on!" She bounded to the closet door, cracking it open an inch to peer out. "All clear!" she called, pulling the door open all the way and making her way to the bedroom door.

"Wait up," Jack mumbled, racing after her.

She eased the door open enough to peer out. "Coast is clear, let's make a run for the stairway."

"Okay, on three," Jack said, counting to three before they made their dash down the hallway to the stairs. Cate's run was less dash and more hobble in her domed skirt with all its flounces, but they made it unseen. They climbed the circular stairs approaching the tower room.

As they rounded the bend, bringing the tower room door into full sight they both spotted the glow emanating from beneath the closed door. "Look!" Cate breathed.

Jack nodded. "I see it. Point proven," he whispered. "Now, let's go."

"Just a second. We can't tell what's happening in there."

"Nope, and unless you brought your x-ray vision googles, we will never know."

"I didn't but..."

"Cate, let's just go."

"Just listen! This stairwell goes to the ground level. We could take a quick peek from outside. See if we spot anything."

"No, no, absolutely not!"

"Okay, you stay here, I'll go."

"Cate, I can't do that!"

"Looks like you're going with me then." Cate smiled. "The longer we spend arguing about it the longer we're here."

"Oh, Cate," he said, rolling his eyes, "I hope you don't come across any more mysteries. Let's go."

Cate nearly leapt for joy, except her ruffled skirt kept her feet firmly on the ground. They descended the stairs, making their way to the ground level and outside without being accosted.

Cate scrambled to the area of the yard where the tower was visible, Jack close behind her. She turned to view the tower windows. She was met with black nothingness. Confused, she changed positions, looking at another of the tower windows. Again, blackness stared back at her. She gave Jack a puzzled glance. "We just saw the lights."

"Maybe the person left. Perhaps there isn't anyone living in the tower room."

"What are the odds in the few minutes it took us to walk here that person left?" Jack opened his mouth to answer but Cate answered for him. "It's low, I promise."

"Well, it's dark now, Cate."

Cate stared at the windows for several more moments. "Or are the windows blacked out? So no one could see light?"

"Oh, come on," Jack began, "how..."

Cate interrupted him. "Jack, look!" she exclaimed, pointing to the window.

Jack's gaze followed her finger. He saw a flash of light from the tower window. Warm, yellow light gleamed from within the tower.

"I knew it!" Cate exclaimed, clasping her hands together in delight. "Blackout curtains to make it appear that no one is there!"

The source of the movement revealed itself. A woman's silhouette appeared in the window. She gazed out into the moonless, darkened sky for a moment before allowing the drape to slip from her hand and cover the window again.

"We should go," Jack said, feeling a sudden urgency.

Cate read the urgency in his voice and agreed. They made their way back to the hallway, creeping to the bedroom. They were lucky to not run into anyone along the way. Most family members were at dinner with most staff serving them.

Jack breathed a sigh of relief as they entered the closet and set the watch back to its normal speed, returning them to their time.

As soon as they were back, Jack loosened his collar, letting out another sigh of relief. Cate's mind was already spinning out of control.

"So," she blurted, "there IS someone in the tower room. A woman, not just someone, a woman. And they are trying to hide her presence. That has to mean something. But who is it? Why is she there? She must be the mysterious 'S' from the note. Randolph was hiding her in the tower. But why? If he was madly in love with Victoria why did he bring her?"

"Cate, slow down, my heart is still returning to normal speed. I can't keep up with all your questions."

Cate paced the floor, barely hearing him. "They are definitely hiding her. But for what reason?"

Jack shook his head, not knowing any of the answers. Cate pondered it for another moment before turning to face him. "Are you thinking what I'm thinking?"

"Somehow I doubt it."

"We need more information," Cate said, eyes wide. "We need to go back."

Jack hung his head in his hands. "Oh, Cate, I somehow figured we weren't thinking the same thing."

"Really?" Cate asked, shocked. "How are you NOT thinking that?"

"Go back? Nope, definitely wasn't thinking that, Cate. I hate going at all, let alone going back to a time when a man is about to commit murder to continue to hide a secret woman in the tower room."

"So, you do imagine there's more to the story, and it somehow involves the mysterious 'S!'" Cate exclaimed, ignoring his reluctance to return to investigate further.

Jack looked incredulous. "Oh, Cate." He sighed. "You

always know just how to twist what I say to support you." He laughed. "You're one amusing lassie, when you're not dragging me back to a time when I have to wear a ruffled collar and almost get killed."

Cate rolled her eyes at him. "You're so dramatic. We weren't almost killed."

"I was so almost killed!" he countered. "By my heart, when it almost attacked me."

Cate rolled her eyes again but couldn't stifle a giggle. "Oh stop," she said. "Be serious, we need a plan." She turned pensive again. "Hmm, when can we go again? We need a plan that allows us to investigate and perhaps talk to a few people. I realize the party is coming up and you'll be busy getting things ready but I'd like to eke some time out this week." Cate babbled, allowing her thoughts to spill directly from her brain to her mouth.

"Whoa, whoa, Cate. Slow down." Jack held up his hands in front of him to signal for her to stop.

"Oh, please don't tell me you're not willing to investigate this! We learned way more than we knew when we first started! And even then you determined it was worth looking into!" Cate argued. "Now we confirmed the existence of a mystery woman and we suspect there may be more to the murder than the story from the articles, we need to press on!"

Jack sighed. "Oh, Cate," he began.

Cate let her shoulders sag. "It's my family, it's important to me. I realize I didn't know them, but I have no other family. The ghosts of my past are all I have."

He sighed again. "You're lucky I like you, Cate."

Cate clasped her hands together under her chin, a smile spreading across her face. "So, you'll go with me?"

"Yes, you'll just go without me and I don't want that," he started, "BUT we only go with a plan I like. And we won't just talk to random people. And we're definitely not going to tell Randolph anything we know. We're going to leave the past as intact as we can."

"Deal," Cate said, agreeing to his terms. "How's Wednesday?"

"As good as any day I guess."

"That gives us time to formulate a plan and make at least two trips before…"

"AT LEAST TWO?" Jack exclaimed. "Wait a minute…"

"Possibly two," Cate interrupted him, "if we find out something that needs followed up on. With the party coming up we won't be doing much then and we're running out of time!"

"Time, the one thing we have plenty of," Jack joked.

"We don't! The murder occurs on Halloween! And we'll lose a whole week for the party if not more," Cate lamented.

"I'm now very excited for the party!" Jack added.

Cate batted at him. "All right, funny guy. Well, I guess I'll let you off the hook for now. I'll come up with a plan and we can re-convene tomorrow to discuss it."

Jack wiped his brow. "Whew, sounds good to me. I'm going home and enjoying my modern life."

After changing, they said their goodbyes and Cate headed to her sitting room. She was too wired to sleep and used the time to come up with a plan for her next visit. Cate grabbed her notebook and pen and began jotting down anything that came to mind. After looking at the scenario from multiple angles, Cate circled a few items that she determined would be the best approach. Pending Jack's approval, she considered it best to introduce themselves as distant cousins under the ruse of Jack's business bringing him to the area. This would allow them instant access to the family but still allow them to appear and disappear as they pleased. Further, she determined that beginning some discussions with Randolph was prudent to set the tone for what type of man he was and gather some basic background. She smiled down at her little plan, hoping Jack would approve.

With that settled, Cate roused Riley, who had nestled in her lap while she made notes, from his slumber for one last trip outside before bed. A lazy Riley dragged himself around the yard near the castle, more ready for bed than a walk of any kind. Cate ended up carrying the tired little pup back up to the bedroom, setting him in his bed before climbing into her own.

CHAPTER 9

Cate arose the next morning excited about sharing her plan but also certain Jack would hate it. He really was a stick in the mud when it came to sleuthing, Cate mused. She bounded through her morning routine with a nervous energy. After finishing her breakfast, she took Riley for his morning walk, intent on using the time to recap her plan to Jack.

As Cate and Riley made their way around the back gardens, Riley burst into a full run. Cate was sure if she followed him he would lead her straight to Jack. Riley did not disappoint, dodging around some hedges and straight to where Jack was trimming bushes. As Cate caught up to him, she found him already playing with a twig, pulling and tugging at it attempting to free it from Jack's clutches.

"Well, good morning, Lady Cate," he called, spotting her in the distance.

"Good morning, Jack. Careful, he'll tear your arm off for that prize!" she joked.

"Yes, I can see that. A mighty strong little rascal, this one!"

Relinquishing the branch, Jack told the pup, "Okay, you win, big guy!" Riley, pleased with his new prize, carried the twig a safe distance from Jack and commenced gnawing on it.

Cate approached Jack. "I have our plan all set!"

Jack groaned. "I was hoping for twenty-four hours to recover, at least!"

"Time is of the essence! I spent last night planning, so we weren't delayed!"

"Okay, okay," Jack said, holding up his hands to admit defeat. "So, tell me this plan of yours."

"Well, I think you were right," Cate began, buttering him up a bit. "We need to tell Randolph that we are distant cousins, part of the MacKenzie clan. That will give us access to the household and the family. We can use the ruse that we are in the area traveling while you are on business. That gives us an excuse to stay outside of the castle and come and go as we please. Our priority should be learning the lay of the land, having a brief discussion with Randolph and perhaps a few other household members. Just a casual conversation to see what he's like."

"I have so many objections," Jack began.

"That's perfect," Cate interrupted. "I figured you could imply that you are an attorney."

"Now I have even more objections," Jack said, rolling his eyes.

Cate gave him a look. "I promise not to say anything to Randolph that would even give him a hint regarding what we're doing."

"Okay, okay. I must admit, it seems a reasonable plan and a good way to start pursuing this scheme."

Cate grinned, pleased that Jack approved of her plan. "We should go back in the early afternoon, perhaps right after lunch. We don't want to interfere with a meal or preparation for a meal. Since we're seeing Randolph, it shouldn't be too much of an issue since he likely conducts business during this time."

"After lunch on Wednesday, I guess," Jack agreed. "If we must."

"We must," Cate added with a grin. They chatted for a few more moments before Cate retrieved Riley and continued on their walk. She was excited about their upcoming trip, spending much of the rest of the day planning, reading about and studying the time period and people at Dunhaven during it. On Tuesday, Cate filled her day with her own research and some details of party planning. Compared to her Wednesday plans, she found the work dull. However, it was a necessity, so she pressed on with it, attempting to fill her day so it passed as quickly as possible.

When the sun crested the moors on Wednesday morning, Cate sprang from her bed. Excited as a kid at Christmas, she went about her morning routine. She took Riley on a long walk so that he would be tired and ready for an afternoon nap. She busied herself with games of fetch and spent some time at the loch. Even with her full schedule, the morning dragged by.

After what seemed like an eternity, lunch arrived. Cate enjoyed spending the time in the castle's kitchen, having a lively discussion about pumpkin carving with the Frasers and Jack. Afterward, Cate and Jack excused themselves, under the ruse of estate business. Cate settled Riley in her sitting room for a nap, then changed into her period clothing. When she was ready, she met Jack in the bedroom closet.

They both drew in a deep breath as they prepared to activate the timepiece and return to the 1850s. While not their first trip to the era, it was the first time they planned to interact with anyone. A nervous energy filled them both.

Jack clasped his hand around Cate's and together they rubbed the timepiece until it began to slow. Once the timepiece's second hand had slowed to a crawl, Jack whispered, "I forgot to ask, what's the plan for getting out of here to the front door?"

"Sneak down the back stairs?" Cate suggested.

"As good a plan as any, I suppose," Jack agreed. He cracked the closet door, peering into the bedroom. "It's clear, let's go." Cate followed him for a repeat performance at the bedroom door. Finding the hallway clear, they made a dash down the hall and into the back stairway. They descended the steps, peering out of the door into the gardens. With no one in sight, they crept out of the door and, trying to remain hidden from anyone's sight, made their way to the front door.

"You sure you want to do this?" Jack asked one final time before announcing their arrival with the lion's head door knocker.

Cate nodded, unsure but unwilling to admit it. Jack lifted the knocker and let it thud against the door. Together, they waited for someone to answer the door. Within a few moments, an older gentleman opened the door to them.

"Yes?" he inquired.

Cate nodded to Jack who responded, "Jack MacKenzie and wife here to see my cousin, Lord Randolph MacKenzie."

"If you would be so kind as to follow me, sir, I will show you to where you may wait for Lord MacKenzie." The pair followed the man, whom Cate assumed was the household's butler, to the sitting room off of the foyer. "I shall announce your arrival to Lord MacKenzie at once, sir." He left the room, leaving the doors ajar behind him.

"Good job!" Cate whispered after he departed.

"Yes, good job me. I got us into your own house!"

Cate made a face at him but offered no further commentary. The two sat on pins and needles waiting for Randolph to arrive. Within a few moments, two men appeared in the doorway. Cate recognized Randolph from his painting in the gallery. The butler preceded him, introducing him upon entering.

After dismissing him, Randolph approached Jack, who stood to greet him. "Lord MacKenzie," Jack said, not quite sure what to do but extending his hand for a handshake. "It's a pleasure to meet you, sir. I'm a distant cousin of yours, Jack MacKenzie."

"Jack MacKenzie, I can't say I've heard of you, laddie, but family is always welcome at Dunhaven Castle," Randolph said, grabbing his hand in a firm handshake.

"Ah, this, sir, is my wife, Catherine. I sent word ahead through the post of our arrival. It appears you haven't received my letter."

Jack's quick thinking impressed Cate. He knew enough to fib that they had sent a letter announcing their arrival. The mail in this era was far from dependable. It would be believable that the letter had never arrived.

"I haven't. The only thing you can count on with the post is that you can't count on it!" Randolph joked.

As Randolph approached her, Cate, knowing the customs of the time, did not stand to greet him. Instead, she extended her hand, palm facing down for him to take. As was customary, he brushed her hand, bowing to her. "Mrs. MacKenzie, a pleasure."

"Likewise, Lord MacKenzie," she answered.

He cocked his head. "Do I detect an American accent, lassie?"

She smiled, answering, "You do, Lord MacKenzie, I hail from the other side of the pond."

"I see. Welcome to Scotland, then! And please, call me Randolph. We're all family here." Turning to Jack, he said, "Please, sit down. Can I offer you a scotch?"

Unsure of what to do, Jack sat, glancing at Cate. Cate gave a slight nod, motioning that he should accept the offer. "How kind of you," Jack accepted.

Randolph poured two glasses of scotch. "Anything for the lady?"

"No, thank you," Cate declined.

"Don't tell me you're a teetotaler, Mrs. MacKenzie," Randolph said, laughing as he handed a glass off to Jack.

Cate smiled at him as he sat across from them. "No, but I typically only enjoy those beverages at a much later hour."

He smiled at her then turned toward Jack. "What brings you to my fair land, cousin Jack?"

"Well, as I explained in my letter, I am in the area on some business. I hoped that I could meet some family while here. I apologize again for arriving unannounced."

"Bah, nothing to worry about, cousin! And what is your business?"

"I am an attorney, mainly land dealings and holdings," Jack lied, before taking a large gulp of scotch.

"I see. Interesting. And you'll be staying on with us at Dunhaven Castle?" Randolph inquired.

Jack glanced at Cate. "Eh, no, sir," he stammered.

"We've taken a place of our own, on the outskirts of town," Cate explained. "With Jack's extended business here, we considered it best to set up our own household."

"Nonsense! You're family! Cancel your contract and stay here. You're an attorney, I'm sure you can find your way out of it."

Jack laughed. "While that may be, I am also a man of my word. I'd not cancel a contract out of turn."

"Man of your word, eh? Good man. Honest and independent, just like a Mackenzie." Randolph nodded to him in approval. Jack offered him a smile in thanks. "Well, surely you'll dine with us often while you're here, I hope?"

Jack began to answer when Cate interrupted him. "How gracious of you, we are delighted to accept your invitation at a time that suits you and your wife, Victoria."

"Perhaps Monday? Victoria is throwing together a little soiree, nothing fancy, I'm certain she'd love to have you attend."

"We are happy to accept," Cate answered him.

"Wonderful! I understand the festivities begin at six o'clock. Oh, I'm sure Lady MacKenzie would love to have you for tea, Mrs. MacKenzie. It will be nice for her to have a female friend for tea. I do feel rather sorry for her, moving here to the fringes of civilization."

"We shall plan to arrive at six," Cate responded. "It's such a lovely castle, I'm sure she is contented with such a home despite its remote location," she added.

Randolph smiled at her over his scotch. "Such a gracious wife you have, cousin. While it's true Lady MacKenzie wants for nothing, her happiness is still vital to me, as I'm sure yours is to my dear cousin."

Cate smiled at him to acknowledge his compliment.

"It certainly is! Well," Jack said, finishing his scotch, "we won't take up any more of your time this afternoon. Thank you for meeting with us and I look forward to dining with you and Lady MacKenzie soon."

"Of course," Randolph said, standing as Jack stood. Cate also rose. As she did, Randolph took out his pocket watch, checking the time. It didn't escape Cate that it was the same timepiece that hung around her neck, hidden under her dress. "Anything for family." The statement struck at Cate's core. This was her ancestor, holding the gold timepiece she would inherit over one hundred years from now. The impact of the moment was staggering. After checking the time, he shook Jack's hand, then brushed Cate's, nodding to her. "I shall look forward to seeing you both again soon." Approaching the wall, he pulled a cord hanging from the ceiling. Within moments, the butler returned. "Ah, Thomson, Mr. and Mrs. MacKenzie were just leaving, if you could show them out. And please collect their address so that Lady MacKenzie can correspond with Mrs. MacKenzie about an invitation to tea."

"Very good, m'lord," he answered. Randolph left the room and Thomson guided Cate toward a desk where she could pen her address using a quill and paper. Cate felt as though she were in the stone age as she penned the note. Thanking the butler, she folded it and handed it to him. She expressed that they could see themselves out and did not need to trouble him further.

"It's no trouble at all, Mrs. MacKenzie," he responded, leading them into the foyer. Cate had hoped to have gotten rid of him with her subterfuge, but the man remained glued to their sides. She preferred to take a direct route to the bedroom rather than risk running into someone on the less direct route. They had gotten lucky once, but would they do it again?

Cate had to think fast. As they approached the door, Cate drew on any dramatic skills she had, throwing her hand across her forehead and swooning into Jack's arms. "Oh!" she cried, grasping him so as not to fall. "I am so faint!"

"Cate!" he exclaimed, unaware that she was faking.

"Oh, dear," Thomson muttered. "Is the lady quite all right, sir?"

"I don't know, perhaps she should lie down?"

"Oh, yes, yes, if I could only lie down." Cate moaned.

"Of course, madam. Sir, if you could help her up the stairs, I will see to finding her a bedroom to rest in until she has recovered."

Jack, still not cognizant of Cate's clever deception, lifted her to carry her up the stairs. With the butler in front of them, Cate risked a glance at Jack, giving him a wink. He screwed up his face as she returned to playing unsteady before realization dawned on him.

The butler led them down the upstairs hall, taking them to a bedroom near the one they needed to reach. Opening the door, he stood aside allowing Jack to enter and place a woozy Cate on the bed. "Shall I call a doctor, sir?"

"No," Jack responded, clasping Cate's hand like a dutiful husband. "It's likely the journey has been too much for her. I'm sure she only needs a moment to rest and recover, then we will be on our way. Please, don't let us keep you."

"Thank you, sir. I will check back with you in the event that you should need anything or the lady's condition worsens."

"Thank you, Thomson." With the dismissal, the butler exited the room, leaving the door ajar.

Moments after he exited, Cate ceased her sick act, popping her eyes wide and sitting up. "Wow, I can't believe that worked!" she exclaimed, trying to keep her voice quiet. "Hurry! We'll make a run for the bedroom!"

"Best idea I've heard all day," Jack agreed. The pair crept to the door, checking for anyone in the hall. Spotting no one, they made a dash across and down the hall, entering the bedroom and racing to the closet. Cate removed the timepiece from the folds of her dress. Both of them clutched it, rubbing it in unison. The second hand speeded up, soon returning to keeping normal time.

Even Cate breathed a sigh of relief this time. "Oh," Jack

said, putting a hand over his heart, "I always feel so much better when we're home."

"What an incredible experience though! My ancestor, Randolph, right there in front of me! And did you see the watch? He held the same watch that I inherited. It really is mind-blowing," Cate said, excitement filling her voice.

"That's one way of describing it, I suppose. Clever stunt, I was becoming concerned about navigating back to this closet without being caught."

"Thank you!" she said, grinning at him.

"And, I must admit, that was quite an experience. Randolph seems to be quite an interesting character, I rather liked him!"

Cate smiled again. "I did, too! And now, do you still find it believable that he killed a man because he gave a questionable glance at his wife at the table?"

"I suppose it's plausible. He was very family-oriented."

"Oh, come on, Victoria's happiness is vital to him, anything for family, honest and independent, that's what a MacKenzie is! Does he sound like a man who kills someone over a glance, then lies about it?"

"Perhaps he snapped? And maybe guilt got to him?"

"He didn't seem like a hothead," Cate said.

"No he didn't," Jack admitted. "He seemed like a right fellow, I felt bad lying to him."

Cate nodded. "A necessary drawback. But consider how much better it will be when we prove his innocence and he can live a happy life with his wife and child!"

"IF we prove his innocence," Jack corrected. "Now, I better get back to work. I'll leave you to come up with a strategy for Monday, well Sunday for us. I will be on pins and needles all week."

Cate beamed. A trip to the past she wouldn't have to twist Jack's arm on! "Don't worry, I'll have a plan locked down in no time!" Cate winked at him, turning to leave the closet.

"Oh, Cate," Jack said, stopping her. Cate turned back to face him. "Before you leave, what did you write on the paper for our address?"

"I didn't," Cate admitted. "I wrote a note stating to leave any correspondence with the postmaster until we had set up our household. I hope that works."

"Ah, good thinking," Jack said. Cate nodded to him, smiling, before leaving the closet and returning to her bedroom suite to change. She could barely contain her excitement over the entire encounter. The promise of another trip to the past had Cate bursting with anticipation. Details raced through her mind about the upcoming excursion. She strategized what she should wear, when they should arrive, back stories, manners of the period that she would need to apprise Jack of and many other aspects. Only four short days, she reflected. Four days too many by her count.

She curled up with Riley after changing her clothes, her mind in a daze. She wondered as she lounged if they should jaunt back before Sunday to check their mail. Jack would never agree, but she figured she would ask, anyway. The worst that could happen is he didn't agree.

With her plan sketched out, she gathered Riley for a walk before dinner. Cate gazed at the castle with new eyes as she walked with Riley. She pictured Randolph raising his family here, or rather, missing that opportunity due to the circumstances thrust upon him. She marveled at the castle, at how much different it was yet how unchanged. The castle in Randolph's time had not yet included the additional wing. Cate stared at the wing, picturing the castle without it.

Her gaze shifted to the tower. Cate's mind returned to the mystery she was trying to solve. Who was this mysterious woman Randolph kept in the tower? And for what purpose?

Randolph seemed personable, friendly and in love with his wife, not like the type of man who kept a woman imprisoned against her will.

Cate shook her head. Staring at the tower room provided no answers. She was forced to wait until Sunday to get any more information or do any further exploring. Even if she could convince Jack to take another trip back before then, it was unreasonable to expect that she would visit the castle. One uninvited trip this week would be enough.

Cate spent the rest of her day and evening attempting to read while daydreaming about the past. The following day she again sprang from her bed, excited for the day. She searched out Jack on her morning walk with Riley and suggested that they make the effort for a quick trip back to check on any correspondence that they might have received. It took some convincing, but Jack eventually agreed. Cate persuaded him by suggesting that not checking on their correspondence might be suspicious. While Jack was anxious about being caught on the castle's grounds, Cate advocated that they go in the early morning, when most of the family would be asleep and the servants not roaming about in the castle. They agreed to go on Friday morning.

Cate sat on pins and needles for the next twenty-four hours, nervous anticipation filling her. Despite it being a short "business" trip, Cate was still excited. Any length of time in another era exhilarated her. Even with her anticipation building, she slept that night but was up bright and early before the sun rise to ready herself for the trip. They had agreed to leave before breakfast around 6:30 a.m. Since time passed more slowly in the present when they were in the past, they should have plenty of time to travel to town on foot, inquire about any correspondence left for them and return without being missed.

Cate met an already prepared Jack in the bedroom closet

right on the dot of six thirty. He sighed as she held the watch out for him to grasp. "You'd think I'd be getting used to this by now but I'm still a bundle of nerves," he admitted.

Cate nodded. "Just wait until we have to dine with them. This is an easy trip!"

"Don't remind me," he said, shuddering at the notion. "Okay, let's go check our mail."

They grasped the watch together, rubbing it in unison. Within seconds, the second hand slowed, and they slipped back into the past. They cautiously made their way out of the castle, meeting no one at this hour of the morning. Most of those already up were in the servant's areas, busy readying for their day.

The sun was just cresting the moors as they set off toward town on a path obscured from most of the castle's view. The walk, while not difficult in general, was taxing on Cate lugging her awkward period clothing with her. Jack pronounced his newfound appreciation for modern clothing as well, more than once during the trip. After a small struggle, they made it to town, heading straight to the postmaster.

Their efforts were rewarded. The postmaster had one letter from Lady MacKenzie for Cate. They thanked him then hurried back to the castle. By now, the household would be stirring but with careful timing they made their way back to the bedroom closet undetected. They returned to their own time with no issues. Jack breathed his customary sigh of relief after they were back.

Cate was like a giddy child. "I can't wait to read it!" she said, brandishing the letter in the air in front of her.

"Well, I can wait to hear about it, I'm going to change before breakfast and head down there. I'm starving."

"Me too," Cate admitted. "Time travel makes me hungry." Even Jack laughed at her terrible joke. The two parted ways to change before breakfast. Cate placed the letter from

Victoria on her side table in her sitting room, giving it a forlorn glance as she exited the room for breakfast.

She ate her breakfast in the library, checking her email and completing a few other tasks as she ate. Her mind continued to return to the correspondence waiting for her upstairs. Before she could read it, she promised Riley his morning walk. Despite her obvious interest in the letter, she still enjoyed watching Riley romp around the grounds.

After returning to the castle, she curled up on her chaise to read the letter. With careful precision, she unsealed the wax seal. It was amazing how different the paper felt and the handwriting was. She marveled at it even before unfolding it, running her hand over the name written on the outside: *Mrs. Jack MacKenzie*. Cate held back an eye roll at the salutation with no mention of her own name at all.

She unfolded the letter, appreciating the elaborate penmanship before reading the brief correspondence.

Dearest Cousin Catherine -

I learned from my dear husband, Lord Randolph MacKenzie, of your recent arrival in our little hamlet. I am most eager to make your acquaintance. My husband has informed me he has already invited you to our small party on Monday, 13 October and I am delighted that you have already accepted. Please arrive at Dunhaven Castle at five thirty in the evening, a time prior to other guests.

I look so forward to meeting you in person. I am sure we will become fast friends. As I expect our meeting will be a success, I would also invite you to do me the honor of paying a call for afternoon tea on Wednesday, 15 October. You may express your acceptance in person when we meet. I expect you have much to do in setting up your household and do not expect correspondence to be at the top of your list.

Yours in friendship,
Victoria

Excitement coursed through Cate as she read the letter. Dining with her ancestors was both thrilling and overwhelming. She glanced at the letter again, appreciating all the sentiment that a handwritten note from this era carried. It was so different from receiving correspondence today, most often hastily typed and lacking any warm regard or personal sentiment.

A list of next steps filled Cate's mind. She would need to prepare Jack for the manners expected from a visiting couple for a dinner party, since they would not be seated near each other for dinner, as was the custom in 1856. Cate would also need to inform Jack they must travel back again on October fifteenth in order for Cate to attend tea with Victoria. At least for that visit, Jack need only to find a spot to hide out and wait for Cate to finish her business. She imagined the news that they would be making two visits to the past in a matter of only a handful of days would go over like a lead balloon.

As Cate imagined the ramifications of telling Jack the news, Mrs. Fraser knocked and entered with a tray of lunch. "Didn't mean to be presumptuous, but I thought I'd bring your lunch early. Since you have a meeting with that woman this afternoon," she said, referring to Mrs. Campbell, "I figured you may want to eat early."

"Thank you, Mrs. Fraser, good idea!" Cate answered, folding the letter and placing it on her side table. In her excitement, Cate had almost forgotten about her meeting later. What a perfect way to spoil her fun, she mused. Either way, it was necessary. She would have to wait until tomorrow to discuss plans further with Jack.

After lunch, party planning details consumed Cate's afternoon. The meeting left her spent, but they accomplished a good deal. As she watched Mrs. Campbell's car pull away from the house, she found herself longing for her staff dinner. Despite the early hour, she made her way to the kitchen. She had left Riley with Mrs. Fraser for the afternoon while she met with Mrs. Campbell.

Upon arriving at the kitchen, she found Mrs. Fraser wiping off a wet Riley. "What happened to you?" Cate asked the pup.

"Went and got himself a mess again," Mrs. Fraser answered her. "I let him out earlier and the little monkey disappeared on me again and got caught in that rain storm that passed through."

"Oh, Riley." Cate shook her head at him as Mrs. Fraser set him down on the floor. "What is with you and your disappearing acts anymore?" The pup offered no answers beyond a mischievous gleam in his eye.

"And how did your meeting go today, Lady Cate?"

"Very well, I believe. Although, I am exhausted. The details of this party seem endless!"

"I would have thought the company was the most exhausting part of that meeting," Mrs. Fraser said, offering a coy smile.

Cate returned her smile. "She does seem to make even the simplest task rather tedious," Cate admitted, "but she has a good handle on planning an event of this magnitude. For that, I am appreciative, I wouldn't know where to start."

"Ah, I don't believe that, Lady Cate. As bright as you are, I expect you'd do just fine on your own!"

"Thank you for the vote of confidence, Mrs. Fraser!

Speaking of planning, have you planned your pumpkin carving? We're only two weeks away from the party!"

"Oh, I have. I've got a special design in mind, but no one is getting any details before the contest!"

Cate laughed. "Fair enough. I haven't even contemplated mine. I'm so pleased everyone liked the idea enough to chip in. Even Mr. Smythe and Gayle are excited to create their own pumpkin carving for the competition."

"I think it's a fun idea, Lady Cate. No doubt Isla didn't agree but I think it's splendid."

"Thank you. Yes, she was concerned about it not being what she called 'appropriate' but it's all in good fun."

Mrs. Fraser nodded in agreement. They chitchatted a few moments longer, with Cate pitching in here and there to help with dinner preparations as much as Mrs. Fraser would allow. Cate enjoyed a long dinner and conversation with the Frasers, Jack and Riley.

After dinner, Cate made a list of the fine points of dining in the 1800s she wanted to discuss with Jack before their dinner invitation. She reviewed it and, once she was satisfied, retired for the evening.

The following morning, Cate took a long walk with Riley before spending the rest of her day researching for her book. She tried to focus her energy even though she found herself distracted much of the time. The day dragged by with evening finally approaching. The sun hung low on the horizon as Jack met her in the library after dinner.

Cate pulled out her list to share with him. His eyes widened at the length of it and he asked if she could provide a cheat sheet that he could hide in his hand. Cate laughed despite Jack's insistence that he wasn't joking. She assured him he would be fine. The quick thinking he displayed on their last visit made her confident he'd breeze through the dinner.

With the rules squared away, Cate let Jack head home for the evening. They planned on meeting tomorrow around four to dress. They would then travel back and leave enough time to sneak out of the castle and to the front door for their five thirty call. On his way out, Jack expressed his genuine hope that he would sleep tonight. Cate agreed, stating that she was far too excited to sleep. It wasn't excitement that threatened to keep Jack up, he confessed.

CHAPTER 10

Cate spent most of her night tossing and turning with anxious anticipation. When morning came, Cate watched the sunrise from her chaise before taking Riley for a long walk. She spent the rest of her morning watching a movie and going over and over her list in her mind. The timepiece was a constant fixture in her hand. After a while, she stopped closing the face, afraid it would break off from her constant opening of it.

When four o'clock approached, Cate met Jack at the front door, ushering him in and off to change. In the meantime, she took Riley for a last walk before her trip, then nestled him into his bed near the fireplace in her sitting room.

Cate had selected a ruby red gown with lace detail at the top, a bustle in the back and a train. With it, she wore a matching capelet for the evening chill. She pulled her hair into a chignon, complete with a ruby hair comb. Preparing for the dinner took her longer than for her other trips. She was glad she had left plenty of time for them to dress.

When she was ready, she made her way to the bedroom

to meet Jack. He was already waiting for her in his formal dinner wear.

"Wow, that's quite a dress!" Jack said as she tried to make her way through the door in the hooped skirt and crinoline petticoat.

"It is a bit unwieldy, I must admit," Cate said, hoping she was able to sneak anywhere on the estate in this much fabric.

"Please don't fake faint again. I don't think I could navigate holding you in that dress," Jack laughed.

"I'll have to try another type of subterfuge," Cate said, leading the way to the closet.

Jack followed her, taking a deep breath. "I hope I don't do anything wrong," he said, wiping a bead of sweat from his brow.

"You'll be fine, I'm sure! If you do anything that wrong, I'll kick you under the table," she said, grinning at him and holding the timepiece out.

They both grasped it and started the process to return to 1856. Within moments, they were standing in the bedroom closet in another century. Cate was careful to calculate a time when most others in the household would be dressing for dinner assisted by their servants. This should leave a clear path for them to make it out of the castle. Once on the grounds if anyone caught them, it would be far easier to explain.

They still moved cautiously until they were outside. Once outside on the grounds, they both breathed a sigh of relief. Checking the time, they realized they were too early to present themselves for dinner. Instead, they strolled to the loch, remarking how little some things had changed in over a century. As the time approached five thirty, they made their way to the front entrance. Jack used the door knocker, and Thomson greeted them.

"Welcome back to Dunhaven Castle, Mr. and Mrs.

MacKenzie. May I take your wrap, ma'am?" Cate removed her capelet, handing it to Thomson. "Lord and Lady MacKenzie are waiting in the east sitting room, if you'll follow me." They followed the butler to the sitting room where he announced them as they entered.

"Ah, cousin Jack," Randolph said as they entered, "glad you could make it to our little party." He approached Cate, grasping her hand and bowing to her. "Mrs. MacKenzie, lovely to see you again."

Cate acknowledged his greeting. Behind him, she saw Victoria, seated on a loveseat. Cate understood why her beauty were renowned, she was a very attractive woman with delicate features, beautiful dark, exotic eyes, and an exquisitely shaped mouth. Her dark hair was swept up, framing a delicate neck around which hung a beautiful emerald necklace.

Cate and Jack approached her as Randolph introduced her. Her smile lit up her face. Jack approached, delicately taking her hand, imitating Randolph and bowing to her.

"Lady MacKenzie, a pleasure to make your acquaintance."

Cate went next, giving a slight curtsy and conveying a similar sentiment.

"Drinks?" Randolph asked, making his way to the bar cart.

"I'll have what you're having," Jack answered, sitting across from Victoria. Cate chose a seat with her on the loveseat.

"I'll have a small sherry," Cate answered, noticing Victoria already sipping one.

"I hope you are feeling better, Mrs. MacKenzie," Victoria began.

"Yes, I am, thank you. And please thank Thomson for his hospitality when I took ill. After a few moments of rest, I felt strong enough to travel back home. We weren't able to locate him so we took our leave causing no further disruptions."

Victoria nodded. "And I hope you didn't find it awkward to arrive earlier than our other guests but I hoped to spend a small amount of time with family only."

"Not at all, and thank you so very much for extending the private invitation," Cate answered.

"Of course. I understand from my husband that you will not be staying with us. I hope the stories of our home haven't put you off."

"Oh, Victoria, please, let's not start with that," Randolph said, handing drinks all around.

"The truth of the matter, Lady MacKenzie, is that we considered it best to establish our own household given that we were unsure how long we may be staying. We did not want to upset your household if our plans unexpectedly changed."

"It's no upset at all and I understand how important family is to my husband. But if you shan't be staying with us, I do hope you will accept my invitation for afternoon tea?"

"Lady MacKenzie, I accept your gracious invitation."

"Wonderful. I hope you will be a fixture on the property despite not taking up residence here."

"Yes, please consider our doors always open to you," Randolph noted. Cate nodded to him, he held her gaze longer than she expected. Odd, Cate ruminated to herself, he seemed to be staring at her. It made her uncomfortable for a few moments before Victoria began speaking again.

The women made further conversation about how the move was going for the couple while Randolph and Jack discussed business and the prospect of an upcoming shooting party.

Soon after, other guests began arriving. Cate and Jack did their best to mingle amongst the others with Victoria and

Randolph providing a good bit of the small amount of background information on their newly arrived family members.

At dinner, Cate and Jack found themselves seated across from each other as was the customary practice. Despite the trepidation they both experienced about trying to make conversation with people from centuries prior to theirs, they made it through dinner. Cate watched each of the footmen present in the dining room. Which one, she wondered, was the servant who would be murdered? It was impossible to tell without knowing their names. Cate scrutinized their movements as closely as possible, trying to glean any details she could about them. None of them seemed to pay particular attention to Victoria. Cate recalled the reported motive for the murder was too intimate a glance shared between Victoria and the victim. Cate questioned the motive, witnessing no such glances at this dinner party. She rejoined Jack at post-dinner drinks and they were briefly able to compare notes before beginning to socialize again.

Cate planned to leave the party earlier than other guests so they could sneak to the bedroom and return to their own time while everyone was still occupied with others in the castle. After giving her signal to Jack, she announced to Victoria that the couple would depart despite the early hour. Cate feigned tiredness from her journey.

"Leaving?" Randolph asked, overhearing Cate's conversation with Victoria.

"Yes, I'm afraid so," Jack stepped in, "I'm afraid the journey has been taxing on Mrs. MacKenzie."

"I understand," Randolph said, "If it isn't too much, I hoped to have a brief word with both of you before you left."

Cate and Jack shared a glance. Cate gave him a slight nod signaling he should accept the invitation. She wasn't sure they had much other choice. "By all means," Jack said, nodding to Randolph.

"Wonderful, follow me, we can speak uninterrupted in my study. Victoria, please excuse me, I shan't be long."

The pair followed him from the room. Cate's heart was racing as she trailed him down the hall. This was unusual; she couldn't imagine what it was about. Randolph opened a set of double doors leading to the small study. Cate was familiar with the room from her experience with the castle. The two entered and Randolph made his way to his bar cart, pouring himself a drink before standing behind his desk.

Cate and Jack stood in bewildered silence. "Well, now that we are alone, I was hoping you'd tell me who you really are," Randolph began.

Cate glanced at Jack, shocked and without a clue what to say. Jack began, "I'm sorry? I'm your cousin, Jack. We aren't closely related, I believe..." Jack stammered around.

"Yes, yes, I know the cover story," Randolph said, waving his hand in the air. "Cousins, distant, a letter was sent but never arrived. You're staying on the outskirts of town, but I inquired after you and no one heard a thing. In a town this size, the arrival of a new MacKenzie would have been the talk of everyone, so I have my doubts that your story is true."

"Well, we..." Cate began, likewise stammering. "We're not... we didn't..."

"Perhaps I'm asking the wrong question," Randolph interrupted her. "Rather than WHO are you, perhaps I should ask WHEN are you from?"

Cate froze. She eyed the timepiece sticking out of his pocket before glancing at Jack.

"I'll take that as an affirmation that my theory was correct," Randolph said. "You're time travelers. Future, I'd say, since neither of you are one of my parents or grandparents."

Cate was the first to answer. "Yes, you are correct."

"I'd ask what you're doing here but I shouldn't know

that," he said, sipping his drink. Cate smiled at him; she appreciated his understanding. "Well, now that I am aware of the circumstances surrounding your visits, that should make whatever you're here to do easier for you."

"Sorry about lying to you," Jack said, "but you can imagine the position we're in, I'm sure."

"Absolutely," Randolph agreed.

"Thanks for your understanding. We'll be taking our leave now and returning to our own time. Please enjoy the rest of your evening," Jack said.

"Oh, before you leave, Catherine, you will still attend tea with my wife?"

"Yes," Cate answered, surprised he was asking.

"Oh good, I worry about her adjustment to country life. I'm certain it would make her happy."

Cate smiled at him again as she and Jack turned to leave. "One more thing," Randolph said, stopping them. They turned back, and he eyed each of them. After a moment more he spoke, "If you're time travelers, that means one of you is a MacKenzie and one of you is a Reid. I'm going to bet you're the MacKenzie." He pointed to Cate.

"I am," Cate answered, "yes."

"Ah, I knew it, I knew it. She's got the MacKenzie spunk," he said to Jack. "But, by golly, you're a Yank!" he exclaimed to Cate.

"A little too much, in my opinion, sir," Jack answered, grinning.

"And you've all the practicality of a Reid," Randolph added.

"A little too much, in my opinion," Cate mimicked, grinning back.

Randolph smiled at them. "Well, I won't hold you back any further, I'm sure you know the way to wherever will return you. I look forward to seeing you both again and good luck to you in whatever it is you're trying to do."

"Thank you," Cate said to him before they left the room.

They hurried without a word to each other up the main staircase and to the bedroom closet. They returned to the present, where Jack breathed another sigh of relief.

"Wow," Cate said.

"You aren't kidding," Jack said, "how did he figure it out? Are we the worst time travelers ever?"

Cate laughed. "He strikes me as being intelligent. And we had some rather large gaps in our story in retrospect."

"Our second meeting only and he calls us right out. I didn't think I was going to stay upright."

"Silver lining, we don't have to sneak around as much. Now he knows, I get the impression he also realizes we're doing something back there and that if push came to shove he'd cover for us."

"Yeah, I'm not sure I want to push our luck on that."

"Me either, I agree we should continue to be careful but at least some pressure is off."

"I could use some of your optimism, Cate."

"Or my spunk." She laughed.

"You have that to spare, lassie. Oh, I can't believe we have to do this again in two days."

"Hey, you've got it easy! You just have to stay hidden. I have all the hard work."

"Speaking of hard work, did you notice anything out of the ordinary during the dinner?"

"I didn't. If there is an affair, it's well hidden. Although, I don't believe that story. I'm not sure which servant it was from the men that were serving tonight, but I didn't see anything suspicious."

"Neither did I. It would be helpful if we could identify the servant."

"I agree. It doesn't help that there will be no pictures of him. We only have his name. Our best bet is to continue to travel back and spend time in the household and hope to identify him by his name."

Jack scowled. "Not what I wanted to hear. But I agree."

"We're almost halfway through the month, leaving us only two-and-a-half weeks to get more information. It doesn't help that in less than a week we'll be tethered to our time for a week."

"I can't say that I'm upset being tethered here as you put it. But we'll do what we can before your guests arrive and after."

"Thanks, Jack. I think it's time we get out of these clothes."

"I agree. And you're welcome. I'm actually starting to find this interesting. Randolph seems like a good man, I like him. I hope we can help him. I hope you're right about his innocence."

Cate smiled at him, glad that he was appreciating the experience now. That would make things easier. "I'm glad! Now, let's change out of these clothes," Cate said.

"I'll second that."

"Me too. I agree with you on the clothing perspective!"

"Oh, wow! You mean you agree with me on something? I'm flattered!"

She rolled her eyes at him, laughing. "See you tomorrow, Jack."

"See you tomorrow, Cate. I'll let myself out when I've changed into normal clothes."

Cate toddled back to her room, gaining a new admiration for the women of this century. Wearing these dresses was not an easy feat. Neither was undressing alone, but she managed, feeling as though she was wearing nothing but air in her normal clothes compared to the weight of the evening dress.

She was exhausted after the evening, not only from traipsing about in the dress but also from the demanding social engagement. The tension she experienced most of the night hit her like a palette of bricks. After changing, she took Riley out for a short walk then cuddled under a blanket on her chaise with Riley curled on her lap. It didn't take long before she was nodding off. With that, she turned in early, sleeping well despite the day's excitement.

CHAPTER 11

She was still riding the high of her experience the next morning. Her upcoming trip the following day was at the forefront of her mind. She was eager to spend more time at the Dunhaven Castle of the past. It seemed even Jack was in high spirits today. She met him as she and Riley walked to the loch. He didn't complain once about their upcoming trip to the past, even when Cate mentioned it.

Cate spent over an hour selecting the dress she wanted to wear for her tea with Victoria. After a long while of debate, she selected a pink and white striped gown. It was the gown she had tried on when she first arrived at the castle. She remembered back to that day. She assumed she had lost Riley, having inadvertently traveled to the past without realizing what she had done. She panicked when she failed to find the little pup, running through the house in the dress like a crazy woman. She had run into one of the maids, who, not knowing who Cate was, had fled from her, assuming she was a member of the undead. Cate chuckled at her experience. How little she had known then.

After lunch, Cate spent the time doing some research. While on a break, she found an email waiting from Molly.

Cate! We're less than a week away! I'm so excited! I can't believe in four days I'll be on a plane to England and in five I'll be in Scotland staying at a castle with a Countess! I have been talking nonstop to anyone who will listen about my upcoming trip! I think Jeff is getting annoyed with me. Well, I can't tell if he's more annoyed that I keep reminding him about your turn of good luck or if he's annoyed by my lack of focus on the job. Either way, in four days, I won't have to think about him or work or Aberdeen for ten whole days! I am counting the days down!

FOUR TO GO!
Molly

Cate smiled at her computer screen. Molly's enthusiasm for her upcoming trip thrilled her. While Cate was disappointed that her time traveling would be on hold while Molly and her other guests stayed with her, she was pleased to have her old friend with her.

Before Molly's arrival, though, she had a few trips to the past to make. She answered Molly, stating how eager she was for her arrival and that she, too, was counting down the days. After finishing her email, she went back to her work, concluding just before dinner.

After dinner, Jack dropped by the library. He sought her out to go over the plan for traveling to 1856 the following day. Cate was impressed to find Jack interested in the trip, she didn't have to twist his arm for this one. In addition to his interest, he also had an entire plan for putting his time to good use while Cate enjoyed tea with Lady MacKenzie. Jack's idea was to travel to town and put in a few appearances to cover their tracks. His appearance should get people talking about the new MacKenzies in town. Since Randolph drew some of his suspicion of them from the lack of scuttlebutt in town, Jack wanted to remedy that. Afterwards, Jack would go to the castle to pay a quick call on Randolph before collecting Cate for the return trip. Cate admitted, it was a good plan and use of his time while she visited with Victoria.

Despite having a solid plan for the visit the next day, Cate tossed and turned most of the night. With two trips under their belt and Randolph aware of who they were, Cate wasn't plagued by nervous energy but rather filled with pure excitement. She felt they had far less to lose now and was excited to experience socializing in another era.

Regardless of her lack of sleep, Cate sprang from her bed the next morning. She went about her morning chores with an added bounce in her step. As she sat on the banks of the loch after her morning walk with Riley, she gazed at the castle. Her upcoming visit consumed her mind. She imagined the tea, served in a porcelain tea set, or perhaps a silver one. In her mind, she pictured a multilevel serving tray arranged with tea sandwiches, scones and cookies. She envisioned Victoria in a blue dress, or perhaps rose, her exotic eyes peering at Cate over her teacup as she made polite conversation with her new cousin.

Cate smiled at the vision she concocted in her head. Soon enough she would ascertain firsthand what the tea set looked like, what fashions Victoria would wear. Checking the timepiece that hung around her neck she found it almost time for lunch. She stood, brushing herself off and collecting Riley to return to the castle.

Right after lunch, Cate prepared for her trip. She had several hours before her tea date but she was too excited to wait. She fussed with her hair, trying several styles before settling on one. She took Riley for another brief walk and then, around 2:30 p.m., started the process of dressing.

Cate was glad she left ample time to get ready. Although she was wearing a day dress, dressing was still complicated. She managed after a good deal of trying to pull her outfit together. After making herself presentable by 1850s standards, Cate tottered down the hall, carrying her skirts. Jack was waiting for her, already dressed and ready to tackle his plan.

The two entered the closet and used the timepiece to travel back to 1856. Unnoticed, they made their way out of the castle and traveled a ways from it before parting ways. With a wave to Cate, Jack made his way toward town. Cate turned back toward the castle.

As she approached the castle's main entrance, she smoothed her skirts, fussed with her hair and knocked on the door. Thomson answered the door within seconds.

"Mrs. Jack MacKenzie to see Lady MacKenzie," Cate said.

"Yes, please come in, Mrs. MacKenzie. Lady MacKensie is expecting you. Right this way," Thomson said, leading her down the hall toward the tea room. He announced her arrival upon entering the room, stepping aside to allow her to enter.

"Mrs. MacKenzie, welcome. I am so grateful that you could join me for tea." Victoria already sat at the table. She was holding a baby, not yet a year old. As Cate entered the room, Victoria nodded to the woman standing nearby. The woman rushed to relieve Victoria of the child, exiting the room in an instant. "Please sit down, Mrs. MacKenzie."

Cate approached the table, taking a seat next to Victoria, removing her gloves as was the custom at the tea table. Victoria was already pouring the tea for her into a porcelain cup with red roses decorating it. "Thank you for the invitation, Lady MacKenzie. I appreciate how welcoming you have been in my first few days in Dunhaven."

Victoria smiled at her, offering her a tea sandwich. "Please, call me Victoria, we're family. And how have you been finding our little hamlet?"

"Quite charming, Victoria." Cate nibbled on the sandwich and sipped her tea.

"I detect an American accent. Where in America are you from?" Victoria inquired.

"The midwestern United States. You may know of Chicago? This was the closest large city to where I was raised."

Victoria nodded her head. "And how did you meet my dear husband's cousin, Jack?"

Cate stuck to the backstory that she and Jack had prepared. "I was visiting my aunt in New York. Jack was traveling on business. We were seated next to each other at a dinner party hosted by one of my aunt's close friends."

"How charming," Victoria said.

"And how did you meet Lord MacKenzie?" Cate asked.

"Randolph was in London, as was I, staying with relatives. We attended a ball together. After the ball, he sent me a sonnet and asked to court me. I declined but his enthusiasm proved too much for me. He sent notes and flowers almost daily until I agreed to be courted."

"How romantic," Cate answered. Her mind recalled the letters she found when first exploring the castle. She knew the sonnets well, having read them with great interest several times. Randolph had been quite the paramour, expressing his heartfelt emotion many times to woo the beautiful Victoria into a courtship and marriage.

"Yes," Victoria reflected. "How are you settling in to your new home? I am disappointed you are not staying with us. It would have been lovely to have family stay in the castle."

Cate sidestepped the question. "We are settling in nicely, thank you for asking. Are you and Randolph the only family in the castle?"

"Primarily. Randolph's younger brother, Lorne, stays with us now and then. He offers little companionship to either of us. Other than our staff and Ethan, our infant son, we are alone."

Victoria didn't mention any other person in the castle. So either Victoria did not know about the tower's occupant or it was being kept a secret. "It must be quite a change from your London life."

"Yes," Victoria said with a wistful gaze out the window. "Quite a change for me."

"How do you find Scottish country life?"

"Peaceful," Victoria answered tactfully. "How long do you and Mr. MacKenzie plan to stay in our little hamlet?"

"We are uncertain, but at least through the end of the month. Perhaps through part of November."

"Oh!" Victoria exclaimed, her eyes lighting up. "Then you'll attend our Halloween Ball on All Hallows' Eve! Please say you will!"

"It sounds delightful, thank you for the invitation."

"What a fortunate turn of events. I am so pleased to have family attending." Cate smiled at her. "You should dine with us again before the party."

"We would love to dine with you again."

"Oh, you shall do so more than once, I hope."

"Thank you for your gracious hospitality," Cate answered.

"Will you be able to join us for a private dinner party two days hence?"

Cate contemplated a moment. "I must check with Mr. MacKenzie, but I believe our schedule would accommodate it, yes."

"Wonderful. I am so pleased."

"Well, have you ladies solved all the world's problems?" Randolph said, entering the tearoom. Jack trailed behind him.

"Oh, Randolph!" Victoria chuckled. "We have not but we have decided that Mr. and Mrs. MacKenzie shall dine with us two days hence and that they shall attend our ball on All Hallows' Eve!"

"Divine! I am so pleased," Randolph answered. "I do hope you'll join us often for dinner at the castle. It's splendid having family nearby."

"As much as our schedule permits and without us wearing out our welcome!" Jack answered.

"Magnificent!" Randolph answered.

"I had one request, if it's not too much to ask," Jack said.

"Ask away, cousin!" Randolph said.

"I hope you don't view this as ill-mannered, but would it be possible to tour the castle? I would like to see it all."

"Well, certainly, old chap. Shall we do it at the upcoming dinner party?" Randolph clapped him on the back.

"That sounds perfect, yes," Jack answered.

"Then we shall see you in two days forth and shall give you the grand tour of our family's home!"

"Well," Jack began, "I suppose Catherine and I should be on our way."

Cate stood, thanking Victoria for the hospitality. "I'll walk you out," Randolph offered.

"Thank you," Jack answered. The three exited the room, with Randolph leading them to the main stairs.

"I shall leave you here, dear friends. I know not the reason you are here but if I may say, I hope it keeps you returning to us. I haven't seen such a pleasant and cheerful look on my wife's face in months."

Cate smiled at him. "We plan on it. We'll see you in two days!"

"I bid you both a fond farewell until then," Randolph said. He turned and departed down the hall, not glancing back.

Cate and Jack made their way to the bedroom, returning to their own time. Jack breathed his usual sigh of relief. Cate patted him on the arm. "Good going getting us the tour of the castle!" she exclaimed.

"Thanks," Jack grinned. "I expected you would appreciate that."

"Let's see how he handles the tower when we tour the castle."

"I'm interested in that, too. He seems like a nice chap. I hope we don't find anything untoward."

Cate snickered. "Did you just say chap?"

"Sorry." Jack laughed. "I guess the past is rubbing off on me." He loosened his collar.

"Anyway, I can't imagine anything untoward. He seems enamored and very much devoted to his wife. He dotes on her. After talking with him I'd be shocked if he was the rogue everyone made him out to be."

"Perhaps he's a fantastic actor."

"Perhaps. But he seems so genuine."

"I guess we shall see," Jack responded.

Cate nodded in agreement. "Well, I'm going to change and get ready for dinner."

"Great plan. We need to devise a plan for the upcoming dinner. Although, this should be an easy one. We're off the hook with Randolph, no other guests to worry about, and I'm starting to get used to the 1800s!"

"Wow! Are you beginning to enjoy this?"

"I wouldn't go that far, Cate." Jack laughed, shaking his head.

Cate made her way back to her bedroom suite to undress, happy to change back into modern clothes. She took Riley for a quick walk before dinner then spent the rest of the evening lounging on her chaise.

The following day Cate spent relaxing. Although she enjoyed her trips and savored every moment of her excursions to the past, time difference was proving more difficult than she was prepared for. Akin to jet lag, Cate found herself fatigued from living her double life. She spent hours in the past. Upon coming home, however, only a short period of time had passed. The result was her days were longer than twenty-four hours.

Cate was glad for the relaxing day. She devoted her day to researching and spending time with Riley. She enjoyed her weekly lunch with her staff. Afterwards, she met with Jack under the ruse of going over estate business. In reality, Jack wanted to outline the plan for their upcoming dinner party. Cate was pleased that he was coming around to time traveling.

After their meeting, Cate went back to the kitchen. Riley had been chewing on a bone over lunch and Mrs. Fraser suggested Cate leave him while she attended to her business. As she approached the kitchen, Cate heard Mrs. Fraser's voice carrying down the hall, "Now where could that have gone? Have you seen it, little Riley?"

Cate entered the kitchen. "What's going on?" she questioned.

"Oh, well, I'm afraid my old age is catching up to me."

Cate furrowed her brow. "What?"

"I could have sworn I set out two pieces of meat for tonight's dinner. But I cannae find the smaller one of them. I must not have put it out. Well, looks like I'll have to make do with what I have. It'll be enough, but I won't be able to put any away for sandwiches over the weekend. In case your guest wanted a quick snack."

"Aww, well don't give it a second thought, I'm sure we'll be just fine without it, Mrs. Fraser. Nothing to worry about."

"Aye, you're right, Lady Cate." Cate gathered Riley and his bone. She intended to spend some time selecting her next dress before settling in her sitting room for a lazy afternoon. Eventually, Cate selected a demure dark blue gown, much less grandiose than her previous dinner gown since they would only dine with family.

Satisfied with her selection, she resumed her research, spreading out on the floor of her sitting room. She was still engrossed in her Dunhaven Castle history project when Mrs. Fraser delivered her dinner.

After dinner, she cuddled on her chaise with Riley, streaming a movie on her laptop. She made it three quarters of the way through before she found herself dozing off. Taking that as a cue, she put herself to bed.

Following her early night, Cate awoke refreshed. She would spend another day on pins and needles in giddy anticipation of her upcoming dinner party. It had been years since Cate had any family. When her parents died, she assumed she was alone, with no family to speak of. Although Randolph and Victoria's familial connection spanned generations, time travel had made them seem like immediate family.

Cate had already excused both herself and Jack from dinner, using the excuse that they had a few errands for the estate to take care of in town. With that news, Mr. and Mrs. Fraser had left the castle early, heading home for a quiet dinner. That left Jack and Cate alone to dress and travel back for their dinner party.

Cate felt the familiar excitement creeping into her body as she watched the second hand of the timepiece slow to a crawl. Within an instant, they were whisked back to 1856. Sneaking from the castle, they made their way to the front door where Thomson greeted them. They reentered the castle, this time as guests. Thomson showed them into the sitting room where Randolph and Victoria awaited them.

"Ah, Jack, Catherine, lovely to see you again," Randolph said, preparing a cocktail for them both.

"Yes, thank you for joining us for the evening," Victoria greeted them.

"The pleasure is all ours," Jack answered. "And I must confess, we are looking forward to the tour."

"Yes," Cate added, "I am fascinated by your home. There is nothing comparable in my country."

"Are there no grand homes in America?" Victoria inquired.

"Grand homes, yes. Castles, no," Cate answered.

"My wife is quite taken with your home," Jack added.

"Well, then we should start the tour!" Randolph suggested, raising his glass to them.

"At your convenience, sir," Jack said.

Randolph showed them out of the sitting room. They spent over an hour touring the house. Randolph pointed out several unique features. Cate found it fascinating to see the castle a mere sixty-four years after it was built. Although countless things had changed, many remained the same.

They concluded their tour, ending back in the sitting room to enjoy a cocktail before dinner. Conspicuously missing from the tour was that particular tower room. Cate took a chance mentioning it during their pre-dinner conversation. "I noticed a turret while Jack and I walked the grounds. Forgive me," Cate said, playing the unassuming female role, "what room was it on our tour?"

"Ah, we didn't visit it on the tour, dear Catherine," Randolph answered.

"Oh, what a pity. I hoped to see it."

There was a pause in conversation. "I'm afraid my wife

has romantic notions about that tower. White knights rescuing princesses and so on."

Randolph roared with laughter. "I'm sorry, cousin Catherine. There are no white knights or princesses. I'm afraid the only thing you'll find in our tower room are chests full of old articles from past generations. I doubt one could even set foot in the room."

Cate cast a fleeting glance toward Jack before offering a smile to Randolph. "Well, there is my romantic bubble burst," she yielded.

"I'm so very sorry to have crushed your quixotic concept of our home. I can only hope to make it up to you with our dinner."

Thomson appeared as if on cue. "Dinner, sir," he announced.

"What perfect timing," Randolph said as they stood to enter the dining room.

As they sat for dinner, Cate feigned forgetfulness. "Oh, how silly of me, I seem to have left my bag in the sitting room."

"Oh, you mustn't worry, nothing will happen to it," Victoria reassured her. "We will all remember to retrieve it before you depart."

"Oh, thank you. I should like to keep it with me. If it isn't too much trouble, perhaps one of your footmen could retrieve it?"

"Of course," Randolph said. Turning to the nearest footman, he said, "Andrew, retrieve Mrs. MacKenzie's bag, wouldn't you?"

Cate was in luck. Andrew was the name of the footman who would soon meet his fateful end. A short, dark-haired, dark-eyed man, Andrew's mouth seemed set in a perpetual scowl. Without a word, he left the room, returning within moments with Cate's bag. Cate hoped her ruse was not wasted on Jack and that he also picked up on the name. Jack gave her a knowing glance and an eyebrow raise. She gave a slight nod to her head.

Dinner conversation turned to the upcoming Halloween ball that Lord and Lady MacKenzie were hosting. Cate showered Victoria with her praise for the idea.

"I hope it is a success and we can make it an annual event! It promises to be so much fun," Victoria responded.

"We are looking forward to it," Cate assured her.

"I am thrilled you are attending. It has made my planning more enjoyable knowing we can share it with family." Cate offered her a smile. "On this subject," Victoria continued, "my dressmaker is coming Saturday mid-morning. We will finalize options for my ball gown. I was hoping you'd not have plans, Catherine, and could call at that time. Perhaps she can design something for you as well? Unless you have a gown already or prefer your own dressmaker?"

"Oh," Cate began, glancing at Jack then her dinner plate, unsure of what to say.

"I expect you can fit it into your schedule, can't you, dear?" Jack encouraged, nodding at her. "You've not found a dressmaker you're fond of."

Cate smiled at him, appreciating his support. "Thank you for the invitation, Victoria. I have given no consideration to my gown. This is very helpful."

"Splendid!" Randolph said, "it appears you ladies have everything under control."

"Oh, but there are so many details to attend to," Victoria corrected.

"Well, all the important details, anyway," Randolph said, winking to her.

The dinner continued with pleasant conversation about the upcoming ball and other frivolities. They finished their night with a nightcap before Cate and Jack, escorted by Randolph, slipped upstairs to return to their own time.

"Well, that was an interesting evening," Cate said after changing their clothes upon their return.

"Rather enjoyable," Jack admitted.

"And very informative!"

"Yes, a clever ruse on your part to elicit the name of the servant."

"Lucky, too," Cate said, "Randolph chose Andrew. And he omitted the tower room from the grand tour! We know it's not full of boxes, we've seen a woman there."

"Yes, I found it interesting how Randolph side-stepped that when you asked about it."

"I wonder why," Cate pondered.

"I don't know. But if he is lying about it, I can't imagine it's for any good reasons."

"I'm afraid I can't argue with you," Cate admitted. A sinking feeling filled her. Perhaps Jack had been right. Maybe Randolph was a madman, clever at hiding his murderous tendencies. "Perhaps I'll learn something at my fashion show with Victoria on Saturday. Thank you for the encouragement to accept her."

"Well, you need a dress, I'm sure. Although, I'm not pleased you'll be going on your own."

"I'm rather sorry about it too," Cate acknowledged. "I was hoping you could have taken a peek around the place while I enjoyed my fashion show."

"Gee, and here I thought you cared, Cate." Cate grinned at him.

"I'll also admit I will miss you. The only times I've traveled alone were by accident! And they were scary!"

"That's because you assumed you were seeing ghosts!"

Cate laughed. It was true, when she had stumbled upon the

secret, she hadn't understood it. She had inferred that the castle was haunted. "Well, it's a lot more fun this way. But I'm sure I can handle a small shopping trip while you pick up Molly from the train station. Thank you again for offering to get Molly. I didn't want her driving for hours by herself in a foreign country."

"My pleasure, Cate. Just don't be late from your little shopping excursion! I don't want to explain where you are to anyone!"

"I'll make sure to keep an eye on my time!" she said, winking at him. "Now, I suppose I should let you go home. We both need rest before the meeting with Mrs. Campbell tomorrow."

"Yes, these extra hours in my day are really becoming exhausting. So is Isla Campbell. So, I will bid you adieu m'lady!" Jack bowed extravagantly.

"Good night, Jack," Cate answered as she let him out the front door. She meditated on his last statements as she climbed the stairs and strode to her sitting room. She had also been experiencing the fatigue of her double life. Furthermore, Isla Campbell was exhausting. Their three-hour meeting loomed over Cate. She needed all the rest she could get. She gathered Riley into her lap, turning a movie on for background noise as she wrote a few notes from their latest travels. When she finished her notes, Cate turned in early.

CHAPTER 12

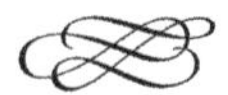

Cate dragged herself from bed the following morning. While she had slept well despite her evening's excitement, she dreaded the planning meeting. Today's promised to be a humdinger. With a week to go before the party, Mrs. Campbell wanted to discuss every detail. She had insisted Jack and Mr. Fraser be present to account for the exterior decorating plan.

Cate shortened her walk with Riley to accommodate the meeting, scheduled for 9 a.m. Mrs. Campbell arrived fifteen minutes before her scheduled time. This time, Cate was prepared for her early arrival. She met her at the front door, showing her into the library to begin their discussion.

"I can hardly believe we are less than a week away!" Mrs. Campbell exclaimed as she entered the library with Cate.

"It has snuck up on us, hasn't it!" Cate answered her.

"Oh, and I am so glad you both could join us, Jack and Charlie," she said, greeting the two men. "Forgive me for taking up your day, but I am finicky about every detail. We must strive for perfection with this ball."

"A noble goal," Jack answered.

"I agree," Cate added. "Where shall we begin?"

"Well, I believe we should begin with the external decorating scheme," Mrs. Campbell answered, sitting in a nearby armchair.

Mr. Fraser opened his folder. He spread his design, notes, and orders across the table. "I have made…" he began.

Mrs. Campbell interrupted him. "Yes, Lady Cate showed me your design. I found it…" She paused. "Quaint. I had a few ideas to spruce it up. Give it a more sleek, modern design." Mr. Fraser sat straighter in his chair, disheartened by Mrs. Campbell's assessment of his design.

Mrs. Campbell began to remove notes from her own folder. "Oh, that won't be necessary," Cate interjected.

Bewilderment crossed Mrs. Campbell's face. "Oh, while I realize Charlie has presumably made the required arrangements. I deemed that…"

This time Cate did the interrupting. "He has not only taken care of all the required arrangements, but I considered the design perfect."

"I appreciate your candor, Lady Cate. Although, my concern stems from the clash it may provide to the interior design that we have planned."

Cate shook her head. "Mr. Fraser's exterior design will not be changed. I don't consider the designs clashing, but that they provide a complimentary contrast."

"Surely there's some room for…" Mrs. Campbell tried again.

"The design will remain unchanged. That is final." Cate stated. "Now, let's proceed. Mr. Fraser, you were saying?"

Mr. Fraser nodded, offering an appreciative smile to Cate. "Aye, as I was saying, there are several elements involved in my design. Banners are ready and we will hang them on Monday. Trimming is complete, we will make final adjustments on Monday to the gardens. I arranged everything needed for the lighting. Lighting will arrive on Tuesday. Bailey's farm is bringing the pumpkins and cornstalks for us on Wednesday. We are, from our end, ready to go, Lady Cate!"

"Wonderful," Cate answered. "Mrs. Campbell, how are we with your arrangements?"

Mrs. Campbell, a frown still on her face, began, "Would it be possible to do a walkthrough to envision the exterior proposal?"

"Yes, we will complete a walkthrough of both the interior and exterior."

Mrs. Campbell gave the briefest of smiles. "Wonderful," she said in a monotone voice. "Well, on my end, all arrangements are taken care of, also. Linens have been ordered and will be delivered to the town library on Monday. Tables and chairs will arrive on Wednesday. Lighting and other decorations are also coming Wednesday. The musicians have been confirmed. I approved all final menu choices with the caterer yesterday along with our final numbers. Which, if I may add, are fantastic. This event sold out weeks ago. It is the event of the season!"

Cate smiled at her. "I'm glad this has been a success so far. With all your planning and attention to detail, it will be a very grand event."

"Oh, I do hope so!" Mrs. Campbell exclaimed. "Well, shall we begin the walkthrough? I'm eager to see the gardens and get a clearer picture of the vision. And we need to discuss the final interior design and placement."

"Sure!" Cate answered. "Let's move to the ballroom."

The group moved through the castle to the ballroom. They exited through the massive double doors leading outside. They began with the gardens. Mr. Fraser and Jack had them in exquisite shape. They looked enchanting and would, without question, add to the ambiance of the party.

Mrs. Campbell was less enthused about the design but admitted that the gardens were well-kempt. And, while the design was still more quaint than she imagined, she was satisfied with the end result. Cate held back rolling her eyes at the remark. Satisfied was a far cry from the word Cate would have used to describe the design.

At Mrs. Campbell's insistence, the men stayed on through the interior walkthrough and design discussion. If they needed to assist with decorating, Mrs. Campbell wanted to be sure they had a firm handle on her vision.

When they had fleshed out every minute detail down to the number of prongs on the appetizer forks, Cate ushered them to the kitchen for lunch to conclude the meeting. Mrs. Campbell feigned confusion about being steered downstairs, surprised that Cate ate with the staff. She had assumed, as she stated on their way downstairs, that she would enjoy a private luncheon with the Countess.

When lunch ended, Cate almost skipped to the front door to see Mrs. Campbell out. Cate sunk into one of the large leather armchairs in the library after watching Mrs. Campbell's car disappear down the drive. It was an exhausting morning. Still, they had accomplished everything they needed to. Cate was pleased with the progress and looking forward to the party.

She smiled to herself. Prior to the party, though, she had plans to look forward to. She picked Riley up to take him for a long afternoon walk. As they walked, she contemplated her full day tomorrow. She'd start with her dress fitting with Victoria for the upcoming Halloween ball in 1856. Upon returning from that, she was enthusiastically anticipating Molly's arrival. In just over twenty-four hours, her friend would join her at the castle. She couldn't deny the excitement building inside her.

She enjoyed a leisurely evening, her last night alone in the castle before guests arrived. It would be nice to have life in the castle, although she had gotten used to being alone here. She no longer checked dark corners for ghosts or found the moonlit rooms unnerving. Instead, Cate laid in bed admiring the shadows created by the moonlight in her room. She dozed off, dreaming of ball gowns.

The following morning, Jack left the estate early, making the long drive to Edinburgh to retrieve Molly from the train station. Cate readied herself for her trip to the past. Mrs. Fraser was busy with preparations for the soon-arriving guest. Cate was able to slip to the bedroom undetected in her day dress and back to the past.

Cate snuck down the backstairs, made her way to the front door and knocked to gain entrance. Thompson showed her to Victoria's private sitting room.

"Oh, Catherine!" Victoria rushed to her, giving her a warm embrace and a kiss on her cheek. "Please come in, sit down. May I offer you tea?"

"Thank you, tea would be delightful."

Victoria poured them each a cup of tea. "My dressmaker should arrive any moment. Have you thought about design, color, fabric?" Victoria was like a giddy schoolchild.

"I hadn't. I hoped to see what you selected so I may complement it."

"I'm so eager to show you my selection. I've chosen a burgundy ensemble with a drop waist. I plan to try the new bodice style, with the front closure. The button detail it adds to the bodice is quite alluring."

"It sounds lovely," Cate answered.

"I was thinking, Catherine, with your fair skin and light eyes, perhaps something in sapphire. I believe it would be very becoming on you and a nice contrast to my dress. Oh, I don't mean to be overbearing though if you prefer another color."

"No, I think that may be the perfect selection," Cate answered, musing the color would work well on her.

Victoria squeezed Cate's hands. "Oh, how fortunate I am that you have traveled to us, Catherine!"

"I agree!" Cate answered. "Victoria," Cate continued, sipping her tea, "I don't mean to be improper, but I hoped I could ask a candid question?" Victoria cocked her head, but gave a slight nod to encourage Cate to continue. "Your footman, the one who retrieved my purse, Alexander, was it? Has he been with you long? I feel as though I've seen him before. He seems so familiar to me."

"Oh, you mean Andrew? He is new to the household. We had a…" Victoria stumbled. "An incident. It left us rather short-handed. Andrew was not highly recommended but, well, given the circumstances, we accepted him."

"Incident?" Cate questioned, then added, "oh, I hope I'm not prying."

Victoria offered a tight-lipped smile, "Of course not, you're family. Several months ago one of our footman left, in the middle of the night, in fact. He claimed to have seen strange people wandering the estate. The final straw was when he was rousted from his bed by what he called a screaming banshee."

Cate raised her eyebrows. Victoria continued, "Oh, how this must sound. I assure you, there is nothing wrong with our home!"

"I don't doubt that, Victoria," Cate assured her. "I'm rather surprised to hear that a grown man gave in to such nonsense."

"I quite agree, Catherine. However, it seems these tales abound at every turn. The village is filled with them."

"People love gossip."

"Quite. Especially when the rumors are stoked by our servants."

"Your runaway footman?"

"And others. Just a few months ago, Lorna, one of our housemaids, ran screaming through the house to our housekeeper carrying on about having seen a woman at the top of the stairway."

"Indeed! She must have been imagining things." Cate sipped more tea, nibbling a biscuit.

Victoria shrugged. "She claimed the woman was shouting at her, babbling incomprehensible nonsense, frantic about something." She shook her head, dismissing it. "I don't know. I believe the girl to be unstable, perhaps."

Cate's mind returned to when she had moved in a few months before. Prior to her discovery about her true inheritance, she had inadvertently time traveled to this exact time. The maid had not been crazy, she had seen Cate standing at the top of the main staircase. Cate had shouted to her to help find a missing Riley. She remembered the poor maid fleeing from the room at the sight of her. "The mind can play many tricks, particularly in a house this large," Cate explained it away. Cate hoped the young maid didn't recognize her if they came across each other now.

"How judicious you are, cousin Catherine." Victoria smiled at her. After a light knock, the door opened. Two women stepped into the room. "Madame Bisset, m'lady," the maid announced.

"Ah." Victoria rose. "Please come in Madame Bisset. It is my pleasure to introduce my cousin, Catherine MacKenzie. Mrs. MacKenzie will also attend our ball. We would like to discuss her dress with you."

"A pleasure to meet you, Madame MacKenzie," the woman answered in a thick French accent. "Countess Victoria," she said, kissing Victoria on each cheek, "I have some lovely new designs for you to consider."

"We are excited to see them. Please, sit. Shall I pour you tea?"

"Thank you, Countess." Madame Bisset sat between the two women at the round table. She placed a portfolio in front of her, opening it.

"Oh, please show Mrs. MacKenzie the design for my gown first. Then we'll consider Catherine's dress."

Madame Bisset pulled one design from the pile, showing a large hooped skirt, a bejeweled bodice with button detail down the center. "How charming," Cate exclaimed.

Victoria beamed, proud of her selection. "And now, cousin Catherine, we'll find you something equally charming. Oh, Madame Bisset, we deemed a sapphire blue may be an attractive color for Mrs. MacKenzie. Do you agree?"

Madame Bisset considered it, eyeing Cate up and down. "Yes," she said, after a moment, "quite fitting, Countess."

The ladies spent another hour going over designs, discussing options and adjustments. Cate settled on a hooped skirt with a ruffled bottom and black lace details. The bodice included a ruffled top. Victoria pronounced that she had the perfect sapphire necklace to fit the neckline and insisted that Cate borrow it for the evening. Madame Bisset gathered Cate's measurements, and they concluded their tea. Cate remained for a few moments after Madame Bisset departed. The two women chatted about what a lovely morning they enjoyed before saying their goodbyes. Cate asked Victoria if she could stop by the library to borrow a book, stating that she and Jack planned to be traveling for several days. Cate could not visit with Victoria until October twenty-eighth. After Victoria showed her to the library, Cate assured Victoria she could see herself out after she made her selection.

Left alone, Cate grabbed a book and snuck back to the bedroom closet to return to her own time. Once returned, she made her way to her bedroom to change before lunch. After lunch, she hoped to help Mrs. Fraser with some preparations before Molly arrived late this afternoon.

Mr. and Mrs. Fraser had already settled into their own room in the castle, planning on staying while guests were visiting. Cate hated to have extra work thrust upon them. Mrs. Fraser assured her she enjoyed doing it, but Cate still felt a measure of guilt. Despite having adapted to many aspects of Scottish country castle life, Cate was not sure she would ever be used to having a staff.

Cate used her lunch to reminisce about her morning meeting. Her new, special made ball gown elated her. Guests on the estate and her own upcoming Halloween ball would help distract her from the long wait to try her gown.

After lunch, she helped Mrs. Fraser, as much as Mrs. Fraser permitted, before taking a quick afternoon walk with Riley. Cate monitored the time, not wanting to be late to greet Molly. Each glance at the time piece was accompanied by a pang of disappointment that she would not see her newfound family for several days. However, each second that ticked past also filled her with excitement for her friend's arrival. Cate returned to the castle to freshen up after her walk with Riley.

CHAPTER 13

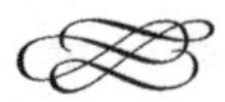

Cate waited with Riley as the car drove down the drive toward the castle. She had asked Jack to text her when they were near to the castle. She aimed to be waiting at the door when Molly arrived.

As the car pulled alongside the castle, Cate spotted Molly waving from inside. As soon as the car came to a stop, Molly's door popped open, and she leapt from the car. "CATE!" she squealed. "Oh, my! It's so great to see you!" She ran to Cate, wrapping her in a giant hug. "And hello, Riley! Oh, come here you sweet little boy!" Molly extended her arms to hold him and Cate allowed her to take the little pup. "Oh, you both look so great!"

"It's good to see you, too, Molly," Cate answered. While excited, Cate's introversion made it undetectable. "How was your trip?"

"Oh, my gosh! Look at this place!!" Molly's eyes darted from one thing to another, sheer excitement filling her. "Huh? Oh, the trip? It was fine, great! Oh, sorry, I'm just overwhelmed by this whole thing. I mean, I can't believe this is your home!" Molly was nearly breathless with excitement.

"It is incredible!" Cate answered. "Would you like to see the inside?"

"Yes!!! I'm dying to explore every part!"

Jack chimed in before they could enter the castle. "I'm taking the luggage to the Rose Room, right?"

"Yes, that's right, thanks, Jack!" Cate answered.

"Oh, oh my gosh, my luggage, here, I can get it." Molly scrambled to grab her suitcase.

"Nay, I wouldn't have it, lassie. I'll carry your luggage up," Jack admonished with a grin. "You'll get the royal treatment here!"

"Aww, thanks," Molly said. Cate put her arm around Molly to draw her into the house. "I already feel like I'm getting the royal treatment with the chauffeured ride from the train station and now luggage service to the, what was it? The Rose Room, did you say? I could get used to this, Cate!"

They made their way through the double doors into the foyer. Molly's eyes were wide. "CATE!" she exclaimed, "this is unbelievable! I can't believe you live here! I am so jealous!"

Cate smiled at her excitement, remembering her own reaction to seeing the castle's entryway months ago. Mrs. Fraser approached them from across the foyer. "Oh, Mrs. Fraser, what great timing," Cate said, waving her over. "Please come meet my friend, Molly."

"It's a pleasure to meet any friend of Lady Cate's," Mrs. Fraser said.

"Molly, this is my friend and housekeeper, Mrs. Emily Fraser," Cate introduced her.

"Lady Cate," Molly giggled, "Oh, how far you've come, honey! It is a pleasure to meet you, Mrs. Fraser." Molly nodded to her given the absence of a free hand.

"I just came up to determine if there was anything Ms. Williams needed after her trip," Mrs. Fraser said to Cate.

Cate looked to Molly. "Oh, no," Molly said, shaking her

head, "no, I'm all good! Thanks, though. And, please call me Molly!"

Mrs. Fraser smiled. "A pleasure to meet you, Molly. Well, I'll begin dinner preparations then." Mrs. Fraser turned on a heel to return to the kitchen.

Cate raised an eyebrow at her last comment. It appeared she wouldn't stand on ceremony with Molly, obliging her by using her first name. Molly was hugging Riley close, asking him if he was enjoying castle life.

"Well," Cate began, "I'll show you to your room. Jack should have your luggage up there soon. You can freshen up before dinner. If you need anything, I'll show you where to find me."

"Thanks, Cate! Oh, I'm so excited to check out my room. Even if it's in the dungeon, it'll be better than my current place."

"I haven't found a dungeon yet. Not enjoying the new apartment?" Cate asked as they made their way up the staircase.

"Ugh, no," Molly answered, rolling her eyes, "it's cramped and crappy. Just horrible. I swear I spotted a cockroach or a mouse or something gross behind the fridge, too."

Cate grimaced. Molly was really having a rough go of things following the divorce. Unable to continue payments on her house, she had no choice but to sell and move into a small apartment. Guilt coursed through Cate over her recent stroke of good luck.

They made their way down the hallway, weaving their way through to the wing with Cate's bedroom. Molly marveled as they made their way. They arrived at a bedroom a few doors down from Cate's. "Here we are. I'm right down the hall," Cate pointed. "Through those double doors if you need me." Cate opened the door and allowed Molly to enter first.

Molly's jaw dropped. "CATE!" she exclaimed again. "Cate, it's beautiful!" Molly gawked at the room. Cate had selected a large bedroom, decorated in a mauve-rose color and appointed with dainty, feminine details. It boasted a large fireplace with a loveseat and a comfortable armchair and ottoman, grouped around the fireplace making a cozy setting. Across the room, a four-poster bed stood against the wall. It also contained an en-suite bathroom for Molly's convenience.

Cate smiled. "I imagined you might like it, it's one of my favorite rooms!"

Jack arrived with the luggage. "Where would the lady like her luggage?" he asked.

"Oh, gosh, just anywhere is fine!"

"Maybe by the wardrobe, Jack?" Cate suggested.

"All right, easy enough." Jack wheeled the luggage over to the wardrobe. "Anything else you might need?"

"No, I don't think so, thanks!" Cate answered.

"M'lady!" Jack said, giving his usual bow before leaving the room.

"He's too much, Cate," Molly said, cracking up over his extravagant manner.

"Yes, he's quite the comedian," Cate agreed. "Well, I'll let you get settled." Cate took Riley back from Molly. "See you for dinner around five thirty. I'll pick you up right here!"

"Good thing," Molly said, "I'll get lost!"

"It can be overwhelming! It overwhelmed me, too, when I arrived. But you'll learn it!"

"Too bad by the time I do, I'll be ready to leave." Molly frowned.

Cate smiled at her, giving her arm a squeeze. "See you soon, Molly!" Cate left her still gawking around her room.

She returned to her bedroom with Riley in tow. She had little to do since she had freshened up before Molly arrived.

Instead, she relaxed with a book before taking Riley for a short walk. Afterward, she made her way to Molly's door, giving it a light knock. Within seconds, Molly opened the door. She had changed her outfit from jeans and a sweatshirt, choosing a pair of black leggings and a burgundy tunic for dinner.

"Oh, Cate! You said casual was okay, right? Is this okay?"

"It's perfect," Cate answered, smiling at her. "Is this a new 'Scotland sweater'?"

"It is, yes, do you like it?"

"I do! It's a gorgeous color, it looks great on you!" Cate said.

"Aw, thanks, honey."

"Ready for dinner?"

"Am I ever! I am starving! Traveling really makes you hungry," Molly admitted. "Lead the way, Cate!"

Cate and Riley led her to the dining room. Mrs. Fraser was setting out the last dish of the dinner. "Lady Cate and Molly, I hope you enjoy your meal! I have a special dessert prepared for you both afterwards. Lady Cate, I'll serve that in the library whenever you are ready."

"Thank you, Mrs. Fraser! Please enjoy your dinner."

"Cate, have I told you how jealous I am of your life?" Molly said, as Mrs. Fraser left the room. "This dining room is beautiful. Well, the whole house is! Castle I should say!" Molly began serving herself after Cate dug in.

They made light conversation during their meal about Molly's trip, the latest goings on in Aberdeen and at Aberdeen College. Molly informed her that Jeff, Cate's old department chair, was struggling to fill many of the department's needs. After Cate left, he'd had to cover most department events himself, unable to convince anyone else in the department to do the extra work. This didn't surprise Cate, when she had worked as an adjunct faculty member at

Aberdeen she had done most of the extra work within the department. Her extra efforts had been in an attempt to be transitioned into a permanent faculty member, but to no avail.

After their meal, Cate took Molly to the library. She planned to give Molly her gift then, she had it set out by the fireplace. Mr. Fraser had built them a roaring fire to relax by after dinner. "Oh, wow, Cate! I continue to be awed by your home! Oh, this fire looks so cozy!"

Cate and Molly settled into the armchairs near the fireplace. Riley opted for his usual spot on the rug, cuddled close to the warmth of the fire. Mrs. Fraser arrived with a tray of her homemade cookies and two steaming mugs of hot chocolate. "This will keep you warm on this chilly October night!" she said, setting the tray down on the ottoman nearby.

"Thank you so much, Mrs. Fraser."

"If you need anything else, let me know, Lady Cate!"

"We'll be fine, Mrs. Fraser, and we'll clean up after ourselves. You are free to retire for the evening," Cate assured her.

"I'll see you in the morning, then, Lady Cate. I hope you sleep well, Molly." Mrs. Fraser left the room, pulling the doors closed behind her.

"Mmm, this is the best hot chocolate I have EVER had," Molly said, sipping from her mug.

"She is a fantastic cook! You'll like these cookies even better!" Molly took one from the tray, nodding her head to confirm that Cate was correct in her assessment. "I have another surprise I hope you'll like, too!"

"More surprises?" Molly mumbled, mouth full of cookie. "Wow!"

Cate retrieved the gift bag and handed it to Molly. "A welcome gift, of sorts. I hope you like it!"

"Aww, oh, honey, you didn't have to do this! But I'm so glad you did!" Molly grinned, pulling the tissue paper out. She grabbed the blanket out of the bag first. "Oh, this is beautiful! It's so soft and cuddly! I love it!" She reached back in, pulling out the book and photo album next.

Cate explained, "The book discusses the haunted castles of Scotland. It not only mentions Dunhaven Castle, but that it's considered to be haunted. I thought of you as soon as I spotted this since you were so concerned it was haunted."

Molly giggled. "I did tease you about that, but see, someone else concluded it was haunted, too!"

"The one with the picture of the castle is a photo album. You can keep all your memories of Scotland in there."

"Aw, Cate," Molly said, clutching it to her chest, "I love them, all of them! You didn't need to buy me anything though! The invitation to stay was enough!"

"I enjoyed the shopping and I'm so glad you like everything."

Molly was still clutching the gifts to her. "I do, I really do." She closed her eyes, taking a deep breath. "I needed this, Cate," she said, her voice breaking. A tear rolled down her cheek. "I'm so sorry, I'm sorry."

Cate's heart went out to Molly. She reached over, rubbing her arm. Molly sighed, wiping her tears away with a hand and sniffling. "I'm okay, I'm sorry. I didn't want to ruin our first night."

"You're not ruining anything, Molly," Cate answered. "There's no need for an apology."

Molly nodded. "It's just that I feel..." She paused. "So stupid. Just so incredibly stupid. It's so embarrassing." Cate responded with a smile. Molly grasped her hand, giving it a squeeze. "I just can't believe it still sometimes. I can't believe Tom cheated on me, with my own student assistant. What's worse, I introduced them. I took her out to lunch with Tom and myself to thank her for being a great assistant." Cate listened without responding, allowing Molly to get it out. "Great assistant, huh? And he just continues on with his life while mine is blown apart. We had to sell the house, I had to move into some crappy little apartment because I can't afford anything else, meanwhile, she moved in with him! They're playing house together somewhere; it makes me sick."

"It's not your fault, Molly. This is all on Tom AND your assistant," Cate offered.

"Yeah, yeah, that's what everyone tells me. Accompanied by that sad, pitying look in their eyes. I hate even walking around town. I feel like the laughingstock. I wish I didn't have to go back."

"I'm so sorry, Molly," Cate offered.

Molly continued, "I mean, my sister said I could stay with her for a bit, IN HER BASEMENT." Cate made a face. "Yeah, exactly! Like that's inviting! She couldn't even offer me a spot in her kids' playroom, which is essentially her fifth bedroom! Says she's 'full up' now that she's taking care of Ted's mom." Molly rolled her eyes. She sniffled again, taking a deep breath and shaking her head, "but that's enough of my misery. I will not let Tom and Aimee ruin the trip I have looked so forward to! At this moment, my life is perfect! I am in Scotland, with one of my very best friends, in her CASTLE. I will not spend my time moping! Now, give me another one of those cookies, because I am also NOT counting calories on this trip!"

Cate smiled at her and squeezed her hand. She picked up the tray, offering a cookie to Molly. They spent the rest of the evening talking about Cate's transition to Scottish life. Molly insisted that Cate give her the grand tour of the castle and grounds the following day. Cate warned her that it was quite a tour and she hoped Molly had brought a supportive pair of walking shoes, but Molly wasn't put off. Knowing that the upcoming party would soon absorb Cate's time, she wanted to see it all first.

Given the plan for Molly's first full day in Scotland, they turned in early, after finishing their hot chocolate and cookies and cleaning up their mugs. They said their good nights with Cate expressing her hope that Molly slept well her first night in the castle.

CHAPTER 14

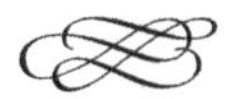

Cate watched the sun cross the horizon over the moors the next morning as she walked Riley. It painted the sky with bright oranges, reds, and yellows. She wondered how Molly had slept and if she was awake yet. She hadn't knocked on her door before bringing Riley out, not wanting to disturb her if she was still asleep. She planned on collecting her just before heading to breakfast.

After Riley had his fill of frolicking in the yard, Cate gathered him into her arms and returned to the castle. With the sun painting the windows of the castle bright yellow, Cate couldn't tell if there were lights on in Molly's room. She entered through the front door rather than the servant's entrance, making her way to Molly's room. Cate waited a few moments after knocking but received no response. She tried again, this time knocking louder. Again, nothing. She called Molly's name, but this elicited nothing.

Cate headed down to breakfast, not wanting to be late for when Mrs. Fraser set everything out. She would check back on Molly later. Perhaps she hadn't slept well and was sleeping in.

Cate made her way to the kitchen via the dining room to check in with Mrs. Fraser. She wanted to check that the Frasers had slept well. As she approached the kitchen, she heard voices and laughter floating down the hallway. Surprisingly, Cate noted the voices were of two women. She recognized Mrs. Fraser's voice and after a moment, identified the other as Molly's. So that was why Molly wasn't answering her door when she knocked, Cate realized.

Cate reached the kitchen doorway, peering in at the scene. Molly was stirring the oatmeal, discussing easy ways to keep the oatmeal from sticking or becoming lumpy with Mrs. Fraser.

"Now, I knew most of those tips, Molly, but that last one I cannae say I've heard before. I will have to try that," Mrs. Fraser, a towel slung over her shoulder, said, as she prepared oatmeal toppings to take to the dining room.

"It works like a charm, I promise!" Molly answered.

"Oh, good morning, Lady Cate," Mrs. Fraser said, turning and spotting her in the doorway. "You're sneaking up on me again."

"Sorry," Cate laughed, "I just got here, I didn't want to interrupt!"

"You'd never be interrupting, Lady Cate," Mrs. Fraser assured her.

"Good morning, Cate!" Molly said, a big grin on her face.

"Good morning, Molly. How did you sleep?"

"Great! Best night's sleep I've had in a while. That bed is fabulous! I was up early, so I figured I'd pop down and see if I could lend a hand with anything." Molly nodded to the pot she was stirring. "Make myself useful."

Cate smiled at her as Mrs. Fraser answered, "And what a hand she is! She knows her way around a kitchen, this one! Well, that should be about it. If you ladies would like to head up to the dining room, I'll bring everything up."

"Oh, I assume the oatmeal goes in this server here?" Molly asked, already starting to pour it in. "I'll carry this up if you want to bring the toppings."

"I can help," Cate offered.

"Nay, Lady Cate," Mrs. Fraser refused. "Besides you haven't got a free hand." She nodded to Riley in Cate's arms.

"Oh, he's capable of walking." Cate laughed.

"We have a handle on it, Lady Cate," Mrs. Fraser assured her. "Don't we, Molly?"

Molly nodded. "We sure do!"

Cate watched the scene unfolding in front of her. Mrs. Fraser was checking the oatmeal as Molly poured it into the server. Mrs. Fraser marveled that, true to Molly's word, there wasn't one lump and the bottom of the pot was clean. The two women shared a good rapport. An idea formed in Cate's head. She would follow up on it later when she had a moment to speak with Mrs. Fraser alone. For now, both Mrs. Fraser and her stomach were urging her to eat her breakfast.

Cate led the way upstairs with Molly and Mrs. Fraser following her. Cate and Molly served themselves oatmeal as Mrs. Fraser poured water for each of them. After checking that they had everything they needed, Mrs. Fraser returned downstairs for the staff breakfast.

Molly and Cate settled at the table. Cate fed Riley a few dog biscuits that Mrs. Fraser set out for him each morning before diving into her own breakfast. "I'm so glad that you slept well," Cate said, blowing on her oatmeal to cool it.

"Oh, I did, honey. Best night's sleep I've had in MONTHS. I was asleep before my head hit the pillow. I don't think I even moved."

"That's great, Molly. I was concerned that you had a bad night. When I knocked this morning and didn't get a response, I worried our ghosts may have gotten you!"

"Nope, great night! That's why I got up early. I felt so

good I thought I'd see if I could lend a hand to your housekeeper, Mrs. Fraser. She seems so nice. Hey! I thought you said there were no ghosts!" Molly laughed.

"We have no ghosts, I promise. I'm only teasing. But sometimes it can be tricky relaxing in a different bed."

"Oh, honey, I'll have no trouble relaxing in this place!" Molly waved her hand around. "Like I said, I love this place! It's such a nice change from the peeling paint and dirty wallpaper in my new place." Molly rolled her eyes. "I can't wait to see the whole place. Say, how d'you sleep? I hope you have enough energy to show me EVERYTHING and I mean everything!"

"Plenty of energy here!" Cate assured her. "And I'm sure Riley will love to show you his loch."

"I can't wait to see it, Riley!" Molly said to the little dog.

They finished their breakfast, discussing more of Cate's new life. Molly, true to her word, did not want to discuss any more of her situation. She found her new life "depressing" and didn't want to be reminded of it as she was living her "dream vacation," according to her.

Cate obliged her, trying to keep the conversation light. Although, she still experienced a sense of guilt discussing her recent good fortune when Molly's luck seemed to be on the downturn.

After breakfast, Cate asked Molly if she preferred to begin inside or outside with her tour. Easygoing Molly let Cate choose. Cate opted to begin outside, allowing Riley to have his post-breakfast walk as was typical. Molly met Cate in the foyer after running back to her room to grab one of her "Scotland sweaters" to bundle up in before heading outside.

The air was cool and crisp outside with brilliant sunshine. Riley bounded in front of the two women as they walked down the path that led to the back gardens. Molly marveled at the landscaping and the gardens. The scenery, Cate agreed, was idyllic. Light fog still clung to the tops of the moors that surrounded them. They continued on to the loch, Molly playing fetch with Riley and his favorite blue ball.

As they settled on the banks of the loch, Molly remarked on how breathtaking she found the scenery. Cate couldn't agree with her more. Riley settled in between them for a rest after his long tour of the grounds. Together they laughed over Cate's story about how concerned she was before moving from Aberdeen that she wouldn't find an area as beautiful as Aberdeen Park. Molly remarked that she was sure Cate considered herself foolish after arriving. Cate agreed.

They spent another half hour chitchatting about the area and the grounds of Dunhaven Castle. Cate timed it so they were back in time for lunch at the castle. Mrs. Fraser had insisted on preparing a lunch for them, despite Cate's insistence that she could handle lunch arrangements since it was Mrs. Fraser's day off. Over lunch, Molly asked about the town of Dunhaven. Cate promised Molly a tour tomorrow before Gayle's arrival in the late afternoon. She wanted Molly to have the entire experience, although her schedule would fill up later in the week with the party approaching.

Molly assured her she would be fine relaxing at the castle and if she was feeling adventurous, she would make her own way into town if she wanted a second trip. Following lunch, Molly jumped from her seat, insisting on the grand tour of the castle.

Cate obliged showing Molly every detail that she knew of the castle so far. They ended their tour back in the library, where Mrs. Fraser would serve their dinner. Curling up in the armchairs near the fire, Molly chattered about everything she had seen within the walls of the castle. She was enthralled by the castle's beauty and fascinated by the history within its walls. She conceded that she was a tad bit jealous of Cate's good fortune, adding that she would have moved here in a heartbeat.

They ate a quiet, cozy dinner before retiring for the evening, both of them tired after their excursions inside and outside of the castle.

The following morning, Cate was up bright and early to walk Riley before their trip to town. Mrs. Fraser offered to look after the little pup so the women could shop unencumbered. Cate appreciated the offer since not all shops were dog friendly. Since she wanted Molly to have the freedom to shop in any store, she took Mrs. Fraser up on the offer. Before they left, Cate apprised Mrs. Fraser they would lunch in town, but would arrive before Gayle was expected to be at the castle later this afternoon. Cate discussed final dinner arrangements with Mrs. Fraser before giving Riley a kiss on the head and heading upstairs to collect Molly for the trip.

On their way into town, Cate quipped that she hoped Molly had left room to pack all the souvenirs. They also planned on picking up Molly's costume while in town, which Molly jested she was glad she did not have to pack or she'd need a third suitcase.

Cate parked the car near the center of town and the two women began their tour of the town. Molly fell in love with Dunhaven as Cate had, finding the small Scottish town to be full of charm. Cate and Molly had a ball shopping for souvenirs. They were happy to get off their feet at lunchtime, choosing the pub for a midday meal. Molly, always the adventurous eater, chose the Scotch Broth while Cate had her usual, fish and chips.

They spent a short while after lunch finishing up their shopping, then picked up the costume before heading back to the castle. Cate helped Molly carry her loot upstairs. As they set the bags near her suitcases, Molly confessed she may have over-shopped. Checking her watch, Cate said she'd be back to collect Molly in about half an hour to wait for Gayle's arrival. Cate was excited for the two women to meet.

Cate took Riley for a quick walk before returning to collect Molly. Gayle had decided to rent a car and drive herself to Dunhaven. The car was just coming into sight down the drive as the two women, Riley in Cate's arms, stepped out of the castle. Jack approached from around the side of the castle, ready to assist with luggage.

Within moments, Gayle eased the car to a stop a few feet from the front door. Jack opened her door for her, offering his hand to help her out of the car.

"Hello, Gayle!" Cate said, "how was your drive in?"

"Hello, Cate," Gayle said, smoothing her sweater over her slacks and reaching out to embrace Cate. "It's so lovely to see you again, dear. The drive was not too bad, but I will admit, I am stiff! And hello to you sweet Riley!" Gayle gave him a pet under the chin, getting down on his level to greet him.

"Aww, well, I hope a night in one of our beds will ease that!" Cate answered. "I'd like you to meet my friend, Molly Williams."

"Hello, Molly," Gayle said, extending her hand, "it's a pleasure to meet you. Cate has told me nothing but wonderful things about you!"

"Cate always was a fantastic liar!" Molly laughed, shaking Gayle's hand. "A pleasure to meet you, too, Gayle."

"Shall we head inside?" Cate suggested. "Mrs. Fraser should have dinner ready in about an hour. I put you in the room you stayed in on your last visit. You can unwind and freshen up after your long drive."

"That would be lovely, Cate," Gayle responded. "And thank you, Jack, for retrieving that luggage."

"My pleasure, ma'am!" Jack responded, carrying the luggage in behind them.

"Molly, I'll be right down after showing Gayle to her room. Would you mind taking Riley into the sitting room for me?"

"Sure, Cate!" Molly responded, happy to relieve Cate of the cute pup.

Cate made her way up the stairs with Gayle. The two chitchatted about the upcoming party and Gayle's costume. Cate left her in her bedroom to relax and change prior to dinner then made her way back to the sitting room to spend the hour before dinner with Molly.

Cate found her sitting on the floor near the fireplace with Riley, stroking the dog's fur. "Oh, he's loving that," Cate said, entering the room.

"Me, too!" Molly said, laughing. "It's cozy here by the fire. Oh, I just love it here. And I love everyone's accents, they all sound so posh!" Molly joked.

Cate laughed. "It sounds normal to me now. It sounded so strange to me when I first came."

"So, Gayle is the secretary for your attorney, right? The guy who sprung the big news on you?"

"Yes, Gayle is his assistant. She helped me move into the castle. She's so friendly and kind-hearted, she made my transition so much easier. I was delighted when she said she could attend the party."

The women chatted a few more minutes before heading to dinner. Dinner went effortlessly. Cate's companions were both avid talkers, keeping the conversation flowing which made entertaining easy for introverted Cate. By the end of the night, Gayle and Molly had even planned a trip to town together the following day, leaving Cate available to deal with an unexpected meeting request from Mrs. Campbell. The librarian had phoned moments before dinner stating that she had an "emergency" that couldn't wait until their Wednesday meeting to be discussed. Cate could hardly wait to see what the woman considered an emergency, but with the party fast approaching, Cate set aside some time the following day to meet with her. Everyone retired early that evening, Cate and Molly spent from their shopping trip and Gayle from her long drive.

The next morning, Molly and Gayle spent breakfast discussing their trip into town. Molly wanted to pick up a few additional things even though she confessed to Gayle she had little clue how she would get it all home. Gayle was content to explore the town with Molly and was sure she'd find a few purchases along the way.

"Poor Cate," Gayle lamented, "you won't have any fun staying home today."

"Oh, that's okay. I can have fun in Dunhaven whenever I want!"

"Oh, that's a very good point, Cate," Molly chimed in. "She lives here so she shouldn't get to have as much fun as us, anyway! We're on vacation!"

"Good point," Cate agreed. "Spend as much time as you'd like in town, ladies! Don't feel bad for me, I'm sure Mrs. Campbell will keep me busy!"

"Deal," Molly said, "looks like we're free to shop 'til we drop, Gayle!"

"Yes, it does!" Gayle agreed. "Well, shall we be on our way?"

"Let me just grab one of my new cardigans and meet you at the car."

"Sounds like a good idea. I'll do the same. Enjoy your party-planning, Cate." Gayle said, standing from the table.

The two women disappeared from the room in a cloud of girlish giggles as they continued to discuss their shopping excursion. Cate was left with Riley staring at her, expecting a walk. "Well, it's just you and me, kid," she said. "Shall we get a walk in before Mrs. Campbell arrives?"

Riley leapt to his feet in answer. Cate gathered him into her arms and made her way to the front of the house. Riley frolicked on the grass as she waited to see her friends off to town. After they pulled away, she called Riley over to head down their favorite path to the loch. The two enjoyed a brisk morning walk before Cate returned to the castle to prepare for her emergency meeting with Mrs. Campbell.

Mrs. Fraser had already shown the librarian into the sitting room, grumbling to Cate that the woman had arrived well before her appointment and had the audacity to seek Mrs. Fraser out in the kitchen to ask where she should wait. Cate went to the sitting room, Riley in tow, for her meeting.

"Mrs. Campbell, lovely to see you again, although I'm sorry it's because of an emergency!" Cate said, walking through the door, Riley in her arms.

"Oh!" Mrs. Campbell exclaimed as she saw Cate enter, "oh, you've brought the dog." She eyed him like a bug. "Hello, there."

"Yes," Cate said, setting him next to her on the loveseat as she sat down and motioned for Mrs. Campbell to do the same. "Oh, you aren't allergic, are you?"

"Oh, no, nothing like that. I just thought he might be a distraction, well, I hope not," she said, waving her hand in the air as if to dismiss her comment.

"He shouldn't be, he's well-behaved. I hope we can resolve whatever issue there is quickly, to set both our minds at ease."

"Yes, so do I!" Mrs. Campbell said.

"So, what is the issue?" Cate prompted.

"Oh, yes, yes, I'm sorry, I'm just not thinking today, ever since I got the call yesterday. Here is the long and short of it, I ordered burgundy tablecloths for all the tables we'll be setting up in the ballroom and various areas. The tablecloths they sent are red." Mrs. Campbell paused, closing her eyes as if unable to deal with the horror of the situation. "Of course, I called at once to complain. However, according to them, there isn't much that can be done. The tablecloth company can't locate enough burgundy on such short notice. We'd either have to drive to Edinburgh to pick up half of them or use the red."

Cate was speechless. She never would have dreamt that the color of tablecloths for a party would constitute an emergency. Yet, here she was, faced with that exact situation.

"I know, I know," Mrs. Campbell continued when Cate failed to answer, "it's a travesty. Everything we've done is planned around the burgundy, napkins, decorations. Since it's so impactful, I wanted to leave the final decision to you, Lady Cate. I was so flabbergasted; I didn't know what to do."

After a moment, Cate collected herself and answered, "Well, given the circumstances, I say we just go with the red. It will be very dramatic!"

"Really?" Mrs. Campbell answered, seeming more flabbergasted by Cate's choice than by the mistake.

"Yes. As you stated, there's little we can do now. None of us can spare the time to drive to Edinburgh to pick up more tablecloths. We'll have to make the best of it."

"Oh, yes, I suppose so. Well, I hope they don't clash with the draperies in that room."

"I'm sure it will be fine. We can describe the color as 'blood red'. Very Halloween-oriented!"

Mrs. Campbell gave her a tight-lipped smile. "How enterprising of you, Lady Cate. Yes, we shall make the best of a bad situation. And we shall ask for a discount! I will see to that myself!"

"A very good idea, Mrs. Campbell," Cate said, standing. "I know you'll negotiate a good discount. And crisis averted!"

With some reluctance, Mrs. Campbell also stood. "I

suppose so," she admitted. "Well, if you're positive you're satisfied with the solution, then I guess I can be on my way."

"I am certain we can make the red work! It will provide a lovely contrast to the other décor. If things are too match-y, it may seem drab."

Mrs. Campbell gave her a wide-eyed smile, still horrified by the situation. "Ah," she began, not sure how to answer.

"If anyone can pull off this look, Mrs. Campbell, I'm sure it's you and Dunhaven!"

Bolstered by Cate's confidence in her, Mrs. Campbell raised her chin and broadened her smile. "I'm up to the task, Lady Cate! You can count on me!"

"That's the spirit!" Cate said, walking her to the door.

"Well, I shall see you tomorrow then for the initial setup. I pray there will be no other crises waiting 'round the corner to spring on us!"

"Fingers crossed!" Cate said, crossing her fingers as Mrs. Campbell exited the castle. "See you tomorrow, bright and early!"

Cate closed the door after Mrs. Campbell's car pulled down the driveway, sighing and rolling her eyes. She checked the timepiece that hung around her neck. About an hour before lunch remained. It was a perfect time to have the discussion she had been planning with Mrs. Fraser.

Cate wound her way down to the kitchen, knocking on the door jamb on her way in to announce her arrival. "Ah, Lady Cate, is the pest gone?"

Cate laughed at her description. "Yes, Mrs. Campbell has left."

"And what, pray tell, was the emergency?"

"The linen company sent red tablecloths instead of burgundy."

"Oh, heavens! Well, that certainly was an excellent reason to interrupt your day! That woman is a ninny. I'm sorry,

Lady Cate, I should be more charitable, but I just cannae tolerate that woman."

"It's okay, Mrs. Fraser. I marveled at the alarm it caused her, too. There wasn't much anyone could do. The company cannot send the correct color because they don't have enough stock. We'd have to drive to Edinburgh to collect the correct ones, which no one has time to do. Long story short, I told her we'd stick with the red and make do, despite her apprehension that it will clash with anything and everything else that we'd planned."

"Was she expecting you to send someone to Edinburgh, or worse, go yourself?"

"I had the distinct impression that's what she was hoping for. Since that is not an option, red it is!"

"A wise choice, Lady Cate. The red will be fine." Mrs. Fraser gave her a nod of her head before waving a bone in her hand for Riley. Riley's dark, almond-shaped eyes gleamed with excitement as he danced on his hind legs. "Here you are, little Riley, a nice juicy bone for a special little boy!" she said, handing it off to him. "I'll have your lunch ready soon, Lady Cate. I'll bring it up to the library."

"If you have a moment before lunch, I'd like to speak with you about something, Mrs. Fraser."

"I always have a minute for you, Lady Cate. Do you mind if I continue to prepare lunch while we talk?"

"Not at all. I can help a little, too!"

"Now don't trouble yourself at all, Lady Cate, I can do it," Mrs. Fraser said, shooing her away to a seat at the table. Cate yielded to her demands, taking a seat at the table before launching into her request. "Now, what did you want to discuss, Lady Cate?" she asked as she bustled around the kitchen.

"Well, I know that you've been considering retirement after finding a suitable replacement to train. As much as I'll regret the day you retire, I realize that it is something we need to plan for, even though I hope it's still several years off."

"Aye, and I have mixed feelings about it, too, Lady Cate. But don't you fret, I'll still be around on the estate and I hope you'll let me visit from time to time!"

"Mrs. Fraser, you are welcome to visit or stay anytime you'd like!"

"Thank you, Lady Cate. There's nothing to fuss over yet. I haven't had any luck finding a suitable replacement to train yet!" She shook her head in disbelief. "Seems no one wants to go into service these days!"

"About that," Cate started. "I had an idea that I wanted to run past you. Now, I'd only consider it if you are one hundred percent on board with it. If you have even the slightest reservation, I won't ever mention it again. And please don't feel obliged to say yes for my sake, only if you're comfortable and agree."

"My goodness, Lady Cate," Mrs. Fraser said, coming to a dead stop, "well, I'm all ears but I'm a little nervous given that disclaimer!"

Cate smirked. "I had an idea for a replacement for you and someone who can relieve you of some heavier chores until you retire. My friend, Molly."

"Ms. Williams?"

"Yes. I should tell you I haven't mentioned it to her at all, so she may not even be interested. I will only mention it to her if you approve of the idea. She hasn't been having an easy time of things lately. She's struggling to make ends meet and to get back on her feet after the rug was swept out from under her. A change of scenery might be just what the doctor ordered!"

"Or just what her ladyship ordered." Mrs. Fraser nodded her head. "And very kind of you to think of helping her."

"Again, I don't know if she'd accept. I haven't mentioned the idea to her. I wouldn't do that until you've had time to consider it and let me know your thoughts. Take a night or two to sleep on it before you give me your answer."

"I don't need to sleep on it, Lady Cate. I would be happy to take Molly on to train, if she wants the job."

"Are you sure?" Cate asked, excited by the news but wanting to be sure Mrs. Fraser was certain.

"Aye. Molly's been a good friend to you and she's a good lassie. Besides, in the end, the choice is not mine but yours."

"No." Cate shook her head. "The choice is half yours, Mrs. Fraser. These are your last few years here. I want you to be happy. You will work closely together in training her. It's important to me you are comfortable with the choice. So, are you sure? Please take all the time you need to consider it."

"I needn't any more time to consider it." She shook her hand again before continuing. "I like Molly, she's good around the kitchen. I'd feel more than comfortable leaving Dunhaven and you in her care once I'm fully retired, which won't be for several years if I have any say in it." Cate smiled at her, unsure of how to respond. While she was thrilled for Molly, she was fond of Mrs. Fraser and hated to see her retire. She didn't want Mrs. Fraser to feel pushed out, nor obliged to stay. Cate found it a fine line to walk. "Well, there it is, you have my blessing, Lady Cate. Extend the offer to Ms. Williams!"

"Okay, I'll speak with her about it before she leaves!"

"I hope she accepts, Lady Cate. I think she'd be a wonderful addition to the castle! You know, it's a shame what that man, if you can call him that, did to her. But his loss will be Dunhaven's gain if she accepts!"

"I hope she accepts too, Mrs. Fraser. I'll let you know as soon as I have her answer." Cate beamed at her. As the conversation ended, Jack and Mr. Fraser came through the door.

"Ah," Jack said, "Lady Cate! Joining us for lunch today?"

Cate thought a moment. "Well, it isn't my normal lunch day, but since I'll miss it tomorrow, I'd like to stay today if you'll have me." Since no one minded, Cate stayed, glad she did not miss lunch with her staff this week. After clearing a few additional details with Mrs. Fraser about Mr. Smythe's arrival, she enjoyed an afternoon walk with Riley. They settled on the banks of the loch and Cate's gaze focused on the castle.

Jack and Cate had not visited the past in nearly a week. Cate was itching to get back to her investigation. While she enjoyed hosting company and her excitement was increasing for the upcoming Halloween ball, she missed her excursions to the past. She missed immersing herself in another era. She missed experiencing time with her relatives, even if they were from another century. She missed trying to help them. They were at such a critical juncture in their investigation, too. Cate finally felt as though they were getting somewhere. They had identified the servant, witnessed a woman in the tower room and had made tremendous inroads with Randolph and Victoria, despite Randolph realizing they were time-travelers. Even though time almost stood still while they were in the past, party preparations kept them too busy for a visit. With the party fast approaching and company on the estate, she could not steal away nor ask Jack to spare a second for it.

She returned her focus to the present. There was still so much to do. Tomorrow would kick-start full swing of party preparations. Cate took a deep breath. She would need all the stamina she could muster, leaving no energy to live a double-life. Cate planned on pitching in and doing her fair share of the work for party set-up.

She enjoyed the last few moments of quiet solitude before returning to the castle to prepare for dinner. As she approached, she spotted a car winding down the driveway. It was Molly and Gayle, returning from their trip to town. Cate bypassed the back door, heading to the front of the castle to greet them.

They spilled out of the car with dozens of packages. "Oh, Cate!" Molly exclaimed, "I think I may need extra luggage and an extra seat on the plane to take all this back."

"I hope they can get the plane off the ground with all of that!" Cate laughed.

"She might have to make two trips," Gayle quipped.

"Only if I can stay another week here between," Molly added.

Cate relieved the ladies of a few packages. She ushered Riley into the castle with everyone else, and they climbed the stairs with all their packages. They all went their separate ways to freshen up before dinner then met in the dining room for a casual dinner. They discussed the jam-packed days that lay ahead of them. Both Molly and Gayle offered to pitch in with any last-minute details. Cate was grateful to have such friends. Given the work ahead of them, they opted for an early evening.

CHAPTER 15

After breakfast the next morning, Cate and crew met in the ballroom. Riley elected to spend the day in the kitchen chewing a new bone courtesy of Mrs. Fraser. Cate covered the general plan for the setup with Molly and Gayle. As she concluded her overview, Mrs. Campbell arrived. "Oh, reinforcements have arrived, I see," she commented.

"Yes, and ready to work!" Gayle answered.

"I've gone over the basic plan with them. Today is the delivery and setup of tables, chairs, and so on inside and most of the exterior decorations. Tomorrow we work on the decorations inside."

"And pumpkin carving!" Molly exclaimed.

"Yes, pumpkin carving," Cate agreed.

"You Americans and your pumpkin carving," Mrs. Campbell said, with a shake of her head.

"I think it's fun, too!" Gayle added. "Are you sure you won't join in the competition, Mrs. Campbell?"

Mrs. Campbell issued a polite but disingenuous smile.

"Positive. Well, the truck with the tables and chairs should arrive any minute."

They stood in awkward silence for a few moments until Jack entered, announcing the delivery truck had arrived. Mrs. Campbell remained in the ballroom to coordinate anything coming in. The others followed Cate to the truck to coordinate and assist with unloading.

It was quick work with everyone's help; the truck was unloaded just inside of two hours. The repositioning and setting up of all items took far longer. They completed the basic set up of the furniture after a working lunch.

They had just finished lunch when the trucks carrying the decorations for outside arrived. The cornstalks and pumpkins seemed endless. It took the better part of the afternoon to unload the materials from the trucks. Everyone worked until late afternoon, finishing about half of the setup. They planned to finish the rest first thing the next morning. They broke from their work, allowing everyone to freshen up before Mr. Smythe's arrival.

Cate, Gayle and Molly reconvened at the castle's driveway as Mr. Smythe's car pulled down the drive. Jack arrived just as his car slowed to a stop, ready to assist with the luggage.

"Hello, Mr. Smythe," Cate greeted him, "it's so nice to see you again. How was your trip in?"

"Cate, hello. The trip was pleasant. I completed a good amount of paperwork on the train." Cate smiled, somewhat to herself, the man's work ethic was limitless. Gayle followed Cate in greeting him.

"I'd like you to meet my friend from the States, Molly Williams," Cate said, motioning to Molly.

"Hello!" Molly greeted him. "It's nice to meet you."

"The pleasure is all mine," Mr. Smythe answered, shaking her hand.

"Mr. Smythe, I've put you in the Blue Room, as usual," Cate informed him.

"I'll take the luggage up straight away," Jack said, emptying the boot of the car.

"Thank you, Mr. Reid," Mr. Smythe answered.

"Shall we?" Cate asked, motioning to enter the castle.

The group made their way inside. "I trust you didn't put your pumpkin carving design in your luggage, Mr. Smythe," Gayle teased. "Jack might try to peek at it."

"I've got it here in my pocket," he said, patting his breast pocket. "I take no chances." Cate giggled, betting his last statement was more truthful than a joke. "If you ladies don't mind, I'll take my leave to freshen up before dinner."

"Okay. We'll see you at dinner," Cate answered.

Gayle and Molly entered the sitting room while Cate excused herself to retrieve Riley before dinner. Cate meandered to the kitchen. Mrs. Fraser appeared to be in a frenzy as she entered.

"Mrs. Fraser!" Cate exclaimed. "Is everything all right?"

"It's getting there, Lady Cate, it's getting there."

"What happened? What's wrong?" Cate asked.

"I had to make a quick change for our dinner this evening. I was short one piece of meat." Cate furrowed her brow, not understanding. "Your little monkey stole one right off the table and disappeared with it this afternoon."

"RILEY!" Cate exclaimed, dismayed. "Shame on you!"

"Oh, don't blame the poor pup. I practically left it right under his nose. All he had to do was jump on the chair and grab it. It's only natural that he'd take it."

"It's so unlike him, Mrs. Fraser. He's typically well-behaved. I am so sorry. I should have checked in with you earlier to ask if you needed help. I wasn't thinking! I shouldn't have left him with you, you have so much extra work. But, as I said, he's not usually like this!"

"Oh, it's nothing to worry about, Lady Cate. I was able to adjust the recipe. Besides, with the stories you've told me about your cooking, I'm not sure you could have helped. Oh, I'm only joking, Lady Cate." Mrs. Fraser winked at her.

Cate laughed. "You are correct, though. Can I do anything to help?"

"Under any other circumstances, I would decline, but since I am behind, would you fill the water and wine glasses upstairs?"

"Yes, I can manage that task!" Cate declared, retrieving the water pitcher from the refrigerator and the opened wine bottle from the counter.

When Cate returned after completing her task, she found Mrs. Fraser's kitchen back in its usual order. "See, Lady Cate, I told you I had it under control."

"I never doubted it, Mrs. Fraser."

"Now, out with you, back to your guests!" Mrs. Fraser pronounced, waving Cate out of the kitchen after she retrieved Riley.

Cate climbed the stairs to the dining room, finding Molly and Gayle already there. "Ah, there you are, Cate!" Gayle said.

"Sorry," Cate apologized, "a minor kitchen disaster courtesy of Riley."

"Uh-oh. What have you done little fellow?" Gayle queried.

"The little thief tried to abscond with our dinner!"

"Oh, no! Riley! I hope you weren't successful! I'm starved!" Molly said.

"Don't worry, Mrs. Fraser has it under control." Cate answered.

"I'd expect nothing less!" Gayle said, as Mr. Smythe entered the dining room.

They were seated for dinner just as Mrs. Fraser entered with the meal. The group enjoyed their dinner, making light conversation as they ate. Cate wondered what Mrs. Fraser had done to "salvage" the meal. It was delicious. Had Cate not discovered the scene in the kitchen before dinner, she'd never have known anything was amiss. After a brief night-cap, everyone retired for the evening, exhausted from their long day.

CHAPTER 16

Cate arose early the next morning, despite feeling a few aches and pains from her previous day's work. She took Riley for an early morning walk, planning to leave him in her sitting room with a bone for the day. She didn't want him causing any more hassles for Mrs. Fraser. After breakfast, everyone, even Mr. Smythe who was actually wearing casual clothing, convened in the back garden to finish the exterior decorating.

They spent their morning setting up hay bales, cornstalks and pumpkins, adjusting lights and arranging other decorations. Cate worked with Molly on the displays closest to the ballroom doors.

Cate positioned a few pumpkins on top of a hay bale, asking Molly if the angle looked correct from the doorway. She received no response. "Molly? Molly?" Cate called, turning to determine why there was no response.

She found Molly staring at the castle. "What? Oh! Sorry! A little to the left, honey."

"Everything okay?" Cate asked.

"Oh, yeah, yeah." Molly waved her hand in the air. "Just me being a downer."

"What's wrong? Allergic to hay bales?"

Molly laughed. "No. Just realizing the party is tomorrow. I'm still looking forward to it, but… well, it also means my trip is almost over. I'll be so sad to leave."

Cate guessed the moment might be opportune to discuss her idea with Molly. "Molly," she began, "what if you didn't have to leave?"

Molly roared with laughter. "Oh, honey, if I didn't have to leave I'd consider my life perfect." Cate smiled at her. She gave her a confused stare. "Do you know something I don't? Did Mr. Smythe tell you I have a long-lost relative with a castle to give me?"

"No," Cate said. "But… I had an idea."

"An idea?"

"Yes. Mrs. Fraser, my housekeeper, is planning on retiring in the next few years. She was hoping to find a replacement to train, but so far she hasn't had any luck. I remember how much you love to cook and bake. And after I saw you two in the kitchen together the last few days, I spoke with her and asked if she thought you might be a fitting replacement. She agreed that you'd be a wonderful selection. So, I'd like to offer you the job if you'd like to have it. I realize it may be a surprise and that you may not have an answer, and that's fine. Please take all the time you need to consider it. Oh, and I realize, also, that this may not even be something you'd consider. That's okay, too, you're under no obligation here, Molly," Cate babbled, as was her tendency when she was nervous. She glanced at Molly. "You can… what?" she asked, noticing Molly grinning at her.

"Oh, Cate," she said, tears forming in her eyes. "Stop your babbling and give me a hug." She drew Cate into a tight embrace. "Thank you for the offer. Your kindness makes me warm all over."

"Oh, Molly, I just want to help. You seemed so unhappy when you came. But, please, you're not obligated to..."

Molly interrupted her. "Cate, I would LOVE to work for you."

The admission stunned Cate into silence for a moment. "You would?"

"Yes! Oh, this wasn't one of those things where I was supposed to decline politely was it?"

"No!" Cate exclaimed. "I'm thrilled! I just assumed you might need some time to consider it! It's a big move!"

"Nope, there's nothing for me in Aberdeen. You're right, my life was miserable before I came. I hate living in that town now. I need a fresh start, and nothing's fresher than a new country! I have been so happy since I've been here, it's the happiest I've been in months. I don't want to leave, but it will be easier knowing I'm coming back... for good!"

Cate smiled, giving Molly another hug. "I'm so glad you accepted, Molly. There are a million arrangements to make. We have a lot to discuss, salary, start dates, living arrangements and all of that. Oh, I want you to live at the castle, if that's okay! There are so many details, but it'll be so fun discussing them!"

"If that's okay? I couldn't imagine a better place to live! Oh, Cate! I'm so excited! I believed the best day of my life was the day I arrived here. But I was wrong. Today is the best day!"

Cate smiled at her. "We better get this display finished before we get in trouble for slacking!"

"Yes, I don't want to be fired before I even start," Molly joked.

Cate and Molly focused their attention on completing the display on each side of the door. With Molly's work ethic now bolstered by her excitement, they made quick work finishing it.

The garden decorations took the better part of the morning. After the group ate lunch, they gathered in the ballroom to put the final touches on the décor there. By mid-afternoon, everything was in order. After one final walkthrough, Mrs. Campbell was satisfied. The group disbanded to freshen up before dinner.

Cate strolled through the ballroom and gardens one final time before heading up to her room. Festive Halloween décor adorned the ballroom. Blood red linens covered the tables placed around the room. Seats were placed along the outskirts of the room, adorned with burgundy chair skirts. Cate smiled to herself recalling the tragedy of the mismatched linens.

Pushing out the massive doors, Cate entered the garden outside. It was transformed into a magical fall wonderland. Hay bales, pumpkins and cornstalks greeted her at every turn. Lights were strung to allow guests to enjoy the gardens well after the sun set. Cate made her way to the far end of the garden, peering back at the castle. Banners swung lazily in the breeze, lending a regal air to the castle.

There were a few final touches that needed completing. The largest was the pumpkin carving. Each of them, Mr. and Mrs. Fraser, Jack, Cate, Molly, Gayle and even Mr. Smythe were carving one for the pumpkin carving contest. Cate considered it the perfect way to get everyone into the spirit of the party. Her gaze focused on the tower. She wondered what Randolph and Victoria were doing. She longed to travel back, to visit with them, to investigate further. She would soon enough, she reminded herself. For now, she must live in her own time, enjoy her own party.

Forcing her mind back to the present, she figured she had better freshen up and take Riley for a quick walk. The plan afterwards was to meet in the kitchen for the pumpkin carving party to commence. Mrs. Fraser planned a light dinner of sandwiches while they worked. Cate strolled back into the house and to her sitting room. She expected Riley to greet her, however, she found the room empty. A wave of panic swept over Cate until she saw the note on her side table. Mrs. Fraser, despite the fiasco yesterday, thought the pup would be too cooped up for the day. She had "rescued" him from the room, taking him to the kitchen with her for the day.

Cate changed and fixed her makeup and hair then went straight to the kitchen. She found Riley watching Mrs. Fraser set out the sandwiches. "Good afternoon, Mrs. Fraser," Cate said. "No incidents today, I trust, Riley?"

"No incidents, Lady Cate. He's been the picture of perfect behavior."

"I'm glad to hear that. Riley, did you thank Mrs. Fraser for rescuing you?"

"It was my pleasure. I hated to see him alone all day."

"Well, thank you for taking care of him, Mrs. Fraser. And these sandwiches look great! Oh wow!" Cate exclaimed, eyeing the kitchen table, "you have been busy!" The table was not only set for dinner, but Mrs. Fraser had also created individual carving stations at each place setting. Each place setting was complete with a pumpkin, a bowl for seeds and scrapings from the inside, and a set of carving knifes.

"Aye, Lady Cate. I couldn't help much with the decorating so this is my contribution."

Cate smiled at her. "You more than contributed by providing us all with lunch! It's going to be a fun evening!"

"I quite agree. I cannae wait to carve my winning pumpkin!"

"Your winning pumpkin, is it? Pretty confident, Mrs. Fraser," Cate teased.

"That I am, Lady Cate!" Mrs. Fraser quipped.

Cate laughed. "Oh, I have some great news, Mrs. Fraser."

"Oh?"

"I spoke with Molly earlier this morning and she has accepted the position to follow in your footsteps as the housekeeper! There are lots of details that still need to be discussed, but it looks like we've at least got your replacement settled."

"That's wonderful news, Lady Cate! Although, I won't be leaving until I am satisfied with her work."

"I'd expect nothing less, Mrs. Fraser."

Molly joined them next. "Hi girls! I figured I'd pop down and see if I could help with anything."

"Hi, Molly! I just told Mrs. Fraser the good news! That you'll be returning to us to learn her position and take over once she retires."

Molly squealed with excitement. "I'm so excited, I can barely contain myself. It took all in me not to send Jeff my letter of resignation the moment I went to my room. I was too lazy to type it all on my phone, though! But I will send it the moment I get back!"

Cate smiled at her. Mrs. Fraser said, "Molly, I'm so pleased that you'll be joining us. Lady Cate made an excellent suggestion to bring you on."

"I'm excited to start! I wish I didn't have to go home!"

"Well, Miss Molly, you can start right now by setting out a plate of biscuits from that tin in front of you." Mrs. Fraser nodded to the tin on the preparation table.

"Sure thing!" Molly responded.

"Don't worry, you'll be back before you know it, Molly. We'll figure out the details this weekend before you leave, then you'll have something to look forward to!" Cate assured her.

The ladies discussed a few more minor details about

Molly's new position before Mr. Fraser and Jack joined them, followed within minutes by Gayle. Mr. Smythe was the last to arrive, stating he had spent an extra few minutes making adjustments to his award-winning design.

They each selected their pumpkin and carving station. It took about three hours to dine and complete their carving. The group enjoyed the project and the roasted pumpkin seeds they made as a by-product of their carving. They set their finished products in a row on the table. Everyone agreed it would be a tough competition, admitting all the carvings were excellent. Mr. Fraser offered to place all the pumpkins in the garden the following morning. The pumpkins would be numbered, with the carver's name revealed only after the votes were counted.

After the carving task was complete, they all enjoyed hot chocolate and cookies in the sitting room before retiring before the big day. Cate found it difficult to sleep that night. The excitement of the past few days coupled with the anticipation of the party proved too much for her. Instead, she wandered the halls of the castle. Her attention turned from her upcoming party to the All Hallows' Eve ball being hosted by Randolph and Victoria. A murder would occur that evening. She had met the victim. But she was no closer to discovering why he was murdered nor by whom. More questions remained than answers. She was eager to continue her investigation.

She roamed the halls until she found herself at the tower room. Turning on the light, she stared at the box-filled room. "What happened here in 1856?" she inquired of the room. She closed her eyes trying to imagine a scene in which the footman she met ended up with his skull smashed and defenestrated. She imagined an enraged Randolph committing the act. Something about the scenario didn't quite fit. Perhaps it was the mysterious "S," the woman she and Jack had witnessed peeking from the tower room. Was it madness from being locked in the tower room that drove her to it? If this theory was correct, why would Randolph confess?

Closing her eyes, Cate tried to picture the woman they had witnessed at the window smashing Andrew's skull repeatedly. An idea occurred to Cate as she struggled to picture the scene. The blunt object that served as the murder weapon was never mentioned beyond the initial article. What served as the murder weapon? Was the object never found?

Authorities must have searched the room and castle grounds. Yet Cate could not recall any reports of the murder weapon. Cate opened her eyes, regarding the room. Could the murder weapon still be here? She had completed a thorough search of the room before. There was one place she hadn't looked, she recalled. The wardrobe stood off the floor about half a foot on raised legs. When Cate searched the room before, she had been so astonished by her discovery of the secret compartment and the note inside she had failed to check under it.

Cate skirted the boxes, kneeling on the floor in front of the wardrobe. She peered underneath, not seeing much. The room's light was not bright enough to pierce the darkness under the wardrobe. She cursed herself for not bringing her cell phone. She considered retrieving it, then decided she would make do without it. Steeling her nerves, she closed her eyes and reached a hand underneath, blindly feeling around.

After a moment, she pulled her hand back, too nervous to continue. Her mind ran through various scenarios in which her hand found something she'd rather it didn't. She would return in the morning with a flashlight. Dusting off her hands, she placed them on her thighs to stand. A moment of impulsivity struck her, and she reached under the wardrobe one last time before leaving.

Her hand struck something. She instinctively pulled her hand back, afraid of what she might have touched. She pressed herself against the floor, squinting into the shadows but to no avail.

She stretched her arm under again, feeling for the object. Her hand found it again. She touched the object in several places. It was cold and felt metallic. She grasped it and pulled. It was wedged against the back leg. She tugged with all her strength. After some work, the object moved. She grabbed hold of it and pulled it out from under the wardrobe.

Cate stared at the unearthed object. A thick layer of dust obscured every surface of the object. Cate blew on it, sending a cloud of dust billowing into the surrounding air. After a few sneezes, she wiped more dust away and beheld the object she had recovered.

It was a brass globe atop a rectangular stand, she surmised it was a paperweight. It was heavy. Cate studied the object, turning it over in her hands. She turned the object over, exposing the bottom. The object nearly slipped from her hands as she viewed the bottom. A thick smear of rust-colored material covered the bottom. Cate's heart skipped a beat. Was she holding the murder weapon from a centuries old murder in her hands?

Cate got to her feet, still clutching the brass globe. She wasn't sure if it was blood that stained the bottom of the paperweight, but she was determined the find out. She carried the object to the kitchen, seeking a plastic bag to place the object in. After washing her hands, she carried the object to her sitting room, placing it on the side table of her chaise. She sat for several moments staring at the object.

This couldn't be the murder weapon, she surmised. The authorities would have searched this room. Why hadn't they found the object? Yet, what else could produce the stain that sullied the bottom of the paperweight.

Cate checked the timepiece hanging from her neck. It was after midnight. Cate yawned, perhaps sleep would come to her now. She would leave her mysterious find in favor of her bed.

Despite her wanderings, her sleep was fitful. Nightmares filled her dreams as her mind concocted diverse scenarios of murder and mayhem within the castle.

The rising sun pierced through the windows, greeting Cate the next morning. She sighed, kicking herself for roaming around the castle half the night. But, tired or not, she had a full day ahead of her. She dragged herself out of bed, dressed and collected Riley for his morning walk.

The castle was abuzz with activity following breakfast. Final touches were being added to the décor in the ballroom and the gardens. Cate admired the line-up of pumpkins for the contest as she walked the gardens, checking on the final arrangements.

Cate had given everyone the day off to prepare for the party this evening. She found Mrs. Fraser reading a book in the library. Caterers descended on Mrs. Frasers kitchen to begin preparations for the party, chasing the woman from her haven. She snatched a tin of her shortbreads before being ushered out.

"It's nice to see you with your feet up, Mrs. Fraser," Cate said, plopping into an armchair nearby.

Mrs. Fraser shook her head. "Chased from my own kitchen, I was."

"Good thing, it's your day off!"

"Aye, you mentioned that, but I still don't understand what we will eat for lunch."

Cate grinned at her. She had told Mrs. Fraser that she would make arrangements for lunch on Friday but hadn't told the woman any details. "Don't worry, Mrs. Fraser, I have it covered!"

"I hope it's not cereal!" Jack said, entering the library.

"And what's wrong with that? I'd even spring for the kind with marshmallows," Cate retorted.

"You hear that, Mrs. Fraser. And you worried about our lunch."

"Oh, Jack," Cate said, "I had a question about something if you have a minute."

"Sure, what did you need?"

"Come with me, I'd like you to take a peek at something." Cate bent to retrieve Riley, not finding him at her feet. Instead, he had leapt onto Mrs. Fraser's footstool, curling up in the blanket draped over her feet. "Oh, Riley," Cate said, shaking her head, "you look like you've made yourself quite comfortable there! Come on, lazy bones, let's go."

"Oh, why not leave him, Lady Cate? He's nice and comfy. Not to mention, he's keeping my feet warm!"

"Thanks, Mrs. Fraser," Cate said. "We won't be long."

"Take your time, Lady Cate! Both of us are cozy here!"

Cate and Jack exited the library. Jack followed Cate down the hall. "Everything okay with the party preparations?"

"Yes. It has nothing to do with that. I found something I'd like you to take a glance at."

"Care to give any more explanation?"

"Yes, but not just yet. I want you to look at it first and give me your impression."

Jack followed Cate to her sitting room. She picked up the bagged object from her side table and handed it to him. He accepted it from her, bobbling the heavy object. "Wow, it's heavy." He glanced at it, turning the bag and its contents around in his hands. "Something I'm supposed to notice?"

"Turn it over," Cate answered.

"Oh, is that blood?" he asked upon seeing the stain.

"I'm not sure, but that's what I thought."

"Where did you find this? And why do you think it's blood? I mean it looks like blood but why would there be blood on this paperweight?"

Cate stared at him. "I found it in the tower room, wedged under the wardrobe. The same one where I found the mysterious note from 'S.'"

Jack screwed up his face before realization dawned on him. "You think this relates to the murder?"

Cate nodded. "Yes. Well, that's the most obvious idea in my mind."

"Cate, surely the police would have found this when the murder occurred. What are the chances the murder weapon lay hidden in the tower room for over a century?"

"I wondered about that, too. But I re-read the articles about the murder last night and this morning. When the body was first found, they assumed he had died from the fall. They wouldn't have looked for a murder weapon. They would have presumed the fall killed him, whether or not it was an accident. It was only after the autopsy that they realized he was dead before he fell. By the time they searched for the murder weapon a week had already gone by. They could have easily missed it!"

Jack pondered the information. "It's a long shot, but you could be correct. They found that he was killed by blunt force trauma to the head, right?"

Cate nodded again. "Yes, that's right. This is the sort of object that may have struck the fatal blow."

"Or it could be rust and discoloration from being stuck under the wardrobe for years."

"I have a method to tell if it's blood," Cate countered.

"I'm all ears."

"We can put a few drops of peroxide on it. If it's blood, it will bubble. If not, it won't!"

"Worth a try, I guess. Do you have some?"

"Yes, let me grab it." Cate disappeared from the room, retrieving a bottle of hydrogen peroxide from her bathroom and an eye dropper. She returned to the room, saying, "Okay, open that bag and let's try this."

Jack opened the bag, withdrawing the item. Cate filled the eyedropper with peroxide then dribbled a few drops onto the stained surface. Within seconds, the surface bubbled and fizzed. Cate and Jack shared a glance.

"So, it is blood," Cate said.

"Looks that way," Jack agreed. "You may be right, Cate. We may have a murder weapon in our hands."

CHAPTER 17

Cate stared at the item Jack held. She wasn't sure if it helped them, but she considered it progress. "I'm not sure if that makes me feel better or worse," Cate admitted.

"Well, it tells us where the murder occurred, most likely."

"Yes, I'd say it's likely the murder occurred in the tower room. I doubt someone bludgeoned Andrew to death somewhere else then went to the tower room to hide this object after throwing his body from the window there."

Jack nodded in agreement.

"Well," Cate said after a moment, "I expect we've learned all we can for the moment from this." Cate relieved Jack of the object, setting it on the side table in its bag. "We should go grab Riley and head to lunch!"

"Ah, yes, your infamous and mysterious lunch. We wouldn't want the cereal to get soggy."

Cate made a face at him, rolling her eyes and shaking her head. "Come on," she said.

The pair returned to the library where Cate retrieved Riley. She asked everyone to meet her in the dining room, where they would eat her surprise lunch. As the group gathered in the dining room, Cate waited at the front door for her lunch delivery. After receiving it from the delivery man, she carried it to the dining room. She pushed through the doors, carrying her bounty.

"Lunch is served, American style!" she exclaimed.

"Yay!" Molly cheered. "Pizza! Oh, I hope there is pepperoni!"

Cate laughed. "There is pepperoni, cheese, mushroom and green pepper!" Cate announced. Cate had paper plates supplied and sodas with plastic cups, determined to have no work to do for clean-up.

"Why, Lady Cate," Mrs. Fraser said, "I expect I might enjoy this lunch!"

Cate smiled at her, appreciating her willingness to accept pizza for lunch.

"Mmm," Jack said, already diving into his mushroom slice, "this might be your best cooking ever, Cate."

"And you assumed it was cereal!" Cate retorted.

Even Mr. Smythe seemed to enjoy the pizza and soda luncheon.

After lunch, Cate and Molly cleared the plates and cups, taking everything to the kitchen to dispose of. Riley trailed behind them, following them into the kitchen. The room was abuzz with activity. Caterers bustled around preparing dishes, serving trays and unpacking food. The exterior door swung open and closed in an endless cycle as people traveled in and out.

Cate and Molly were about to leave after tying up the trash bags when Riley bolted through the open back door. "RILEY!" Cate shouted after him.

She ran to the door, watching the pup bound across the yard and out of sight. Cate ran a few steps into the yard. "RILEY! RILEY!" she called, "COME BACK HERE!" She shouted for several more minutes to no avail. He was nowhere in sight and was not listening to Cate's commands to come back.

This was unusual for Riley. Only a few weeks after arriving, Cate had foregone his leash when walking with him in the yard. Riley was a well-behaved pup, in general. The furthest he ever ran from Cate was around a corner to meet his friend, Jack.

Cate called him again. She marched further into the yard, shouting at the top of her lungs. Cate worried that the activity in the house had frightened him.

"Maybe we should enlist help. We still have some time before we need to get ready!" Molly said, joining Cate.

"Yes, perhaps we should. I'm concerned he ran off because of all the excitement in the house. I'm afraid it may have frightened him. I don't want him to get too far from the house and become lost."

"Sure, honey," Molly said. "We'll find him! He couldn't have gotten far." Cate nodded to her, glancing back over the yard. "Tell you what, you stay out here, keep calling him. I'll go get the others."

"Thanks, Molly," Cate said, patting her arm.

Within minutes, Molly had the search party organized. Cate addressed them, "Thank you all for helping. He went over the ridge over there. I've never seen him run so fast. I'm sorry for the trouble, I just don't want him to become lost if he is frightened."

"Of course, Lady Cate, we're happy to help you look," Mr. Fraser reassured her. "Mrs. Fraser and I will head to the loch, the lad enjoys it there."

"Molly, Gayle and I will go to the back garden and see if the chap has gotten himself into the decorations there," Mr. Smythe offered.

Cate nodded. "Thanks."

"That leaves us," Jack said, "we'll follow where he ran over the ridge. Meet back here in twenty minutes whether or not you find him so we can figure out our next course of action."

They agreed to the plan then split up to search for the small dog. The last thing Cate needed today was a lost Riley. He meant the world to her, she would be heartsick until she found him. Worry creased her face as they set off over the ridge.

Cate traipsed at lightning speed across the yard. Her eyes searched every corner of the landscape, hoping to spot a glimpse of the tiny dog. As they crested the hill, they searched the horizon. There were no signs of Riley. Cate sighed, calling to him again. They saw nothing.

"Should we continue?" Cate asked.

"Yes, but which way?" Jack questioned, searching the horizon again.

"Oh, I don't know," Cate said, her voice wavering.

"Hey!" Jack said, struck with an idea, "isn't the folly along that path there? You've found him there a few times before, haven't you?"

Cate's eyes widened. "Yes! Oh, maybe he ran there! At least I hope so, anyway. Come on, let's hurry."

Cate hurried to the path with Jack dashing behind her. The folly came into sight a short distance away. Cate dashed toward it, calling Riley's name. There was no sign of him, but she hoped that he was nearby.

They reached the folly. Jack thumbed on his flashlight before entering. Despite the sunny day, the interior was dark and dimly lit. "Riley!" Cate called, her voice echoing off the stone. Jack swept the flashlight around the walls. "Riley!" Cate called again.

A whimper emanated from across the room. Cate raced toward it. "Over here, shine the light over here," Cate instructed.

A stone bench ran the length of the back wall. Cobwebs and leaves adorned it, making it difficult to see underneath. As Jack trained the light under it, something dashed out, almost knocked Cate over.

"RILEY!" she exclaimed as the little pup leapt into her arms. "Oh, Riley! Why did you run off? Thank goodness we found you!" Cate said, squeezing the dog close to her.

Jack was still eyeing under the bench with his flashlight. "That's interesting," he commented.

"What is?" Cate asked, recovering from her panic with Riley safely back in her arms.

"There's some garbage here, it looks like." Jack picked up a red object from amidst the debris. "Yum-yum Bones. Isn't this one of Riley's treat bags?"

"Yes, it is," Cate said, approaching Jack. As she did, Riley wriggled out of her arms again, dodging back under the bench. "Riley! What is so interesting under that bench?"

"Perhaps he left a treat from his treat bag," Jack surmised. He shined the light under the bench, following Riley. "Or not."

"What is it?" Cate asked, kneeling on the floor and following the light. She blinked a few times to adjust her eyes, then gawked at Jack. Glancing back under the bench she detected not one pair of eyes staring back at her but two. "Is that…"

"Another dog it looks like."

"Come on, Riley, come here," Cate encouraged. Riley trotted out from under the bench, glancing between Cate and the other pup. "I think he's trying to tell us something."

"Yes, I think so. And by the looks of it, he's been trying for the last month. I see what's left of Mrs. Fraser's steak here, a torn open bag of treats and some other food scraps." Jack reached under the bench, coaxing the other dog out. "Come on little fella, come on. We won't hurt you."

With Jack's coaxing, the other dog crept out from under the bench. Riley whimpered, wagging his tail at Cate. The dog stood just taller than Riley but was otherwise similar in size. He appeared to be gray and white, however, it was difficult to tell since dirt and mud smudged large portions of his fur. His fluffy tail was curled in a tight pigtail over his back.

"Oh, hello, little guy. Are you a guy?" Cate asked him, kneeling and extending her hand to the dog. Extending his neck, the dog sniffed Cate's hand before attempting to retreat under the bench.

"Oh, no you don't," Jack said, snatching him before he could hide again. "Looks like Riley has found a friend, Lady Cate."

"Looks like it. Well, I suppose we better take them both back to the house. We can inquire about lost dogs in town later. For now, we should get him cleaned up and fed. Poor thing, it seems he's been hiding here for quite a while."

"Yes, it does. But it looks like Riley has kept him well fed."

Cate scooped Riley into her arms. "Indeed, he has. And it also explains all of his naughty behavior of late. Oh, Riley, what have I told you about bringing home strays?" Cate joked, giving the pup a kiss on the head.

They hiked the path back to the house, arriving last. "We found him!" Cate shouted from a distance, lifting Riley in her arms.

Molly applauded the announcement. "And then some!" Jack added.

"Is that…" Gayle began, unable to finish.

"Another dog?" Molly finished for her.

"Yes," Cate said, as they closed the distance between them. "We also found the remnants of your stolen steak, Mrs. Fraser. And a bone from the other piece of meat you thought you had forgotten in the freezer."

"So, I haven't gone senile! The little bugger stole it, too, did he?"

"He did," Cate admitted. "I'm sorry!"

"No apology needed, Lady Cate. It looks like he did it for the right reasons. Hello, little pup," Mrs. Fraser greeted him.

"Well, with the emergency over, everyone can return to their party preparations! I will give this little one a bath and something to eat."

After everyone welcomed Riley and his new friend, they dispersed. Cate offered both dogs a bowl of food. The new pup ate it with vigor. The poor animal still seemed to be hungry despite the amount of food Riley had been providing him with.

After they ate, Cate used the washbasin in the laundry to give the second dog a quick bath. She wrapped him in a towel and carried him to her bedroom, Riley trailing behind. Once Cate had the dog toweled off, she set him on the floor, watching him interact with Riley. Riley carried a ball to him, setting it down in front of him. He then retrieved a bone, dropping that in front of the other dog, too. He nudged it toward him, encouraging his canine friend to chew it. The little gray and white pup snatched the bone, carrying it a few feet away and settling in to chew it. Satisfied, Riley curled in his bed, watching the other dog as his eyes became heavy.

The scene was heartwarming. Cate adored Riley. His obvious concern for the other dog touched her heart. He was a sweet dog. She was hoping no one owned the dog. Riley could use a friend.

Cate smiled at them. She would have to settle that later. Now, she needed to ready herself for the party. She left the two dogs while she applied her makeup and swept her hair into an up-do. She was becoming an expert at these given her practice when she traveled to the past. Cate opted for a dramatic makeup look to match her blood red with black trim ball gown. Cate's costume was an ironic choice, hailing from the very era where she and Jack were time traveling. A fitting choice, Cate surmised.

Before slipping into her costume, she checked on the dogs and took them for a short walk before the party. She found the two nestled together in Riley's bed, Riley's chin resting on the other pup's back as though protecting him. She smiled at the scene before rousting the two from their slumber for a walk. Not wanting to take a chance, Cate used a leash and harness on both dogs. After their brief trip outside, she returned them to their bed. Riley didn't seem to mind sharing. Cate smiled at the two as they settled together, Riley with a big yawn.

Satisfied that they were content, Cate slipped into her costume. In most cases, a costume gown like this would be uncomfortable, but Cate was growing accustomed to this style of clothing. She checked the gold timepiece hanging from her neck. She had a few minutes before she needed to be downstairs. She spent the time giving Riley and his friend a little TLC.

A knock sounded at her door. "Yes?" she called.

"Just me," Jack's voice answered, "can I come in?"

"Yes, you can! Everything okay?" Cate asked.

"Yes," Jack announced, entering the room already in costume. "I just wanted to see how Riley's little buddy is doing."

"He seems fine. Riley has been sharing his bed with him. He's still shy with me, but he seems to have a friend in Riley."

Jack stooped down to pet the two dogs. Riley climbed from his bed to give Jack an appreciative lap to his face. "You're still my best buddy, Riley," Jack told him. "And kudos to you for taking care of your little friend."

Cate smiled at them again. "I wonder if he belongs to someone."

"We can ask around at the party tonight," Jack suggested.

Cate sighed. "I'm almost hoping he doesn't. It would be nice for Riley to have a pal."

"I suppose we'll find out soon enough! May I escort you down, Lady Cate?" Jack asked, standing and giving an extravagant bow.

"Thank you," she said, adding a curtsy. Jack offered his arm and together they made their way down to the ballroom. The room hummed with activity as the caterers began their preparations for food service. Drinks were being set out, warming candles lit and appetizers placed on trays. The band was setting up and testing their instruments. Everything seemed in order. Molly joined them, her costume a take on Marie Antoinette. She beamed with excitement.

"This place looks great!" Molly said. Gayle and Mr. Smythe joined them, each of them dressed in clothing from the seventeenth century. Mr. Smythe looked at home in the formal clothing. Mr. and Mrs. Fraser were right behind them. Cate awaited their arrival, dying to see Mrs. Fraser's top-secret costume. Mr. Fraser had selected an old-fashioned Scottish outfit, complete with a kilt. Mrs. Fraser wore an eighteenth-century hooped skirt in a blue tartan fabric. She looked regal and Scottish to the core.

Cate loved the outfit, telling Mrs. Fraser how fitting she found her costume. If there were to be a costume competition, everyone agreed Mrs. Fraser stood a great chance of winning.

Chimes rang throughout the house. "That would be Mrs. Campbell, I'd bet," Cate said. "I'll go meet her and then I had better get ready to greet guests!"

Cate made her way to the front door, opening it to Mrs. Campbell, dressed in a regal ball gown. "Good evening, Mrs. Campbell! Please come in!" Cate ushered her through the door and to the ballroom.

The woman was pleased with the setup, but within moments was issuing orders to ensure the party came off without a snafu. Cate left the ballroom with the very capable Mrs. Campbell in charge. While Mrs. Campbell had volunteers to welcome the guests and escort them to the ballroom, Cate wanted to be there to greet all the guests when they arrived.

She didn't have long to wait before her first guests arrived. The guests, many townsfolk from Dunhaven, were excited to see the castle. Most had never seen the interior of the castle, despite it dominating the landscape of the town for their lifetimes. Cate found herself excited to greet them and meet those she hadn't met yet.

When the bulk of the guest list had arrived, Cate left the greeters at the door for the remaining stragglers and joined everyone else in the ballroom. The party was in full swing. Music filled the air along with talking and laughing. The caterers mingled with champagne and hors d'oeuvers.

Cate made her rounds, speaking with each guest again. She made sure to direct them to the pumpkin contest and encouraged them to vote. After Cate had been sure she had spoken to everyone and any new arrivals, she found Molly and Mrs. Fraser hovering near one of the food stations. She joined them, finding them critiquing the assortment and presentation. "Can't you take one night off?" she joked.

"I find it enjoyable to critique cooking that isn't mine," Mrs. Fraser retorted. "Besides, Molly and I are comparing notes as a beginning step to her training."

"I don't mind," Molly chimed in. "I'm so excited to start, I don't even want to go home!"

"Look at it this way," Cate said, "it's just a small detour to collect all your belongings!"

"A tiny one if I have any say in it," Molly said.

"I'll be speaking to Mr. Smythe about the paperwork

before he leaves. I hate to make him work on his vacation. But I don't think he ever takes a vacation."

Cate left the two women to continue their critique of the catering. She caught Mrs. Campbell as she was taking a break from circulating amongst the guests to micro-manage some of the caterers. She asked the woman to oversee the pumpkin carving competition vote so that the results were above reproach.

After squaring that away, Jack approached. "If you have a minute, Lady Cate, I think I may have found the owner of the extra dog." Cate's heart sank. She had hoped to keep the dog and the appearance of the owner disappointed her. Yet, she understood, knowing how she would feel if she lost Riley and someone else found him and wanted to keep him.

Jack led her to a couple outside admiring the pumpkin carving. "Lady Cate, this is Mr. and Mrs. Frank and Cara Bailey, owners of Bailey's farm."

"Oh, yes, we met earlier. You provided all the pumpkins, cornstalks and hay bales. Thank you!"

"I think they also may have provided the new addition upstairs," Jack added.

"Aye," Frank said. "I think you may have ended up with one freeloader from the Bailey farm, Lady Cate."

"He's just upstairs if you'd like to take a peek," Cate offered.

"I don't want to interrupt your party, Lady Cate," Frank said.

"I think I can slip away for a few moments, follow me."

Cate led them upstairs to her suite, showing them all into the bedroom. Riley and friend were curled in his bed. The two lifted their heads to peer at the newcomers, too lazy to get up.

Frank glanced at Cara, nodding his head. "Aye, that's him," Frank said. "He looks right at home here!"

Cate smiled, despite a pang of sadness. "I'll bet he misses his real home."

"He never really had a 'real' home, Lady Cate," Cara said. "Our dog had puppies a little over a year ago. We found homes for all of them except this one. He's very reserved and never stood out to anyone considering adopting one of our pups. About a month ago, he disappeared. We searched and searched for him but never found him. I suppose he was hiding out here on your estate."

"Aww, what a shame. He's very cute! Poor baby, getting lost!"

"It appears your dog has taken quite a liking to him!" Frank said.

"Yes. Riley has been sneaking off to see him for the entire month, I believe. He's been supplying him with as much food as he could steal, too." Cate laughed.

"What a fine friend!" Cara said. She glanced at Frank who nodded again. "Lady Cate, I don't suppose you'd be interested in providing a home for him? It looks like Riley likes his new friend."

"Oh!" Cate exclaimed. "I... Well... I'd love to!" Cate blurted. "I mean, only if you're sure. After a year, you must be attached to him. I don't want to take him away from you!"

"Nay, Lady Cate, we always hoped he'd find a good home. It seems he's found a fine one here. Living on a farm, we have many animals. This poor pup seems to need more attention than we can give him. But I'm sure he'd receive nothing but the best care here!"

Cate smiled. "Then I wholeheartedly accept. I think Riley will be thrilled he's staying." Cate rubbed the new dog under the chin. "Did you hear that? We will get you your own bed for your new home!"

"He'll have the royal treatment now!" Jack said. "What will you name him, Lady Cate?"

An idea struck Cate and she turned to the group. "I think I'll name him Bailey!"

Satisfied with the results, everyone returned to the party downstairs. Cate was thrilled about being able to keep Bailey. She would bet money that the prospect also thrilled Riley. When they returned to the party, it was in full swing with music, dancing and revelry. Mrs. Fraser was introducing Molly to everyone in the room, making everyone aware that Molly was her successor and protégé. Although quick to dispel rumors she'd soon be retiring, she seemed to be enjoying her moment as the proud peacock with her new peachick. Mr. Fraser's gardens were a hit, with many people escaping the warm ballroom into the cool, crisp autumn air. It helped that the gardens looked magical with their hanging lights and autumn décor. No matter what activity they were participating in, it seemed everyone was enjoying the party. Mr. Smythe had already commented to Cate that he considered the party to be a success. Gayle hadn't left the dance floor since the music began. Molly's unwavering grin made it apparent that she was enjoying herself. Jack's loud laugh with friends confirmed his enjoyment.

As Cate entered the ballroom, Mrs. Campbell sought her out. They had the results from the pumpkin carving contest and were ready to announce the winner. Mrs. Campbell also suggested it might be an appropriate time for Cate to make a small speech to the group.

Despite having been a college professor, speeches were not Cate's forte. However, she recognized the importance of addressing the group. Still, she planned on keeping it brief. She thanked everyone for attending, stating that it was a pleasure to meet each and every one of them. Cate gave all the credit for the party's success to Mrs. Campbell. Her concluding remarks hinted at another party and the hope to make the Halloween party an annual event.

When finished, Cate handed the microphone back to Mrs. Campbell, who had a few announcements of her own to make. Following her remarks, she announced that the winner of the pumpkin carving contest had been determined. Before announcing it, they would reveal the carver of each pumpkin. Jack created a pumpkin carved with the image of Riley near a shrub. Mrs. Fraser's entry was a cornucopia. Mr. Smythe's pumpkin was carved with an image of Lady Justice. Cate, Molly and Gayle each created versions of the traditional jack-o'-lantern. Once the owner of each pumpkin was revealed, Mrs. Campbell asked the band for a drum roll.

"The winner of the first annual Dunhaven Castle Halloween Ball Pumpkin Carving Contest is..." She paused, adding drama to the moment as everyone waited with bated breath for the announcement. "CHARLIE FRASER!"

Applause broke out throughout the room along with cheers from Cate, Mrs. Fraser and Jack. Mr. Fraser's pumpkin design had been a replica of Dunhaven Castle. He had carved and peeled the pumpkin for a dramatic effect with a tremendous amount of detail.

Cate was thrilled Mr. Fraser had won. His design was flawless and well-deserving of the win. The man's quiet ways often failed to get him the recognition he deserved. On this occasion, though, he had captured the glory.

Cate returned to Mrs. Campbell's side. She retrieved a trophy hidden away behind a table skirt. It was a secret addition to the party only Cate and Mrs. Campbell knew about. Cate had ordered a trophy for the winner. Their name would be engraved along with the year of their win. She was overjoyed to hand it over to Mr. Fraser after a few pictures of Lady Catherine with the winner.

Following the award ceremony, Mrs. Campbell

concluded by inviting everyone to enjoy the rest of the party. Music commenced again and chatter filled the room.

Cate poured herself a glass of punch and made her way to the edge of the room, overlooking both the ballroom and the gardens. She watched life pass her by, as the cool autumn air caressed her skin, cooling her off after her moment in the spotlight. Cate reflected on her time in the castle. From the time she stepped foot onto the property, she had felt an incredible sense of ease. She had never experienced such a homey feeling as she had here. She sensed that Molly had the same sentiment about Dunhaven.

The party wound down within a few hours. Cate said her goodbyes to most guests before returning to an almost empty ballroom. Her own guests, staff and Mrs. Campbell remained. After a few moments of conversation with Mrs. Campbell, the woman also said her goodbyes. Cate saw her off.

Everyone was exhausted after a fabulous night, yet they decided to meet for a nightcap after changing. Left over energy from the party kept them up for another hour, discussing everything from Cate's new dog to Mr. Fraser's win. Finally worn-out and sleepy, the group parted ways for a much needed rendezvous with their beds.

CHAPTER 18

Cate spent some extra time in bed the next morning. Everyone planned on sleeping in. Even both dogs enjoyed a lazy morning. Cate enjoyed the sunrise, painting the cloudless sky with vivid purples and pinks. The Halloween ball had been a rousing success. The weather had been perfect, dry and cool, a perfect fall evening. Mrs. Campbell was already talking about the next event as she left the castle. She dubbed it "Christmas with Lady Cate," intent on hosting a winter celebration with the castle bedecked in holiday splendor.

Cate was pleased the event went well. And while the idea of planning another party exhausted her, she agreed it was an excellent idea. It gave her a great chance to meet her neighbors and allow everyone a chance to enjoy the beauty and splendor that she enjoyed daily. At least Mrs. Campbell seemed content to allow Cate the weekend to recover, suggesting that they meet on Wednesday to discuss the next event. She had suggested Monday, but Cate had asked to postpone until mid-week.

Cate pushed the next party from her mind, determined to focus on a lazy weekend with her friends. They had no plans which, in Cate's mind, were the best plans. She couldn't wait to discuss plans for Molly's return. She smiled, stretching, motivating herself to get moving.

Hopping out of bed, she dressed for the day and collected both dogs for a morning walk before breakfast. She found Molly outside enjoying the view, wrapped up in one of her now infamous "Scotland sweaters."

"You will need a lot more sweaters," Cate said.

"I KNOW!" Molly bellowed. "CATE!!!!!" she squealed. "I am so excited!"

"So am I!" Cate exclaimed.

Molly took one of the leashes from Cate. "I'm telling Jeff as soon as I get home, I'm giving him my two weeks the day I am back!"

Cate smiled at her. "We need to discuss so much. When do you plan to move?"

"Tomorrow? Do I even need to go back?" Molly joked.

Cate understood the impulse. She gazed at the scenery surrounding them. Although she was likely biased, she found it one of the most beautiful spots on earth. The rolling hills, the way the mist clung to the moors, the sky painted like a picture, the way the colors reflected onto the castle's stone giving it a magical glow; all of it created a setting that couldn't be more perfect. "You don't HAVE to go back," she answered, "but you may want a few items from home."

"Sadly, you're right. I do need more than a week's worth of clothes and a travel toothbrush. Although, I won't need much else, will I? Not that I have much, a handful of cheap pieces of furniture in my awful apartment. But I still need to deal with it. What did you do with your stuff?"

"Donated most of it. I took my clothes and a few personal

keepsakes. But furniture, kitchenware, my car, all of that went to charity."

"I think I will do the same. You have no idea how happy it makes me to say that. Wow!"

"It makes me happy, too! I'll be counting the days until you are back and in your Rose Room! Let's continue this discussion over breakfast. We can discuss timelines with Mr. Smythe. He took care of all my paperwork for my move."

"I can't wait. Will I become a Scottish citizen?"

"I think so!" Cate wrapped Molly in a hug, excited to see her friend so energized. It was a contrast to Molly's arrival. While she had been excited to visit, Molly's first night had been an emotional one. She had broken down in tears recounting how tough the last few months had been on her. The difference one week later was astounding. No longer dwelling on the past, Molly was focusing on the future.

The women walked back to the castle. As they entered the dining room, they found Mrs. Fraser fussing over some food on the sideboard. Cate scolded her for bothering on her day off. She insisted that Mrs. Fraser sit at once and let Cate make a plate for her. The rest of the group soon joined them. Everyone helped themselves to the à la carte cold breakfast.

During breakfast, the conversation turned toward Molly's upcoming move. With Mr. Smythe's advice they nailed down a rough date for her return. Much to Molly's delight, with Mr. Smythe's recommendation and Molly's own estimates for tying up loose ends, she would be back to Dunhaven by mid-December. Everyone was thrilled that she would be back for the holiday season. Cate double-checked that she wouldn't rather postpone until the new year, spending Christmas with her family and coming to Dunhaven afterwards.

Molly was candid, admitting that she preferred to spend Christmas in Dunhaven with her new family. She much preferred the Rose Room to her sister's basement. Mr. Smythe assured her he would have all paperwork completed for her as her early Christmas present.

They all had plenty of time to continue discussing arrangements. The group enjoyed a quiet weekend on the estate. Cate enjoyed having the company. She was torn, however, missing Randolph and Victoria, her family from the past. She longed to travel back to the past, excitement building for her dress fitting appointment on Monday. It helped ease the disappointment she would feel when all her guests left.

On Sunday, the group took one final trip to Dunhaven together before everyone departed Monday. Mr. Smythe drove back alone while Gayle and Molly drove together to the train station. Both women were glad to have the company for the long drive and train ride. Molly had a late flight back to the States. She didn't return to work until Thursday, when she planned to hand in her resignation and begin preparing to move to her new home.

Cate watched the cars disappear down the drive. Mr. and Mrs. Fraser and Jack joined her, waving as everyone departed. Everyone returned to their respective duties. The castle was too quiet. Riley and his new friend, Bailey, provided a wonderful distraction to combat the silence. The two pups enjoyed wrestling, playing with a ball, tugging on toys together. Cate relished watching the two of them play. Riley seemed to enjoy his new companion, rolling around the floor like a puppy again.

Cate was also relieved to be time traveling today. It would aid in diverting her attention and filling her time. Plus, Cate was ecstatic about trying her dress on today. She never had tailor-made clothes before. It was quite a different experience to modern-day shopping. Excitement was building for Cate to see the results of her dress selection.

Jack was her traveling companion once again. He planned to meet with Randolph while Cate and Victoria shared girl time. Cate also tasked him with looking for the murder weapon in the castle. She hoped to identify the location of the object and hence, the location of the murder.

The fated day was approaching. Cate wasn't sure what she hoped to achieve. At the very least, she wanted to help her ancestor avoid going to jail for a murder he didn't commit. A part of her questioned if preventing the murder would be the best scenario. After a lengthy discussion with Jack, she ruled that out. Reminding her of his grandfather's warning, Jack cautioned her that changing the past too drastically threatened the entire future.

While the conversation frustrated her, Cate agreed. If the poor unwitting servant did not succumb to his fate, the ripples throughout time could be incalculable. Cate hated the inability to intervene to prevent a man's death, but she understood that she could not.

She pushed the frustrations of her tied hands from her mind, directing her attention back to her dress. Cate checked the gold timepiece hanging around her neck. One hour to go. She collected both dogs and climbed the stairs to her sitting room to prepare for her trip.

When she was ready, hair swept up, dressed in a hooped skirt and crinoline underskirt, she made her way to meet Jack. Slowing the watch, they traveled back to 1856. They traversed the usual circuit down the back stairs and around to the front of the castle. Thomson greeted them. He left Jack to find his way to Randolph's study while he showed Cate to Victoria's sitting room.

Victoria rose and greeted Cate with an embrace.

"Cousin Catherine," Victoria said, kissing her cheek, "it's lovely to see you again. And how were your travels? I hope your journey did not tire you too much."

Cate followed her to the table she had arranged for tea. "Excellent. I have this for you. I hope you are keen on it." Cate removed a silk fan. Before visiting, she had searched high and low for something to return with for Victoria. She was careful to select something fitting for the time period.

"Oh!" Victoria said, clapping her hands together before taking the fan from Cate. "It's lovely, Catherine! How grateful I am that you thought of me while on your tour."

"How has your dress come along?" Cate asked as Victoria set the fan aside.

"I'm very pleased with it. I had a fitting last week. The color is striking, I shall be a standout! As will you in the sapphire gown! Are you eager to see it?"

Cate's smile radiated, showing her excitement. She nodded her head. "I am! I must confess patience is not a virtue I possess. I was most eager for our trip to end!"

"If I may also confess, it is not my virtue either. I was impatient for your return, also! I have missed you!"

Before Cate answered, Thompson opened the door, announcing Madame Bisset had arrived. The woman glided into the room followed by two servants carrying garments. They placed the garments on a nearby chair, following Thompson out of the room after delivering their packages.

"Countess and Mrs. MacKenzie," she said, throwing her arms around both women as they approached her. "I trust you both are well?"

"We are," Victoria answered. "Please, sit down. Let us have some tea."

"Lovely," Madame Bisset said, sitting at the table. "Oh, Mrs. MacKenzie, I am so pleased with your gown! I hunted for the perfect fabric, I had it re-dyed to be the exact color we discussed. Oh, it is truly lovely, simply marvelous. When paired with Countess MacKenzie's gown, you two will be dazzling."

"I am so eager to see it!" Cate said.

"As am I," Victoria agreed. "We have been discussing it all morning. Oh please, may we see it now? Catherine, you wouldn't mind postponing your tea for a moment to model for us?"

"I thought you'd never ask!" Cate exclaimed.

"Just a moment, I'll ring for my ladies' maid, she can assist you, Catherine."

Within moments, Bryson, Victoria's ladies' maid, arrived. "Oh, Bryson." Victoria waved her in. "Please assist Mrs. MacKenzie in trying Madame Bisset's creation! We are impatient to see it!"

Bryson motioned for Cate to follow her to the dressing room, carrying the gown with her. Bryson's proficiency in working with various garments outdid Cate's on her best day. She had Cate ready in record time.

"How's it coming, Catherine?" Victoria called in. Cate appeared in the doorway. "OH!" Victoria exclaimed. "Madame Bisset, you have outdone yourself again! Oh, Catherine! It's incredible! We shall be the belles of this ball! Are you pleased with it?"

"Very!" Cate exclaimed. The details on the gown were exquisite. The frills, trimmed in black lace over the deep sapphire color, fell delicately to the floor. When Cate moved, the fabric sashayed and flowed around her like water gently floating along in a stream. Madame Bisset had added beading details on the off-the-shoulder sleeves. "It is extraordinary!"

Victoria rushed to a jewelry armoire nearby, removing a necklace. "Come, Catherine, envision the entire ensemble." She led Cate to a mirror, placing the necklace around her neck. The sapphire necklace sparkled around Cate's neck, matching the neckline well. "It's perfect! Oh, please say you will borrow it!"

"I couldn't decline, Victoria," Cate said, "it is too perfect!"

"Splendid! I am so pleased!"

Madame Bisset fussed over the dress, pinching it here and bunching it there. She commented that it fit very well, just a few minor adjustments to bring it to perfection. Cate returned to the dressing room to change out of the evening gown. She hated to take it off, it was beautiful.

After changing, she returned to the tea table, finishing her tea and light snacks with Victoria and Madame Bisset. They talked fashion and the upcoming ball. Cate felt like a schoolgirl, giggling over lace details and accessories.

They saw Madame Bisset off, spent a few more moments chattering about the upcoming party, then Victoria walked Cate to Randolph's study to meet Jack. A man unknown to Cate exited the room as the ladies entered. The foursome spent a few moments chatting, however, Randolph seemed distracted, checking the gold time piece several times.

Jack suggested they be on their way, perceiving Randolph's anxiety. Randolph agreed, excusing himself from seeing them out, stating they were family and could do so on their own. Victoria said her goodbyes, leaving Jack and Cate in the hallway to find their way to the front door.

"That was something. Tell you when we get back." Jack started toward the main staircase when Cate tugged him back. "What?" he questioned.

"I think we should follow Randolph," she whispered.

"Follow Randolph? Why?" he said, lowering his voice.

"Didn't you notice how troubled he seemed? Kept checking his watch, he was distracted. We should follow up on that."

"Perhaps he had something important to do," Jack countered.

"Or perhaps this ties into the murder. We're days away, and Randolph is uneasy and agitated. I think we should at least check it out."

"Okay, okay. But we cannot, under any circumstance, prevent this murder from happening. I'm not even sure we should help Randolph stay out of jail, but I understand your impulse to protect your family."

They hurried down the hall in the direction Randolph had gone earlier. Cate spotted Randolph walking down the path leading to the loch. They dashed out of the castle, making their way to the path. They were careful not to get too close to Randolph, but they kept him in sight.

As they approached the loch, Cate and Jack found a spot behind a large tree, concealing them but allowing them a full view of the loch. Randolph continued to approach the water. When he was on the bank, another person emerged, approaching Randolph. Cate recognized Andrew, the footman who was soon to be murdered.

She smacked Jack in the chest. He rolled his eyes at her, loathe to admit she was right. They watched as the two men conversed. It was clear they were arguing from their gestures and postures. After a few moments, the argument became heated. Randolph grasped the footman by his collar, shaking him before lobbing the man backwards. He stormed toward the castle past Jack and Cate's hiding spot. They shrunk back into the shadows of the large tree.

"Now what?" Jack said, his voice just above a whisper.

"Let's follow him," Cate said, pointing to Andrew, who was still smoothing his ruffled clothing.

"I was afraid you would say that," Jack admitted. Within a few moments, Andrew made his way down the path passing them. They waited until they could follow him without being spotted.

They entered the castle. Andrew was nowhere in sight. "Let's split up," Cate suggested, taking the stairs upward.

"That's a terrible idea, Cate," Jack began.

"We don't have a choice, I'm not taking no for an answer," Cate said, sprinting up the stairs two at a time.

Jack groaned behind her but she was already on her way. She had a specific destination in mind: the tower room.

Breathless, she made it to the second floor and scurried down the hall toward the turret stairs. She peered up the curving stairway, craning her neck as if it would help her see through the stone walls. Gathering her skirts, she started up the steps.

As she climbed, she glimpsed the open door at the top. She sped up, approaching the open door. She was within eight steps of the door when Andrew appeared at the top. Spotting her, he slammed the door behind him, locking it.

"Something I can help you with, Mrs. MacKenzie?" he sniped at her.

"Oh," Cate said, quick to react, "yes. I seem to have lost track of my husband. Have you seen him?"

"I have not seen him, madam."

Cate swallowed hard, continuing, "Are you sure? I could have sworn I saw him ascending these very stairs!" Cate approached the door.

"You are mistaken, Mrs. MacKenzie. If you'll excuse me, I must return to my duties." He stepped down from the landing.

"Oh, but…" Cate said, stopping him.

He paused, turning around, annoyance plain on his face. "Yes, Mrs. MacKenzie?"

"I wondered… might I have a quick look around the tower room? I'd love to see the views."

"No, you may not, Mrs. MacKenzie. Now if you'll please excuse me."

"Really?" Cate continued. "I'll be quick!"

Andrew turned to face her again, climbing the stairs to

her level. "Perhaps you should concentrate on locating your husband,"

"What would the harm be?"

"You should learn to mind your own business, Mrs. MacKenzie," he said, bringing his face close to hers. "Shall I ask Thomson to assist you in finding your absent husband?"

In an instant, Cate felt unsafe. Andrew's demeanor changed from annoyed to threatening. Cate forced a weak smile. "No, thank you. I'm sure I'll find him," she whispered.

He nodded to her, staring at her as she descended the stairs. She glanced back once. Andrew loomed at the top of the stairs. She quickened her steps, rushing to the bottom of the tower stairs. She almost toppled into Jack as she rounded the bend.

"How did I know I'd find you here," he said.

"Ah, Mrs. MacKenzie," Andrew said, rounding the stairway behind her, "I see you located Mr. MacKenzie. I shall call off the dogs."

Jack gave Cate a puzzled look. "Yes, I ran into Andrew while looking for you," Cate covered, "I'm sorry I lost track of you somewhere."

"Well, you found me!" Jack assured Andrew.

"How fortuitous. Mrs. MacKenzie seems to have an innate ability to lose precious things then wander about searching for them in places she shouldn't."

"Excuse me?" Jack questioned him.

"Mrs. MacKenzie shouldn't be wandering the halls of the castle, sir."

"Mrs. MacKenzie and I are family, sir. Lord and Lady MacKenzie have graciously opened their home to us. I don't believe either of them intended it to have the restrictions you are implying."

"You misunderstood me, Mr. MacKenzie." Andrew smirked. "I'm only concerned about the lady's well-being.

The castle has many dangerous places, including the tower room which is filled with many trunks. She may be hurt should one of them fall on her."

"How kind of you to exhibit such concern for my wife, I will be sure she is cautious in future visits."

Andrew forced a smile and nodded to him as he pushed past them down the stairs.

"I think we should head back," Cate suggested once he was out of earshot.

"Great idea," Jack agreed.

They wound through the halls to the bedroom. Slipping inside, they set the watch back to normal time, returning to their time. Jack breathed a larger than normal sigh of relief. "Don't do that again," he admonished.

"Do what?" Cate asked.

"No splitting up. I don't even want to travel back, yet I know you'll never agree!"

"We must go back. Victoria will be crushed if we don't attend the party."

Jack rolled his eyes. "Yes, yes, I realize that. Randolph made it clear how much Victoria was enjoying your time together. But I think we need to have a serious conversation about dropping this murder investigation, Cate."

"Why?"

"Cate! Did Andrew not give you the same vibe he gave me? He was threatening us, in particular, you."

"I don't..." Cate began.

"No, no, no, no, no," Jack said, waving his arms in the air, motioning her to stop her answer. "I don't want to hear you defend him. It was obvious; he was threatening you."

"Which only makes me more curious!"

"Bah!" Jack exclaimed, waving his arms in the air again.

"Think about it! I caught him leaving the tower room. He was attending to whoever is hidden in there. Who is it? Why are they hiding her? Why is he privy to the secret? Why was he arguing with Randolph?"

"I don't know the answer to any of those, but given what we saw today, it is possible that Randolph killed him. You witnessed the hostility between them firsthand."

Cate contemplated for a moment before responding. "I still disagree. Randolph would not have put his family in harm's way by doing that, even if he is prone to losing his temper."

Jack shook his head again. "I don't want you alone with that man again."

Cate didn't answer. She understood his concern, yet she was reluctant to make any promises. "We should attempt to gather more information in the remaining days we have. Do you have time for a quick trip tomorrow and maybe Wednesday? I'll come up with some excuse to visit."

Jack shook his head. "Oh, Lady Cate, I will never win. Okay, okay, whatever you say, boss. I'm beginning to look forward to this guy being gone."

"He will be soon enough. That's why we need to gather as much information as we can before he makes his exit."

"Okay, but ONLY because we are already committed to this investigation. And, no splitting up!"

"Same time, same place tomorrow!" Cate said.

"Guess so," Jack acquiesced.

"Oh, hey, what did you want to tell me when we got home?" Cate inquired.

"Oh, I had almost forgotten in the excitement," Jack said, smiling, "I met my great-great-great-grandfather."

Cate grinned. "Malcom Reid? Was he the man we passed on our way into Randolph's office?"

"None other. That was... strange. I can see the appeal though. You must feel the same with Randolph and Victoria."

Cate smiled again. "It is, they are my family. I feel a connection to them, no matter how odd that may sound."

"I understand, Cate. Meeting Malcom was… staggering, mind-blowing. I now understand your enthusiasm for time travel."

"I'm glad you met him," Cate answered. "I'll bet you'll be seeing more of him."

Jack wrinkled his nose. "Okay, okay, I guess that's a good thing." He grinned.

They parted to change clothes and return to their normal day. Cate spent a large part of the day enjoying the grounds with Riley and their newest friend, Bailey. Cate hoped to eventually train Bailey so she wouldn't need a leash and harness for him. Riley was well-behaved and, his latest excursions to assist Bailey notwithstanding, was trustworthy enough to walk with no restrictions.

While Cate walked with her pups, her mind mulled over the growing mystery in 1856. Things seemed to be reaching their breaking point, hurling toward a precipice with Cate powerless to stop it. It was amazing, even knowing that tragedy was about to strike, Cate still seemed incapable of altering the situation. Perhaps despite any interventions, some events were destined to happen.

Cate second-guessed herself, questioning if she had been more aggressive in her early investigation if they would have had a better chance of preventing the upcoming tragedy. Cate shook her head. Not only could they not interfere to prevent the man's death, but if they had been any more aggressive in their investigation, it may have tipped their hand. Although, they had done a poor job of covering their tracks, Randolph had seen right through their weak facade.

Cate sighed, sitting down on the banks of the loch with Riley and Bailey at her side. Her pondering turned to contemplating the conversation she had witnessed on these same banks only hours ago. She cursed their inability to hear the words being exchanged between Randolph and Andrew. Even without the exact statements, it was clear they were arguing. It was also apparent that Randolph was annoyed, perhaps even angry. His aggressive behavior disconcerted Cate. What if her entire theory was wrong? Perhaps an innocent man was not punished. Perhaps Randolph was guilty.

"I confess," she said to the two dogs, "I have no clue what I'm doing. Now, don't tell Jack. But I'm worried. What do you think, Riley? Should I press on?" The little dog didn't answer. "How about you, Bailey?" He, too, was mum on the subject.

Cate surmised the only way to find answers was to continue their investigation. Resolute in her plan, Cate focused her energy on enjoying the rest of her day.

Before dinner, Cate received an email from Gayle thanking her for the stay and informing her she and Mr. Smythe were back in London. She had seen Molly to the airport for her late-night flight. Gayle looked forward to seeing Molly again in a few short weeks when Molly arrived in Scotland permanently.

The email eased Cate's nerves, it was nice to know two of her three guests were settled. She now awaited an email from Molly, stating she was home safe and sound. She'd have a good while to wait, not expecting to receive the all clear from Molly until Tuesday afternoon.

Cate opted to eat dinner with her staff. Friday was her typical day to have a staff dinner, however, the castle was far too quiet this evening after the bustle of the weekend. Mrs. Fraser assured her she wasn't intruding, and everyone understood Cate's impulse to seek company. They enjoyed another delicious meal courtesy of Mrs. Fraser, discussing the events of the week, Molly's new position, Cate's new addition and Mr. Fraser's pumpkin carving win.

Jack asked if a "Christmas with Lady Cate" competition was in the cards. Mr. Fraser joked that he'd likely win, so perhaps they should consider having his name engraved on the trophy before it was sent. They shared a hearty laugh. Cate helped clean up following dinner, as much as Mrs. Fraser permitted her. She gathered both dogs, retiring to her sitting room to enjoy a movie before turning in for the night.

CHAPTER 19

Cate rose before the sun the next morning. She paced the floor of her sitting room, leaving Riley and Bailey sleeping in the bedroom. She planned her trip for today. Jack hadn't mentioned glimpsing the globe they presumed was the murder weapon yesterday. Perhaps in the excitement of the encounter with Andrew he had forgotten. Or perhaps he hadn't found it anywhere in the castle. If the latter was true, they needed to explore that further today.

Cate settled onto her chaise. The sun was peeking over the horizon. Clouds dotted the sky, diffusing and reflecting the sun's rays. When the sun made its debut, Cate rose, dressing for the day and shuttling the pups outside before breakfast.

Jack met Cate in the library following breakfast. After Jack informed her he had not seen the suspected murder weapon, they discussed the plan for their morning visit. They would keep to the shadows, searching for any clue they could find. Cate suggested they split up to explore. Jack reminded Cate they were not supposed to be traipsing around the castle alone after the incident yesterday. Not agreeing, Cate argued they had a better chance of being caught if they spent more time there. Jack agreed to consider the idea. They planned to meet in a few hours in the usual spot.

Cate took a morning walk, playing fetch with Riley and teaching the game to Bailey. Time crawled as Cate waited for her trip. As mid-morning approached, Cate placed the pups in her sitting room occupied with bones provided by Mrs. Fraser. Despite their plan to stay hidden, Cate dressed for the olden era and fixed her hair in case anyone spotted them. Afterwards, she met Jack in the bedroom closet. They slowed the watch, slipping backward to a bygone time.

After a few minutes of spirited, whispered arguments, Jack ceded that they would split up to investigate. Cate was pleased to have won the argument, having a plan she was certain Jack would not approve of. Cate would peek around the upstairs, while Jack would check the downstairs again. They would meet back in the closet in thirty minutes.

Sneaking into the hallway, they parted ways. Cate poked around a few upstairs rooms where she was almost certain not to find anyone. She found nothing of interest and spotted no sign of the murder weapon.

Cate stood at the bottom of the turret stairs. She stared up, sighing, fingering the tower key she held around her neck. This may be disastrous, she conjectured. What did she expect to find? What would she do if she found someone inside? How would she explain? She would answer those questions when and if the situation faced her.

One by one, Cate climbed the stairs to the turret. Each step she took solidified her resolve. She must open the tower door and determine what or who waited inside. She also needed to determine if the murder weapon was in that room. As she rounded the bend, the tower door loomed ahead of her.

She paused for a moment, second guessing her plan. She shook her head, shaking away any doubt. Setting her jaw, she plodded up the remaining stairs. She tried the doorknob. It was locked. A shaky hand grasped the key, pulling it from around her neck. She inserted it into the lock. As she turned the key, a voice boomed behind her.

"Oi! What do you think you're doing there?" Hastily, Cate grabbed the key from the lock, hanging it around her neck and tucking it into her dress before turning to face the voice's owner. An indignant Andrew was storming up the steps.

"I… I…" Cate stammered.

"You what, Mrs. MacKenzie?" he demanded, meeting her on the landing.

Cate swallowed hard. "I thought I heard a noise, someone crying," Cate lied.

"And you took it upon yourself to investigate it, roaming through someone else's home uninvited?"

"Not someone's. My family's," Cate reminded him.

"Your husband's family. Mrs. MacKenzie, you are not a member of this household regardless of your husband's relationship to Lord MacKenzie. You should not be poking your nose where it is not welcome," Andrew barked. He grabbed Cate's arm roughly, dragging her down the stairs. "Now…" he began when they reached the bottom of the stairs.

"Excuse me," a new voice shouted, "unhand my wife, sir!" Jack marched toward them.

"Your wife, sir," he said, emphasizing the last word and dropping Cate's arm, "has been skulking around the castle. Again. I caught her at the tower door."

"I would hardly call it skulking. My cousin, Lord MacKenzie, has given us free access to the property, including the castle. You have no business telling either of us where we are or are not permitted," Jack argued.

"Yes," Cate added, "what are you hiding up there?"

Andrew gave them an annoyed stare accompanied by a smirk. "I'm merely stating that you, madam, should take care when roaming the estate. You may find yourself in harm's way."

"I don't appreciate the veiled threat," Jack retorted.

"No threat at all, sir, just friendly advice. Now if you will excuse me, I have several duties to attend to." Andrew turned on a heel, climbing the steps to the tower.

"Thanks," Cate said, glancing up at Jack.

"Let's go," Jack said, motioning for her to precede him down the hall.

Cate acquiesced without a word, plodding down the hall and back to the closet. Together, they reset the watch to normal speed, returning to their own time. Once back, Jack could no longer contain his frustration. "Are you mad?" he shouted.

Cate sighed. "I'm sorry. I found nothing in the bedrooms. We need more information, information that's only in the tower room. They're hiding something there, something very important." Cate paced around the floor of the bedroom.

"Are you kidding me, Cate? Do you hear yourself? That man has threatened you, twice now! He caught you somewhere you shouldn't have been, manhandled you down the steps and who knows what he would have done next if I hadn't shown up. And all you can think about is what he's hiding?"

"Yes, all those things you mentioned means it must be something big! Besides, what were you doing there? You must have had the same idea I did."

"I doubt that. I finished downstairs and didn't see you anywhere upstairs. I suspected where you were. I hoped I was wrong, but I wasn't." Jack loosened his collar with a sigh.

"We need to go back tomorrow. Try to find something, anything out. We're two days away from the murder."

Jack breathed another sigh, shaking his head. "Cate, I really think we need to rethink this."

"We can't. We need to follow through. No tower runs this time, I promise. Let's go back and observe. We're so close to the murder, there's got to be some telltale signs. We have to use everything we know to get information."

Jack considered it. "Okay," Jack yielded. "But no more stunts. I'm serious, Cate."

Cate held her hands up in surrender. "I have that meeting with Mrs. Campbell tomorrow about the next party. We can go after lunch, mid-afternoon?"

"It's a plan."

They parted ways, Cate heading back to her suite to change and spend some time with Riley and Bailey. Despite the wonderful distractions the pups provided, Cate found herself unable to concentrate on anything but the impending murder. Tomorrow marked one day prior to the murder's occurrence. They were no closer to the solution. The only thing Cate had accomplished was making an enemy.

She put it out of her mind. There was nothing she could do tonight. She settled for the evening with a book and her two best friends.

CHAPTER 20

The next morning brought a thick fog to the area along with threatening clouds. The gloom matched Cate's mood. Their lack of progress frustrated her. She hoped to make more headway today.

First, though, she had a party planning meeting with Mrs. Campbell. The librarian and historical society president wanted to capitalize on the rousing success of the Halloween ball. With the momentum of the previous party still rolling, Mrs. Campbell wanted to nail down a few details and get an announcement released pronto.

Party planning exhausted Cate, however, she knew it was a positive event for the town. Plus, she loved sharing the castle with others, even if it was for only one night. She met Mrs. Campbell at the front door, prepared for her fifteen-minute-early arrival.

Mrs. Campbell bustled into the house, carrying an armful of materials. "Lady Cate!" she exclaimed. "You were so right to postpone this meeting until mid-week! It gave me a plethora of time to research and plan. My mind is just overflowing with ideas. Not only for 'Christmas with Lady Cate'!

What about 'New Year with our Newest MacKenzie,' or 'Cupid and Lady Cate,' the first day of spring celebration, Burns' day. There is no end to my list."

Cate's eyes grew wide at the last statement. Still, the woman's enthusiasm was becoming contagious. "Well, it sounds like we have quite a bit to talk about then!"

Cate led her to the library, and Mrs. Campbell spread her materials across the desk. "Let's start with the Christmas party. I'm thinking plaid!" Mrs. Campbell spent the next two hours discussing dates, details, décor, and announcements for the Christmas event. They wrapped up discussing the potential for a few other events, to which Cate agreed.

The meeting was productive. Her mind hadn't dwelled on the centuries-old mystery for the entire meeting, a surprise to Cate. She found herself eager to host another party. Mrs. Campbell's design ideas were splendid and Cate was sure the castle would, once again, look stunning.

Mrs. Campbell took her leave just before lunch with a long to-do list. An equally long list existed on Cate's end. Cate glanced at the list. She chuckled, sure that the work involved on this list would be preferable to Jack than his next task on the estate.

Cate pocketed the list, planning how to broach the topic during lunchtime conversation. Luckily for her, the topic arose when Mrs. Fraser asked about her meeting with Mrs. Campbell. Cate launched into the bevy of details provided by Mrs. Campbell. She produced the list of items. Jack and Mr. Fraser perused the list, glancing at each other after a moment.

"It sounds lovely to me, Lady Cate! And Molly will be here for the party, she'll be so pleased!" Mrs. Fraser exclaimed.

"Yes! She will be thrilled!" Cate noticed the glance shared between the two men. She raised her eyebrows at them.

"Is she serious about number four?" Jack asked.

"I told her we'd need to consider whether that was a practical option."

Jack read it from the list. "Snow machine in the event it doesn't snow?!?!"

Cate shrugged. "She wants all the magic and majesty of a Bing Crosby White Christmas."

"I'll hope for snow," Jack answered.

"Me, too," Cate admitted.

"It doesn't matter to me if there's snow or not. Not eating my own cooking is magic enough for me!" Mrs. Fraser laughed.

"Speaking of, I thought perhaps we should consider a catered meal on Christmas Day, too! I'd like everyone to have the holiday off."

"That sounds lovely, Lady Cate. Leave it to me," Mrs. Fraser said, "I know where we can get a good Christmas meal."

"Okay," Cate agreed. "I'll cross that off my list. Sorry to add to yours!"

"'Tis nothing, Lady Cate," Mrs. Fraser assured her. "Do you think we'll be having guests in the castle again?"

"I'm not sure. I plan to invite Mr. Smythe and Gayle, but given that it's Christmas, they may prefer to spend it at home."

"Well, you just let me know and I'll plan accordingly," Mrs. Fraser said, patting her hand.

They finished their lunch, speaking further about some other details that would need taken care of before the party. The event was two months away. They would need to sort out details on their end soon. They planned to meet on Thursday afternoon to go over design ideas and sort out decorations already at the castle.

After lunch, Cate took the dogs for a short walk before

returning to her bedroom to dress for her trip to 1856. She had no plan, unusual for her, but planning hadn't helped her in the past. She hoped to find something, anything before the party tomorrow night and subsequent murder.

She hated feeling this helpless, but she was determined to press on. After dressing, she met Jack in the closet. They slowed the watch, returning to 1856. Sneaking down a set of backstairs, they exited the castle and made their way to the front.

"It makes me nervous that we don't have a plan," Jack said, knocking on the door.

"I know what you mean, but I'm not sure what we can do except observe and gather more information," Cate said with a shrug. "We're so close to the murder, something, anything may be a clue or tip us off. We just need to keep our eyes and ears open."

"I like that. Observe only, good idea," Jack said as the door opened.

"Ah, Mr. and Mrs. MacKenzie," Thomson said. "Please come in." They entered the foyer. "I shall announce your arrival."

"We're not expected, I hope it's not an inconvenience," Jack said.

"I'm sure it won't be. You're family, sir. You can wait in the sitting room."

Cate and Jack moved to the sitting room to wait as Thomson announced their arrival. They didn't have long to wait, Randolph soon joined them.

"Jack, Catherine, lovely to see you," Randolph said, striding toward them to shake Jack's hand and kiss Cate's.

"My apologies, we come unannounced. My wife has borrowed one of your books and wanted to return it as soon as she had finished."

Randolph waved his hand at them. "Think nothing of it,

you're family, family is always welcome." Randolph poured drinks for the men as Victoria entered the room, hurrying to Cate to give her a hug and kiss. "You have missed little, my dear, just our cousins apologizing for disturbing our peace."

"You are never disturbing us," Victoria assured them.

"We apologize for coming unannounced. But I have finished with the book I borrowed and wanted to return it."

"You needn't make a special trip, but I will not object as I do love to see you," Victoria said, ringing the bell on the wall to alert the servants of a request.

"Truth be told," Cate said, "I hoped to return this and select another."

"By all means! I must make time to read, as you do, Catherine," Victoria said, as Thomson entered the room. "Thomson, please bring some tea for myself and Mrs. MacKenzie."

"Right away, Lady MacKenzie," Thomson said, leaving the room.

The foursome made polite conversation, discussing the upcoming ball. Excitement was building for the festivities. They made plans for Cate and Jack to arrive early so Cate could dress at the castle. Victoria insisted this was most convenient for Cate. Tea arrived, delivered by Andrew, who seemed surprised to see Cate and Jack. He offered a fleeting smile that resembled more of a smirk as he set the tray down near Victoria.

When they finished tea, Victoria ushered Cate upstairs to show her the necklace she planned to wear, a new gift from Randolph for the occasion. Jack seized the opportunity to excuse Randolph from playing host. "Well, I shan't keep you any longer, cousin. I'm capable to wait for my wife's return on my own. I'm sure you have business to attend to."

Randolph checked his watch. "Yes, if you don't mind

waiting alone, I do have something pressing that requires my attention."

"Not at all, cousin."

"I dare say though, you may be in for a long wait. I fear ladies discussing clothing and jewelry may take longer than discussions in the House of Lords!" Randolph roared with laughter at his own joke before disappearing through the door.

Jack smiled as he left. Randolph might be correct. Either way, it gave him a chance to take one last peek around. He had detected nothing that hinted at the upcoming tragedy.

Cate and Victoria scurried down the hall in a cloud of giggles. Neither noticed Andrew on the servant's stairway. Victoria steered her to her suite. A large jewelry case sat on a table. Victoria hastened to it. "Wait until you see it, cousin Catherine. It is simply marvelous!" She opened the case. The necklace gleamed and sparkled. In the center of the necklace was a large ruby. Smaller rubies decorated the sides. The piece was spectacular.

"Oh! Victoria, it's beautiful!"

"Isn't it?" Victoria giggled. "And it is a perfect match for the red dress I planned for the ball. It seems Randolph pays attention when I speak! He has matched the stone perfectly!"

"It will look exquisite with your dress!"

There was a knock at the door. "Come in!" Andrew entered the room. "Andrew? What did you need?"

"I apologize for the interruption. Mrs. MacKenzie, I believe you may have dropped this." He handed her a small slip of paper.

"Oh, how kind. Thank you, Andrew," Cate said, accepting the paper. "I am so clumsy!"

"Thank you, Andrew," Victoria said, dismissing him. He

exited the room with a curt smile. Cate shoved the note into her purse, feigning admiration for the necklace a few more moments. After a polite amount of time, Cate excused herself, expressing her excitement for the upcoming ball and telling Victoria that she would show herself to the library to select another book.

Cate embraced Victoria then left the room. She traveled downstairs to the library, hastily returning the book before digging the paper out of her purse. She read the note.

Catherine– I must see you, it's urgent. Meet me at the loch at 3:30.

-Randolph

Cate dug the timepiece from the folds of her dress, checking the time. It was almost 3:30 p.m. already. Cate huffed, gathering up her skirts and fleeing from the library to the nearest exit door. The note slipped from her hands, fluttering to the floor as she raced from the room to meet Randolph.

Once outside, Cate ran down the path toward the loch. As she approached, she saw no one. She hurried toward the loch, hoping she hadn't missed him. Perhaps this was the break she had been waiting for. She couldn't lose this opportunity.

She approached the edge of the loch, out of breath. She panted, scanning the area for Randolph. As she turned, a figure raced toward her side. It was Andrew. Before she could react, Andrew grabbed her by the arms. "You really don't know when to stop, do you, Mrs. MacKenzie?"

"Let go of me," Cate yelled, struggling.

"I've got a good thing going here. I will not allow you to ruin it for me!" he shouted.

"What thing is that?" Cate demanded.

"I told you to mind your own business. You couldn't do that, could you?" he roared at her, backing her toward the loch.

Cate struggled, but she was no match for him, especially in this clothing. "Let go," she cried. Step by step, he pushed her back toward the loch. Her feet splashed into the icy water. The bottom of her dress soaked through as it swirled over the water's edge. She struggled to push back onto the bank, but she was engaged in a losing battle. The water crept further up her legs as the bank descended.

"You are a problem, Mrs. MacKenzie. Now, you won't be," he growled. He gave her a massive shove, toppling her backward into the loch. Cate expected the bottom to be nearer than it was. There was a steep drop-off in the loch's bed behind where she had been standing. She lost her footing as she toppled backward, icy cold water surrounded her. Clawing at the water, she struggled to stay afloat. She kicked her legs, but they became entangled in the fabric of her slips and skirts. The dress weighed heavier and heavier on her as the water penetrated the fabric. She thrashed wildly for a moment before she slipped below the surface. She reached toward the light as she sunk further.

CHAPTER 21

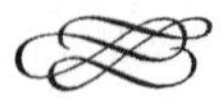

Suddenly, the surface of the loch came closer. Hands grabbed her, and she was pulled upward. She broke through the surface, gasping for air. She was dragged ashore, still gasping and choking. "Cate! Cate! Are you all right?" Jack asked, looming over her as she laid on the loch's bank.

She gulped a few last breaths of air before nodding her head. "Yes," she said, still catching her breath. "I'm okay." She sat up after a moment. Jack fell backwards onto the bank, soaked through, a heavy sigh escaping his lips. "Thank you," Cate murmured. She took another moment to catch her breath before saying, "Lucky you found me when you did."

"Aye, damn lucky. If I wasn't so relieved you're alive, I would let you have it for sneaking off like that. No splitting up, remember?"

"Yes, I remember. But I got a note from Randolph. Well, that's what it said, anyway. It told me to meet him at the loch and I had no time to find you."

"I know. I found the note on the library floor when I was poking around. I came as quickly as I could. Not fast enough to stop that bastard from tossing you into the loch, but at least fast enough to stop him from killing you. Cate, you've got to be more careful!"

"I know, I know," Cate conceded, acknowledging the foolishness of her actions. "I'm sorry. I wasn't thinking." She wrung the fabric of her dress out as best as possible. "I suppose we should get back. I'd like to get home and change into something warm and dry."

"Me, too. Assuming we still can, that is."

"Why wouldn't..." Cate began before the realization struck her. "THE WATCH!" she shouted.

"Aye, the watch," Jack answered.

She pulled it from the folds of her dress. She clicked open the cover. The second hand ticked ever-so-slowly, but it still ticked. "It's still working, hopefully it's not damaged."

"Let's not wait to find out. Let's go," Jack said, standing and offering her a hand to right herself. "Let's go before it breaks."

"Okay," she agreed, accepting his help. They hastened to the castle, into a back entrance, up to the closet and prayed as they rubbed the timepiece. Cate breathed a sigh of relief as it sped up. "Oh, I hope that worked and we're home," she said as the timepiece ticked normally.

"Only one way to find out," Jack said.

They left the closet. Cate ran down the hall to her bedroom suite. If they were home, she should find two small dogs waiting for her there. She burst through the double doors. Two tiny pups lifted their heads, eyeing her. Cate beamed at them. "Riley! Bailey!" she cried. Both dogs ran to her. She knelt on the floor, gathering them into her arms. "We're back!"

"Thank heavens," Jack said behind her.

Cate agreed. "At least we haven't broken the watch."

"It may be better if we had."

"No. We still have the murder to solve and Randolph's reputation to save!" Cate said, standing.

"Yes, I realize that. But I'm less happy about it now than I was before. This is becoming dangerous and we've taken a reckless chance that may have stranded us in the 1800s!"

"It's more dangerous because we're on to something!" Cate said. "What is in that tower room that has Andrew so apprehensive that he's willing to kill for it?"

"I can't believe you're still so interested even after what happened," Jack said, shaking his head. "Oh, Lady Cate, I'll never figure you out."

Cate turned serious. "To be honest, I am still shaken by it. I guess it's how I deal with anything unpleasant, throw myself into the 'research' I'm working on."

"That, my dear Lady Cate, is called avoidance." Jack grinned. "I'm going to get out of these wet clothes. You should do the same." Jack walked to the door, turning back to face Cate before exiting. "M'lady," he said, with a grand bow.

Cate shook her head at him. "Jack," she said before he left.

"Yeah?"

"Thanks again. You're a lifesaver."

"Oh, that's a terrible joke, Lady Cate, just terrible."

She grinned sticking her tongue out at him as he left.

Cate was never so glad to get out of her period clothing as she was today. She laid the outfit and its undergarments out in her bathroom to dry and re-dressed in a warm sweater and a pair of leggings.

She spent the rest of the afternoon cuddled under a thick blanket enjoying a movie on her laptop. She attempted to read, but found herself unable to focus, her mind dwelling on the frightening incident from earlier in the day and the impending murder. The notion struck her she may have died before she was even born. The ripple effect of her untimely death may have stranded Jack in 1856.

Much of her consternation centered on her inability to stop the inevitable. If she couldn't prevent the murder, what else was she powerless to stop? Were their trips to the past going to achieve anything? Would she be able to salvage anything of Randolph's reputation or prevent him from going to jail?

Cate concluded she could only do her best. She had to try. Perhaps being present on the night of the murder would offer her some clue as to why Randolph had confessed or what circumstances prompted the murder to begin with. If she couldn't prevent it or prevent Randolph's confession, at least, perhaps, she could understand why Randolph confessed. Until tomorrow evening, she'd have to wait, wonder and worry.

CHAPTER 22

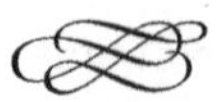

Cate spent a restless night and morning pacing the floor of her suite. The day crawled by with Cate checking her watch often. She spent lunch and the better part of her afternoon re-reading all the materials she had gathered on the murder and the trial. She wanted to have a firm grasp on all the details so she could recognize any potential clues.

After what seemed an eternity, the moment for Cate to ready herself arrived. She eyed her previous dress as she slid on her underskirts. It still lay spread out on several towels, drying, still damp from her excursions yesterday. The sight gave Cate a jittery stomach. She was less shaken than she had been yesterday, but the incident was still disturbing. As was the idea a murder would occur in the castle while she was present.

She chased the doubt from her mind as she slid her dress on and fastened it. She put the final touches on her hair and clothes before giving her two pups a hug and kiss and leaving them in her bedroom. She met Jack in their usual spot. Jack was carrying a garment bag with his formal attire for the evening.

"Ready?" she asked.

"As I'll ever be. You?"

"I think so! I'm nervous, I'll admit, but I am ready."

"Then away we go!!" Jack said, placing his hand over hers to slow the watch.

Within ten minutes they had arrived in 1856, snuck out of the castle and were being greeted at the front door. They were ushered into the castle and Cate was shown to Victoria's suite, while Jack was offered a separate bedroom to change. The castle was abuzz with activity, reminiscent of Cate's own party. Servants bustled here and there, preparing for the onslaught of guests to arrive.

Victoria was in a dressing gown as Cate entered her room. "Ah, cousin Catherine!" she exclaimed, leaping from her seat to embrace Cate. "I thought you'd never arrive! I must confess, I've been a ball of nerves all day. I'm like this before all my parties. Oh, I do hope the party is a success."

Cate was heartsick. Victoria was brimming with excitement, yet Cate knew the tragic end to the party that awaited them. She also knew the fate of the family members she had gotten to know and care for. Randolph would be sentenced to prison. Victoria would become a recluse after the investigation, trial and sentencing of Randolph. Ethan would grow up without a father.

Cate pasted a smile on her face and tried to match Victoria's excitement. "I have been excited all day!"

Victoria hugged her again, squealing with excitement. "Let's have some champagne!" Victoria poured two flutes from a bottle chilling nearby. She handed one to Cate and took a sip from her own. Cate took a sip of champagne as Victoria guided her to the dressing table. "Come, let's get you ready! Bryson!" she called, "Bryson!" She sat Cate down. "What are you thinking about your hair?" She fussed with a few locks. "I'm thinking let a few locks flow down like this. What do you think?"

"Pretty! I've never worn it like that!"

"Oh, Jack will be surprised! He'll love it! He won't be able to take his eyes off you!" Victoria winked at her.

Cate smiled back, hoping the sadness she felt didn't creep into her expression. "Bryson, here's what we're thinking. You can do that, can't you?"

"Oh, I can try," Cate offered.

"Nonsense! Bryson is a fabulous hair stylist. Relax and let her work her magic!" Victoria sunk into an armchair across the room, sipping champagne, as Bryson began her work on Cate's hair. Her deft ability impressed Cate. She had Cate's hair swept into the updo Victoria suggested much faster than Cate could have.

"How is that, m'lady?" Bryson asked Victoria.

"Excellent! Yes!" Victoria approached Cate. She fussed a bit with the style then agreed it was what she had envisioned. "Now, time for the dresses! Oh, yours first, yours first!"

Cate gave a genuine smile. She was excited to wear the dress again. Sincere excitement filled her as Bryson brought the dress over. Cate was unaccustomed to being dressed by a ladies' maid. More to the point, she was unaccustomed to being undressed by a ladies' maid. Cate found it awkward to be undressed with multiple people milling around the room. She sipped more champagne to ease her nerves.

"Oh, we should have planned for you to stay the night. I hate to think of you having to collect your belongings and carry them home."

"We'll be fine," Cate said. "Don't give it another thought."

"At least let us send you in a carriage."

"Nonsense," Cate argued. "We'll be fine. I am an American, after all. We excel at this!"

"Let's postpone this discussion until after the party," Victoria said, not willing to give in. "Oh, that color looks just lovely on you!"

Cate glanced in the mirror. The dress, still unfastened, hung around her frame. The sapphire color was flattering against her creamy skin. Victoria's selection was spot on. Bryson finished fastening the dress. Cate twirled in the dress. "What do you think?"

"It's perfection! Now, the necklace!" Victoria fetched it from a nearby jewelry box and placed it around Cate's neck. "The final touch! Stunning!"

Cate smiled. "Your turn!" she said, turning to Victoria, grinning. Cate switched places with Victoria, taking a seat in the armchair, sipping the rest of her champagne.

"That color is beautiful!" Cate said, admiring the red dress. "It complements your skin so well!"

"Isn't it? Yes, it is a good shade for my coloring. I was not blessed with the creamy complexion you have, Catherine."

Cate refrained from laughing, having always hated her pale skin. As Bryson finished fastening Victoria's dress, Cate spied the necklace box on the dressing table. She set down her champagne flute and retrieved the necklace from the box. "Now, your finishing touch!" she exclaimed, placing the necklace around Victoria's neck.

"Thank you! Come, look in the mirror," Victoria said, pulling her next to her so they were both in front of the mirror.

"Beautiful ladies!" Bryson chimed in from behind them.

"Thank you!" they answered in unison.

"Oh, Catherine, I'm so excited!" Victoria squealed,

squeezing Cate's hands. A knock on the door interrupted them from further conversation. "Yes?" Victoria called.

"May we enter?" Randolph answered.

"Oh, just a moment!" Victoria called back. She reached to her dressing table, snatching a bottle of perfume. "Here," she said, spraying some on Cate and then herself. "Now we are ready!" she called.

The door swung open and Jack and Randolph strode into the room. "Well, if these aren't two angels descended straight from heaven in front of us, cousin." He took Victoria by the hands, admiring her, then kissing her cheek. "You look lovely, my dear. Simply lovely."

"Thank you, husband. How kind. And how handsome you are!" Victoria answered.

Jack made his attempt to follow suit. "So, this is the infamous dress. It has lived up to its potential. You look beautiful, Catherine." He kissed her cheek. Cate held in a giggle at his act.

"Thank you. I must thank Victoria for the necklace, it's a perfect match!"

"Oh, it pales when compared to your beauty, cousin Catherine!" Randolph said. "Well…" he checked his watch, "we should proceed downstairs. Guests will arrive soon! Shall we?" he offered Victoria his arm. She accepted. Jack followed suit and Cate threaded her arm through his. They followed Victoria and Randolph to the ballroom.

"The ballroom looks lovely, Victoria," Cate said as they entered. The room was decorated in black lace with red accents. An orchestra group set up, testing their instruments. The sudden realization that Cate and Jack lacked any dancing skills for this era hit her. Her passing knowledge of a waltz would be no match for the attendees. She hoped to keep off the dance floor as much as possible.

Victoria checked with the staff, fussed over the décor and

then returned. "I suppose it's passable," she said in answer to Cate.

"Nervous, darling?" Randolph asked her.

"As always, yes," she admitted. "I want to make tonight a success."

"I'm sure it will be, my dear. Now, we should ready ourselves to receive guests. They should arrive any moment now."

Cate removed herself from blocking the entry way, dragging Jack behind Victoria and Randolph so they could greet their guests first. She noticed Andrew across the room, delivering a few items from the kitchen. He did a double take when he spotted her before turning on a heel to leave. Nervous butterflies rattled in Cate's stomach at the sight of him. On one hand, the prospect of facing the man who almost drowned her overwhelmed her. On the other hand, she felt pity and sorrow for him, knowing his fate.

"Your friend looks happy to see you," Jack whispered, also noticing Andrew's reaction.

"Yes, he seems downright tickled," Cate answered.

"Don't go sneaking off anywhere out of my sight."

"Don't worry, I won't," Cate agreed.

"Good, it'd be a terrible shame to ruin that dress."

Cate gave him a light smack with the back of her hand then changed the subject as the first few guests arrived. "It's interesting, though, to see the similarities and differences between our Halloween ball and theirs."

"Lucky for us, the biggest difference was no one was killed at ours."

Cate nodded in agreement but said no more as Randolph and Victoria called them over to introduce them to their first batch of arrivals. As more guests poured in, Cate and Jack stayed close to their hosts to be introduced to other guests.

Once most introductions were complete and the influx of

guests died down, the foursome separated, moving around the room to mingle. Victoria wanted Cate to chat further with old friends from London. She ushered Cate around the room skillfully, entering and exiting conversations like a professional. Cate was impressed. After a few hours at her own party, she had been exhausted from playing social butterfly. Victoria seemed to thrive on it.

Cate attempted to keep an eye out for any strange occurrences despite the dizzying array of conversations she enjoyed. In particular, she paid careful attention to Randolph's whereabouts. Knowledge of his whereabouts were crucial for Cate to determine if he was innocent.

She spotted him moving through the guests across the room, Jack in tow. He must be introducing Jack to guests as Victoria was with Cate. Good, Cate thought, Jack will be able to account for Randolph's location for a large part of the party.

While Cate and Victoria conversed with a duchess, the name and lineage of which Cate had already forgotten, Randolph and Jack approached, providing refreshments for both ladies.

Cate wanted to swap notes with Jack. She checked the time, there was only one and a half hours remaining before the body would be discovered. Jack's glass was half-full. Cate tried to signal with her eyes for him to finish it. After a few attempts, he understood, downed his drink and announced that he needed to retrieve another. He offered to return with refreshments for anyone else, but no one needed a refresher. Cate excused herself with him.

"I didn't think you would ever pick up on that," she said as they walked away.

"Your skills at charades are weak, Lady Cate."

They retrieved a new drink for Jack and retreated to a

corner to talk. "Well?" Cate said, monitoring the party. "Anything interesting on your end?"

"Nothing of note. I've heard enough about land deals, the House of Lords, and almost everyone asked me if my wife knew anything about the impending conflict in the States. But no hints why someone will soon be murdered."

"Randolph was never away from you, right?"

"Never. What about on your end?"

"I heard less than you! All my talk was about marriages, births, parties and clothing. Oh and one discussion about the best painter for a handsome portrait."

"Do you think Victoria may have killed him? And Randolph covered for her?" Jack asked. "He seems protective of her."

"But why?" Cate questioned, as they watched Randolph and Victoria laughing with a group of friends. "It doesn't fit her personality at all and she doesn't seem to have much to hide. In fact, she seems an open book in the discussions I've had with her."

"I just can't figure out who else he'd be covering for if he didn't do it."

"I don't know. It must deal with that mysterious woman in the tower. Now would be a perfect time to meet her but we can't leave the party."

"And we will NOT split up," Jack insisted.

"No, you're right. I don't want to end up thrown down the tower stairs by Andrew. I'd end up dead before I was born!"

Further conversation was stunted when Randolph tapped his glass, signaling everyone to silence. A hush fell over the room. Randolph shouted from the center of the room, "Welcome everyone to our first Halloween Ball!" The crowd responded with applause. Randolph waited for them to die down before continuing. "My wife, the beautiful Victoria, and I are so glad you could join us! I would like to take a moment to thank each of you for joining us on this chilly October evening. From those of you who traveled from afar to those of you who live in our own town, we are so pleased to have you at Dunhaven Castle! Now, I won't drone on and on, but I want to take one more moment to recognize the efforts of my exquisite and magnificently talented wife, Victoria, who put all this together. Victoria, my dear, you have outdone yourself. This ball will be remembered for years." The last statement was like a knife to Cate's heart. How haunting those words were just one hour before a murder. "Please everyone, let's raise a glass to my beloved Victoria," Randolph continued. Everyone raised their glass. "And now, without further ado, let's dance!"

The room burst into applause. Animated conversation reignited, and the orchestra readied to play their first waltz. Randolph led Victoria to the middle of the floor to begin the dancing. Cate and Jack inched toward the wall, hoping to avoid the dance floor.

Cate glanced at Jack. "I'm hoping to avoid any dancing," she said, "I imagine it would be a dead giveaway that we're not from this century."

"No kidding. I've got no idea what they're doing," Jack chuckled.

"At least we can easily account for Randolph's whereabouts!"

Cate and Jack kept to the outskirts of the room for several dances. After a few rounds, Randolph and Victoria, who had switched partners several times, approached.

"Wallflowers, are we?" Randolph asked as he approached.

"I'm sorry to say we are," Jack admitted.

"Oh, surely, cousin Jack, you'll dance with your lovely wife!" Victoria said.

"I think she'd prefer I didn't. I've two left feet, and her toes would never survive it!"

Cate nodded in agreement. "I'm happy to watch the fun," she added.

"Nonsense, cousin Catherine!" Randolph exclaimed. "I shall have the next dance and I shall not step on your toes!"

"Oh, really, that's not..." Cate began.

"Now, I won't take no for an answer," Randolph insisted, taking Cate's hand and pulling her to the dance floor.

"Don't worry, cousin Catherine, I'll keep Jack company while I rest for the next round!" Victoria laughed, waving her on.

A wide-eyed Cate issued a panicked glance toward Jack as Randolph swept her away. Randolph led her to the center of the floor. "I'm not much of a dancer..." she began.

"Poppycock! Follow my lead, you'll be fine. This one is easy, I shall show you. If you don't catch on, we shall simply tell everyone dancing in America is altogether different! Place your hand just so. Excellent! And off we go. Just like this. One, two, three, one, two, three, one, two, three and turn, one, two, three, one, two, three, that's the way." While Cate was less than perfect, Randolph made it easy, as promised, whisking her around the floor. Cate relished the experience, grinning from ear to ear as she improved with practice. It was as enjoyable as promised and Cate was sad for the dance to end. She applauded, curtsying to her partner while still breathless from the experience.

Randolph began to speak to Cate but was interrupted. Andrew approached, whispering in Randolph's ear before disappearing. "Please excuse me, cousin Catherine," Randolph uttered, appearing distracted, "there is something urgent I must attend to."

"By all means," Cate managed as Randolph turned to leave. Peering around, she spotted Jack in their favorite corner. Victoria was being led to the dance floor by a new dance partner. Cate widened her eyes to signal Jack to follow her.

"What's up?" he asked, joining her as she scurried to keep up with Randolph.

"Andrew just said something to Randolph. He seemed agitated and excused himself to attend to 'urgent business.' Something's up, we need to follow him."

"Did you see where he went?"

"Yes, down this hall. There!" Cate pointed to a light streaming from an open door.

Jack nodded, holding a finger to his lips. They crept toward the open door. As they approached, they overheard loud voices from within.

"... will NOT continue to be threatened in my own home!" Randolph shouted.

"Don't look like you've got much choice the way I see it," Andrew answered.

"Do not presume to tell me what I have and haven't," Randolph blasted back.

"What you have is a secret whore," Andrew snarled.

"How dare you, sir!" Randolph retorted.

"How dare I? How dare I? How dare YOU! Asking me to wait on your whore, fetching her this and that, all the while asking me to keep quiet about it. And nothing in it for me." There was a scuffle. Cate moved to peer through the crack in the door. Randolph had Andrew by the collar.

"Now you listen to me you sorry excuse for a human, this ends tonight! I shall pay you what you ask and you shall vacate this property and never return."

Andrew squirmed from his grasp. "You'd turn me out on the street given the information I have on you? That wouldn't be wise."

Randolph smirked. "Any tale you tell now will be the sour

grapes of a released staff member. No one will believe you. Now collect your things and go AFTER you've attended to Sonia."

"You're making a huge mistake, friend. You've no idea the lengths I'll go to to protect what's mine. Just ask Catherine MacKenzie."

With that he spun and exited the room. Cate pushed Jack backward, flattening him against the wall. In his rage, Andrew stormed past them, never noticing them in the shadows.

"Do we follow him or stay with Randolph?" Cate questioned.

"He looks like he's going to the kitchen, we can't very well go there…" Jack began when a figure loomed at the door.

Randolph stood in the doorway, spotting them in the shadows. "Catherine… Jack…" he stumbled, trying to compose himself, "I must apologize for my prolonged absence. I hope I haven't been missed."

"Randolph…" Jack began.

Cate pushed Randolph back inside the room. "Randolph, we must speak with you. We overheard your conversation with Andrew. He must leave the house now!"

"Catherine," Randolph questioned, "what is the meaning of this?"

"Perhaps you should be the one explaining that. What is the problem with Andrew? We saw you the other day at the loch and overheard you tonight. What is he threatening you with? Who is Sonia?" Cate fired questions at him.

"I can't answer those questions, Catherine, I'm sorry."

"Damn it, Randolph, now isn't the time to be tight-lipped!" Cate exclaimed.

Randolph appeared shocked at Cate's forthrightness. "She's only trying to help, Randolph," Jack chimed in. "We need the answers to those questions."

"Why? What do you know?"

Cate glanced at Jack, rubbing her forehead in frustration. "Nothing we can share," Jack responded.

"I'm afraid I'm the same with nothing to share. But perhaps you can answer this. Why did my footman suggest I ask you about the lengths he's willing to go to in order to protect what's his?"

Cate sighed as Jack began, "We can't…"

Cate interrupted him. "He pushed me into the loch yesterday after catching me wandering in the castle a few times. I almost drowned. I was lucky, Jack pulled me out before anything happened to me."

"My God, Catherine! Are you alright? You should have informed me at once!"

"It's difficult to explain. I don't… this time traveling is so difficult to navigate. You must accept there are things we can't share with you."

Randolph considered her statement for a moment. "I understand. But I ask you to offer me the same consideration."

They were at a stalemate, neither side willing to reveal additional information. "I've relieved him of his position. He'll soon be gone from this house, so he shan't be bothering you again." Cate's heart sank. She prayed that whatever she and Jack had done in the past had changed events enough that Randolph was correct. Her scientific side told her that wasn't the case, yet she still held on to hope. "Now, we should return to the party before we are missed."

Cate nodded in reluctant agreement. Checking a nearby clock, she noted that it was almost the time that the body would be discovered. Perhaps, in the end, they had avoided the horrible mess. "You go ahead without me, I need a moment. I'll be right behind you," Randolph said. Cate glanced at Jack again. "Now, go! I'll be fine!"

Cate and Jack acquiesced, exiting the room and heading toward the ballroom. "Do you suppose we should have left him?" Jack asked.

"I'm not sure we had a choice," Cate admitted. "It's almost time for the murder anyway, maybe we somehow avoided it." She shrugged, defeated for the moment.

They entered the ballroom, the party was still in full swing. Music filled the air accompanied by laughing and enthusiastic conversation from the revelers. Victoria approached them, smiling. "There you are! Have you seen Randolph? He seems to have disappeared." She scanned the crowd for him.

Cate plastered a smile on. "Oh, he was right behind us. We were discussing a painting and stepped out to view it. I'm afraid it was our fault! He should be here any moment."

"A painting?" Victoria questioned. "He left my ball for a painting?"

"Yes, a family portrait," Jack added. "My sincere apologies, Victoria. I'm afraid I was somewhat overzealous in asking about an ancestor. Randolph is a gracious host."

"Yes," Cate agreed. "Again, we're so very sorry for stealing him away!"

"No apology needed, dear cousins. I was hoping to have another dance with him though."

"I'm sure he'll be here any moment," Cate assured her. They waited together a few more moments before Victoria spotted him.

"Ah! There he is!" Victoria exclaimed. Randolph approached them, smiling, seeming unruffled. He kissed Victoria on the cheek.

"Viewing a painting while we have a ball occurring? Honestly, Randolph! You are such a terrible host!" Victoria teased.

"Well..." Randolph began, when he was interrupted. A

blood-curdling scream ripped through the air. The noise startled the guests, most of them grinding to a halt mid-dance. The band one-by-one stopped playing as another scream and shouts came from outside the ballroom.

One of the servants, who had run toward the scream, raced back inside toward Randolph. "M'lord, you had better come quick."

"What is it?" Victoria asked, concern crossing her face.

Cate and Jack shared a glance, knowing what awaited Randolph. "Stay with Victoria," Jack suggested, following Randolph and the servant outside. Cate waited behind, unhappy about her role, but unsure if she wanted to view the body. Within seconds, a limp form was carried through the door and sat in a chair. The woman, the source of the initial scream, had fainted dead away after realizing what her gaze had fallen upon while walking the gardens.

Victoria, Cate in tow, rushed to her side. "What's happened? Is she all right?"

"Merely fainted, Lady MacKenzie," her companion replied.

"Bring smelling salts and some brandy," Victoria ordered a staff member.

"Excuse me," Cate said, leaving her to attend to the unconscious guest.

Cate made her way to the gardens. She followed the path toward a small grouping of men that included Randolph and Jack. As she approached, she saw the limp form of Andrew sprawled in an unnatural pose. Blood pooled under him, his eyes stared straight ahead. Cate's stomach turned at the sight. She squeezed her eyes shut, blocking out the image.

"My God, Catherine!" Randolph shouted. "You shouldn't be here."

Jack turned and caught sight of her. "Cate! Catherine," he corrected, approaching her, "you don't want to see this, go inside." Cate nodded to him. "We'll talk later," he said, turning her away from the scene.

Cate returned to the ballroom. Victoria continued to hover over the ill woman, who was now recovering. As she startled back to consciousness, Victoria handed her a brandy to sip. The sobbing woman sipped the drink with a shaky hand. "What is it? What caused you to take such a turn?" Victoria asked, smoothing the woman's hair.

"Oh, it was simply awful! Too awful to speak about," she sobbed.

Victoria looked to her companion for an answer. Before he could provide it, Cate stepped between them. "Victoria, perhaps we should give her some room and discuss this in private."

"Discuss what? What has frightened poor Louise so? Why won't anyone tell me."

Cate tried her best to usher Victoria away from the growing scene, but she failed. Whispered turned to gasps, gasps to louder expressions of shock and horror. Cate pitied Victoria as Louise's companion informed her. "Why, m'lady, she saw a body. Someone has died this Hallow's Eve, fallen from the turret it looks like. It appeared to be one of your footmen."

"What?" Victoria gasped.

"Not died, murdered!" another guest chimed in.

Victoria swooned. Cate, along with a nearby gentleman steadied her. Randolph, Jack and several others rejoined the group. Victoria searched his face for answers. "Randolph?" she breathed, shaking her head in disbelief.

Randolph put his arms around her. "I'm sorry, my darling," he said, then raised his voice, "and I'm sorry to all our guests. There has been a tragedy tonight. I fear that young Andrew, one of our footmen, has met with an accident that cost him his life." Gasps rung throughout the room as

Randolph confirmed the rumor. "The police have been sent for. I ask that all of you please remain calm and within the ballroom until they have arrived. Thank you for your patience and please, despite the dreadful news, continue to enjoy the refreshments while you wait." He nodded to the staff to continue serving beverages to the rattled guests.

Victoria was beside herself. "How could this happen?" she questioned.

"Come, darling, please sit down." He guided her to a chair.

She sat on the chair before springing back up. "Oh, I should…" her voice trailed off, unable to suggest something suitable to do.

"Just rest, darling." Randolph soothed her. "The police will be here any moment."

"Are you all right?" Jack asked Cate.

"Yes, thank you. I'm fine. I wish I hadn't seen the body, but yes."

They kept a distance from the reeling Victoria so she did not overhear their conversation. "Did you spot anything of interest?" Cate inquired.

"Nothing more than we already know," Jack answered. "The fall didn't kill him, as we read."

"It's that obvious?"

"Yes," Jack said. "It was obvious."

"It couldn't…" Cate began when Randolph interrupted her.

"Catherine," he called, waving her over. Cate hastened to him with Jack following behind. "Could you please stay with Victoria? She's taking it rather poorly, I'm concerned. There are many things I should attend to, but I am reluctant to leave her."

"Certainly," Cate assured him. "Jack can help with anything you need."

"Thank you, both. Jack, please follow me."

Cate stepped toward Victoria, placing her arm around the woman's shoulder. She offered her a consoling smile, not able to offer much else in the way of comfort. "How could this happen?" Victoria asked.

Cate could offer no answers. Within a few more minutes, the first round of police arrived. They swept past the ballroom to the crime scene. Randolph and Jack, met them outside with a few other men. They conversed for several moments before two officers entered the ballroom.

"Good evening, everyone," one shouted to the crowd. "As you well know, a member of the MacKenzie staff has died this evening. We do not know the circumstances surrounding this death, it appears it may be accidental. Still, we should like to speak with each of you before you leave tonight. If you would please form two lines at the door, you will need to speak with one of us before leaving. Please form two lines, thank you! Please move in an orderly fashion, thank you!" The officer continued to instruct the partygoers until everyone had formed two lines and they commenced questioning the guests.

Victoria glanced up at the lines of her guests. The band had begun to gather their instruments and join the line. "Oh," Victoria moaned, her voice faltering, "oh, what a mess." Tears formed in her eyes.

"Victoria, perhaps we should remove ourselves from the commotion and retire to your suite. I'll inform the police of our location, you can rest," Cate suggested.

"Perhaps you are right, I feel lightheaded."

"Come, let's get you settled." Cate helped her from the chair. Along the way, she found Bryson, suggesting that the woman accompany them to help settle her mistress. Once in the privacy of Victoria's suite, Cate left her in Bryson's capable hands while she returned to the ballroom to help see guests off.

When the last guests departed, the police asked to speak with the staff then the family members. Randolph organized the staff to be questioned, offering them the night off from their clean-up if they did not feel up to the task given the circumstances.

Jack rejoined Cate for a moment. "We better get our stories straight. We only have a few moments."

"I plan to stick to the truth as much as I can," Cate answered. "We were with Randolph discussing a painting then returned to the party. A few minutes passed before we heard the scream."

"What about Andrew?"

"Nothing. I don't plan on mentioning our run-ins with him. We'd have little reason to have had many conversations with him. It shouldn't be a stretch."

"I agree. We say as little as possible."

Cate nodded as an officer approached them.

"Mr. and Mrs. MacKenzie, we'd like to speak with each of you. Perhaps Mrs. MacKenzie first so she may return to Lady MacKenzie and rest." Cate found the statement amusing despite the circumstances. She nodded her agreement. "If you'll follow me, Mrs. MacKenzie, you can have a seat right here."

Cate recounted her version of events to the officer. She left out any hint of conflict between Randolph and Andrew or herself and Andrew. "I'm so sorry to put you through this trouble, Mrs. MacKenzie," the officer whispered. "I don't have any further questions for you. If it wouldn't be too much trouble, could you show me to Lady MacKenzie's room so I may gather a statement from her?"

"Yes, I would be happy to," Cate agreed.

Cate led the officer to Victoria's room. She knocked at the door and entered first, explaining to Bryson that the officer wanted to speak with Victoria. Bryson conceded she wasn't sure Victoria could offer any answers but they were welcome to try. She would situate Lady MacKenzie in her arm chair and Cate could show the officer in. Cate retrieved the officer from the hall, showing him into the bedroom.

"Hello, Lady MacKenzie," the officer began. "I'm terribly sorry about this imposition, but I won't be more than a moment." He asked her to recount where she was when the body was discovered. Victoria struggled to respond, her answers confused and nonsensical.

"She was in the ballroom the entire time," Cate offered.

"Yet, you were not, Mrs. MacKenzie, so you cannot attest to that, is that correct?"

"Correct, although we were not gone for long. She was there when we left and when we returned. I believe she was enjoying a dance with a gentleman whose name I don't recall. She was with us when the body was discovered."

"I see. Well, I shan't trouble you ladies any further. Good evening, Mrs. MacKenzie, Lady MacKenzie. I can show myself out and back to the ballroom."

He exited the room. "OH!" Victoria exclaimed bursting into tears, covering her face with her hands.

Cate rushed to her side. "Perhaps you should lie down, Victoria."

She uncovered her face, it was a mask of heartbreak. "I desired a party everyone would remember. I suppose I achieved that," she choked through her tears.

"Oh, Victoria, I'm so sorry your party was ruined."

"How shallow I must sound," Victoria said, wiping tears from her face. "A man is dead. A man who was in my employ, in my household for months and my first concern is my party."

"You don't sound shallow, Victoria. This evening was important to you. There is nothing wrong with being upset."

"We shall once again be the talk of the town." She exhaled a ragged breath.

Cate understood her trepidation. According to what she read, things would only get worse. Even without the chain of events about to unfold, a murder on the estate would provide the town with juicy gossip for months. She did not blame Victoria for the dismay and turmoil she was experiencing.

"Yet this, too, shall pass, Victoria. Soon, they will move on to discuss the next sensational story."

Victoria burst into tears again. "What a disaster. Oh, I couldn't bear this without you here, cousin Catherine. Thank you," she said, grasping Cate's hands.

Cate smiled at her. "Come now. You should rest, Victoria."

Victoria nodded, allowing Cate to help her to her bed. Cate covered her, then sat on the edge of the bed. "Try to sleep," she said.

Victoria nodded to her. Cate stroked her hair as she closed her eyes. Exhausted from the excitement of the party and the tension that followed, Victoria drifted off in seconds.

A quiet knock sounded on the bedroom door. Bryson poked her head in. Cate held a finger to her lips, signaling her to stay silent. Cate delicately stood and crept to the door.

Randolph and Jack stood in the sitting room. Cate pulled the door closed behind her, signaling to them to keep quiet. "Victoria is asleep," she whispered.

"How is she?" Randolph asked.

"Upset. Perhaps the sleep will do her good," Cate answered.

"You are calming for her, Catherine. Thank you." He squeezed her hands.

"Randolph, we need to speak to you," Cate said.

A knock sounded at the door. "Sir," a footman said, peering in. "You're needed downstairs."

Randolph nodded. "You two will return tomorrow, please?" Cate and Jack nodded after sharing a glance. "Good. Speak with you then. Excuse me."

Randolph followed the footman. "Well, I guess that's our cue," Jack said.

"Yes, seems so," Cate agreed. "We should travel home."

Jack nodded. "Just let me check on Victoria one more time," Cate said. She crept to the room, inched the door open and peered in. Easing it shut, she returned. "She's asleep," she said.

"Good. Okay, let's go," Jack said.

"Oh, just a second. Let me leave her necklace here," Cate mentioned, unclasping the necklace and returning it to its box. "Okay, now I'm ready."

They made their way to the bedroom closet, setting the watch back to their time. Despite spending over eight hours in the past, only half an hour had passed in the present time. Cate yawned. Time traveling produced the same side effects as jet lag. It felt more like midnight than mid-afternoon to both Cate and Jack.

"I am exhausted," Cate said, "but I'll never be able to settle."

"Same here," Jack admitted.

"We have a little time before dinner. Want to compare notes?"

"Can I change first? I've been in this monkey suit all night, it's stiff as a board," Jack complained.

"Yes, I'd like to change too. This dress is beautiful but wow is it heavy! Meet you in the library?"

"Perfect," Jack agreed.

CHAPTER 23

Cate dragged herself to the bedroom to change clothes. "What a night!" she exclaimed to Riley and Bailey. They cocked their heads, listening to her babble. "I suppose the two of you don't understand, it's still afternoon for you! Oh Riley, Bailey, what a mess. I hope we can help poor Randolph. Come on, let's meet Jack in the library and see what we can learn!" At the mention of Jack's name, Riley leapt to his feet, his tail wagging. He loved visiting his friend. Bailey studied him, giving a slight wag to his tail. Riley danced as Cate gathered a notebook and pen along with the newspaper clippings about the murder. He nudged at Bailey, exhibiting his excitement and encouraging Bailey to join in. "Okay, little buddies! Let's go!"

Riley dashed down the hall after Cate opened the door. Bailey raced to keep up with him. The black and white dog barreled down the stairs and sprinted to the library. Bailey hurried behind him. The two dogs burst through the open doors, Riley galloping straight to Jack.

"Well, hello, little fella!" Jack said, lifting him into his arms. Bailey approached Jack, eyeing the scene cautiously.

"And hello to you, too, other little fella!" Jack tousled Riley's fur, and Riley gave him an appreciative lick on the face. When Cate entered the room, she found Jack kneeling down, still holding Riley, giving a tentative Bailey a quick head rub.

"The new addition isn't as keen on me as Riley," Jack said, standing as Cate entered.

"I'm sure you'll win him over. Riley took an immediate shine to you, which is unusual for him. Bailey is more bashful than Riley. I'm sure he'll come around soon, though! He's had a tough start!"

"Aye, but he's living the life of… well, Riley now." Jack gave a hearty laugh as Riley cocked his head quizzically at the mention of his name.

Cate groaned at the joke. "You should take your act on the road."

"I'll keep my day job, thanks," Jack declined. "Or my night job, or whatever I've got here. I feel like I've lived through two days already and it's not even suppertime yet."

"Yes," Cate said, wincing, "time traveling is exhausting!" They collapsed into the armchairs near the fireplace. "The only thing keeping me awake is fretting over Randolph and Victoria. I feel terrible for them both."

"Aye, so do I. I expected it and it still was a shock. I can imagine they are both reeling. Well, unless Randolph expected it, too."

"He couldn't have done it though, right?"

Jack pondered a moment. "I don't know. Perhaps he could have. We weren't with him the entire time. There was a gap between when we returned to the party and when he returned."

"Yes, but was it a large enough gap for him to have committed a murder? I don't imagine so."

"It would have been a tight window but may be possible."

It was Cate's turn to contemplate the statement. "Really

tight," she answered after a few moments of recollection. "It's safe to assume the body was thrown from the tower window based on where it landed, would you agree?"

"Yes, I'd consider that a reasonable assumption."

"Okay, so that means Randolph had to leave his office, locate Andrew, kill him with the globe paperweight by striking him with multiple blows, toss his body from the tower, discard the murder weapon in the tower room and return to the ballroom all within that small time frame. It doesn't seem possible."

"Well, assume Andrew was in the tower and Randolph knew it."

"Okay, that's a safe bet. And it would shave some time off, but still, that's a tall order to go to the tower, murder someone, throw his body out the window and make it back to the party within... what would you estimate it at? Perhaps five to seven minutes?"

"No longer than that, yes. And yes, that is a tall order."

"We could try it out and time it," Cate suggested.

"It's not a bad idea, although I was rather comfy here." Cate rolled her eyes at him. "Okay, okay, Lady Cate, we'll try it."

They left the dogs playing with a ball in the library and went to the room that served as Randolph's office. "Okay, now, as soon as I leave, you go to the tower room, unlock it, pretend to bash someone multiple times with a paperweight, heave their body out the window then meet me in the ballroom," Cate instructed.

"I never realized how teacher-like you really are, Lady Cate. Okay, got the time ready on your phone?"

"Yes. Oh, give me a few moments head start. We didn't see or hear Randolph leave his office when we were walking down the hall."

"Got it."

"Okay, here we go!" Cate said, starting the timer and leaving the room. She walked to the ballroom on the same route they used at the party. She stood in the cavernous space, now empty, waiting for Jack. She watched the seconds tick by on her app. Time seemed to move agonizingly slow. She was beginning to doubt she was correct in assuming Randolph did not have the time to commit the murder.

Cate paced the floor. The timer reached the five-minute mark. No sign of Jack yet. It wasn't time to breathe a sigh of relief just yet. Cate increased her speed, pacing double-time in an ever-widening circle.

As Cate rounded the corner in the far end of the room, Jack appeared in the doorway. He was out of breath, beads of perspiration on his forehead. "Time?" he gasped.

"Seven minutes, forty-eight seconds."

He doubled over, letting his hands rest on his knees. "I had a few thoughts along the way," he breathed.

"Let's go back to the library," Cate suggested. "Looks like you need a rest!"

"Great idea, Lady Cate!"

They walked to the library, Jack caught his breath as he sunk into his armchair. "So," Cate began, "that window is really tight. You were forty-eight seconds over the time frame we came up with. So, I'm not sure it helps." Cate frowned in speculation.

"But," Jack said, "as I spent a few moments thrashing my arms around pretending to murder someone with a brass paperweight something occurred to me. This is a close contact crime. Is it likely that he'd end up with no blood on him?"

"Oh, great point and I didn't see any."

"Neither did I. And I doubt he had time to clean it off. I ran so we could determine the shortest amount of time Randolph would have had to commit the murder."

“By the sound and sight of you, it was much faster than Randolph would have. He wasn’t out of breath and wasn’t perspiring when he rejoined us.”

“Maybe he’s in better shape than me,” Jack suggested. Cate shot him a look. “Thanks for the vote of confidence.” Jack laughed.

“Okay, we’ve ruled out Randolph as a suspect.”

“I agree. The possibility is remote.”

“One thing settled: Randolph is not the murderer. Two questions remain. Who is the real killer and why does Randolph cover for them?”

“Between the guests and the staff, there were over one hundred people. There’s no way we could keep track of where everyone was, this is impossible, Cate.”

“It’s not. Would Randolph confess to a crime he didn’t commit for the vast majority of the people there?”

“Good point,” Jack conceded.

“That narrows the list. There are only two people I imagine he would protect.”

Jack mulled it over. “Victoria. She’s the only one I can come up with.”

“Victoria, yes. He’d do anything for her. But she’s not the murderer. I doubt she left the party for even a second. It’s not her he’s covering for. There is someone else, though. And I’d put money on the fact that she is the murderer.”

“Who?” Jack questioned, crinkling his brow.

“Sonia.”

“Sonia?”

“Yes, the woman he told Andrew to attend to before he vacated the castle. Sonia.”

“We don’t even know who Sonia is or what she means to him.”

“She’s the woman from the tower. It fits! The body falls from the tower. Randolph sent Andrew to the tower. The woman there murders him. When the investigation draws too much attention, Randolph confesses to divert the attention away from Sonia."

"That's a great theory, Cate, but it reminds me of a certain cheese."

"Huh?" Cate said, wrinkling her brow in confusion.

"Your theory is like Swiss cheese, it's full of holes."

Cate frowned at him. "It's a darn good theory if you ask me. And I love Swiss cheese."

"Come on, Cate. Think about it, really consider what you're suggesting. To start, what is the motive? Why would Sonia, who we don't know is even the tower lady, kill Andrew? Could Sonia possess the strength it takes to inflict the injuries Andrew sustained? Even if she did, does she have the strength to toss his dead body out of a window? From what we saw of her, which was only a glimpse, I understand, she appeared to be a smaller woman. No larger than you. Do you think you could have beaten Andrew and tossed him from a window?"

Cate sighed. They sat in silence for a few moments, each ruminating over the discussion. Jack had many good points. However, not many other theories made sense. In fact, no other theory held any weight in Cate's mind. Cate had no means to confirm a motive for Sonia. But she realized Andrew was no angel, so her motive could be anything. Randolph also seemed protective of Sonia. He refused to speak to Cate and Jack about her at all. Andrew accused Sonia of being a fallen woman, Randolph's fallen woman. That story still did not ring true to Cate, either. Regardless, Cate could answer none of Jack's questions. Then Cate remembered something.

"There's something else," Cate said. "When I had my unfortunate incident with Andrew…"

Jack gave her a wide-eyed stare. "Unfortunate incident? Is

that what you're calling it now?"

Cate bit her lower lip. "Sounded better than saying when Andrew almost drowned me," she joked, attempting to lighten the mood. "Anyway, when the 'thing' happened, Andrew mentioned something about having a good thing going that he wouldn't let me ruin. Could that play into it?"

"A good thing going?" he asked. "As in his position at the castle, perhaps?"

"But how would I ruin that?"

"By telling Randolph that he was rude and manhandled you."

"He'd kill me over that?"

"Who knows," Jack said, rubbing his eyes.

"I'm tired, too." Cate yawned. "We're spinning our wheels. We need dinner and a long nap!"

As if on cue, Mrs. Fraser arrived with Cate's dinner tray. "All finished with your estate business and ready for dinner, I hope!"

"Ah, estate business is never finished," Jack responded, standing.

"That's the truth!" Mrs. Fraser agreed. "But time for a break! Now, come on, you," she ordered, pushing Jack toward the door, "let's leave Lady Cate to a quiet meal. She looks as though you've tired her out with all your estate business."

Cate spent her meal mulling over their discussion but coming to no new conclusions. Her overtired mind failed to process anything new. Instead of dwelling on it, Cate attempted to read. Her mind often wandered back to the mystery, however, she only ended up frustrated. Her musings turned from solving the mystery to her family. She worried about Victoria and Randolph. Concern for what they must be living through filled every crevice of her mind. Anxiety coursed through her. But she would not solve anything tonight. After a brief walk with the dogs, she turned in for an early bedtime.

The sheer exhaustion of living through one and a half days in twenty-four hours put her to sleep within seconds. Cate awoke in the same position that she fell asleep in. Out of sheer exhaustion she had never moved throughout the entire night.

CHAPTER 24

Cate remained tired regardless of how well she slept. However, her concern for Victoria and Randolph forced her out of bed early. She was dressed and walking the dogs before the sun rose over the moors. She viewed the sunrise from the banks of the loch, recalling her last visit here that had almost been fatal.

Cate and Jack agreed to travel to the past to assess the situation in the late morning and return prior to lunch. Cate hoped to leave the couple some time to recover from the situation before checking in on them. She used the morning hours to work on her research. Before settling into penning a chapter, she checked her email, finding an email from Molly. The subject read I DID IT! Despite her unease, Cate chuckled at the subject line.

Hi Cate! Well, I did it! I quit! Told Jeff yesterday and gave my two-week notice! He wasn't happy, asked me to stay until the end of the academic year but I've got better things to do!

Speaking of, WOW, how did you do this when you moved? I am so excited but I looked around my cramped little apartment and wondered how I still have so much stuff?!?! I already stopped to get boxes, I will start packing this weekend. Where should I send everything?

I haven't broken the news to my sister yet, I'm waiting so I can savor the moment. I'm just waiting to hear from my ex, too. Won't take long for word to filter to him through the grapevine in this town!

I hope everything is going well for you there. I can't wait to be back "home" (and I really can't wait to call Scotland home!). Miss you, Riley and Bailey!

Love you guys!
Molly

The email brought a smile to Cate's face. She was so pleased Molly accepted her offer and would soon call Scotland home. Cate tried to imagine the look on Jeff's face when Molly resigned. It was likely similar to when she had done the same. Cate almost felt sorry for him.

Clicking the reply button, Cate emailed Molly back giving her the address and some encouragement for the packing that lay ahead of her. She told Molly the Rose Room was awaiting her. She also told her about the planned Christmas event at the castle, sure it would thrill Molly to know she'd be at the castle in time for the party.

With the email on its way, Cate returned to her work. She pushed herself to write two paragraphs before giving up and deciding to dress for her trip. She took the dogs for another brief walk before donning her age-old clothing. Cate beat Jack to the closet, arriving fifteen minutes early. She paced the floor of the closet, impatient to go.

Jack arrived. "You're early!"

"Ready?" Cate answered.

"Anxious?"

"Yes. I won't deny it. I'm nervous. I feel sorry for Randolph and Victoria. Even if we learn nothing, we can at least support them."

Jack smiled at her. "I understand. I feel the same way. Randolph didn't commit this crime. It is a shame his family is destroyed by this. I still can't figure out why he does it."

"Let's hope to get some answers today. Let's not push too much, though. I realize we only have a limited amount of time but I think we should proceed with caution."

"Ohhh, what is this I'm hearing? Lady Cate wants to proceed with caution? I can't believe my ears!"

"Oh, stop," Cate said with a chuckle. "I'm being serious!"

"I'll believe it when I see it, Cate. Now, come on."

They activated the timepiece, sending them back to 1856. Thomson met them at the door, ushering them into the house. He showed them to Randolph's office. Two police officers exited the office as they entered.

"Jack, Catherine. Thank you for coming. Catherine, Victoria is in her room. She has not emerged from her room. But I'm sure she would see you."

"I will visit her in a moment. Are there any developments regarding the investigation?"

"The officers told me they expect the autopsy to occur early next week. They're bringing in a coroner from Edinburgh. I don't understand what they expect to find. The man fell from a third-story window."

Cate wrinkled her brow. She knew what they would find. It appeared Randolph did not, still believing Andrew died from the fall.

"Randolph, what did you discuss with the police yesterday?" Cate inquired.

"The standard questions, same as they asked everyone, I assume. My whereabouts, information about Andrew, any issues I've noticed as his employer."

"What did you tell them?" she continued.

Randolph gave her an odd look. "The truth," he began. "I told them I last saw him alive when I fired him. I imagine you overheard that. We then spoke for a few minutes before returning to the party."

"We weren't with you returning to the ballroom," Jack said. "Did you tell them that? We did, I hope it hasn't caused any trouble."

"No trouble at all. I arrived in the ballroom only a few moments after you. I spoke with a few servants then returned to the ball. They can confirm my story."

Cate and Jack shared a glance. So this was the alibi disclosed in the early news articles before Randolph confessed.

"I'm glad. I have been worried all night. If you'll excuse me, I'll go to Victoria now," Cate said, unwilling to push things any further. Cate considered asking about Sonia but was sure Randolph would refuse to discuss her as he had last night. Plus, she was concerned about Victoria and would like to visit with her and offer any comfort she could.

Cate snaked through the castle's halls to Victoria's suite. She knocked on the door, calling to Victoria.

Within a moment, Victoria opened the door. She appeared weary, drained from the incident. "Oh, Catherine," she muttered, "please come in. I'll ring for tea."

"How are you, Victoria?" Cate asked, taking her hand as she sat down.

"I suppose I'm carrying on. Thank you for helping last night. Randolph told me you saw the guests off. Thank you. I wasn't up to it. I shall be known as a terrible hostess, I suppose."

"Everyone will understand," Cate assured her.

Bryson arrived with a tea tray, leaving it with Victoria after checking if anything else was needed. "I can't thank you enough, Catherine, for your help not only with the guests but also for what you did for me last night. Oh, I was so distraught. Thank you for comforting me when I needed it." Victoria poured tea for Cate and herself.

"I didn't do much," Cate said. "Did you get any sleep?"

"Yes, yes, I did. Although I still am exhausted. I cannot wait for this mess to end. I haven't been able to face anyone yet. How did you sleep? Oh, you had to travel home after that, I feel awful. You should have stayed with us."

"Don't trouble yourself over it, Victoria. Randolph offered," Cate fibbed, "but we did not want to disturb the household at such a time. I slept little. I experienced a restless night. I worried about you."

"Oh," Victoria said, grabbing Cate's hand, "you are such a dear, Catherine."

"Randolph said the coroner should arrive early in the week to complete his investigation," Cate said, sipping her tea.

"What a nasty business. I cannot wait for it to end."

"I understand," Cate said. "Hopefully soon." Cate changed the subject, asking how Victoria would celebrate the upcoming Christmas holiday. The two women chatted for a while about the holiday, Victoria's son, Ethan, winters in Dunhaven and more before Cate suggested she should find Jack and depart.

"Thank you, cousin Catherine, for providing a distraction for me today. I do appreciate your stopping by."

"You're welcome, Victoria. Jack has some business this weekend, but I will check in again on Monday with you if that's suitable."

"Most suitable. In fact, please join us for dinner on Monday if you can."

"I shall share the invitation with Jack but I believe we are free."

"Wonderful. I shall see you then." Victoria embraced her, kissing her on the cheek.

Cate navigated to Randolph's office, finding Jack there with Randolph and Malcolm, discussing a few estate items. "Sorry to interrupt," she said after knocking, "I'm just here to collect Jack."

Jack stood, saying his goodbyes to Malcolm and Randolph. "When can we expect you again?" Randolph asked. "I hope soon."

"Monday," Cate answered, "for dinner."

"I shall look forward to it," Randolph answered. The men exchanged handshakes and Jack and Cate departed, making their way to the closet and returning home.

"Change and meet to discuss before lunch?" Cate suggested.

"Sure, meet you in the library," Jack answered.

With both of them in regular clothing, they met in the library to go over anything of note from their latest trip.

"We can confirm that Randolph had a solid alibi, now. If servants saw him after we did, there's no way he had the time to kill someone and return to the ballroom," Cate said as they sunk into the oversized armchairs by the fireplace.

"Right, so we have that confirmed."

"Nothing of note on my end from Victoria. So far, she's holding up okay. It's taken a toll, but she's doing fine. I imagine the real issue will come when Randolph confesses. Perhaps we can avoid that."

"I don't see how. I've got nothing on my end. Randolph acts like nothing happened, he won't even discuss it. We spent most of the time discussing estate business. He asked about the circumstances of your mishap with Andrew."

"What did you tell him?"

"I danced around an explanation, saying Andrew caught us on the way back to the time travel location and wasn't happy about it."

"Did he buy that story?"

"I think so, yes."

"Anything else?" Cate asked.

Jack shook his head. "No, nothing of note. Although, can I just say how weird it is to discuss estate affairs with my great-great-great-grandfather?"

"No stranger than it is to discuss fashion with my great-great-great-grandmother." Cate laughed.

"You win, estate business has changed less than fashion," Jack chuckled.

"Well, anyway, it looks like we're on hold until Monday. I told Victoria we'd visit then, and she invited us to dinner. I'm hoping the autopsy results are in. That's when the real action begins. Until then, Randolph will tell us nothing."

"I agree. He's tight-lipped, and he will remain so until something precipitates a major change."

"Right, like him confessing to a murder he didn't commit to protect Sonia. I hope we can prevent that but I'm not sure."

"We may have to let it play out. We're not supposed to be changing things, remember?"

Cate scrunched up her face. "Yes, I know. But I intend to prevent Randolph from going to jail and ruining his and Victoria's futures. I'm just warning you," she said, shooting him a glance.

"I realize that. I won't try to stop you. You're protecting your family. I'd do the same if it was Malcolm accused. Rules be damned."

His answer pleased Cate. Having her partner in time travel in agreement with her was crucial to an outcome she could live with.

"Well," she said, standing, "it looks like you're off the hook for the weekend."

"Oh boy," he answered, standing also, "you mean I only need to go through forty-eight hours in the next forty-eight hours?"

Cate chuckled. "Yes, two whole days of only twenty-four hours each." As much as Cate wished to settle the situation in 1856, there was nothing she could accomplish at this point. And she, too, would enjoy living the "simple life" again.

"What will you do with your normal twenty-four hour days?" Jack winked at her.

"Fret, most likely," she admitted. "I'll try to keep my mind off things by working on my book and maybe getting a few things ready for Molly's arrival."

They spent a few more moments discussing Molly's impending move before disbanding for lunch. Cate spent her lunch making a list of things to do before Molly arrived, trying to focus her energy on the present.

CHAPTER 25

Her weekly dinner with her staff aided in relieving her mind of some of the stress she felt waiting for time to pass. The rest of the weekend dragged. Cate spent her time training Bailey with Riley's help. She reassessed the Rose Room, noting a few changes she wanted to make before Molly's arrival. A quick trip to town allowed her to pick up some "housewarming" gifts for Molly. While she had plenty of time before Molly's arrival, the activity helped distract her. She rounded out her weekend with a quiet, rainy Sunday reading with the dogs cuddled on either side of her.

When Monday rolled around, Cate was again a bundle of nerves. The autopsy was being performed today. The situation would spiral from here. Randolph would find out that the fall didn't kill Andrew, but blunt force trauma caused his death. Within hours, Randolph and Victoria's lives would change. Randolph would unexpectedly confess to a crime he didn't commit, that he couldn't have committed. Within days, the police would charge Randolph with the murder of Andrew Forsythe. Within weeks, Randolph would be sentenced to prison, leaving behind a devastated wife and infant child.

Cate spent the day reviewing the case again, unable to push it from her mind. In mid-afternoon, Cate readied for the trip. As she and Jack set the watch back to 1856, her hands trembled. She feared what they would find when they arrived.

Jack knocked at the front door. Cate wiped sweaty palms on her dress. Thomson answered, ushering them inside. Victoria swept into the room, her face a mask of worry.

"Thank God you're both here, cousins. Please, come quickly."

"What's happened," Cate asked.

"It's terrible. The police are here speaking with Randolph. Andrew did not die in the fall. He was hit on the head, that's what caused his death. A blow to the head." She wrung her hands. "Well, blows, there were multiple. This has now changed the entire investigation. It's now considered murder. They are questioning Randolph further and want to search the castle. What a disruption. Oh, I am so sorry, we may be late for dinner."

"Don't worry about dinner, Victoria. I'm glad we are here to wait with you. Let's sit down."

"Oh, yes, let's sit down. Oh, Jack, you're an attorney, aren't you? Perhaps you could join Randolph in speaking with the police. I'd feel so much more at ease knowing you were there, that he had legal advice from someone we can trust, from family."

"Ah..." Jack hesitated, having no real expertise in law.

"He would be more than happy to," Cate answered for him. She gave an encouraging node to Jack.

"Oh, thank you," Victoria said, leaping from her chair to embrace Jack.

"That's what family is for," Jack said, laughing with unease. "Catherine, a word before I join Randolph?"

Cate squeezed Victoria's hand before leaving the room with Jack.

"Cate, are you crazy?" Jack whispered when they were alone in the hall. "I'm not an attorney."

"No, but you're aware of the specifics of the case. You know where this is heading. The 'legal advice' is the easy part, tell him to remain silent! Just make sure he doesn't confess to a murder he didn't commit. And don't let them search the house without a warrant. You can stall them until we can brainstorm, just tell the police they aren't allowed to do what they want to do without a judge signing off."

"You watch too much *Law and Order,* Cate."

"Good thing I did!"

"Maybe you should be the lawyer," Jack said, adjusting his collar.

"I can't, there aren't women lawyers yet, remember? Come on, you can do it! I have faith in you."

Jack nodded. "Okay, here goes nothing."

He took a deep breath and headed down the hall to Randolph's office, giving Cate one final glance and a salute before disappearing. Cate smiled before returning to Victoria. The two women sat together in nervous anticipation, making limited and distracted conversation.

After half an hour, Randolph and Jack joined them. Victoria sprang from her seat, rushing to them. "What happened?"

"They're gone for now," Randolph told her.

Cate studied Jack, searching for more answers. "They cannot search the castle until they have a warrant to do so. I expect them to return, but we will be prepared when they do. This will not be chaos, they will respect your rights and your home."

A smile spread across Cate's face and she winked at Jack. His new role suited him.

"Thank heavens and thank you, cousin Jack," Victoria said, fanning herself as she collapsed into a chair. "What a mess."

"Indeed," Randolph agreed. "With any luck it will be cleared up soon and we can return to our lives."

"Do the police have any suspects?" Cate asked.

"They haven't said," Randolph answered. "Andrew had several questionable associates, though. It doesn't surprise me this was his fate."

"Just terrible," Victoria said, shaking her head.

"Enough of this talk tonight," Randolph said, pouring a drink and handing one to Jack.

Victoria agreed. "We should go in for dinner, I imagine Cook is beside herself with the delay."

"Yes, I expect you are correct, my dear. Shall we?"

The foursome went to the dining room. The first course served was a soup. Cook sent her apologies if it was no longer piping hot, but the delay was unexpected. The main course was served, and the quartet engaged in light conversation, attempting to avoid discussing the ongoing murder investigation. Halfway through their dinner Thomson interrupted them, approaching Randolph to whisper in his ear.

The expression on Randolph's face transformed in an instant. He whispered a response to Thomson who nodded and left the room. Within minutes he returned, whispering again to Randolph. Randolph flung his napkin onto the table in disgust. "How dare they intrude on our dinner!"

"What is it?" Victoria asked.

"The damned police," Randolph said, standing. "They have sought Judge Darrow over his supper to obtain a warrant."

Jack stood also, prepared to follow Randolph to speak to

the police. As they turned from the table, the doors burst open. Several police officers stormed into the room.

"What is the meaning of this? How dare you interrupt my meal!" Randolph shouted as they entered the room.

"Allow me to handle it, Randolph," Jack said, stepping between them. "May I see the warrant, please?"

One officer handed him the paperwork, adding, "You'll find everything in order. We shall begin our search posthaste."

"Just a moment." Jack held up his hand.

"Mr. MacKenzie, please stand aside and allow us to conduct our business. The warrant is in order."

"I..." Jack began, searching for an argument but finding none. Victoria joined Randolph, putting her arm on his shoulder. Cate glanced over Jack's at the paperwork. "It appears everything is in order."

"Right, boys, let's begin!" the officer ordered.

"Just a moment!" Randolph shouted. "No one will lay one finger on anything in this house!"

"Lord MacKenzie, you must not interfere with this investigation, please stand aside."

"There isn't a need for a search," Randolph insisted.

"Do you have information that would suggest a search is not warranted?" the officer asked.

"Yes..." Randolph began.

"Wait, Randolph," Jack cautioned. "do not say another word." He turned to the officer in charge. "I'd like a private moment with my client."

"If your client has information about the murder, I'd like to hear it."

"And you shall," Randolph insisted.

"Randolph, please, I must insist as your legal counsel that you remain silent."

"Enough of this charade, boys, search the house."

"There's no need, I tell you! The murderer is right here. It was me. I am the guilty party. I killed Andrew Forsythe."

Victoria gasped, Jack's head sunk, Cate's stomach turned over. Randolph, in a desperate attempt to stop the search of his home, confessed to a murder he did not commit.

"You?" the officer questioned the unexpected turn of events.

"Yes. I did it. I created a false alibi but I can no longer live with the guilt."

"Randolph, please," Jack insisted.

Randolph waved him off. The police officer, eyes wide, shook his head, saying, "Randolph MacKenzie, I place you under arrest for the murder of Andrew Forsythe."

"Oh my God," Victoria exclaimed, swooning. Cate raced to her side, sitting her in a chair. One of the other officers handcuffed Randolph.

"I suppose you can lead us to the murder weapon," the lead officer asked. "Otherwise, we still must conduct the search."

"I can tell you where it is, but I doubt you'll find it. I threw it in the loch the day after the murder."

"We'll try dragging the loch tomorrow morning. It's too dark now," the officer said. "Come along, Lord MacKenzie, we need to take a formal statement from you at the station."

Cate leapt to her feet from Victoria's side. "Jack," she whispered, "you must go with him."

"What for?" Jack whispered back. "He is a murderer, he's murdered any attempt I have at a defense!" he continued, his voice thick with sarcasm.

"Still! Go with him, try to minimize the damage. And try to find out why he's doing this!"

Jack sighed and nodded, "Okay, okay. I'll see what I can do."

"Good luck."

"I shall go with my client. He is not to be questioned unless I am present," Jack said, returning to his normal voice.

"Very well. You both can follow me," the officer said.

"Oh no!" Victoria cried, "Randolph!" She sprang from her chair throwing her arms around him. "Please," she begged the officer, "please do not take him."

"Lady MacKenzie, please stand aside."

"No!" she wailed.

The officer nodded to another who pulled her away. "Don't touch me!" she shouted.

"Get your hands off of my wife!" Randolph bellowed, approaching the officer. Chaos ensued as the police restrained both Victoria and Randolph.

"Victoria, please," Cate said, grabbing her by the shoulders, "this will not help. Please, let Jack straighten it out."

Tears fell from Victoria's eyes. "Yes," she gasped out. "Please, cousin Jack, help him." She flung herself into Jack's arms, sobbing. Jack consoled her, promising to do his best. Cate pulled her away, sitting her in a chair while the men cleared the room.

As the room cleared, Cate requested Thomson to fetch Bryson, directing that Victoria should be taken to her room to rest. Thomson disappeared to fetch the ladies' maid below stairs. With Bryson's help, Cate took Victoria to her bedroom suite. Bryson dressed her in her nightclothes and situated her in bed. Cate took her brandy to settle her nerves.

"Why is this happening?" Victoria croaked before downing the glass.

"Try not to worry, cousin. Jack will do whatever he can to settle this."

"Yes." Victoria nodded. "Yes, Jack must help him. Or…" her voice trailed off.

"Do not even think it, Victoria," Cate prompted. "Please

close your eyes and try to sleep. You have had a severe shock."

"How can I sleep with Randolph..." Her voice trailed off again, unable to verbalize the situation.

Cate adjusted her covers, taking her hand. "Please try to rest. Perhaps when you awaken, he will be returned. You'll want to have all your strength then."

Victoria nodded, squeezing Cate's hand. "Please stay, Catherine. Ask Bryson to make up a room. You mustn't return home alone, anyway."

Cate nodded. "I shall wait here for Jack to return," she promised.

Victoria nodded again, satisfied and closed her eyes. The shock and anxiety of the events took a hard toll. The tea Bryson prepared with the addition of the sleeping draught also aided and she drifted off to a fitful sleep. Cate removed herself to the sitting room, asking Bryson to fetch her when Jack returned.

She collapsed into the armchair near the fireplace. The tension wore on Cate, too. She found herself tired yet unable to rest. The fire danced in front of her as she stared into it, her mind incapable of settling. She spent an hour fidgeting in the chair, jumping at every noise, hoping it was Jack returning.

After an hour, Cate rose from the chair to pace the room. She peeked in at Victoria who was still asleep, moaning as though suffering from a bad dream. Cate entered the room, taking her hand and stroking her forehead until she was quiet. She returned to pacing the sitting room floor until weary. She sunk into the arm chair again, letting her head rest against the wing. Her eyes were heavy, she closed them for a moment and drifted off to sleep.

CHAPTER 26

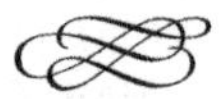

Cate shook all over. Startled, she bolted up, her eyes snapping open. "Cate," Jack whispered, giving her a light shake while kneeling beside her.

"What? What time is it?" she asked, her voice groggy with sleep. Confusion flashed across her face before the realization of her whereabouts set in.

"Almost 2 a.m. You fell asleep. Come on," Jack said, standing and offering his hand for her to join him.

"Where are we going?" Cate asked, still out of it.

"Home, silly."

"Home? What happened with Randolph? I should check on Victoria," she said, standing.

Jack stopped her. "Bryson is with her. We can talk about what happened when we get home and out of these clothes."

Cate nodded, still drowsy. She glanced back toward Victoria's room. Worry clouded her mind, but she hoped Victoria slept through the night. She followed Jack to the closet and returned to their own time.

"Whew, what a night," Jack said when they were home.

"Yeah," Cate agreed. "I bet you are tired."

"You aren't kidding."

"Do you want to discuss everything tomorrow after you've had some sleep?"

"No. I'd rather do it while it's fresh in my mind. Besides, I'll not be responsible for you laying awake all night wondering what's happened."

Cate gave him a small smile. "I appreciate that. I would like to know."

"Let's change. We have about thirty minutes before dinner."

"I'll ask Mrs. Fraser to send a tray up for you with mine, in the name of estate business. We can talk over dinner then you can go home straight after."

"Perfect. I'll meet you in the usual spot?"

"See you in the library as soon as I'm changed and have taken the dogs for a quick pit stop."

Cate returned to her bedroom suite, greeted the dogs then changed. She was tired despite dozing off; she couldn't imagine how tired Jack must be. "Okay, boys," she said to Riley and Bailey, "let's go for a quick walk before dinner."

On her way out, Cate asked Mrs. Fraser to send both her dinner and Jack's to the library, offering to carry one tray up on her own. After a short walk with the dogs, Cate returned to the kitchen to collect her tray and accompany Mrs. Fraser to the library.

Jack was lounging in an armchair, appearing close to dozing off. "Here we are, lazy bones," Mrs. Fraser joked, setting his tray in front of him.

"Thanks," he answered, yawning.

"Now dinnae you go getting used to this treatment. I'm only doing it just this once," Mrs. Fraser warned.

Jack laughed. "I wouldn't dare, Emily, I wouldn't dare."

"I'm glad I did, I dare say you look like you're coming down with something!"

"Ah, I just didn't sleep well enough last night," Jack said.

"We'll see," Mrs. Fraser said, "best you eat all your dinner and try to stave off whatever bug you caught. You sure you want to hang around this one, Lady Cate? I hope he doesn't breathe his germs onto you. Can't your business wait until your well?"

"Afraid not. I won't breathe in her direction," Jack promised.

"Well, I suppose I'll go eat my own dinner far, far away from the germs." Mrs. Fraser laughed, shaking her head as she walked away.

Cate sat down across from Jack, setting her tray on the table in front of her. Jack stabbed a few pieces of the meal with his fork, already digging in. "Hey," Cate chided, "stop breathing in my direction."

"Very funny, Lady Cate. You know very well I'm not sick."

Cate giggled before diving into her own meal. "Okay, so what happened? What took until two in the morning? And did Randolph come back with you? What did he tell the police? Is he sticking with his story?"

"Whoa, whoa, slow down, Cate," Jack said. "One thing at a time. I'll go over everything I remember then you can ask questions."

"Okay," Cate answered, waiting for him to begin.

He took a few more bites of food before beginning. "Okay, so I tried my best, but Randolph is sticking to his story so far. I spent hours trying to talk him out of it, trying to find out why he confessed. I even told him we knew he couldn't have done it. He refused to change his mind. He refused to tell me who he was trying to protect. Kept saying he realized what he was doing, and he was guilty." Jack ate a few more bites of food, washed down with some water. "I gave him my 'professional opinion' about what he was doing, he didn't care. The police questioned him. I did my best to minimize the amount of questions and, after a while, they gave up. Told me they'd finish questioning him tomorrow. Speaking of, we need to be back tomorrow morning at nine for Randolph's questioning."

Cate nodded in agreement. "I don't get it. Why is he doing this? It has to be Sonia."

"He wouldn't say. What a mess. I fully expect to lose my first and hopefully only legal case."

"Well, your client isn't doing you any favors," Cate stated.

"No, he is not."

"How bad did the questioning go? What did he admit to?"

"Not much, thanks to my superb legal maneuvering. And what he explained fell short of making much sense. That's why the police want to question him again. And why I was able to postpone it until tomorrow."

"What do you mean?" Cate asked.

"The explanations he provided did not add up upon close inspection. He's lying, and it's obvious at times."

"Any specific discrepancies you remember?"

"He couldn't identify the murder weapon. Said he didn't remember what he grabbed to hit him with. When they questioned him on how he knew what item to throw into the loch, he flip-flopped, said he remembered what he hit him with at the time and directly afterwards but can't remember now."

Cate raised her eyebrows. "That sounds made up. I remember the news story mentioned the police being skeptical. I'll bet this is why."

"There was another time they asked about his supposed alibi. He said he had time to commit the crime and talk with the staff. Later he said the staff lied on his behalf at his request."

"Is he still at the police station or did you get him out of custody?"

"I'm not THAT good of a fake lawyer, Cate." Jack laughed. "No, he's still in custody. Spent his night in a cell."

Cate shook her head at the situation. "Perhaps you'll have better luck tomorrow. I could speak with him, maybe that will help."

"It can't hurt. Although, we can't give him any information. You can't tell him what will happen to him or even hint at it."

Cate nodded in agreement. "You're right. But I can try to convince him, anyway."

Jack nodded to her. "How is Victoria taking it?"

"Not great. I got her to sleep. Once she wakes up and finds out Randolph is still in custody, I can imagine it will send her into a tailspin."

"I would expect so, yes."

"I'm hoping my talk with Randolph kills two birds with one stone. Convince him to stop this charade and make sure he's okay so I can report back to Victoria and set her mind at ease."

"You're optimistic."

"I'm sure I'll fail at this, but I have to try to change this."

"Are you going to be okay if it turns out we can't?"

Cate froze, deep in thought. The notion had crossed her mind before but she had dismissed it, trying to remain positive. "I'm not sure if okay is how I'd describe it but..." She paused, still pondering it. "At least we tried. That's all we can do."

Jack nodded to her. "I just don't want you upset over something that we very well may not have the power to change."

Cate considered his comment a moment. He was right. Perhaps the past was unchangeable, perhaps this was all for naught. She couldn't believe that, she wouldn't believe that. If they failed, Cate would be dismayed, but she would realize they tried. And she would learn from this experience. "I'm sure I'll be upset, but we have to try. If we can't change it, I'll accept that."

Jack stared at her a moment before setting his fork on his empty plate. "Well, that about does it for me. If you don't mind, I will head home."

Cate smiled, "I don't mind. Just leave that tray, I'll take it down with mine."

"And have Mrs. Fraser scold me tomorrow for making Lady Cate carry both trays? No way, lassie. I'll take them BOTH down myself. She's already mad at me for breathing my bogus germs on you."

Cate laughed. "Okay," she said, giving in, "you take them."

Jack gathered up the trays. Before exiting he bowed extravagantly. "Good evening, m'lady."

Cate rolled her eyes, shaking her head and holding in a laugh. "Good night, Jack," she groaned.

Cate spent the rest of her evening in an ineffective attempt at reading a book. Her mind could not focus on the words printed on the page, often drifting to her ancestors and their current plight. After a while she dozed off. The book slipped from her lap, clattering to the floor and startling her awake. She blinked a few times, awakening slowly. Two pairs of eyes peered at her from the floor. "Oh, sorry! Did I startle you when I dropped my book?" Riley leapt into her lap, Bailey followed him. Cate gathered them both into her arms, kissing each on the head. "We better get to bed before I fall out of the chair next!"

After a quick trip outside, Cate climbed the stairs to her bedroom suite and snuggled beneath the covers. She dropped off to sleep within moments.

CHAPTER 27

Cate arose the next morning as anxious as she was the day before. She practiced what she planned to say to Randolph over and over in her head. She revised and adjusted it, attempting to create a speech that wouldn't fail. After an hour, Riley and Bailey seemed more than convinced. Cate hoped her speech had the same effect on Randolph.

She appreciated the early appointment with the police and dressed to meet Jack early. They planned to meet at eight fifteen since they had to walk to town. Jack did not want to be late, his nerves getting the better of him. He expressed his hope that Cate could convince Randolph to change his current plan of action. Cate promised to do her best, not at all convinced she could pull it off.

They arrived at the police station with fifteen minutes to spare. Cate suggested she visit with Randolph before their questioning was scheduled. At first, the police refused, but with a little convincing on Jack and Cate's parts, they agreed to allow Cate five minutes to visit with Randolph. Jack wished her good luck with her venture, sending her into the interrogation room.

Cate sat in the small, sparsely decorated room. The chair was hard and uncomfortable, she fidgeted, trying to ease the cramp developing in her back. An officer led Randolph through the door, his wrists in thick handcuffs. She smiled at him as he sat across from her.

"Five minutes," the officer reminded her, then stood at the door.

"May we have privacy, please?" Cate asked.

"I'm not to leave you alone with the prisoner," he answered.

"Please?" Cate asked again, "if you could step just outside the door."

With a nod of his head, the officer stepped outside the door, hovering at the entrance. Cate turned toward Randolph. "How are you?" she asked, reaching for his hands.

He withdrew them from the table. "Catherine, you shouldn't be here."

"I had to come. I must speak with you."

"Please, Catherine, go to the castle, take care of Victoria. She is, in all likelihood, beside herself with worry and distress."

"She is, and for no reason, Randolph."

"There is a very good reason, Catherine. Her husband has just confessed to murder. She is confused, anxious, distraught. She needs you. Go to her."

"I'd like to share good news with her once I see her."

"I'm afraid there may be none to give."

"Why, Randolph? You are innocent. You must end this madness!"

Randolph remained silent. Cate continued, "Why have you done this? Who are you protecting?"

"Officer!" Randolph shouted.

"Randolph, please!" Cate pleaded. "You must listen."

The officer entered the room. "We're done here," Randolph said.

"No," Cate disagreed. "Randolph, don't do this."

"Mrs. MacKenzie, if you please." The officer motioned toward the door.

"I'm not finished!" Cate exclaimed.

"Go to Victoria, Catherine. We're finished," Randolph said.

Cate sighed as the officer approached her, making it clear the visit was over. "Please think about it, Randolph," Cate added before leaving the room.

She stalked to the entryway where Jack waited for her. "Any luck?" he asked.

Cate shook her head. "Afraid not. He wouldn't listen to anything I said."

"Great!" Jack sighed. "Well, looks like I'm in for a fun morning."

Cate didn't envy him. Randolph was being impossible. There wasn't much Jack could do. She shook her head again. "Do what you can. I'll see you back at the castle."

"Be careful, Cate. Wish me luck."

"Good luck! You'll need it," Cate said, giving his arm a squeeze.

She departed, turning to give Jack a wink and a wave before leaving him at the police station. Cate plodded out of town, her heart heavy at her failure. What would she tell Victoria? How could she rationalize Randolph's choices? How could she assure Victoria the situation would work out? She had no answers to these questions. Her uncertainty slowed her pace to a crawl.

She glanced ahead; the castle loomed in front of her. She pictured Victoria inside, longing for news of her husband. Tears formed in her eyes, threatening to roll down her cheeks. She pursed her lips, raising her eyes to the sky. She took several deep, steadying breaths. After a few moments, she had composed herself. She continued toward the castle, assuring herself that she possessed the strength to survive this ordeal.

When she arrived, she knocked on the door and Thomson greeted her. "Thank goodness you are here, Mrs. MacKenzie," he said, taking her coat. "Lady MacKenzie has taken a terrible turn upon finding out Lord MacKenzie did not return last evening."

"Oh, no," Cate sighed. "I had hoped she wouldn't become to upset over it before I could be here."

"Please go to her room. Perhaps your visit will cheer her."

"I will and I hope so. Thank you, Thomson."

Cate wound through the halls to Victoria's room. She knocked at the door and Bryson ushered her into the room. "Thank goodness you've come, Mrs. MacKenzie. She's been like this all morning," Bryson said, wringing her hands.

Cate stepped into the room. Victoria was propped in her armchair. She was pale, her lips white. Her eyes were glazed, and she stared straight ahead. "Thank you, Bryson. You may go."

Bryson nodded to her, glancing toward Victoria before exiting. Cate approached Victoria, kneeling beside the chair and taking her hand. "Victoria," she said gently, rubbing her hand, "Victoria? It's Catherine." Cate gave her a gentle shake.

Victoria blinked a few times, focusing on Cate. "Catherine!" she said as though just realizing Cate was there. "Is Randolph with you?"

"No," Cate said. "He is with Jack. They are at the police station."

Victoria's eyes filled with tears. "Oh," she cried.

Cate hoped to stave off the negative reaction before it capitulated into a full fit. "Do not worry, Victoria. Jack is with him. He'll take care of Randolph."

"He spent his entire night in jail," Victoria sobbed.

Cate sat back in the chair next to Victoria's. "Yes, he did. Jack did all he could, but he could not convince them to release Randolph last night. I'm sorry, Victoria."

"Please don't apologize, Catherine. I know Jack is doing all he can and I thank him for it. However," she said, a few tears spilling onto her cheeks, "I cannot dismiss my anguish over Randolph."

"I understand," Cate said. "I can imagine how worried you must be. But, Victoria, you must remain strong for Randolph's sake." Victoria dried her tears with her handkerchief, sniffling. "I saw Randolph this morning. He looked well, tired but all right. He was, however, concerned about you."

Victoria's sobbing intensified. "Just like Randolph," she croaked. "Always worried for someone else. Oh, Catherine, I cannot believe he is a murderer. Am I being foolish?"

Cate reached out, rubbing Victoria's arm. "No, Victoria, you are not. I do not believe it either and neither does Jack. I do not understand why he confessed, but I am certain Randolph is no murderer."

Victoria clasped Cate's hand in hers, smiling. "Thank you, Catherine," she said, her eyes filled with tears.

"I'd like to be able to tell Randolph that you are doing all right under the circumstances and allow him to focus on himself."

"Yes," Victoria said, sniffling then breaking down in sobs again.

Cate stood then perched on the arm of Victoria's chair, wrapping her in an embrace. After a moment, Victoria patted Cate's arm. "Thank you, dear Catherine." She dried her eyes again, sniffling. "Thank you. You are right, I must be strong. I can be with your support." She returned the hug. "Oh, I must look a fright," she said, pulling away.

Cate smoothed Victoria's hair, wiping away a few tear stains. "Why don't you splash some cool water on your face? You'll feel better."

Victoria nodded, rising from the chair. She went to her bedroom, pouring water from her pitcher into the basin and using it to clean up. Cate followed her into the bedroom. "Shall we get you dressed?"

"Yes, perhaps then my mood will improve."

"Oh, Victoria," Cate said, "I understand how upsetting this is but you must remain strong for Randolph and for your son, Ethan."

"He is too young to understand," Victoria noted.

"But he can sense your upset, the upset of the household. He'll need your strength now more than ever."

"How do you do it, Catherine? How do you remain so positive and focused? My head feels as though my brains have been scrambled."

Cate pondered her question a moment. "When I was younger, my parents passed away in an unexpected accident. The shock left me the same feelings you are experiencing, but I realized I had no choice but to continue moving on with my life." Cate approached Victoria, grabbing her hands. "I do, however, understand what you mean. But give yourself time, Victoria, the shock will pass."

"Oh, Catherine, I'm so sorry, I did not know. You've never mentioned about your parents."

Cate shook her head, dismissing it. "No need for an apology. Now, let's pick a dress that will brighten your day."

"Perhaps something in blue, not too ostentatious given the circumstances but not depressing."

"We'll get through this, Victoria."

"Thank you, Catherine."

Victoria called for Bryson. Cate helped Victoria dress and when Bryson arrived, she tamed Victoria's hair into a low bun. Victoria asked her to have tea sent to the solarium and to have Ethan brought there also. Victoria, at Cate's encouragement, wanted to keep her son close.

The two spent an hour fussing over Ethan and sipping tea. Victoria smiled once or twice during the hour. The time spent with her infant seemed to improve her mood.

As the noon hour approached, Thomson entered. He informed Victoria that Cook wanted to speak with her regarding the menu for the week. Victoria excused herself, leaving Ethan on Cate's lap. As she departed, Thomson turned to Cate. "Mrs. MacKenzie," he whispered, "I wanted Lady Mackenzie distracted. Mr. MacKenzie has returned. He has asked to see you. I'm afraid the news may not be good. I did not want to upset Lady MacKenzie."

"Thank you, Thomson," Cate said. "I will take Ethan and meet him in the library."

"He is waiting in the foyer." Cate gathered the child into her arms and made her way to the foyer to collect Jack.

"Oh, Cate, I hope Thomson was discreet," Jack said as she approached.

"He was. Victoria is distracted, let's talk in the library."

They hurried down the hall, shutting themselves in the library to speak. "What's happened?" Cate asked once in private.

"It's not good, Cate. I mean, it's not terrible, but it's not good." Cate waited for him to continue. He shook his head. "The questioning did not go well. He's giving conflicting information, contradicting himself."

"That's not good."

"That's the good news," Jack said, sighing. "His conflicting information has the police unsure. They haven't charged him yet, but I'm not sure how much longer we can avoid it. I'd guess a formal charge is coming this afternoon, tomorrow morning at the latest."

Cate sighed, her shoulders sagging. "We need a plan."

"You aren't kidding, one that is Randolph-proof."

"What do you mean?" Cate asked, her brow furrowing.

"He's impossible. I suggested he consult with a more experienced attorney in these types of cases before plowing ahead with his admission of guilt."

"And?"

"And he flat-out said no. Then threatened to fire me if I didn't do what he wanted." Jack rolled his eyes.

"I cannot believe he is being so stubborn! How frustrating," Cate said, shaking her head. "How are you holding up?"

"I don't know. It's incredibly frustrating, but then again, I'm making this up as I go. I feel like I live on a bad episode of a legal drama."

Cate understood his distress. He was thrown into a murder investigation as legal counsel for an innocent man intent on proving his own guilt. He possessed no legal training and was representing a client who preferred not to cooperate in his own defense. "What now?" Cate asked.

"Unless he's charged, there's not much."

"Do you need to return to the police station?"

"There's no need for me to return today, but I'm not sure I want to face Victoria. Thomson seemed to think the mere sight of me may cause a fit."

"She is doing better than when I arrived this morning, but yes, Thomson may be right. I'm afraid the slightest thing will send her reeling."

"Ah, what a mess. Can't he see what this is doing to his wife?" Jack asked, throwing his arms in the air.

"Why is he protecting this other woman at Victoria's expense?" Cate sighed, brooding over the situation. After a moment, Cate's gloomy expression changed, her eyes becoming bright, her lips parting in excitement. "Jack! Do you suppose you could go to the station and make sure they don't charge Randolph until tomorrow morning at the earliest?"

Jack's brow furrowed. "I'm not sure I can pull that off but I can try. Why?"

"I have an idea. It would require us to return this evening, but I have an idea."

Jack opened his mouth to follow up with a question when Thomson knocked then entered the room. "Pardon the interruption, but Lady MacKenzie is finishing up with Cook. Perhaps you should return to the solarium, Mrs. MacKenzie."

"Thank you, Thomson." Thomson nodded then exited, closing the doors behind him.

"I'd better go."

Jack nodded. "I'll do what I can at the police station then come back for you. Cate, I'm not going to like this idea you have, am I?"

"Not one bit."

"I was afraid of that," Jack said. "Can't wait to hear it so I can really detest it. Wish me luck!" Jack gave her a salute as he left the room.

"Good luck!" she called after him.

Cate returned to the solarium. She arrived prior to Victoria and was seated and settled with Ethan before Victoria entered. She never suspected Cate had left.

Victoria suggested they move to the dining room for lunch. The ladies lunched, trying to keep conversation light. As they finished their meal, Thomson arrived again. "Pardon me, Lady MacKenzie, Mrs. MacKenzie, Mr. MacKenzie has returned."

Victoria's eyes grew wide. "Send him in at once."

"Yes, Lady MacKenzie." Thomas nodded, leaving the room to fetch Jack.

Within moments, Thomson appeared with Jack in tow. Cate stared at him for some sign about what happened at the station. Jack gave her a slight nod. Cate breathed a silent sigh of relief. He pulled it off, she didn't know how, but he must have.

"What news of my husband?" Victoria asked.

"The police have questioned him extensively. There will be no formal charge made for at least the next twenty-four hours."

"Will he be returning home?"

"Not yet. But I hope soon," Jack answered her.

"This is good news, Victoria," Cate said, placing her hand on Victoria's arm.

Victoria didn't look convinced but nodded her head at Cate, placing her hand over Cate's.

After a moment, she turned to Jack. "Have you eaten anything?"

"No, ma'am," Jack said, sitting down across from Victoria.

"Oh, let me have something sent up. You must be famished!"

Cate smiled to Jack as Victoria rang for service. It seemed she was returning to her old self a bit. Cate hoped her plan worked, so the trend continued. She hated to see vivacious Victoria reduced to a lonely hermit.

Victoria had sandwiches sent up for Jack which he ate with vigor, starved from the morning's events. As he finished, wiping the corners of his mouth, he thanked Victoria for the lunch. "And I'm sorry to seem ungracious but I have a few things I must attend to. Catherine, we should go and allow Victoria a chance to rest."

"Oh, must you go?" Victoria asked.

"I'm afraid we must," Jack answered for the both of them. "We'll be back bright and early tomorrow morning, I promise. There is nothing to worry about, Victoria. Please try to rest, this will all be over soon." Jack placed his hand over Victoria's.

Victoria clasped his hand in hers, also reaching for Cate's. "Thank you, both of you."

"Jack's right, Victoria," Cate said, "you should rest. This is taking a tremendous toll on you. Please promise you'll rest."

"I shall try," Victoria promised. "Although, I worry about Randolph. I do wish he was home."

"I tried my best..." Jack began. Victoria waved her hand in the air, stopping him.

"I understand and appreciate all that you've done. I'm not suggesting there is a deficiency with your work, Jack. But I would be more settled with Randolph at home. Still, I promise to rest."

Cate squeezed her hand. "Good. As Jack said, we'll be here tomorrow morning."

"Let me ring for Nanny to take Ethan."

"Oh, let me take him to the nursery. We'll show ourselves out afterward."

"Are you certain?" Victoria asked. Cate nodded. "Thank you, Catherine. I shall see you tomorrow." Victoria embraced Jack then Cate, giving Cate a kiss on the cheek.

Cate and Jack took Ethan to the nursery then used a discreet path to get to the closet and return home. Jack breathed his customary sigh of relief after they were back.

"I'm dying to know how you pulled off your legal coup," Cate exclaimed as they returned.

"And I'm dying to know your plan to save a man who doesn't want to be saved," Jack answered.

"Meet in the library?" they said in unison.

Cate laughed. "Yes, after we change, of course."

"Of course," Jack said, also laughing.

CHAPTER 28

After Cate greeted Riley and Bailey, she undressed, stripping off her dress and undergarments in favor of modern clothes. Once changed, she and the pups made their way to the library to meet Jack. He was already there, having changed must faster than Cate.

"Hey, buddy!" Jack exclaimed as Riley bounded over to him. "I missed you! Did you miss me?"

"I expect he did, despite us only being gone for…" Cate checked her timepiece. "Twenty-four minutes."

"This time differential is killing me. I've eaten lunch already, and it's only 9 a.m."

"I know the feeling." Cate sunk into the armchair. "Okay, I can't take any more suspense. How did you pull off the delay in the formal charges being filed?"

Jack collapsed into the armchair next to her. "I threw everything I could at them. Told them he was under duress, tired and not thinking straight. I reminded them that his story did not add up and they needed to consider other suspects because of that. Then I threatened them about a few procedural things and they agreed to hold off."

"Wow, you must have been doing your homework. Been watching *Law & Order*, huh?"

"Yep." Jack laughed. "Okay, your turn. I'm dying to learn how you plan to fix this."

"Randolph will not cooperate, we know that. So it's on us to take matters into our own hands."

"I'm alarmed already," Jack said.

"We need to learn more about Sonia, about what motive she may have had and why Randolph would go to such lengths to protect her. Randolph isn't going to offer us any information."

"So what do you propose we do? Give him truth serum?"

"No," Cate said, shaking her head. "I propose we ask Sonia."

"Ask Sonia?!" Jack exclaimed.

"Yes. Assuming she hasn't run away yet, she should still be in the tower room. We must ask her who she is and what happened that night. She must have killed Andrew. He fell from the tower, or so it appeared. He must have been with her and she must have killed him. We have a key. We'll take it back this evening, speak with Sonia, learn what we can and come up with a plan to proceed."

"What makes you assume she'll talk to you?"

"We must convince her. I think she will."

"Why would she? How are you so sure?"

"Well," Cate conjectured, pondering a moment, "she only has contact with the servant or servants who care for her. Randolph is gone, it was clear she was fond of him. She's got to be reeling, just like Victoria. Only she has no support system like Victoria has. The servants cannot provide her with any help, they have no means to. She may be more accommodating than we expect."

"It's a gamble."

"There isn't much choice."

"You're right. You want to do this tonight?"

"I think it may be best. Perhaps we can sneak back when most of the household is quiet. Then we'll have some time before we return tomorrow to sort through whatever information we receive and devise a plan."

"Okay, agreed."

"Wow, that was easy!"

"You make a good point. And my legal skills leave a lot to be desired. With Randolph's reckless behavior, he will go to jail. I can't stop it unless we gather more information. I don't want to be responsible for ruining Randolph's life."

Cate leaned forward, grabbing Jack's hand. "You wouldn't be responsible, even if we can't stop this. Randolph is calling the shots. There's not much you can do."

"Thanks, Cate. But I still can't help but feel somewhat responsible, considering I am the man's legal counsel."

"I'm sorry about that. I feel terrible having put you in that position."

"Don't. I could have refused, but I wouldn't have."

"We didn't have to use the cover story we did. That's what thrust you into this position."

"I'd still be in this position. He refuses to have any legal counsel. He's only accepting my help because it would seem awkward to Victoria if he didn't accept 'cousin Jack's' help."

Cate smiled at Jack. "Thanks for being a good sport about it."

"No problem, Lady Cate. Now, I suppose some work awaits me."

"Maybe you should rest first? Catch a nap?" Cate suggested.

"I'll be all right. I'll take a quick nap after dinner before we travel back tonight."

"Sounds good. See you later… around eight?"

"Perfect. See you then, Cate."

CHAPTER 29

Jack left Cate in the library. She slouched into the chair, putting her feet up on the table in front of her. She planned her day. Her nerves were on edge considering their trip later. She figured she would spend the rest of her morning enjoying a long walk with the dogs, hoping it settled her nerves. She would use the walk to plan what she would say to Sonia.

Cate retrieved Bailey's harness and leash and returned to the library to collect both dogs. Riley leapt to his feet, dancing on his hind legs at the mention of a walk. Once Bailey was ready, they made their way outside. Cate selected the path to the loch, playing ball with Riley as they walked and working with Bailey on his training.

They spent the morning together. Cate ensured the dogs got plenty of exercise to tire them out for the day. She promised to take them for a short walk in the afternoon, too.

Following her lunch, Cate scoured the castle for clues about Sonia. She searched the tower room again. She re-read the note to Randolph, stared at the sketch she had drawn of him. Cate searched through any documents she could find from the era for even the hint of a reference to the mysterious Sonia. She hoped to find something she could use to further the conversation she planned for this evening. She came up empty.

Cate cursed the lack of information. It did little to help her form a course of action for appealing to Sonia. She was going into the situation blind. And nothing could be done about it. It could not be avoided. Information or not, she must confront Sonia. She must convince her to supply any information she could to aid in resolving the crisis with Randolph.

Cate took the dogs for another walk before dinner, hoping the crisp air would clear her head. She settled on a strategy of appealing to Sonia's esteem for Randolph. She hoped it would work, it must work. They were running out of options.

After dinner, Cate withdrew to her bedroom, planning to rest before their trip to the past. A ball of nerves, Cate found it impossible. Instead, she paced the floor. After a time, she settled on her bed, laptop in hand. She browsed around then checked her email, finding a new message from Molly.

Cate! I shipped the first set of boxes over to you yesterday! They should arrive within the next ten days. Would you let me know when you get them?

I heard from Gayle, too. She has the ball rolling on the paperwork for me to move. I was so excited to hear that. I sent all the information she requested right away so there are no delays. This is starting to feel so real now. I'm counting the days down.

I told my sister, too! She called me over the weekend to ask me if I was coming for Thanksgiving (after she told me she didn't know where she'd put everybody!). I told her I was too busy to come and would have a quiet Thanksgiving alone. When she asked what I was too busy with, I told her I was packing to move... TO SCOTLAND. I also told her I won't be there for Christmas since I will be at my new home in a SCOTTISH CASTLE!!! I don't think I've ever heard that woman speechless, but I did on Sunday!

*You know, I might need more Scotland sweaters. Is it okay if I have them shipped straight to my new home? Well, I should get back to work. I'm counting the days down until I blow this joint, too! Jeff has me doing a complete overhaul of the office 'to prepare it for the new person', painful 'til the bitter end. *Rolling my eyes**

Talk to you soon, Molly

Molly's correspondence always brought a smile to Cate's face. She used the time she had left to answer Molly's email. She, too, was growing excited with each passing day about Molly's arrival. It would be splendid to have her closest friend with her, especially for her first holiday in Scotland. She answered all Molly's questions and reminded her not to forget to shop for a Christmas party dress while she was looking for more Scotland sweaters.

The email left Cate with a renewed sense of purpose and drive. She closed her laptop and climbed off the bed to dress for the trip. Tired from their big day, Riley and Bailey never moved from their slumber, curled together in Riley's bed.

Cate slipped her crinoline underskirts on then her hooped skirt dress. She fixed her hair and put the finishing touches on her outfit. She gave both pups a kiss on the forehead, earning a large sigh from Riley as he stretched and settled back in. "I won't be too long, I hope," Cate promised him.

Cate retrieved the tower room key before joining Jack in the closet to return to 1856. They snuck out of the bedroom and down the hall, creeping toward the tower stairs. They made it unscathed and began the climb to the tower. As they approached the top, Jack asked, "Are you sure about this?"

"We don't have a choice. There are things we must learn and confronting Sonia is the only way we will learn them."

"You're one brave but stubborn lassie, Cate."

"I will take that as a compliment. Let's go, before I lose my nerve."

They climbed the last few steps to the tower door. Cate drew in a deep breath, inserted the key and turned it. She took one last deep breath before opening the door.

Cate let the door swing open, peering inside. The room was unrecognizable. Instead of piled boxes and bare floors, the tower housed a bed, dresser, writing desk, an easel and a large area rug. Candles burned inside, lighting the room. Black fabric covered the windows, shutting out any light from the outside. The only similarity was the large wardrobe, placed in the same spot as it was in Cate's time.

A woman crouched at the wardrobe. She swung around to face them. Cate was surprised to see how young she was, appearing to be only in her teens. Black hair framed her pale face. Her blue eyes were piercing despite their small size. She wore a green cape, tattered and frayed. "Who are you?" she demanded.

Cate stepped into the room, pulling Jack in with her and shutting the door behind them. "We're friends of Randolph's. I'm Cate and this is Jack. Jack is representing Randolph in the case the police are building against him for the murder of Andrew Forsythe. Sonia, is it?"

The mention of the murder investigation perturbed the woman. “Will he be cleared of the charges?”

“That is our goal but we need your help,” Cate said.

“My help?”

“Yes. You must tell us what really happened that night,” Cate urged.

The woman turned her back to them, wringing her hands. “I do not know what you mean,” she said.

“Sonia,” Cate chided, “we don’t have time for evasive answers. If we don’t have the facts, we cannot help Randolph. Sonia, he’ll go to jail! You don’t want that, I know it.” Sonia collapsed onto the bed, tears falling from her eyes. Cate continued, “Sonia, please help us!”

Sonia wiped the tears from her cheeks, composing herself. “How do I know I can trust you?”

“We’re here to help, both you and Randolph. We realize Randolph has been protecting you, both by keeping you in the tower room and by confessing to a crime he didn’t commit. What we don’t understand is why. We need to understand that to help him.” Sonia remained silent. “Sonia, please. Right now, we are your only friends. We only want to help. By the looks of it, you need it. Were you running away? Randolph will be devastated to find out you’re missing.”

Sonia nodded her head. “I must go. I’ve cost this family too much now.”

Cate approached her, sitting next to her on the bed and putting her arms around her. “Sonia, Randolph will be devastated if you leave. We can help, but we must have all the facts. Please, help us help you and Randolph.”

“Please,” Sonia responded, “you musn’t tell anyone about me. Only Uncle Randolph and a handful of people know I’m here. Not even his wife Victoria is aware.”

Cate glanced at Jack. “Uncle Randolph?” Cate questioned.

Sonia wiped tears away. “Yes, Randolph is my uncle.”

"Are you Lorne's daughter?" Cate asked, confused.

"No, Emilia was my mother," Sonia said.

"Emilia?" Cate said, recognizing the name as Randolph's deceased younger sister. "She died from influenza at age fifteen. I wasn't aware she was married nor had any children."

"I'm afraid that's the story created to hide me, the ugly blemish on the family name."

"You mean…" Cate began.

"Yes, my mother died at age fifteen but not from influenza, she died in childbirth. I was a bastard, she was unmarried. My grandparents preferred that I be an orphan. Although that's a fair bit better than my paternal grandparents wanted for me. Uncle Randolph wouldn't allow it. He insisted I stay here, argued with his parents. They couldn't explain the new baby without questions being asked. My father's family wanted no parts of me, nor any potential for scandal on the family name. Uncle Randolph kept me a secret. Oh, please don't judge him for putting me in this room. I've been more than comfortable."

"I understand, and we will say nothing, but you must promise not to leave. We can make sure you remain safe. Now," Cate said, stroking her hair, "can you tell me what happened the night Andrew died?" Sonia wept again. "Shh, shh." Cate soothed her. "I realize how hard this must be, but we need to understand the facts so we can help you both."

Sonia nodded again, breathing deeply, composing herself. "Andrew used to bring me some of my meals. He was a vile man. Accused me of being many vulgar things. He blackmailed Uncle Randolph. At first, he paid, but Andrew demanded more and more. I felt so terrible. I almost left then; I wish I had."

"I'm sure Randolph is pleased you didn't leave."

"I do not agree," Sonia sobbed.

"It's all right, Sonia," Cate said, rubbing her arm, "please, continue."

"That night, that horrible night," Sonia lamented. "Andrew came here. He seemed different. Worse than ever, angry and bitter. He... He..." Sonia stumbled, unable to find the words. "He attacked me," she managed, a few more tears rolling down her cheeks. "He ripped my dress. Said that he'd have his way with me, too, like Randolph." Sonia choked out her words amidst tears, struggling to tell the story. "He..."

"We understand, Sonia," Cate assured her. "You then defended yourself?" Cate asked, prompting her to move forward in the story and allowing her to skip rehashing any vile details she may not wish to relive.

She nodded, regaining her composure. "Yes. I grabbed the first thing my hand reached and hit him." Her shoulders sagged, and she sobbed as she continued. "I hit him. I hit him over and over until he didn't move."

Cate held her closer. "It's all right, Sonia. It's over now. You did nothing wrong." Cate glanced at Jack who shook his head in disgust over Andrew's behavior. After a moment, Cate prodded her to continue. "How did Andrew end up falling from the window?"

"Anna, one of the maids who has always been a loyal friend to me, helped me throw his body over. I didn't know what to do. I did not want Uncle Randolph to see what I had done. Perhaps he would have regretted his choice to help me. We struggled but succeeded in pushing him out the window nearest to this bed. I hoped it would appear as an accident. As though he had jumped. Then Anna assisted me in cleaning up the... mess. When Uncle Randolph told me the police were involved, I prayed they would find it to be an accident. But now..." her voice trailed off again.

"I don't want you to worry, Sonia. We're here to help."

"I don't see how," Sonia said, but regained herself a bit.

"Leave that to us. Can we trust you not to leave?"

"I imagine it would be easier if I did," Sonia argued.

"It wouldn't. Randolph will never forgive himself. Please promise us you'll stay, at least until you speak with us again."

Sonia nodded, "I promise. I will stay… for now."

Cate nodded. "Sonia, before we go, is there anything else you can tell us about Andrew that might help us?"

Sonia reflected for a moment. "Andrew was not a nice man. He was involved in many nefarious things. I often spied him meeting with a man, exchanging things in the middle of the night. I am not aware of what the exact nature of their business was, but I cannot imagine it was anything respectable being conducted in the wee hours of the morning."

"Thank you, Sonia. That is helpful. I apologize for making you relive that night, but I assure you things will improve."

"Thank you for trying to help. And thank you for not judging my past."

Cate smiled at her, stroking her hair. The poor girl was hidden away for her entire life, believing she was a blight on her family, something to be ashamed of. For this reason, Cate pitied her. She needed a plan to help her. She needed to mull over the information and consider her options.

"Try to rest, Sonia. We'll visit again when we have a solution."

"Please let it be soon," Sonia said.

Cate helped the girl remove her tattered cape and settled her in bed. She blew out the candles that lit the room before she and Jack snuck from the room. She shut and locked the door behind her before they returned to the closet and their own time.

"That poor girl," Cate declared upon their return.

Jack shook his head. "And that bastard Andrew."

"Yes. We must come up with a solution. We have to help them!"

"I'd love to, I don't know how we can, though. I'm at a loss. Unless we turn her in for it and hope we can prove self-defense, I don't see a way out of this."

"There must be a way," Cate contended. "I need time to deliberate. Perhaps we should discuss this after breakfast and see if we have any ideas."

"Good idea." Jack yawned. "Despite all the excitement, I'm exhausted. I don't think I can put an idea together. It's cutting it close though, we've got to be back tomorrow afternoon. They will charge Randolph, there's no avoiding it."

"Okay." Cate squeezed his arm. "Don't worry, we'll find a way. Try to get some rest. Are you okay to drive home?"

"Yeah, yeah I can make it," Jack answered. "Hey, you try to get some rest, too. Don't be up all night scheming."

"Who, me?" Cate laughed. "Never! See you tomorrow."

"Yes, you, Lady Cate. Okay, see you tomorrow."

They parted ways, with Cate returning to her room. Riley and Bailey were both excited to see her, leaping on her as she entered the room. Cate showered them both with hugs and kisses before changing her clothes. She took them for a brief walk before settling in her suite. Despite her weariness from the long day, her mind was pulsating with worry. She had no plan to resolve the situation. If they didn't act fast, they may lose the chance to fix it.

Cate shook her head as tears threatened to spill onto her cheeks. She remained on her chaise for another forty-five minutes before surrendering to her growing sleepiness. She climbed into bed, drained and no closer to a solution. Despite her upset, she fell asleep within minutes.

CHAPTER 30

Cate bolted upright in bed, gasping for breath. Confused, she sat dumbfounded for a few moments. As her breathing calmed and her mind settled, she realized the source of her distress. A strange dream had disturbed her otherwise restful slumber. She and Jack had been at the castle in 1856. Sonia was there, visiting. Randolph entertained them with stories of his exotic travel. Victoria discussed an upcoming party. Andrew arrived, threatening to ruin all plans, but in the end, he dissolved away to nothing, blowing away like smoke in the wind.

The dream was silly, yet it still left Cate with an unsettled sensation. She slid from under the sheets and out of bed. Her bare feet touched the cold floor, jarring her awake further. Moonlight drenched the room. Cate took a few moments to stare out over the moonlit landscape. Something about the dream bothered her, she found herself unable to shake it from her mind. She paced the floor for a few moments.

As she settled onto her chaise, a notion struck her. She leapt up, her breath quickening as she vetted the idea. After a few moments of pondering, a smile crept across Cate's face.

It was an unusual idea but it just might work. She couldn't wait to tell Jack; she hoped he agreed. At the very least, they had a direction to move in and a plan they could try.

Excited but still tired, Cate crawled back into bed. Satisfied with her strategy, she fell back asleep and slept until her alarm.

The morning sun brightened the sky, painting it a rainbow of reds, oranges, and yellows. The vivid display matched Cate's sunny mood. She sprang from her bed, rushing to dress for the day. After a brief trip outside with Riley and Bailey, she made her way to the kitchen. She greeted Mrs. Fraser with a happy grin, picking up her breakfast for the morning to take upstairs. She hoped she could finish it without bursting from excitement.

After breakfast, she returned her dishes despite Mrs. Fraser's protests and gathered Jack in the name of estate business. He followed her upstairs where they settled in the library. Taking a deep breath, Cate said, grinning, "I have a plan!"

"Great! I came up with nothing, so I'm all ears. I can't believe it, but I'm all ears for a Cate Kensie plan."

"Keep an open mind. I don't have all the quirks worked out but I think it might work."

Cate spent the next hour detailing her plan to Jack. They discussed it at length, debating various aspects, revising minor details, adjusting pieces, gauging reactions from other parties and settling final elements. When they were satisfied, they glanced at each other.

"Well, Lady Cate, it's crazy but it just might work." Jack laughed.

"Gosh, I hope so," Cate said. "We have to act fast though, we don't have much time."

"You're right. We need to get things in place before I'm due at the police station. They will file charges against

Randolph this afternoon unless we can convince them not to. The only way we can do that is to convince Randolph to recant his story. And the only way he'll do that is if he knows Sonia is safe."

"Will retracting his confession be enough for the police to dismiss him as a suspect?"

"Perhaps not outright, but it should shed enough confusion that they will consider other suspects. At least I hope so."

"Well, it's our only option, so let's change and do this!"

"Okay. And if you've got any good luck charms, now's the time to carry them, Lady Cate. Meet you in the usual spot!"

"See you in a few!"

They separated, each going to don their era-appropriate apparel. Cate moved as fast as she was able, selecting the least fussy dress that she had to make the task easier. When she was ready, she met Jack in the bedroom closet. He was pacing the floor waiting for her.

"Second thoughts?" she asked.

"Nope, not one. Just anxious to get moving."

"Me, too," Cate agreed. "Let's go."

Together, they rubbed the watch, sliding back over one hundred and fifty years. When they arrived, they hurried straight to the tower room. Cate unlocked it and they hastened inside, closing the door behind them. The first step of their plan required them to convince Sonia to trust them and follow their direction.

"Cate!" Sonia exclaimed. "I spent much of my night wondering if I had dreamt you and wondering if you would return."

"We are real," Cate assured her, "and we have a plan."

Sonia listened intently as Cate outlined their plan, summarizing the highlights and positive outcomes. "Do you think this will work?"

"Yes, it will work," Cate pledged, "it has to."

"I trust her," Jack chimed in. "We'll make it work."

Sonia nodded. "All right, then let us proceed."

"Good," Cate said. "Come." Cate stood, pulling Sonia to her feet. "We must gather your things and move you."

Between the three of them, they assembled Sonia's limited possessions, placing them in a suitcase. "Follow me," Cate said to Sonia, lugging the suitcase with her.

"Be safe," Jack said before they left.

Cate nodded. "I'll be back as soon as I can to help."

"Okay. I'll do what I can before you're back."

* * *

Cate led Sonia through the halls, avoiding any contact with other occupants of the castle. They arrived at their destination, a bedroom closet in an unused bedroom. She situated Sonia in the closet, making her as comfortable as possible. "Stay here until either Jack or I come for you. Try to stay quiet. No one should be in here but just in case," Cate babbled as she fussed with a pillow, trying to make Sonia comfortable.

"I have been hidden for years, I understand how to remain unseen."

Cate stared at her for a moment. "You're right, sorry. Well, with any luck, we'll be back soon."

"Go, Cate. And thank you," Sonia said, squeezing Cate's hand.

Cate nodded to her, returning the silent encouragement. Then, she left the room, racing to the tower room to finish helping Jack. He had already made good progress by the time Cate returned. He had stripped the bed, pushed the desk and dresser near the door and rolled up the area rug. Jack also removed the blackout curtains from the windows.

"Wow," Cate marveled, "great job so far!"

"Are you sure you're able to do this in that outfit?"

"I'll try. I picked a less cumbersome dress just for the occasion. Come on, we'll move the desk first."

"Right," Jack said, positioning himself behind the desk, allowing Cate to take the front and walk facing forward. "Ready?"

"Ready. Straight to the unused bedroom."

"And hope no one is there. Okay, on three." Jack counted to three, and they lifted the desk. It was small and therefore not heavy. Cate and Jack managed it without trouble. They tucked it away in a unused bedroom near the tower stairs.

They climbed the stairs again, repeating the process with the dresser. This item they stowed in the storage room a few steps down from the tower room. Cate was glad for the shorter trip with the heavier item. They dismantled the bed, shoving the mattress in the same storage room as the dresser and stacking the frame in the corner of the room. Next, they moved several boxes from the storage area into the tower, shoving them in various locations to make it appear to be a storage area.

Cate huffed as she sunk onto the top of a trunk they had dragged into the area. She wiped a few beads of sweat from her brow, catching her breath. "Okay, part one of the plan finished. Sonia is moved, and the tower room is dismantled. No one would suspect someone has lived here for over a decade."

"Now on to part two. You ready?" Jack asked, holding out his hand to pull Cate up to standing.

Cate nodded, grabbing his hand. "As I'll ever be!"

They made their way out of the castle and began the trek to town. They approached the police station and made their way inside. Jack asked to see Randolph, stating Cate wanted to visit with Randolph first then he wanted a few moments with his client. The desk clerk disappeared into an office for a moment then returned. "Mrs. MacKenzie, if you'll follow me."

Cate glanced at Jack. He gave her a nod of encouragement. Cate followed the clerk to the interview room, where she sat to await Randolph's arrival. An officer led Randolph into the room, seating him across from Cate, handcuffs still on.

"Five minutes," he warned before stepping out.

"Catherine, lovely to see you, but you should be with Victoria."

"No time to waste with niceties, Randolph," Cate whispered. "We have a plan, I'll explain it quickly but you must trust me and do as I say."

"Plan?" Randolph asked.

"Yes, listen carefully. I won't have time to repeat this."

Cate explained the plan to Randolph in as much detail as time allowed. Afterwards, Randolph sat silent for a moment, flabbergasted.

"And Sonia is safe?"

"Safe as houses," Cate said, using a popular Victorian phrase.

"Catherine," Randolph said, "that's one hell of a plan. Do you suppose it will work?"

"I hope so. I had to be creative, you put us in one heck of a mess with your confession!"

"Apologies, dear lady, but I will not allow Sonia's safety to be compromised."

"Admirable, Randolph, but we must also consider your wife's and child's lives. This plan offers everyone a chance at happiness. Now, we just have to hope it works."

The officer returned to the room. "Time's up," he announced.

"Take care, Randolph and listen to Jack," Cate said,

standing and exiting the room. She walked down the hall, passing Jack who was on his way to consult with his "client." She smiled, reaching for his hand to give it a squeeze as they passed. "Good luck!" she mouthed.

"Showtime!" Jack whispered, grinning at her.

Cate exited the police station, beginning the walk to the castle. She could do nothing there, so she would go to Victoria and give her as much comfort as she could while she waited for Jack to carry out his piece of the plan.

Butterflies flitted in Cate's stomach as she tried to imagine what was taking place in the police station. The castle stood tall in front of her. She approached it, giving the door knocker a solid smack.

Thomson greeted her, guiding her into the house. "Lady MacKenzie will be so pleased to see you." Cate followed him to Victoria's suite.

"Lady MacKenzie, Mrs. MacKenzie has arrived."

"Catherine! Come in!"

"Hello, Victoria," Cate said, entering the room and offering the woman a hug.

"Please sit down, tea?" Victoria offered.

"Thank you," Cate said, sitting down. Victoria poured a cup of tea for Cate.

"I'm so glad you're here. I'm a bundle of nerves."

"Jack is at the station now. I hope he brings good news with him today."

"As do I." Victoria shook her head. "I'm so unsure," she said, her voice breaking as she tried to hold her composure.

Cate grasped her hand. "Victoria…" Cate began.

"No, no," Victoria interrupted, "I must press on. Must keep my head up."

"There is nothing to fret over yet. Save your strength, you may not even need to fret! Jack has a plan."

"Let us hope and pray that is the case. I trust Jack," she said, reassuring herself.

"Shall we change the subject?"

"Please," Victoria said, wanting the distraction.

They chatted about anything that struck Victoria's fancy over tea. As late afternoon approached, conversation became intermittent as Cate's mind became distracted by the lateness of the hour. The women moved to the sitting room, enjoying some time with Ethan. Several more tedious hours passed. The nanny took Ethan for his evening feeding and bath, leaving Cate and Victoria on their own to pass the time again.

After another hour, Cate feared for her sanity, sure the waiting would drive her mad. "Should Jack's plan be taking this long? Oh, what if they've charged him?" Victoria cried.

"We haven't any news yet. No news may be good news," Cate tried to assure her.

"But..." Victoria began when there were sounds from the foyer. Cate and Victoria shared a glance, before both of them raced from the room.

Victoria's eyes widened as she hurried through the doors into the foyer. "Randolph!" she exclaimed, rushing to him. "Oh my darling husband." She threw her arms around his neck in a full embrace. "How are you? Have they mistreated you?"

"Victoria, I'm fine, just fine."

Cate's heart melted at the scene she witnessed from the doorway. She glanced at Jack, her heart about to burst with excitement. While interested to know the details, the current result satisfied her.

Victoria released Randolph, turning to embrace Jack. "How can I ever thank you, cousin Jack? You have my eternal gratitude."

"We're not out of the woods yet, to coin a phrase from my

wife, but most of the difficulty has passed. The investigation's focus should move from Randolph. They shouldn't trouble you anymore."

"Oh, what a spectacle I am," Victoria said, standing back, wiping tears from her cheeks.

"Shall we go into the sitting room?" Randolph suggested, "I could use a drink."

"As could I," Jack agreed.

They entered the sitting room, Randolph pouring a drink for himself and Jack after offering drinks to the ladies. Thomson entered to inquire if the party needed anything.

"Champagne," Randolph ordered, "four glasses. We are celebrating tonight!" Thomson left to retrieve the request. Once delivered, poured and each of them held a glass, Randolph toasted, "To Jack. Catherine, your husband is a legal genius."

They all raised their glasses to Jack. "Well, I don't know about that, sir," Jack said, after sipping his champagne. "But you certainly tested my mettle."

"No need to be modest, boy. You got me out of quite a tight spot. I made a serious miscalculation, and you handled it with ease."

"We can never repay you, either of you, cousins," Victoria said. "Catherine, you are to be commended, too. Were it not for you, I wouldn't have survived. And Jack, dear Jack, I cannot thank you enough."

"It is our pleasure," Jack answered for the both of them. Then joked, "Besides, I had to help Randolph. I needed a favor from him."

"We'll do anything, just name it," Victoria said.

"Thank you for being so accommodating without yet knowing the request," Jack said.

"I know the request and I hardly think we're being overly accommodating," Randolph said.

"You know it?" Victoria asked, cocking her head.

"I do." Randolph nodded. "We had plenty of time to discuss it while the police sorted through things."

"Are you both going to play coy? What is it?"

"I've just learned my niece, Sonia, my sister's child, has been orphaned. My sister died birthing Sonia, and now my brother-in-law has passed away in an accident."

"Oh, how terrible for the poor child," Victoria lamented.

"Yes, it is most unfortunate. As her next-of-kin, the duty falls to me to look after her. With my need to travel, it may become difficult. While I realize the imposition this places on you, I beseeched Randolph if she may spend some time at the castle until such time that Catherine and I are settled and can take her in. Perhaps, she could provide companionship for you, Victoria."

"Imposition? Nonsense!" Victoria exclaimed. "She is family. There's no imposition at all. We would welcome her. How delightful to meet a new family member."

"I concur," Randolph agreed. "It's poppycock to think it an imposition!"

"What is her age?" Victoria inquired.

"She is nearly sixteen," Jack answered.

"Oh, what fun we shall have!" Victoria exclaimed. "You were right to come to us. She should not be unsettled, traveling about the country at this age. She must be guided, taught, supported and trained. We shall make sure she is raised to make a fine match and become a true lady. Do not give it a second thought, cousins. I will see to it all. When will she arrive?"

"In fact, she is already here. I traveled to retrieve her last evening, returning early this morning with Sonia."

"Oh, you must send for her at once! And I must send for my dressmaker. We must buy her a new dress or two, perhaps even three, for the upcoming holiday season. We will travel to London, we will attend many holiday parties before and after the new year."

"As you can see, cousin Jack," Randolph said, "my wife has the situation well in hand."

"Yes." Jack laughed. "It appears so. In all seriousness though, I am fortunate to count you as family."

"Well, I agree with my wife. Sonia should be sent for at once. I shall tell Thomson to set an extra place for dinner. Please, cousin, might you retrieve her tonight?"

"I should be glad to."

"Oh, Randolph, please have Mrs. Carmichael prepare the bedroom down the hall from mine for Sonia. You don't mind if she stays with us beginning tonight, do you, cousin Jack?"

"Not at all. It would be preferable that she become settled prior to our departure. This would give her a few weeks to become comfortable while we are here to visit. I shall retrieve her now."

Jack left the room as Randolph rung for Thomson. When he arrived, Randolph instructed him to make the arrangements for Jack's niece, Sonia, to join them for dinner and to stay with them going forward.

Cate sat on pins and needles waiting for Jack's return with Sonia. It was the last piece of the puzzle to fall into place, assuming the situation with the police investigation held out. It would be impossible to tell until she spoke with Jack how likely it was that the investigation would close without further troubling the MacKenzie household.

After what seemed an eternity to Cate, Jack arrived. Stepping into the sitting room again, he said, "May I present my niece, Sonia Morgan." Sonia stepped around him, glancing shyly at Victoria then Randolph.

"Sonia, my dear child, come in. Please, call me Uncle Randolph," Randolph said, bringing a slight smile to Cate's face.

"I should like that, Uncle Randolph," Sonia said, her voice barely above a whisper.

Jack guided her forward as Victoria rose. "Sonia, welcome!" She approached the girl and embraced her, adding a kiss on her cheek. "I am your Aunt Victoria. We are so pleased to welcome you into our family and our home. Please, come and sit down." Victoria led her to the loveseat to sit. "Your journey was no doubt taxing on you. Are you exhausted from it?"

"I am rather tired," Sonia admitted. Cate gathered the source of her weariness was from worry rather than travel.

"Poor child. We shall go to dinner soon, you can retire afterwards to rest. I've had a bedroom prepared for you near mine. I look so forward to your stay. We shall have such fun together, Sonia!" Victoria held Sonia's hands in hers, offering a wide, bright smile.

"Thank you for your graciousness, Aunt Victoria," Sonia answered.

"There is no need for gratitude, Sonia. We are family. Oh, I hope you enjoy fashion. I cannot wait to have my dressmaker in for an appointment with you. You are a very pretty girl," Victoria said, fussing with her hair. "Your complexion is quite light but very attractive. You shall do well in bold colors."

"I shall be excited to have a new dress of any color."

Victoria beamed. "Oh, no my dear, not *A* new dress. We shall buy many new dresses for you. You shall need them, we shall attend many events."

Sonia smiled for the first time. Cate also smiled at the scene unfolding. Sonia would live a full life. Victoria would have a friend and companion. She would no longer feel lonely, far from her old life and friends. All that remained was for the police to clear Randolph of all charges and close the case. Cate hoped it was only a matter of time.

The group enjoyed the rest of their evening. Victoria already began her training of Sonia during dinner, prompting the girl to sit properly, holding her utensils as a lady should and how to make light, entertaining conversation. She reminded Sonia that she, one day, would host her own dinner parties as the lady of a household.

Following dinner, Victoria excused herself to settle Sonia in her new room. Cate tagged along to help. Before the ladies departed, Sonia offered Jack a tight hug and a sincere thank you.

"How touching," Victoria said to Cate. "Do not worry, cousin Jack, she shall be well taken care of. Come, Sonia, let us get you settled in your new bed."

Cate and Victoria led Sonia to her new room. She marveled at the room, asking Victoria if she was sure it was hers. Victoria assured her it was. Bryson had set out the few items Sonia brought. As Victoria assessed the items, she sent Bryson to fetch another nightgown from Victoria's collection, claiming the one Sonia had "simply wouldn't do."

After dressing her in the new nightgown, Victoria settled her in bed. Cate gave her a warm hug which Sonia returned along with a thank you. After a few more moments of fussing, Victoria and Cate left Sonia to sleep. "What a dear child she is," Victoria said as they returned to the sitting room. "Do not worry, Catherine, I shall check on her in a bit to be sure she is settled. I sometimes find myself unable to sleep in a new location so I shall know just what to do."

"She is lucky to have you now, Victoria," Cate said.

"She has not enjoyed the presence of a mother before, poor child, and one can tell. But do not worry, I shall have her up to snuff by next season for her debut."

Cate smiled as they entered the sitting room, rejoining Randolph and Jack. "Have her all settled, my dear?" Randolph asked.

"Settled and snug in her new bed," Victoria answered. "And do not worry, cousin Jack, as I told Catherine, I shall have Sonia prepared to make a fine match in short order. She shall have the upbringing of a fine lady. Oh, Jack, has she any musical training? It is sometimes a good skill for young ladies to possess, it makes them seem clever."

"I do not believe she has, Victoria," Jack answered.

"Randolph, we should arrange for her to learn pianoforte. I do hope she might show some skill for it. We shall see!"

"Of course, my dear. Whatever you suggest."

"I shall make a list."

"Wonderful, my dear," Randolph said. "Well, cousin," Randolph addressed Jack, "as you can see, we have the situation well in hand. I hope this sets your mind at ease."

"It does, sir, it does. I shall feel most comfortable leaving her in your care. You have taken a great weight from my mind."

"We both appreciate it very much," Cate chimed in. "We shall take our leave for the evening. It has been a trying day, I'm sure you both would like to relax."

"Indeed," Victoria answered, "as has it been for both of you. Please get some rest. Will you visit tomorrow?"

"Yes," Jack said. "I'd like to see how Sonia has settled. Perhaps we shall stop in the afternoon for tea."

"We shall look forward to seeing you then," Randolph agreed. "I shall walk you to the door."

They left Victoria in the sitting room while Randolph led them to the foyer. "Jack, Catherine, I cannot thank you enough. I shall forever be in your debt."

"Save your thanks for when we are sure you are cleared of all charges, Randolph," Jack said.

"All in due time, my boy, all in due time. Now, I shall see

you tomorrow. You should have an unfettered path to your destination if you go now."

"See you tomorrow, Randolph," Cate said.

They ascended the stairs, winding through the halls to the bedroom closet. They used the time piece to return to their time. Jack breathed his customary sigh of relief. "WOW!" Cate exclaimed. "I want to hear all about it."

"I want to take a nap." Jack sighed. "Whew, I can't believe it's only been an hour."

"Oh, come on," Cate teased, "I've been waiting all day."

"Actually, you've only been waiting an hour," Jack corrected.

"How are you not excited?"

Jack chuckled. "Okay, okay. I'll admit it, it felt rather good helping both Randolph and Sonia today."

"Rather good? That's it?" Cate asked, raising her eyebrows.

"It felt pretty damned good," Jack admitted, laughing.

"So, out with it!"

"At least let me change!" Jack complained.

"Okay, okay, meet in the library as usual?"

"Meet in the library as usual, Lady Cate."

CHAPTER 31

Cate raced to change, not wanting to waste a second. She gathered the dogs with her and rushed to the library. Jack joined her moments later.

"Wow, Lady Cate, you beat me. You must be anxious to hear this story!"

"I am! I don't understand how you did it, Jack. Now, come on, tell me every detail! Don't leave anything out."

"Okay, okay," Jack agreed, sinking into an armchair. Cate perched on the edge of hers with bated breath. "It wasn't too difficult. Once Randolph stopped insisting he was guilty, I succeeded in convincing the police to consider other suspects."

"Did it take any convincing on your part?"

"Only an assurance that Sonia was safe. I told him you had seen to it yourself, that you'd never let anything happen to the girl."

"And then what? He just told the police to cancel his confession?"

"No, it was more difficult than that. He recanted his statement. The police were not happy. They reviewed his statement over and over from when he confessed and his subsequent questioning. We pointed out all the inconsistencies, which they themselves questioned on both occasions. Then I asked them to review the original statements taken from the night of the party. Randolph's new statement matched that one and the other witness testimony. They realized, as we did when we went through the same exercise, that it was impossible for Randolph to have killed Andrew."

"So, he's off the hook, right?"

"Well, they asked him not to leave the area just yet and they haven't officially removed him from the suspect list, but I expect it's only a matter of time. Still, we should check back until he is no longer considered a suspect. Or until the investigation is closed, assuming that's before the end of the year."

"Wait, did I just hear you suggest we SHOULD time travel?"

Jack laughed. "Yes, my dear Lady Cate, I suggested it. I want to see this through. It's my first big legal win."

"Yes, apparently you are quite the legal genius."

"You know it."

"Did the police mention any other suspects?"

"Yes, they did. I inquired after telling them I hoped my client would no longer be bothered by this. They said they may poke around the grounds but doubted they would find much."

"Because it's been too long since the murder?"

"No, they didn't presume the murder weapon was on the estate."

"Really?" Cate raised her eyebrows in surprise.

"Yes. From the eyewitness accounts of that night, several people told the police they had seen Andrew meeting with another man earlier that evening. The man wasn't someone anyone was acquainted with, but they had seen him with Andrew once or twice before. They appeared to be arguing.

The police assume the man was an associate of Andrew's and murdered him over whatever they were arguing about."

"Sonia mentioned seeing Andrew meeting with someone, too."

"Right. Probably the same man. Based on his description, the police suspect he was a rather disreputable fellow. They assume Andrew was involved in some nefarious things and it cost him his life."

"Wonder what will happen when they find him and he says he's innocent. He may even have an alibi."

"I doubt they'll ever find him. With the trouble, he's probably long gone never to return to avoid any suspicion."

"Gosh, I hope so," Cate said.

"Relax, Cate, we stand a good chance. And a far better chance than we did when Randolph was professing his guilt."

Cate contemplated for a moment. "Hmm, wow, I still can't believe this worked."

"Hey!" Jack exclaimed. "What do you mean you can't believe it worked? You insisted this plan would work!"

"Well." Cate shrugged. "I hoped it would work, but now that it did, I'm shocked it went so smoothly. I mean, Randolph confessed, he was insistent. Then he just recanted, and they accepted it."

"They had no choice. His confession was questionable from the start. That's why I had such an easy time getting them to agree not to charge him right away. Even they questioned if it would stick."

"Wow," Cate whispered, stunned into silence after considering the breadth of the situation.

"Now it's just a waiting game to get the all clear, which I hope comes soon."

"Me, too. You know, we're approaching the end of the year, it's sad to realize we won't be able to visit anymore."

Jack nodded. "Yes, I can't believe I'm about to admit to this but I will miss them."

"Me, too," Cate said, sighing. "Oh, well, I suppose we should start our day… again."

"I suppose so. I'll tell you one thing I won't miss is living two days in the time of only one."

"You and me both. It's evening to me but we haven't even had lunch yet. At least it's helping my terrible sleep habits. I sleep the entire night!"

"And it only took time travel to cure your insomnia. Who would have ever guessed traveling through time would benefit one's health."

Cate gave him an amused look. "Back to research for me and preparing for Molly's arrival."

"Have you heard from her? I'll bet she is excited."

"I have. She's already sent some of her things."

"I'll bet she would have stayed here and never gone back if she could have."

"I agree. She's counting the days down."

"Well," Jack said, standing, "let me know when her things arrive, I'll get them moved. If you need anything else done before she's due here, let me know, I'll get right on it."

"Thanks, Jack."

Jack left her in the library. Cate sat for another few moments, pondering the results of the last few days. After a time, she rousted herself from her daze, deciding to take the dogs for a long walk.

After the walk and lunch, she settled in the library determined to make progress on a chapter of her book. Before beginning, she checked her email, finding the latest report from Molly awaiting her.

Hi Cate– More boxes on their way to you. One more round should do it! Gayle also helped me book my ticket. I am arriving in London on December 15 and will take the train to Scotland on December 16. I think she's planning to contact you to see if it would be best for me to rent a car and drive or have Jack come for me. I'm fine either way, I'll be on cloud nine, you just tell me which is best for you.

I'm wrapping things up in the office with my "complete inventory." Soon, I'll just be finishing my time. Jeff is already interviewing for my replacement so I can train them before I leave.

And I saved the best news for last. I ran into Tom yesterday at the grocery store. He tried to play the nice guy, you know, "hi, how are you, how have you been" blah, blah. I told him great, I don't think he believed me. So, I informed him why I was doing great. I told him I quit my job and wouldn't be in my place much longer. Then I dropped the bombshell about my moving to Scotland. I'm not sure who was more shocked, my sister or Tom. I don't care, but I had a good time telling both of them.

Anyway, only five more weeks!!!!!!!!!!

Molly

Cate sensed Molly's excitement through the email. While her arrival date was less than a week from Mrs. Campbell's Christmas extravaganza, Cate surmised it was best to send Jack for Molly, not wanting them to have to return the rental car. Cate returned Molly's email with this information. While she typed, an email arrived from Gayle, also requesting the same information. Cate answered it as well before moving on to her own work.

While visiting 1856, Cate had discovered several pieces of

information that she deemed interesting for her book. Her personal experience in the past gave her a new perspective. Her book would be one-of-a-kind with its unique information.

She spent her afternoon and evening penning a chapter, her mind able to focus after solving the issue with Randolph. Cate turned in early, sleeping without issue given her long day.

The following morning, Cate longed to return to check on the situation in 1856. Concern plagued her. She wondered how Sonia was adjusting, how Victoria was, if there was any further trouble for Randolph. Cate questioned how she would handle it when she could no longer visit with them. It was heart breaking for her. Still, as of now, she could visit with them and would meet them today. She focused on this idea as she watched Riley and Bailey frolic near the loch.

After lunch, she readied herself, meeting Jack in the bedroom closet at 3:30 p.m. They slowed the timepiece and returned to Randolph and Victoria's time. They traversed the back passages of the castle to the outside then the front door. Thomson greeted them, showing them into the solarium for tea. They found Victoria and Sonia already seated, discussing a schedule of plans for Sonia's musical education. Sonia was dressed in one of Victoria's gowns. Her hair coiffed in a becoming style with a matching ribbon.

As they entered, Sonia stood, curtsying. "Good day, Uncle Jack and Aunt Catherine," she said.

Victoria smiled and nodded, as she took her seat again. She beamed to Cate and Jack, giving them a wink. "Come in and sit down, cousins. Sonia and I were just discussing furthering her education. She is keen on learning an instrument."

Cate and Jack sat at the table. "Hello, Sonia. You look well," Cate said.

"Indeed," Jack added, "how was your first night in the castle?"

"Splendid," Sonia answered. Her eyes sparkled with renewed interest in life. "I slept well. The bed was incredibly comfortable."

"I had Bryson alter this dress for her," Victoria said. "To tide her over until my dressmaker can create some new things for her. The color does well on her. It always made me sallow. Would you agree, Catherine?"

"Quite fitting," Cate concurred.

"I've already sent for the dressmaker and to acquire a piano-forte instructor. Sonia may be keen on learning a language, too. She is quite clever," Victoria said.

"I'm so pleased," Jack said as Randolph entered the room.

"Well, cousins, I'm so pleased you could join us," he said as he approached the table.

Jack stood, shaking his hand. "Randolph," he said, "Sonia looks well. I am so pleased with Victoria's plans for her."

"As am I!" Randolph admitted as both men seated themselves. "I am afraid, however, I have some bad news."

"Oh no, what is it?" Cate asked, her heart dropping.

"I shall no longer require your legal counsel, Jack. The police have cleared me of the murder and removed me from the suspect list. I know how you shall miss sparring with them."

"That's fantastic news, Randolph," Jack said, clapping him on the back. "Although, I will miss the scrapping."

"I could do without it," Victoria noted.

"What of the case?" Jack asked.

"They are searching for some dubious character by the name of Simon Dupree. Involved in all sorts of scandal, that one. He was seen on the property multiple times, including the fateful night. I doubt the police will ever catch up with him. Long gone at the first hint of trouble, I'm sure."

"Undoubtedly," Jack agreed.

"Please may we speak of something more light?" Victoria pleaded.

"Agree," Cate chimed in.

The group of five spent the rest of their meal trying to engage in light conversation. Cate experienced a twinge of sadness as each moment passed. With the case settled and the year drawing to a close, she inched closer to being unable to visit with her new friends.

The fact was made even more real when Jack announced his business would conclude within the next two weeks and they would leave the area. Victoria expressed her disappointment but encouraged them to visit. They promised to try, but Cate realized full well this was an empty pledge.

At the conclusion of their evening, Randolph offered to walk Cate and Jack to the door, mentioning he would like a moment alone with the couple before they departed. They strode to his office, and he closed the door behind them.

"With the year drawing to a close," Randolph began, "I suppose we shan't be meeting much more."

"Sadly, no," Cate said. "As the new year arrives, the time clock will reset, as I understand it. Therefore, our travels using this specific rip would bring us back to relive this same year."

"Correct," Randolph agreed.

Cate was silent for a moment, composing herself. "I… that is, we…" she stumbled. "I wish there was another way. It would be nice to visit."

"I cannot offer any solutions. But perhaps…" he began.

"Yes?" Cate asked in earnest.

"You may find it helpful to consult with Douglas. To this day, I do not understand how he tamed the power in this castle."

"Douglas MacKenzie, the original castle owner?" Jack asked.

"Yes, old Doug, my grandfather. A crafty bugger, that one. If anyone can offer you a way, he can."

"I promise to look into that!" Cate vowed.

"Please, sir, don't encourage her," Jack joked.

"Ah, laddie, apologies, but my encouragement or lack of will not change her mind."

"Probably not," Jack answered.

"Definitely not. She's a MacKenzie, we're a strong-willed lot!"

"You've got that right," Jack agreed.

"I for one am glad of it. Without her willfulness, I might be in prison."

"Aye, that's a likely bet, sir."

"On that note, I wanted to say thank you. Thank you to both of you. I cannot ever repay you for what you've done."

"There's no repayment necessary, Randolph," Cate said to him. "We are so pleased to have helped." Cate offered him a wide smile.

"Even so, my family and I are indebted to you. And now, before this moment turns maudlin, particularly for Catherine, let us part ways. I hope to see you at least one more time before the year is out."

"You will," Cate promised.

"So it's goodbye for now, Catherine and Jack. Until we meet again," Randolph said.

They said their goodbyes, promising to see each other at least once more before Jack and Cate returned to the closet and their own time. Cate spent the rest of her evening glum, knowing they would soon say goodbye for good to her ancestors. She held on to the hope that one day she would meet Douglas MacKenzie and perhaps devise a way to return to visit with Randolph and Victoria as their lives continued.

CHAPTER 32

As the month of November continued, Cate spent most of her time researching and planning for the upcoming Christmas event and Molly's arrival. As the year drew to a close, Cate's time to visit with Randolph and Victoria also grew short. She and Jack found the time mid-month to take one last trip to 1856. Good fortune continued for the MacKenzies of 1856. The police abandoned any hope of finding Andrew's killer. While the case remained unsolved, it had more or less been forgotten, written off as a senseless tragedy among a den of thieves.

They said their goodbyes, stating that, after a brief tour of Britain, they would return to the United States. Cate's eyes welled with tears as she said goodbye to Victoria, Randolph, Sonia and little Ethan, presuming it would be the last time she would see them.

After returning home, Cate dug out the folder containing the articles Mrs. Campbell provided her alerting her to the murder. With a shaky hand, she opened the folder. The article titled "MURDER AT DUNHAVEN CASTLE" sat on top of the pile. Cate dug further into the stack of photocopies, searching for the articles discussing the investigation and subsequent trial and conviction of Randolph. She shuffled through the papers. Near the end of the stack, she found what she was hunting. The article that announced Randolph's conviction now read "MURDER REMAINS UNSOLVED: SUSPECT SOUGHT." Cate skimmed the article. It reported that after a lengthy investigation, which cleared Randolph of all charges, a new suspect had been sought. A known associate of Mr. Forsythe was the top suspect. Anyone having any information should contact the police.

On the top of the page, an article detailed an upcoming party given in the honor of Sonia MacKenzie, cousin to Lord and Lady MacKenzie, at the castle. Cate smiled at the new headlines. They had made a difference. She set the papers on her night table, intending to share them with Jack in the morning.

She spent the next several weeks frequenting the portrait gallery, where she felt close to her ancestors. She spent large amounts of time staring at the portraits of Victoria and Randolph, wishing them the best.

As the month came to a close, Cate filled her time with research, meetings with Mrs. Campbell and preparing for Molly's arrival in two short weeks. Anticipation for Molly's arrival occupied Cate's mind, easing her tendency to dwell on those she had left behind.

During their latest meeting, Mrs. Campbell left a folder with Cate containing another set of articles about Dunhaven Castle's past. That night, Cate climbed into bed. With a dog nestled on either side of her, she opened the folder. It contained several news clippings that Mrs. Campbell put together for Cate's research.

Cate grabbed the first article from the top of the stack. Her eyes widened as she read the headline. The paper, marked from the year 1925, announced in block letters: THEFT AT DUNHAVEN CASTLE. Cate cocked her head to the side. "Well this looks interesting," she said, settling back to discover her next mystery.

Stay up to date with all my news! Be the first to find out about new releases first, sales and get free offers! Join the Nellie H. Steele's Mystery Readers' Group on Facebook! Or sign up for my newsletter at www.anovelideapublishing.com!

* * *

Join Cate and Jack in their next adventure! Help Cate and Jack solve a theft in Holiday Heist at Dunhaven Castle! There's even a little mystery for Riley and Bailey, too!

* * *

Want to her the story from Jack's perspective? Try Murder in the Tower, Book 2 of Jack's Journal!

* * *

If you love cozies, you can also check out my newest series, Lily & Cassie by the Sea. Grab book one, *Ghosts, Lore & a House by the Shore* now!

Love immersing yourself in the past? Lenora Fletcher can communicate with the dead! Can she use her unique skill to solve a mystery? Find out in *Death of a Duchess,* Book 1 in the Duchess of Blackmoore Mysteries.

Ready for adventure? Travel the globe with Maggie Edwards in search of her kidnapped uncle and Cleopatra's Tomb. Book one, *Cleopatra's Tomb,* in the Maggie Edwards Adventure series is available now!

If you prefer adventures set in the past, try my newest pirate adventure series. Book 1, *Rise of a Pirate,* is available for purchase now!

Like supernatural suspense? Try the *Shadow Slayers* series, a fast-paced page-turner! Book one, *Shadows of the Past,* is available now!

Made in the USA
Coppell, TX
04 April 2022